I0589297

The Dreaming Fields
Volume I

THE MAGIC of SCIENCE

M. A. Wakefield

Allgood PRESS

The **Magic** *of* Science
The Dreaming Fields
Volume I

Ominous Productions
HARRISBURG

ISBN: 978-0-9864494-4-4 - [paperback]
ISBN: 978-0-9864494-5-1 - [e-book]

book design | **timmyroland**.com   *cover illustration* | **shutterstock**.com

*For my family, and for everyone who believes in the dream.
This wouldn't have happened without all of you.*

PROLOGUE

Blink.
He forced his eyes open, though the light hurt and made him squint.
Blink. Blink.
He rubbed his face with both hands and sat forward, slowly taking in a familiar scene.
How long was I in the dark?
He didn't know.
Blink.
A sound intervened; a rhythmic, comfortable sound, also familiar. *Creak-thump, creak-thump,* it sang, a well-oiled cadence.
"Hello, Johnny. Welcome back."
She sat in her accustomed place to his left, her smile radiant, her face ancient and wrinkled. A cloud of silver-white hair orbited her head loosely, and she gave off a smell of sweetbread and peppermint tea. She was rocking slowly in her old wooden chair, *creak-thump, creak-thump.*
He began to speak, to formulate a question, something along the lines of where have I been? . . . but she only waved her hand and cackled a laugh.
"Save your queries," she said. "Only one thing counts, and without it the rest is garbage. Do you remember my name this time?"
He studied her warily. Though she was as familiar as the rest of this place, and apparently harmless, she made him uneasy. Something about her . . . but he couldn't remember. He shook his head no.
"I thought not." Her eyes were calm and distant. "So then – the rest is moot. You are what you are, I am what I am, this place is what it is." She gestured, and the world around them took on life, a spreading green ripple that snapped the horizon into place. A serrated ridge of blue-black hills leaned into the sunset sky, on the far side of a cactus-spotted desert as familiar and implacable as the porch on which he sat.

A pine railing circumnavigated the old clapboard house, smooth from many oilings. He leaned forward and ran a finger along its surface. "This isn't real."

"You always say that," she replied calmly. From somewhere inside her faded poncho she produced a pipe, filled it with rich-smelling tobacco and began to tamp it.

He surveyed himself. A rough-spun work-shirt and faded blue jeans gave on worn, comfortable boots. A few memories began to flit in like slow butterflies. His eyes widened, and he drew in a sharp breath. "I have to save them!"

She laughed and snapped her fingers, and a flame appeared above her index finger. She dipped it to her pipe and puffed sweet, tangy smoke into the desert twilight. "And you always say *that,* too. But you can't save them, you already know that. And what's more, you know *why.*"

He regarded her severely for a moment, then let out his breath and nodded reluctantly. "Because . . . because it's already happened, right? It's done."

"That's right."

Far out across the packed dirt, a feral howl faded into tailing echoes. He shivered. "How long . . . how long ago did it . . . I mean . . . "

She waved a hand dismissively. "Long and long again. It doesn't matter." She peered at him thoughtfully, then sat back and smiled, her eyes crinkling merrily in their folds. "I think you're ready."

"Ready for what?"

"Ready to put it all together," she replied. "I'm going to send you back again. And this time you'll get it right."

"Back? You mean . . ." Terror welled, left him wide-eyed and dizzy.

"Yes. You need the whole experience if you're to use it, and you . . . well, you still don't understand." She sighed again. "To free yourself, you must go through it again. You must put right the pieces of yourself that went wrong."

An image floated up from the void, of a beautiful young woman with red-gold waves of hair and eyes the color of emeralds.

"Maia," he whispered.

The old woman rocked and puffed, *creak-thump.* "How much do you remember?" She narrowed her eyes, her voice dropping to a hoarse whisper. *"Who are you?"*

He took a deep breath, then another as the tempo of his heart began to slow. His eyes turned inward, and he began to speak as if by rote, rattling off in a monotone like he was reading from an internal tablet.

"My name is Johnny Perdue," he said. "I was born and raised at Montana Compound – one of five free communities in North America. My parents were part of the original rebellion; they were children then, some of the first to grow up off the grid after the shadow government rose to absolute power. They were killed in action when I was young. I continued my schooling until I was old enough to go on raids myself, but by then the movement had virtually died. It was all we could do just to avoid detection – the Civil Enforcement Corps had gotten stronger over the years, while we had only grown weaker. By the time I was twenty, all active missions had been indefinitely shelved."

"And then?" She spurred him on, her eyes gleaming. Over the horizon, a single star quickened, dull and bloated.

"A friend of mine had compiled a lot of statistical information about government activity in North America. It was too much to share over the pirate network – we were limited to high-frequency code in short-burst radio broadcasts – so I volunteered to take it to Compound West."

She sat back and nodded, satisfied. "Good. Good. That's plenty for our purposes. Are you ready, then?"

Fear surged again. "What . . . now?"

"Oh, stop it," she retorted. "Bending time is no fool's game – you're going to need all your strength." She smiled. "Remember, you're only along for the ride. Try to learn something this time, if you can." She gave a little wave, and the desert scene began to fade. A whistling wind rose from the void behind that scene. Panic threatened . . . but by then it was too late.

"Bye-bye, Johnny."

Blink.

The **Magic** of Science

———

1

She could often see the auras of things; plants mostly, trees and bushes and flowers. Sometimes animals, but only rarely. People she almost never saw; in fact, in her life so far there had been only one.

Her favorites were the flowers. Their lifeglow was unmistakable, like a sizzling electric net that surrounded them and connected them to the earth, to all of creation . . . to herself.

Her name was Maia.

She lived where she had been born and raised, in the valley below the Double Falls, next to the river in a hidden forest encampment, far from the prying, hostile eyes of government. Cities and civilization she knew about, but only as vague ideas from stories and files. After her mother died – two weeks before her fifth birthday, that had been – the folk of the compound worked together to raise her as a community. They had loved her and treated her as their own, so that she rarely wanted for anything.

But as much as she cared for them all, it was the forest that always claimed her first and deepest love. She'd been walking its dusky paths, hung with Spanish moss and creeping tendrils of ivy, smelling dank earth and rotting wood and rich green life, since before her memories began. She felt a connection to the burbling streams, the cascading waterfalls, the profusion of flowers that filled the air with their heady perfume in the spring and summer, that she had simply never felt for any individual human being.

She had deeper secrets as well, things she didn't share with anyone, not even Darby, who'd been her best friend since they were both ten years old.

The first secret was a gift, a thing she had simply discovered one day, quite by accident. She had found that by focusing, she could change the aura of a given plant once she'd *seen* it. She found that she could . . . *add* to it, could make it *more,* somehow. She had no explanation for this, nor did she need one. She had never been taught this skill – as far as she knew, she had been born with it. The same was true in the way she had always just *known* which berries and roots and mushrooms were edible, which ones were medicinal, which ones deadly poison. Every year it seemed that half the kids in the compound came down with poison oak or sumac or some other nasty rash . . . but Maia never contracted anything worse than a pimple.

Her second secret . . . well, that was more complicated, as she didn't even know most of it herself. The gist of it was simple and should have been terrifying, but somehow wasn't. Simply put, there were *holes* where her memories should have been, at various times during the summers of her youth – gaps of two or three days that she couldn't account for, no matter how she racked her memory. It always happened when she was up-valley, collecting stones or camping or simply taking a walk to the Falls. Whatever the nature of these forays, she always came back feeling invigorated, refreshed and focused, with a renewed passion for her life, her compound family and the forest.

But though the overall effect had been positive, she was troubled by her inability to recall what went on during those times, and frustrated. And there were other complications, as well.

The first time it had happened, some of the older compound members were rightfully concerned at her absence, and she'd found herself in a very uncomfortable position upon her return, of explaining where she'd been when she herself didn't know. She'd sputtered out something about camping by the falls and losing track of time, and after some severe talk and a lot of frowns, they had let it go.

The lesson wasn't lost on her. She began taking frequent camping trips by herself during the spring and summer months, establishing a pattern so she would have some way of explaining herself should it happen again.

And it *did* happen – had happened at least twice every year since then, sometimes in the late spring, once in awhile in early autumn. This last time had been only two months earlier, in late July of this year. One afternoon, she'd felt a strong intuition, a tug she had only recently learned to identify; basically, she had just 'felt' that it was time to go up-valley, to her hidden spot by the falls . . . and so she had gone camping.

And had returned three days later, feeling invigorated. Refreshed. Focused. And without a clue as to where she had been or what she'd been doing.

But then . . .

But then, perhaps she did have a clue after all. Because there were always dreams afterward, sometimes for weeks – depthless, timeless visions of a man with a wide smile and flashing eyes. All of the dreams were the same in the end. He beckoned her urgently and bade her remember.

But though she tried, she could remember nothing of her dreams except his face, and the way his eyes shone . . .

And a name.

Milos.

2

The privacy of Simon DaLuge's office, only a few steps from the buzz of Lab One, was like a balm for his senses when he needed to focus, and right now he needed just that. A problem had arisen within the Supercontroller's assimilation program, a discrepancy in the imaging generators that had brought a sudden and malignant suspicion to his already over-wrought mind.

And now the hand-com in his pocket was buzzing; it had been trying to get his attention for some time, but he'd only just noticed it. With a sigh, he stood up and fished the thing out, wincing at the tingling and crackling in his back.

"DaLuge here. This had better be important."

The unit gave a burst of static and a vaguely familiar voice came through. "Sorry to bother you, sir. This is Wheeler, up in level three." The voice was hesitant. "I think you should come up here, sir. We've had a breach."

Wheeler . . . level three . . .

DaLuge wiped a thin sheen of sweat from his upper lip and thought for a moment. Of the entire complex of projects at Clifftop over which he had supervisory control, level three was one of the most unique, and certainly one of the most volatile. He shook his head, suddenly angry that he should have to deal with this ineptness during such a stressful time, only a day after the latest clone had failed.

Failed. That's a nice euphemism, isn't it?

"Well, do what you can, Wheeler. I'll get up there as soon as I can."

The hand-com was silent for a moment, then clicked to life with another short burst of static. Wheeler's voice was lower, more urgent. "Um . . .sir, I'm not sure you understand. We've lost a batch of the mosquitoes."

"Lost? What do you mean, lost? You don't mean . . ." DaLuge's mind clamped shut, wouldn't allow the possibility to even surface there, but he knew it was so, even before the other man's voice came back.

"They're outside, sir. They're gone."

He sat down heavily and ran a hand through his grey mop of hair. Taking a deep breath, he snapped the com unit to his lips. "I'm on my way."

Wheeler's voice held audible relief. "Thank you, sir."

"Heads are going to roll on this one, Wheeler," DaLuge said. "Maybe yours."

The hand-com gave a final burst of static, but remained silent.

Level three was divided into a small research lab – which took up about a quarter of the available space – and several controlled testing rooms for each of the strains of genetically altered insects that were being concocted here.

The mosquito room was a series of permaplast box cages; transparent, but humidified so that their inside surfaces were fogged. The mosquitoes were larger than those found in the wild; they clung to the milky surfaces of the cages, or buzzed back and forth between the flesh pods that sustained them while in captivity. Their eerie whine made DaLuge remember why he hated this room. These days, with the Supercontroller Project well under way and the demands of Lab One taking up all of his time, he only occasionally looked over the raw data from level three, and he hadn't actually been up here in months.

Wheeler was waiting for him at the end of the room, along with a couple of masked and suited technicians, busily running scanners over and around a large louvered wall vent – apparently the source of the breach. An uncommonly tall man, Wheeler was slightly hunch-backed but gangly, his lab coat an ill fit; it seemed to hang from his angular frame. His close-set eyes were worried as they watched DaLuge's hurried entry.

"Sir!" he said, straightening nervously. "My sincere apologies for pulling you away from your work."

"How many did we lose?" DaLuge asked, ignoring the other man's beseeching attitude.

"One full batch. Cage thirty-one, right here on the end."

"Has the area been cleared?" DaLuge gestured at the two workers, who had apparently finished their scans. One of them, a small woman with cropped blond hair, turned toward them and removed her mask. "Clear, sir. No trace of any remaining bugs."

DaLuge didn't know whether to be glad or outraged. The mosquitoes were a risk to anyone who encountered them, which meant he should probably be glad that none of them were left in the room to endanger himself or the staff. However, having an entire batch on the loose was a unique and perplexing problem all its own.

"How did this happen?" His voice had gone up in pitch, and he made no effort to hide his anger.

Wheeler avoided his gaze. "A mix-up during the shift change this morning," he said. "We'd pulled some samples for testing, and, er . . . well, the stun field must have been set at a lower resonance than normal. The bugs woke up and flew the coop before we had the box secured."

"Were you here?"

"No sir. I discovered the situation less than an hour ago during normal rounds." He hesitated for a moment. "I took the liberty of sending the responsible persons down to Psych for re-assignment."

"Good." DaLuge nodded curtly. "And I want you to institute new protocols. Resonance must be logged and signed off before testing."

"Yes, sir." Wheeler looked relieved. "I'll see to it myself."

"Can we track them?"

The large man shifted nervously, foot to foot. "Ah – we're already trying, sir, but their frequency generators were minimally operational, at best. All we know for sure is that they're not here, at Clifftop. They made it outside." He shrugged. "If they stay close, or if they infect someone, we might pick them up."

DaLuge knew the man was trying to sound hopeful, but he shared little of Wheeler's optimism. "Well, they're single-generation, correct? Even if we can't find them, they won't be able to reproduce."

"That's true, sir."

"And how long will they live?"

Wheeler paged through his clipboard. "No more than ninety days, but they shouldn't be virile beyond seventy-five or so."

"Do you know what will happen if these bugs infect someone, Wheeler?"

"Well, no, not exactly, sir, but . . . well, isn't that what they're designed for? To infect people?"

DaLuge barked an impatient laugh. "Eventually, yes. Eventually they'll be used for microbotic colonization, but they weren't ready yet. If they inject someone with the sequencers at this stage, there's no telling what might happen."

Wheeler frowned. "It's highly doubtful they could get far enough to infect anyone, sir. There's not a living soul within three hundred miles of here, and the bugs will most likely die off long before they could migrate that far."

DaLuge's voice was flat. "You'd better hope so. If this happens again it's going to be your ass down to Psych."

He felt better as he turned on his heel and strode from the room; felt better all the way to the lift; felt better all the way back to Lab One, in fact, which was where he received a call from the boss that flattened his good mood completely and left him feeling like he'd just been rabbit-punched.

3

Deep in the bowels of Mephisto Station, in a chamber just above the massive centrifugal engines that supplied the station with gravity, was the office and quarters of Lazaro Sol, Proconsul Senior of the Parliament of Elders, Grand Hartha Wizard of the Thirty-Third Degree, and currently Security Chief of Planet Earth.

A huge, faux-marble permaplast desk dominated the end of the room, beneath a screen no less prominent; the latter covered the entire back wall of the office.

The top of the desk held only a few papers and a small built-in screen. Lazaro Sol bent over it, listened for a moment, then laughed, a raw sound like gravel on gravel. "I don't give a tin shit for your opinion at the moment, Simon," he rumbled. "You have your orders. Activate the Daniel Protocol, and do it within the hour. Randall is leaving here shortly."

He disconnected abruptly and laughed again. "Well, I'd say that got his attention," he said to the only other person in the room, the small man standing opposite his desk. "What do you think, Randall?"

"If you say so." The Agent was dressed in a suit of muted grey. His skin, especially his elfin face, was tinged a lighter shade of grey. A grey felt hat spun slowly between his spidery fingers.

Lazaro Sol leaned back imperiously in his customized black-padded leather chair, an ancient man with a deeply seamed face and glittering black eyes. A hidden servo in the chair hummed to life, lifting him up and tilting him forward slightly so that he looked down at the face of his Agent.

"What do you have for me?" The words were distorted by the ragged wheezing coming from his wrecked lungs, the constant threat of a coughing attack.

"Since you were speaking with DaLuge, you already know that the latest attempt at Contact has failed." Randall's words were perfectly cultured, clipped and free of accent.

"Yes, I know. I didn't get the specifics, but . . ." A look of creeping anger crossed Lazaro's face. He clamped and unclamped his jaw once or twice, trying to stave off the unwelcome emotion, then glared balefully at his Agent. "You were there. Was anything different this time?"

"Each of the cases has been interesting in its own right," Randall said carefully. "You can view yesterday's vid-feed yourself if you wish. I have it right here." The felt hat stopped spinning long enough for the Agent's bony fingers to remove a small plug-drive from the inside pocket of his suit jacket. He handed it across the desk.

Lazaro Sol took the drive and turned it in his fingers distractedly, not really looking at it.

Randall cleared his throat. "There was one more thing, sir. Something I thought you might find interesting."

Lazaro looked up, a preternatural gleam in his sunken eyes. "Well?" The word was a grinding snarl, punctuated by a sudden onset of coughing.

"At least some of your suspicions seem to have been confirmed," Randall said, not looking directly at him. "There appears to be a dissonant faction, as you feared. I saw one Elder, a Senator McElroy . . ."

"Yes, yes, I know of the man." Lazaro waved a hand impatiently. "Mid-level ladder-climber, sponsored by Sol Ashbro, if I'm not mistaken. What about him?"

Randall cleared his throat politely. "Hhmmm. As I was saying, I noticed that he seemed to be spending a great deal of time in and around Lab One in the hours following the attempt. He was talking to various people, including Simon DaLuge. I was unable to get very close, though, as he was accompanied by a Triad Agent and I did not wish to attract attention."

"*What!!?*" Lazaro nearly exploded out of his chair. Servos whined in protest, a thin, keening sound that was out of place in the muted stillness of the office. "How in hell's blazes did this happen? Since when does a simple senator require the aid of a Triad?!"

"I found it interesting, as well." Randall seemed not to notice the red flowers that bloomed in the old man's cracked white cheeks. "The Agent's name is Parker," he continued. "The one with McElroy. I believe his designation is oh-three-nine." He paused again, tipped his head forward slightly. "I hope this information is beneficial."

Lazaro Sol leaned back slowly in his chair, feeling once more in control. His mind was beginning to spin, to sort this new information, to play with it the way a dog plays with a bone. "Yes . . . yes, very much so." He looked up with a benevolent smile. "Thank you, Randall."

The Agent nodded curtly and snapped the grey felt hat back onto his head with a practiced gesture. "Thank *you*, sir."

"One more thing, Randall. You heard me speaking with Simon, I presume?"

Randall's face betrayed nothing but a muscle tic at one corner of his mouth. "The clone?"

"The last one," Lazaro replied grimly. "He's in cold storage at Clifftop. I'll send you the code. Once he's been activated, sedate him and bring him here." He checked his chronometer. "If you hurry, you can make it back to Mephisto this afternoon."

"Very good." Randall turned on his heel and left the room silently. The airlock *snicked* shut behind him, and Lazaro closed his eyes and leaned back with a relieved sigh. For a long, long moment he thought of nothing but trying to relax his tired, over-wrought body . . . but the moment was soon over. The wheels in his mind wanted to spin, and as usual, he let them. A mind, he had always believed, needed a problem to stay at its best, and he had stumbled upon an interesting one.

Why was McElroy with a Triad Agent?

The wheels spun, slowly at first and then with more precision, gears within gears turning behind his cracked, grotesque face, picking up speed, rushing towards the certainty of a conclusion . . . and as he reached for the elusive thread, turning information in his mind like a collection of polished stones, a predatory smile curved at the corner of his mouth.

The hunt was on.

Simon DaLuge strode along the hallway toward the lift bay, hand stuffed deeply into the pockets of his long white lab coat, muttering angrily to himself. *"Gods!* To resort to these measures – it's insanity! What the hell does he think he's doing?" He banged on the lift call button and ran a hand distractedly through his shaggy hair. "Insanity!"

The lift *dinged* open and he slammed in. "Level U9!" He barked to the computer. The door slid shut and the lift began its smooth, whirring descent. DaLuge tore his spectacles violently from his nose and cleaned them vigorously with the tail of his shirt, barely noticing what he was doing. He was livid; no, more than livid. He was incensed and aghast.

"Gods!" He sputtered again, feeling the anger circling in his mind. *"How can he do this?"*

He ground his teeth, finally bringing himself back under a shaky sort of control. He ran his hands over his pockets, looking for his pack of cigarettes, only to remember after a moment that he'd quit smoking nearly five years ago. In place of tobacco, his fumbling fingers pulled a small object from his pocket. He stared at it dumbly for a moment.

It was a small blue plug-drive, an innocuous data storage device of the same type used daily by most of the general public . . . but there was something different about this one. Something dangerous. What was it that Senator McElroy had said during their brief meeting in the abandoned cafeteria? Two days earlier, this had been, right before the most recent attempt at Contact. Simon hadn't believed then that his boss would stoop to this sort of madness, but McElroy had warned him, hadn't he? The senator's words came back to him now.

When the time comes, our coup will be complete and merciless and leave no tracks. You won't be implicated.

A shiver of terror snaked up his spine, and he dropped the plug-drive back into his pocket with nerveless fingers.

Bad enough that I talked to McElroy at all; even worse that I took what he gave me. And why did I bring it with me, anyhow?

But he knew why. And if he actually followed through and did what McElroy had asked of him, there was only one light in which Lazaro Sol would view his actions.

It's outright treason, Simon. Don't candy-coat it. Deal with it.

He knew that Lazaro's plan for the final clone was utter madness, but there was no talking to the man. In the end, as usual, Lazaro got his way. He'd waved aside DaLuge's protests with a shake of his large head. "You're the genius, Simon," he'd growled. "Think of it as your greatest challenge. Do what it takes to figure it out, but *this needs to be done.*"

And of course, here he was an hour later like some highly trained monkey, trying his best to remember anything he could about the backup program Lazaro had requested.

The Daniel Protocol.

He hadn't thought of it in years, though he'd helped Lazaro Sol to design the program while they were in Switzerland, currying favor and trying to rally support among the Elders for Lazaro's brainchild, the Supercontroller Project.

He'd thought the whole thing a bit silly at the time – really, why would they ever want to wake the Supercontroller in real-time? – but he'd humored the old man anyway. After all, what choice had there been? Lazaro had been set on the idea, and if there was one thing Simon had learned over the years, it was that Lazaro Sol always got what he wanted. And, besides that, the Elders paid the bills.

So he'd gone along, certain that with plentiful specimens to work from, he'd never be put in the position of actually needing to use the failsafe.

He laughed bitterly as the lift came to a stop.

Shows what I know.

The door slid open, depositing him abruptly on the cold storage level, nine stories underground. His glasses fogged up immediately in the refrigerated air, making it hard to see, and he had to stop and wipe them off three or four times, cursing floridly under his breath, before he made it shivering into the vault.

The final clone was a barely visible shadow, a silhouette through frosted glass in a chamber at the far end of this little-used room, which he'd modified himself for the purpose of growing and housing the initiate Supercontroller clones.

We built them right here.

He looked around, remembering all the time spent here, and found that he hadn't missed the place much since he'd moved upstairs.

It always felt like a meat-locker.

The clones had been built carefully, their genes spliced and coded to the nth degree by DaLuge himself. Larger craniums for more brain capacity, triple synaptic density for high computational yield . . . in short, a series of super-brains. The smartest and most adaptable minds on the planet, at least in theory, these clones had been built for distance *and* speed.

Simon shivered and blew on his hands for warmth as he waited for the main console to boot, but it wasn't only the sub-freezing temperatures that chilled him. Looking uneasily through the frosted window, he couldn't help but think of what had happened to the last clone, only a few days earlier.

Not to mention the first two.

The console whirred to life and he began working, but part of him kept returning to the failed attempts. He didn't like thinking about them, not only for the sense of personal failure it brought to mind but also for the sheer brutal humanity, the utter horror of the first three initiates' collective fate.

Total meltdown.

The clones had been built for a singular purpose. The goal was to synchronize one of them with the Clifftop motherboard, the largest data-sorting computer in the world; in essence, the initiate would be plugged into the huge mainframe and turned into a computer himself. Once this was achieved, the resulting system would monitor virtually every electronic network and device on Earth, acting as control node for the entire planet.

An ambitious project, this brainchild of Lazaro Sol . . . a thing of breathtaking scope.

Oh, don't be so modest, Simon. It wasn't just Lazaro, or the Elders . . . you played your part, too.

He shut this thought out, focusing his attention instead on re-checking his input fields. Everything must be perfect, now more than ever.

As he worked, he questioned himself again. Was he making the right move? Was it worth it?

I'm not the only one who thinks he's lost it.

Lazaro Sol's rash decision to activate the remaining clone before Contact was only the most recent in a list of questionable moves that went back decades, and was obviously raising more eyebrows than just his own.

Simon had respected the man once; had respected him even to the point of awe at times. The brazen certainty with which Lazaro comported himself was an inspiration, as was the genius and lucidity of his ideas – the current project was only one example of the man's brilliant mind, which had given birth to a string of projects over the years that kept Simon DaLuge as busy as a bee. He'd never been happier than when he had a really good challenge in front of him, and so for years he'd created freely, turning Lazaro's twisted, devilish ideas into reality, always working, sometimes on as many as a dozen projects at a time. Without ever paying any attention to it, he'd built up a formidable retirement account and amassed a small fortune . . . but as time went by, all of his various successes began to feel more and more hollow. Reflection forced him to see a truth that he didn't want to see – that his work had largely been co-opted by the Elders, for use in schemes that seemed increasingly repugnant to him as he grew older . . . though he hardly dared admit this, even to himself.

For the last year, a growing certainty had begun to leave him restless; and irritable; and finally sleepless. He tossed in his bed nightly, more sure by the moment that Lazaro Sol would *never* let him go, that he would die hunched over a table in a laboratory with no windows, un-loved and un-remembered. The feeling became so strong that he'd resorted to sleeping pills at times, with only limited success. It had only been in the last few days, since his covert meeting with McElroy, that he'd gotten any real sleep.

So . . . you're going through with it, then?

Whose voice was that, asking the question?

He shook his head. "It doesn't matter," he said out loud. "It's worth it, if they can pull it off. And if not . . ."

With a single movement, he drew the plug-drive from his pocket and slammed it into the port with an angry, muttered oath.

Death or retirement. Either way, I'm done.

His face contorted in a grimace as his fingers flew across the keys, finalizing the 'extra' information that would be added to the clone's initialization program.

Finalizing my treachery.

As he worked, his thoughts turned to the future that McElroy had dangled in front of him like bait.

The price of treason.

An early retirement was what they'd promised him – an island of his own, somewhere warm . . . the South Pacific, perhaps? All he wanted was a place to live out his days in peace. There would be women, of course, and wine, and a sandy beach, sunblown and effervescent; a library, large enough to house every volume he could ever want, and a laboratory, where he could finally do something *real,* something with social worth . . .

His reverie came to an abrupt end as the outer doors opened with a *whoosh*. He looked up to see Lazaro Sol's personal Agent standing just inside the room. Randall's face was a grey mask, his eyes hollow. He was doing that odd, mildly unnerving thing that he did with his hat, turning it slowly in his hands as if it were made not of cloth but steel, a weapon he might unleash with deadly fury at any time.

"Is everything ready?" The Agent's voice was like oil.

DaLuge felt a small twinge of revulsion, which he masked with a tight-lipped smile. "Of course."

He stood, using the movement as a screen to slip McElroy's plug-drive out of the console and back into his pocket. He stepped to one side and tapped the key to lock in the program and bring up the final executive codes.

"He's all yours."

4

Maia sat on a boulder overlooking the river, sorting through the afternoon's find; mostly agates, periwinkles and a few small snail-shells, which she used to make jewelry, or for accent and decoration on the clothes she made.

She hummed softly as she worked, enjoying the solitude and the late autumn afternoon. The sun had broken through a haze of distant clouds, and now she watched it wash the last of the afternoon away, shafts of gold breaking through the swaying hush of greenness that surrounded her.

When she was done sorting, she wrapped the various items in a few large handkerchiefs she'd brought for just that purpose, then stashed them in the small, hip-slung bag she always took when she went walking. She got to her feet and stretched, noting the lateness of the day in the depth of the forest shadows. She debated on going further upstream, but decided against it – dusk would be falling soon, and as the light faded, the chill in the breeze reminded her that it was growing late in the year.

Summer is almost gone.

She pulled the drawstring tight and turned downstream. She could take her time and still be back to the compound before dark.

The chuckle of water over stone became louder as she made her way along the bank, sometimes wading, sometimes pulling herself along by using overhanging branches as handholds. After a few minutes, the stream-bed widened before rushing over a large boulder into a still, flat expanse; a placid pool where all the little kids liked to swim during the summer – and some of the big kids, too. This was where the path cut away from the river and back to the compound.

The hand-com in the pocket of her faded denim jacket gave a single short burst of static. Surprised, she pulled it out and keyed the receiver.

"Yes?"

"Maia, that you?"

She recognized her room-mate's voice. "Yeah, Darby – I'm at the Mirror Pool."

"Are you swimming? I checked at the rapids, but you weren't there – anyway, it doesn't matter. I'm almost . . ."

Darby appeared from behind a nearby bush, looking flushed. The radio gave another burst of static, then a hum of feedback. Maia shut it off quickly, annoyed by the insolent sound.

Darby grinned and pushed a strand of black hair from her round face. Her cheeks were ruddy, and she seemed excited.

"You'll never guess what I just heard," she gushed. "There's new blood in camp, can you believe it?!"

"Really? Who?" Maia was surprised. New people were rare at Compound West; it had been that way her whole life.

Darby shrugged and fell into step beside her, moving away from the water on a faded path between the trees. "I don't know. Allie told me he's from another compound. I guess he just strolled up on the Grove this afternoon like he owned the place. He's been making the rounds with the Chairman." She laughed and took Maia's arm as they reached the well-beaten path that cut through the neck of trees between the river and the compound.

"Huh." Maia ducked under a limb that overhung the path, holding it up so her friend could pass. "That's interesting."

As far as she knew, Darby herself had been the last outsider to come to Compound West, almost ten years ago now. But Darby was city-born, and that happened sometimes; there were refugees, and outcasts, and rescues. But in her entire life, no one had ever come here from another compound.

"Oh, I bet you're interested." Darby's eyes were mischievous. She grinned and nudged Maia with an elbow. "He is a boy, after all. A jen-you-wine male of the species, and one you've never seen before. That makes it even more 'interesting'."

"Ha!" Maia laughed and mock-slapped her friend across the cheek. "As if I care. That would be the last thing I need, anyway."

Darby grunted a laugh and said something in a low voice that Maia didn't quite catch.

"What was that?"

Darby grinned slyly. "I *said* . . . I think it might be the thing you need the most. I don't know what I'd do without Thad."

Maia grinned a little and shrugged. "Well, I'm not you, Dar."

"Don't I know it." Darby laughed. "Maybe I'll just introduce myself then. I got a good man, but I could always use a spare."

Maia laughed with her friend as they broke from the trees and into a huge, lush grassy meadow, shadowed with the encroaching twilight. Across the meadow, nearly a quarter mile away, was the low hill that housed the main bunker system. Behind it, the forest crept up the sides of the high ridge; quartz-infused granite glimmered in a hundred spots along the rocky, serrated peaks as it caught the last of the day's sun.

"You hungry? I think dinner is going."

Maia laughed and patted her friend's hand. "I kind of just assumed that's where you were taking me."

Darby tipped her head with a knowing wink. "Well, you never know. Maybe the new guy will be there."

The main compound was housed in an underground bunker system, which infiltrated the wide, low hill at the edge of the meadow. Friendly yellow light glowed from the wide, low doorway of the kitchen bunker onto the faded, beaten grass as they approached with a few other stragglers and late-comers.

Maia and Darby made their way down the few steps and ducked through the doorway, straightening up into the wonderful smells of dinner; roasted vegetables with fresh butter, hand-tossed salads made from greens and carrots grown in Abby Carmichle's greenhouse, and Diana Russel's current specialty – peppered venison and rice casserole. Somebody had shot a deer a few weeks earlier, and they'd made the meat count.

They greeted friends and chatted as they went through a short line to the serving table, then piled their food on wooden plates and joined Darby's boyfriend, Thad, at a small table near the edge of the room. He pushed over to make room, greeting them without looking up. He seemed intent on shoveling as much food as possible into his wide, ruddy face, washing it all down with iced anise seed tea from a crude clay mug. Maia took a seat across from the pair, with her back to the wall.

As far as she could tell, the new guy was not In the room.

Darby soon had Thad engrossed in wild speculation about the newcomer: where is he from? and what's he doing here? and is he really 'one of us'?

"I hope he's not a government plant," Thad said in a solemn tone, taking a large bite from a hunk of buttered bread. He lowered his voice for dramatic effect, leaned forward, chewed and swallowed. "You guys know the story about what happened at Southwest," he went on. "Hell, Aldridge himself could tell you, he was there around that time. Anyway, some poor bastard got taken on a raid. No one ever knew what the CEC did to him, but at the very least they bugged him before they sent him back to camp. Compound security was on perimeter alert and saw him coming. They had to *shoot* him, Dar – they splattered his brains all over the –"

"Jesus, Thad!" Darby sputtered. "We're trying to eat here. And we've all heard that story a million times anyway. In the version I heard, the guy killed himself with a cyanide capsule so he wouldn't go back and doom his friends."

"Either way," Thad said truculently, "it's pretty bad out there. Which means you just never know."

"Well," Darby shot back, "What I *do* know is that the new guy was out all afternoon with Jeremieah Aldridge, making the rounds and shaking hands. Do you think the Chairman is soft in the head? If anyone could spot something fishy, he could."

The conversation continued in this vein for some time, but Maia didn't join in, contenting herself instead with healthy portions of Diana's savory fare. She finished the last bite of her rice and took a long drink of water, then leaned back with a happy sigh, letting her eyes rove the room.

And so it was that she saw the new guy before her friends did.

He walked through the low doorway behind Jeremieah Aldridge, stooping slightly to avoid bumping his head, then stood for a moment, blinking and letting his eyes adjust to the relatively harsh light of the muted fluorescents.

She used the moment to assess him.

He was tall and rangy, with shoulder-length dark hair, disheveled and seemingly days past needing to be washed and combed. His face was angular, with pronounced cheekbones that looked hewn from limestone. He was dressed in a familiar way; faded blue jeans, a long-sleeved brown shirt, worn leather boots that looked as comfortable as they were ancient. These things she saw in a moment, without even looking . . . but it was his eyes that finally caught her, holding her gaze for a bare moment as he swept the room. She sucked in a breath, surprised at her own reaction, but even after he had looked away, she couldn't. She had been captured by his eyes . . . but why?

They were watchful and attentive, and seemed sadder than most, as if behind them lurked some unnamed burden . . . but the quality that held her was something else entirely.

It's like he knows something he shouldn't.

The thought rose unbidden, and she pushed it away impatiently.

The Chairman said something to the new guy in a low voice and gestured, and the two of them moved off across the room toward the food table.

And for only a moment, as they did, she saw his aura – almost membranous, like a film of subtle, shifting colored light, superimposed over his body.

She gasped involuntarily and sat straight up in her seat.

"Maia? You all right?" Darby followed her gaze, then elbowed Thad almost violently, causing him to spill tea on his plate, which was luckily quite empty by this point. "There he is!" She whispered loudly. "With Jeremieah Aldridge, like I said."

Maia paid her friend no attention. She was too surprised by what she'd seen, too flustered and curious and awed to listen to Darby. All her attention was focused on the new guy, trying to sustain the vision of his aura, trying to see it again . . . but whatever the magic, it was gone. After a moment, she gave up trying and sat back with a sigh.

Darby was saying something.

"What?" Maia turned to her friend apologetically. "Sorry, I was spaced out."

"Yeah, you were," Darby drawled, drooping an eyelid in a knowing wink. "You sure were. What I *said* was that Allie was right. He *is* cute."

Maia laughed easily along with her friend, but her mind was far away and

racing, her heart thumping.

Did I really just see that? What does it mean?

She didn't know . . . but she did know that she wanted to find out. She wanted that quite badly.

Maia re-filled her cup, this time with hot tea, and stayed by herself at a table in the corner, even after Darby and Thad had excused themselves on the pretext of going for a moonlit walk. "While the weather's still decent," Thad said.

Darby asked if she wanted to come along, but the invitation came off half-hearted and she didn't much feel like it anyway, so she smiled and said thanks but no thanks, and told the two of them to go ahead without her, claiming tired legs from her earlier walk. She knew where the two of them were *really* going anyway, or at least where they would end up – making out at The Knob, an earth-and-rock formation that loomed over the valley floor, about half a mile down-valley, past The Grove. A climb of ten minutes afforded great views of star-studded skies over moonlit peaks, and as much privacy as was necessary for Darby and Thad's never-ending fornications.

She sipped her tea, looking around the room. The regular stragglers were all here; Duke Leighton in his battered fedora and dirty pants, Melby Allen with her quick, quiet eyes and hesitant laugh, Tetra Skanovich and her solemn smile, hair in that single long braid she always wore, like an arrow straight down the center of her back. Twenty or more familiar folk sat singly or in groups, eating, drinking and talking, these faces that she knew so well . . .

My friends. My family. But none of these people are keeping me in this room. It's him.

The new guy still sat with the Aldridges – Jeremieah and Allie and their youngest daughter, Karla, who sat across from the stranger and watched him with big, solemn eyes while she pushed her vegetables around her plate with a fork.

Maia had been covertly watching him for more than half an hour now, but after her initial first impression there didn't seem to be anything specifically strange about him. He carried himself in a laid-back, reserved fashion that appealed to her, but also seemed engaging enough with the folks – and there were several – who'd made their way to his table for introductions and general conversation while he ate. He had smiled easily and shaken hands with them all, and seemed genuine enough. She'd tried to catch his name during several of these short meet-and-greets, but hadn't gotten anything definitive. She thought maybe it started with a 'J', but that was all.

What are you going to do when he leaves?

She didn't want to think about it, but apparently she was going to have to.

The Aldridges and the new guy were getting up from the table and drifting toward the door, and within moments they would be gone.

Without the slightest notion of why she was doing it, she put down her cup and stood up. Shrugging into her jacket, she pulled her knit cap tight about her ears and followed them out the door before she could change her mind.

It was fully dark now, but they hadn't gone far and she spotted them almost immediately, illuminated by the meager, swaying yellow light of Jeremieah's electric lantern. The Chairman led the way, an unmistakable figure with his broad shoulders and his head of short, tight gray curls. Allie's slight figure came behind, holding Karla's hand, and the new guy brought up the rear, walking with a long, rolling gait.

She waited for a slow ten-count, then followed, watching. For a moment, as the group entered the trees, she thought she saw his aura again, a cloud of slowly shifting red and blue that enveloped his dark figure.

And again, she blinked and it was gone.

She had no light, but her feet knew the path like an old friend and she had no trouble keeping up with them. She saw right away that they were going back to the Grove, where they, and many other compound family, had spent the warm summer months.

The Grove was a huge, tree-dotted meadow that stretched for more than half a mile along the valley floor. The camp was composed of masterfully crafted temporary huts – made of light wood frames, tree bark and woven mats of branches – that were built to blend into the stands of birch that dominated meadow. Huge, ancient oaks dotted the Grove as well, their leafy crowns forming a partial canopy overhead; the net effect was that the camp was nearly invisible to satellite or high-fly scans.

Or so they say.

The Aldridges' hut was situated on the near edge of the Grove, so the walk didn't take long, which was something of a relief. Maia's usual attitude towards life and people was to be open, honest and direct at all times, and she was beginning to feel a bit strange, lurking about like this in the dark. When the group reached the Aldridges' hut, she hung back in the mass of shadows at the base of a nearby oak, waiting to see what would develop.

What will you do if he disappears inside and goes to sleep?

But he wouldn't. Somehow, she knew with crystal clarity that he meant to sleep out under the stars, though she couldn't have said why she felt this with such certainty.

The new guy stood outside the Aldridges' hut while Allie and Karla went inside, speaking with the Chairman in tones too low for her to hear. This was perfectly fine, as far as she was concerned – she really wasn't into eavesdropping anyhow.

A few minutes later, Allie re-emerged with a bundle that looked like a blanket or a sleeping bag, and the new guy took it, exchanged a few pleasantries, then excused himself and began walking directly towards where she stood, hidden in shadow. For a moment her breath caught in her throat –

he's seen me!

but then he walked right past her in the direction of the river, boots thumping on the earthen path, humming a fragment of melody to himself as he adjusted his pack and the bundle of blankets Allie had given him.

Again, she waited a long ten count, then slipped silently from her hiding place and followed.

From the movements of the silhouetted form against the shine of reflected moonlight on water, the new guy appeared to be exhausted. He hadn't gone far from camp, just found a nice grassy spot under a tree by the river and rolled out his bed. Now he sat, nearly unmoving, his shadow blending with the night.

Maia moved silently, a little upstream, and found a dead log to lean on. The ground under her felt cool and good, and smelled of the river and the dankness of the forest.

She sat and watched him for a while, hoping to catch another glimpse of his aura, but it wasn't visible. Many other things were, though, and for a while, she focused on the night around her. The trees seemed to sway and dance, and when she tried, she could see their silvery essences superimposed on the moonlit riverbank.

Something moved on the far side of the narrow river, under a tree, and she saw the reflective orbs of a deer's eyes – a buck with a large set of horns. Its muzzle dripped, silent rings opening outward onto the river's surface, and then it was gone in a flash of illumination as the full moon caught it for a second in mid-spring.

She sat up, rubbed her eyes and stretched, wondering how long she'd been sitting here. The form on the riverbank lay sleeping now; she could hear him snoring gently. Without any premeditation, she got to her feet and walked toward him slowly, her moccasined feet padding gently on the grass. She stopped about fifteen feet away, dropped to a squatting position, and looked again for the strange aura she had seen when he first walked into the kitchen bunker that evening.

And there it was – a lightning cloud superimposed around his sleeping form. As she watched, it seemed to pulse and grow, becoming more real, more colorful. With dawning amazement, she realized she could feel his aura the way she could feel shoes of plants in the forest. And, as with the plants, she focused her energy and found that she could make it grow, could add to it . . .as she crouched there in the darkness, the aura turned a deep green.

Suddenly he gasped in his sleep, emitting a low moan. His body jerked spasmodically, and he sat up with a startled shout. "What the – !!!"

The aura had disappeared, and she found herself face to face with the new guy.

"Hi," she said, chagrined and embarrassed, hoping the friendliness of her smile would be apparent in the moonlight. "My name is Maia."

"Christ!" He said with a sharp exhalation. "You scared the shit out of me!"

"Sorry." Now that she had woken him, she felt foolish for having followed him here at all. "I didn't know you were sleeping here. I . . ." She paused, then decided on a bald-faced lie. "I was out for a walk. I'll just be going."

He was in a full sitting position now, the starlight flashing in those deep, deep eyes. He gave her a tired smile, running a hand through his tangled hair. "It's all right. It's nice to meet you. My name is Johnny. You can sit down . . .if you want."

"Sure." She breathed a sigh of relief that she hadn't freaked him out too much, then sat cross-legged on the cool grass, absently picking a stalk and putting it her mouth. It tasted sweetly pungent. "So, um – tell me about yourself."

5

The upended wreckage of the armored truck burns with an oily smoke, the paint bubbling and hissing as it melts. One of the vehicle's compressed-plastic wheels spins lazily, then jerks as a blast-gun charge tears a long hole in it. His mother and father are both there, along with two other people; a man dressed in torn denim and a large woman with angry gray eyes. None of them can see him – he's only an observer here.

His mother has a bloodied bandage over her forehead, and holds a dirty white rag over her mouth and nose. Her eyes are glazed and tired, and she coughs convulsively. His father's face is bleeding profusely from a jagged cut on the cheek, and he wears a fierce expression as he looks around the edge of the twisted wreckage. He fires off two bursts from a battered blast-gun, then throws it away with a curse as it loses its charge. "We've got to go!" he screams.

The clambering roar of a chopper fills the scene, coming up over the barn behind them, lights blazing. A voice, demanding and dispassionate: Throw down your weapons and you won't be harmed. You are under arrest. Throw down your weapons . . .

The woman with the angry eyes hoists her blast gun and screams something unintelligible into the chopper's clattering whine. She gets off one wild blast and the four of them are pounded into the ground by massive worms of blinding light, cut to pieces like beefsteaks on a chopping block. The truck's fuel tank explodes, wiping the scene with a red-orange fireball.

Suddenly, the whole scene began to freeze in place, becoming a slow-motion caricature of itself, and Johnny, instead of being a frightened child, was aware of himself in a contemporary state – that is, he remembered having gone to sleep, in an abstract way, and in a similar detached fashion was aware that he must be dreaming.

The chopper hung overhead, its noise an indistinct crackle like static, its cannons throbbing silently. Johnny sensed another presence and turned to see a man, slightly shorter than himself but thicker in breadth. He had lustrous black shoulder-length hair peppered with gray, and wore thick woven pants – 'breeches' was the word that floated to the surface of Johnny's dreaming mind. He also wore a short robe, open at the neck to reveal wisps of graying hair. The robe was green, and tied around his waist with a woven length of braided deerhide strips.

"Good evening," said the man. "This is not a dream."

There was a sound, like that of fabric being ripped, and the scene dissolved. Johnny awoke with a start.

It took him a moment to remember where he was.

He had been sleeping alone, under trees or beside abandoned creekbeds, for a couple of weeks, and at first he mistook the crouching figure for an enemy – a CEC agent or renegade raider, bent on killing or arresting him.

Almost as soon as the startled cry sprang from his lips, however, he saw that it was a woman – a lovely young woman with curly red hair that sprang from under her rough wool cap and caught the moonlight. Her face was pale, with a slim, upturned nose and a wide mouth. She was smiling, showing her white, even teeth. In the moonlight, her skin seemed almost luminescent, and he saw a spread of freckles across her nose and cheeks. Despite the strangeness of his dream, he immediately forgot it in light of this new development.

"Hi," she said. "I'm Maia."

When he asked her to sit down, it was with very little hope that she would actually do so. He had been traveling for weeks and had been too tired for a shave or even a dip in the river. He knew that his hair probably looked like a cactus in the moonlight, so he was a little surprised when she flopped right down next to him like they'd been friends for years.

She picked a stalk of grass and began chewing on it absently, looking sideways at him. "So," she said. "Tell me about yourself."

"What's to tell?" He lay back on his elbows in the soft grass, gazing up at the stars. "I, uh . . . well, what do you want to know, exactly?"

"You know . . ." She drew her knees up until she was sitting in the lotus position, then rocked forward, hands twisting in her lap. "You know . . . like for instance, who is Johnny? What's your last name, by the way?"

"Perdue." He was relieved to have a simple question to answer. "Johnny Perdue."

She laughed easily. "Well, that's something," she said. "At least we have *that* cleared up."

He grinned. She had such an ambivalent, offhand manner that he began to breathe easier.

Maybe it won't be so hard to make friends here, after all.

"I'm from Montana compound," he said. "That's where I lived until now." His life seemed boring to him, uninteresting. "I brought some technological information with me . . . you know, on a plug-drive . . ."

"How did you get here?" She seemed completely uninterested in the nature of the 'technological information'. "Was it hard for you to leave your friends and family behind?"

He laughed. "I've been asking myself that same question," he admitted. "Because it seems like it should have been harder, but to tell the truth, I really wanted to come. You have to understand," he added, "it's not like it is here. The grid at Montana is so small that no one can really go far from the main camp." He shrugged. "I think it mostly came down to being stir-crazy, if you want the truth. I mean why I left. As far as how I got here . . .well, I hitched a ride from a friend, about half the distance, then walked the rest."

She nodded, her hair bouncing moonlit sparkles onto her shoulders. "You must be tired."

He noticed that, unlike himself, she didn't seem concerned about her appearance; she had taken off her wool cap and was turning it idly in her thin white fingers. Her hair was a little wild and unkempt beneath the cap, but this only made her seem more attractive.

What are you thinking, Perdue?

"I didn't know it was like that," she said. "In Montana, I mean. I guess I just thought all the compounds were like this one." Her tone was sincere.

He shrugged. "Maybe we just didn't try hard enough." He indicated the sweep of the ridge opposing them, the trees, the bright night sky. "This is a good thing, though, all of this. What I would've given for this much room, growing up, I can't even say."

"I can tell that you have a thing for the forest," she said.

He was surprised. "Oh? And what exactly does that mean?"

She wouldn't elaborate, just raised a shoulder and an eyebrow, dodging the question.

⁂

The conversation rambled aimlessly, prompted perhaps by the muting effect of the night, or the way the shadows lent mystery and anonymity to their encounter. Johnny felt an intense liking for her, and kept looking at her out of the corner of his eye as they talked. She was very expressive – she talked with her hands and her face as well as her voice, which was half parts lilt and twang. She was telling him bits and pieces of her own life, touching on points of personal history.

"So I don't remember my father," she was saying, "but I learned a lot from my mom, before she died. They tell me that I look a lot like her, but all I remember is a very intense, warm person who laughed all the time and told me lots of crazy stories before bedtime. She died of pneumonia when I was little." She hesitated. "Do you . . . I mean, um . . . what are your parents like?"

Johnny knew why she had hesitated. They were compound brats, both of them, and it went unspoken that many of those with whom you made your life were missing parents or other family members. Even during these last few years, when action had been minimal, death was a constant companion. Injury, disease, lack of competent doctors and good medical supplies . . . all these added up to a life expectancy somewhere in the mid-fifties for compound personnel.

He took the question head on. "They're dead," he said, holding himself still on the inside. The scars had hardened over the years, the wanting . . . but every time it came up, it brought back the hurt.

Her face was solemn. "I'm sorry," she said softly. Then, hesitantly: "Will you tell me about them?"

"It's okay." He looked at her, aware that here was someone who had, herself, lost both parents at a young age. She would understand. He sighed, took a deep breath. "There's really not much to tell. They used to go on raids all the time. They were very active – no bullshitting around like these days. Anyway, they volunteered for a mission, I'm not even sure what it was . . . probably gathering information and supplies like always."

"Their leaving had never bothered me before, but this time it was different. The night before they left, I woke up screaming in the dark. I had a dream; a nightmare, really. My parents were in it, along with some other people I didn't know. They were hiding, and I could tell they were scared. They didn't know I was there, but I could see them. Some people were shooting at them. I remember blast-gun beams flying everywhere, you know that weird yellow light they give off in the dark?"

He registered her look. "I guess not. Well, they do. I had never seen one at the time, but I never forgot that yellow color. Later, when I actually saw those guns in action, they gave off the exact same light." He furrowed his brow and shook his head impatiently. "Anyway, that's not the important part. All of a sudden this chopper comes up behind them and I hear this huge, booming voice, telling them they are under arrest. One of them starts shooting . . . and then . . ." He bit his lip, narrowing his eyes to fight back the tears. When he continued, his voice was low and raspy. "Anyway, you can imagine how it ends."

He took a deep breath.

"Anyway, I was hysterical. I ran to where they were sleeping and woke them up. I begged them not to go. I knew something bad was going to happen. I told them, but they wouldn't listen."

Maia's voice was soft. "Do you think you really saw their deaths?"

"I don't know. Maybe. I had the same dream four days later – two days before they were set to come back." He blinked a couple of times and took a deep breath. "Anyway, long story short, they never came back."

"That must have been hard."

He nodded. "Yeah. I still have that dream, off and on. In fact, I think I was having it before you woke me up. I seem to remember . . . *whoa*." His train of thought had derailed with unexpected swiftness. He was suddenly aware of a discrepancy, an element that had never been there before.

Good evening. This is not a dream.

"Whoa what?"

He hesitated, his mind clouded. A raft of images broke upon him, none of which he could sort intelligibly. "Nothing." He shook his head and sighed. "It's just a weird dream, that's all. I bet I've had it fifty times."

It seemed only a few minutes, but they must have talked for hours. Before Johnny knew it, he was able to see the undersides of passing clouds, and the outlines of the trees that dotted the riverbank. A chill morning breeze crept down the valley, bringing with it the promise of morning and the first twitters of the waking sparrows. There was a lull in the conversation, and Johnny had the wild notion of inviting her to share his blankets. He quickly curbed this unorthodox thought; on her part, she seemed unaffected by the chill in the air, though she had pulled her wool cap down tight over her ears, and she probably wouldn't appreciate what was sure to come off like a proposition.

"Well," she said finally, getting to her feet with a yawn. She stretched her arms toward the lightening sky. "I'd better go get some sleep . . . oh, shit."

"What?"

She grinned. "Darby's going to give me hell about this. Out all night carousing with the new guy." She laughed lightly, the sound soaking into the new morning. It was a nice laugh, fresh as the dew.

"I don't think we did much carousing," he replied with a grin, "but she doesn't have to find out, either way. You said you like to come out here at night, right? I mean, you were out walking at two in the morning when you found me here."

Her expression clouded for an instant, then she smiled. "True enough. Well . . . " she reached out and grasped his hand with a strong grip. "I better go. It was nice meeting you. We'll hang out later?"

"Absolutely." He hesitated, thinking he should say something more, something to seal the deal, to give presence to the fated feeling he had for her. "Thanks for listening."

Thanks for listening?

"You bet." She raised a gloved hand, a smile playing on her lips. "See you later."

She turned and walked away downstream, not looking back. Soon she had disappeared through the trees, and Johnny lay back in his blankets, pulling his pack under his head as a buffer against the wet grass.

"Thanks for listening," he said out loud, to no one in particular. "Shit."

6

Daniel walked down the long, curving corridor toward his appointment, wondering why Grandfather had summoned him. His feet making almost no sound in the thick red carpet

What can the old man want now?

He was in no hurry, so he slowed his pace, rapping his knuckles absent-mindedly on the smooth metal railing that ran around the perimeter of Mephisto Station's observation level. The result was a hollow pinging that went well with his frenetic thoughts.

He stopped to admire the view, leaning on one of the curved steel struts that bisected the railing at eight-meter intervals. His timing was perfect – the mammoth centrifugal engines, throbbing away indifferently at the core of the Station to create gravity, were just bringing his position to bear on the dark moon around which they orbited. Its pocked mass rose in his view like Olympus, and for a moment he was transfixed by its stark beauty.

He couldn't see the planet itself from here, but this did not bother him. He knew every mile of Earth's surface; every crack and canyon, every range of mountains, every bay, river and ocean. And of course, every city. He'd been studying these details, memorizing facts of history and geography, since he was old enough to be taught.

He rested his forehead on the transparent permaplast and sighed. His breath left no residue on the two-foot-thick, radiation-shielded window. This was due to invisible heating filaments inside the huge slabs of transparent (though tinted) glass-like substance. These filaments were sensitive to heat fluctuations within the station, keeping temperatures normalized to avoid cracking.

He knew these mundane facts out of hand, just as he knew thousands of others. Memorization of facts was the most dominant aspect of his life.

Daniel sighed again and pulled away from the view, nothing now but stars and the coldness of space. He debated staying at the window another twelve minutes, until he could once again be graced by a view of the magnificent gray moon . . . but there was no time.

Grandfather was waiting.

Grandfather looked up from the command screen - built into the top of his huge desk - and tapped a curved, bony finger on the screen to close whatever

statistics or communications file he'd been poring over. His deeply seamed face smiled tightly from small, deep-set eyes.

"Come in, Daniel."

The voice was low and gravelly, yet somehow resonant.

Daniel faced the old man, appraising him for today's mood with veiled eyes. He had always thought Grandfather's head too big for his neck, which seemed hung with extra skin; the Adam's apple jutted like the bony gorge of some predatory bird Daniel had come across in a biology text. Grandfather's whole face, in fact, seemed predatory; he had a curving hooked nose, prominent cheekbones and a wide forehead, deeply creased. Daniel had never seen Grandfather naked,

(Gods forbid! What a thought!)

but he suspected that the old man's entire body was wrinkled in the same manner, covered with deep creases like the landscape of some unfound planet. And then there were his eyes; tiny bits of black steel, burning with cold intensity from the caves of their sockets, always watching, always appraising . . .

Always judging.

Daniel often woke with visions of those eyes playing through his mind. Today they seemed, if not friendly, then at the least relaxed.

"Good morning, Grandfather." Daniel avoided the old man's gaze as he sat, being careful to remain attentive; he didn't want to appear overly lax. "You sent for me?"

The old man sat back, servo motors whirring in his oversized black chair. He steepled his gnarled hands beneath his chin. "Look at me, Daniel."

Daniel met his gaze with icy aloofness, though his stomach was turning over unsteadily. Grandfather always had this effect on him; he represented everything that Daniel aspired to, everything he had been taught to covet. Wealth, of course; wealth was all around, but it was the *power* that came with such wealth, the power to move the political currents of an entire world, that interested Daniel the most.

Grandfather eyed him calmly over his extended index fingers. "I'll get to the point," he rumbled. "I've important business, and I'm sure you'd rather be somewhere else?"

Daniel said nothing.

Grandfather flicked a switch under his desk, then turned to face the huge screen on the wall, which showed a familiar view of Earth, from a position directly over the North American continent. Reflexively, Daniel noted that it must be the feed from Sat3 – of the forty-one working reconnaissance satellites, Sat3 was the only one that would catch that picture at this time of day.

"What do you see, Daniel?"

Daniel shrugged. "What do you want me to see?"

Grandfather grunted, a hoarse cough escaping his lips. He reached for a glass of water and took a sip. "Don't be trite, boy. It's not a rhetorical question."

Daniel glanced back at the screen. "Earth, of course," he said. "I see our planet."

Grandfather's seamed face broke into a slow, hideous grin. *"Our planet,"* the old man said softly. "That's right, Daniel. It *is* our planet. But do you want to know what I see?" He raised a talon-like finger, shaking it twice at the screen.

Again, Daniel did not reply, only waited.

"I see a garden." Grandfather's countenance had softened, becoming almost sentimental, his heavy-lidded eyes withdrawn. Daniel knew enough not to trust this look, and he also knew that he was in for a sermon. He settled into his chair to wait it out.

"Our garden," Grandfather went on, "to do with as we please. Let me ask you something." Again his eyebrow went up, and Daniel could almost feel the tentacles of the old man's mind, probing his thoughts. "What do you believe is the purpose in all of your hard work? The lessons you have learned – you *have* learned, have you not? The years have not been wasted?"

Daniel shifted uncomfortably in his chair, not liking where this was going. "Of course not, Grandfather."

"Well, then, to what purpose do you suppose you have been brought?" The old man rose suddenly from his chair, more quickly than Daniel had imagined possible, given his advanced years. He began to pace the room slowly, a regal figure in a flowing black robe, hands clasped behind his back. "You have done well in your studies. You've learned much, and you will learn much, much more." He stopped, swiveled his large head slowly and fixed Daniel with his glittering black gaze. "But now, my boy . . . now you are about to enter the next level."

Daniel stiffened slightly in his chair, feeling his cheeks grow warm. A bead of perspiration began to form on his forehead, and he and willed it away, regarding Grandfather warily. "What new level?"

The old man smiled again, lips thin over yellowed teeth. "Everything you have learned so far has been merely history – the history of our planet. You've studied the playing field, so to speak, but I have yet to show you how history is used to shape the events of the future." He stopped next to the console and tapped a fingernail against its flat screen. The feed jumped to a different feed, showing a clear long-distance view of the entire North American continent.

"This is the game," the old man said softly, sounding almost reverent.

"The game?" Daniel asked.

"History!" Grandfather said, pacing toward the far end of the room, gliding with his arms folded inside his robe like a picture Daniel had once seen of a monk. *Buddhist,* his mental library asserted. *The monk was from Tibet, home of one sect of the ancient Buddhist religion. Other sects included . . .*

"The game . . ." Grandfather intoned, his voice drowning out the cold voice of fact in Daniel's head. "The game is history! But the stakes are the future. Earth is the playing field. And every person on the planet is a piece which moves to shape events. It is our place, our position, to move those pieces to our advantage." He stopped at the far end of the room and turned to face Daniel.

"We've never discussed the future, you and I," the old man said. "Always the past, or at the very least – as in the case of your geography lessons, or biology, or what have you – the present. But even that present is linked closely to history, because every word of every lesson is someone's interpretation of a past event. Remember *that* if you remember nothing else, Daniel . . . that is, if you are interested in the subtleties of control."

He moved slowly back toward the desk, dark eyes narrowed, watching his grandson. "Do you know what an egg is, Daniel?"

Daniel, though surprised by the question, did in fact know what an egg was. Though there were no animals or livestock on Mephisto station - with the exception of those (usually small rodents, insects or reptiles) used for laboratory experimentation or genetic samples - he had studied his biology well enough.

"An egg," he said. "The embryo of a bird. Variant in size. High in protein. Usually small, oval shaped . . ."

"Yes, yes." Grandfather waved a hand impatiently, ragged fingernails glinting in the light of the small desk lamp. "Well, what would happen if you stepped on an egg?"

A trick question?

Daniel cleared his throat. "It would break," he said.

"Of course." Grandfather gave an exaggerated smile. "It would be crushed to dust. But there's something you might not know. The shell of an egg is extremely strong at its domed ends. It's harder to break than you might think."

Daniel nodded, wondering where the old man was going with all this.

"Human beings are like eggs," the old man continued, settling back into his chair. "They're surrounded by a thin shell that is also extremely resilient. It is the shell of their assumptions about the world they live in. It is filled with all sorts of information about anything and everything; mostly themselves, their tastes, and a selection of memories they keep polished like beautiful stones, to be pulled out and looked at whenever they like. It is the inventory of what makes each of them unique. Now, here's the tricky part. If you place half a gross of eggs in cartons on the floor, you can actually walk on them. Do you know why?"

Daniel's mind cycled back to his physics lessons. "Because the surface area of many eggs is greater than that of a single egg, thereby distributing the pressure . . ."

"Close enough." Grandfather gave a dismissive wave of the hand. "It's not important. But the tricky part happens when you apply this idea to managing entire societies. To build a bridge into the future, we apply the pressure to human beings."

Daniel was intrigued with Grandfather's reasoning. He'd endured the old man's babblings many times, but couldn't remember when he'd been this interested. He suddenly realized that he had moved forward, onto the edge of his seat, his knee twitching nervously.

"How, Grandfather? How do you apply pressure to human beings?"

"Not just me." Grandfather leaned forward, moving his hand back and forth in a conspiratorial gesture to include himself and his grandson. "We! You and I, along with the rest of the Parliament of Elders. The decision has been made, my boy. You are to be initiated . . . and when you are, you'll fully be *one of us!* And *that* is the real reason I called you here today."

Daniel tried to speak, but no words came. He realized his mouth was hanging open and snapped it shut, teeth clicking together. He was attempting to respond to this sudden revelation with something approaching objectivity, but it was too much to take in all at once.

"I . . . I . . ." he stammered, feeling the blood rising in his cheeks.

Grandfather's smile broadened, his forehead standing up in ridged creases. "I can see that you're pleased. I, too, am pleased. It will be a momentous occasion . . . for all of us."

"When?" Daniel asked finally, his voice cracking. He cleared his throat, trying to seem aloof, when in fact his heart was racing, and it was all he could do to keep his hands from shaking. "When will I be initiated?"

"Just under six months, if all goes well." Grandfather's eyes glittered in their dark, wrinkled sockets. "In the meantime, there's much to be done. I personally will tutor you in the final stages of your preparation. You are to be here, in my quarters, no later than zero-eight-hundred hours, six mornings of every seven, starting next week. Understood?"

Six days a week?

Daniel's heart sank as he thought of all the free time he would lose.

Time I'll have to spend here. With him.

But then again . . .

Perhaps he ought to cut the old man a little slack. Grandfather seemed privy to more information than Daniel had previously given him credit for. Also, full initiation as an Elder was nothing to sneeze at, though Daniel had always expected it. But to his knowledge, the youngest member ever initiated was twice his age at the time.

"Are you listening to me, boy? Do you understand what is to happen, or do I need to make myself more clear?"

"Six mornings of every seven. I understand."

It had better be worth my time, old man.

"Good!" Grandfather leaned back in his chair again, his wrinkled face soothing into something resembling paternal fondness. "The reason we're starting next week is that I want you to have time for a little fun. You're going to be working hard, so relax for now. Enjoy the company of your female companions. Entertain yourself. Eat, drink, and be merry, as they say, because by the end of next week, you will be a different person."

"How so?" A ripple of fear chased a cold bolt through Daniel's stomach, and his chest tightened.

Grandfather's mouth hardened into a thin smile and he chuckled dryly, then coughed once and spat something small and black into his water cup. "Let's just say that knowledge and information have an interesting effect on a person." He stood slowly. "Enough for now. I'll see you in a week."

Lazaro Sol leaned over his desk until the reinforced steel door clicked shut behind the clone, then collapsed into his chair with a sigh. He took as deep a breath as he could manage, then let it out slowly, relishing the lack of noise.

Ah, silence. No commodity could be more valuable.

The boy was something of a disappointment, really; the way that each gesture and tic of the face gave away his every thought; his emotions ran very near to the surface.

Especially when he was trying to hide them.

The clone was obviously apt enough, though; they'd run tests before waking him up, and his synaptic activity was off the charts.

The false-memory program, devised by Lazaro Sol with DaLuge's help, was in place. Only time would tell if it would be effective, but it seemed to be working so far.

But he knew better than to take any chances. He'd spend the next week observing the boy, learning the quirks of his 'personality', and preparing a curriculum, as it were, to complete Daniel's indoctrination. His powers of observation were as keen as ever, and he was confident he could do the job.

He thought of the other clones that had undergone the procedure in the Clifftop sub-basement. Daniel had been nothing but an understudy, a replacement, a failsafe. Until the other three had, in succession, succumbed to extraordinary cases of schizophrenia.

That's a nice name for it. Complete and total mindfuck, that's what it was.

The strategy was to be markedly different with Daniel.

Of the some two hundred thousand embryos selected to undergo the original tests, less than a thousand were marked for the genetic manipulation necessary to bring about the required synaptic density. And of those few, only a handful – a paltry four clones – had the proper genetic combinations. The other embryos had been destroyed out of hand.

He'd decided to give the failsafe an identity, to install some sense of normalcy, as the boy would have to live as a person for nearly six months before he could be connected to DaLuge's dream machine. He didn't know if it would make the difference or not, but he couldn't simply sit around and wait to run into the same problem with clone number four. Stressful times called for new courses of action.

Unbeknownst to all but the Council of Twelve, he'd prepared a false-memory program, which was to be installed should the need arise.

After three tries, and three failures - each at astronomical cost - the need had arisen.

The worst thing was that they had little more information than they'd started with. DaLuge seemed to think that the problem was purely mechanical – his view had always been that the initiate clone's psyche was almost completely irrelevant, but Lazaro Sol had a hunch . . . well, more than a hunch, really. It was a feeling of surety in his ailing gut that he'd experienced many times in his long, long life. He'd never been sorry when he followed that feeling, and he wasn't about to change his habits now.

To be sure, the problem could be *partly* mechanical, but Lazaro was convinced that the real issue lay with the sudden shift of Contact, from a benign 'nothing state' (the term was DaLuge's and described the hibernation phase of the inactive clone) to one of full awareness. He believed, in the case of a fully developed brain with no identity whatsoever, that it would simply be too much to handle.

And, if he was right, it would explain the discrepancies between the end results of the first three attempts, the records of which he'd subjected to intense analysis.

The first one had never regained consciousness. After Contact he'd lain strapped to DaLuge's gleaming machinery without moving a muscle, with the notable exception of his eyes. For four hours, they had twitched beneath their sallow lids as if he were experiencing a torrent of hallucinations. There'd been no feedback, no monitor traces, nothing at all. The instruments had appeared to be completely lifeless. And then, suddenly, the clone had expired.

The second attempt had been much more interesting, though ultimately fruitless. The initiate had begun convulsing spasmodically. For a period of maybe thirty seconds, the monitors had spewed mountains of data. Then, his eyes had opened, eyeballs literally pushing out beyond the lids, and had begun screaming, a high-pitched series of unintelligible noises. This had gone on for a minute or so before the clone had abruptly died, apparently of coronary arrest.

Later, when slowed down and translated, the unintelligible noises were found to be a coded computer message originally broadcast during the failed New Years' Coup some sixty years earlier. DaLuge and his team of scientists and engineers had been duly amazed, of course; however, as interesting as this was, it proved nothing except that the initiate had for a brief instant accessed the Elders' war library.

The third attempt, only a few days ago, had been the most gruesome.

Less than a minute after contact, the entire system had gone down. The initiate had emitted an ear-splitting scream before his skull split into two pieces, the flesh of his forehead rising in a red gush of fluid and bone as the inner cranium was exposed to the glaring lights of DaLuge's laboratory. The sound of cracking bone had been disconcerting, even to someone as jaded as Lazaro Sol. He'd been watching the digital re-creation from his private quarters on Mephisto, and had cut the feed so as to avoid the lasting effects of watching as this jagged, pulsing human scene unfolded, a quarter million miles away. At times like these, he appreciated Mephisto Station and the distance it afforded between himself and such atrocity. Not having to be there was an advantage.

He closed his eyes, resting his large head on the back of his chair. It felt good to relax, but he only allowed his body to do so. His mind was moving. As always, there were matters that needed attending to.

He must decide on the best way to proceed with the boy's training, for one.

For starters, Daniel would be controlled by the usual means – clone or no, he was sure to have a ravenous sex drive. Lazaro chuckled to himself at the memories of orgies and sexual deviancy with which he had laced the false-memory program.

Additionally, small daily doses of Elepro - *very* small – were being administered through a pill regimen. Not enough to interfere with his highly charged brain, of course - just the right amount to curtail any questioning tendencies the boy might entertain.

The Parliament of Elders would never approve, of course . . . but they would never know. It wouldn't be the first time he'd taken matters into his own hands. After all, security was his *job*, and sometimes you just had to act unilaterally to get the job done.

In this case, it meant teaching the boy . . . letting him in on a few choice secrets, perhaps. His strategy depended on bolstering Daniel's mind, and more importantly, his identity. Not so much that he would begin thinking for himself, but enough so he could survive the jolt of Contact. After that, the temporary personality would be absorbed and Daniel would be no more than a machine.

Contact . . .

The word was heavy in his mind, and for good reason. *Everything* rode on what transpired during that single, critical moment.

The next attempt was set for the day of the vernal equinox, nearly six months away. He wished he could circumvent those necessary months of preparation, but he would work with what he had, like always.

Phlegm rattled in his lungs and he coughed, then spit into his water cup again. The chunk of stuff that floated there looked a little better today, actually – not so black, a little more green. It settled slowly to the bottom of the glass, a grotesque lump, reminder of how short his time truly was.

Six months. I can live that long.

Maybe not a day more, but by all glorious hells, he would survive for those six months. Too much had been invested. Time, energy, resources . . . oh, the money that had been spent! So much death, and so many wars, to bring the Elders' ancient dream to life.

Next time . . .

Next time he would be there in person. And next time, they would not fail.

7

The day after Johnny Perdue arrived at Compound West, Jeremieah Aldridge gave him a tour through the main compound bunkers. The Chairman – as everyone seemed to call Aldridge - showed him through several housing bunkers and underground storage rooms, briefing Johnny as they went on hidden entrances and exits, of which there were many. Most were buried behind rotting tree stumps or deep in copses of juniper, cedar, and redwood. One came out inside a huge hollow tree at the top of the hill.

Johnny was impressed by the sheer size of the place – the bunker system seemed to cover hundreds of square yards, its tunnels snaking up the side of the valley.

To Johnny, Compound West seemed rich beyond imagining.

When he mentioned this to Aldridge, the older man nodded slowly. "You're right," he said. "But you have to remember, it wasn't always this easy for us. This compound was here thirty years before any of the others. We've had a long time to perfect our techniques. Here, watch your head."

Johnny ducked to avoid being brained by one of the huge timbers which served as bunker doorways here, and blinked out into the sunlight, observing that they were just up-valley of the last outside bunker doorway. Aldridge followed him out, leading the way further up-valley.

"Have you had a chance to look at that plug-drive?" Johnny asked.

"That's where we're headed now," Aldridge replied. He pulled the small device from his jacket pocket. "Uma Peak is meeting us in Control at noon."

"Peak? Any relation to *the* Peak?"

"She's Richard Peak's daughter," Aldridge said. "She's also the unofficial compound coordinator, and she just might be the most capable person I've ever known."

They'd stopped short in front of a tangle of blackberry bushes covering a sheer, ivy-covered rock face some twenty feet high.

"Here we are."

Aldridge pushed aside a clump of berry vines, using his jacket sleeve to ward off the prickling thorns, and Johnny saw a dark space beneath, clear of undergrowth and big enough to allow access. Aldridge ducked into the space, and after a moment Johnny heard a loud click and the squeak of hinges.

"Come on in," Aldridge called over his shoulder. His voice had a hollow sound to it. "Plenty of room now."

Johnny hesitated for a moment, then ducked into the space, trying in vain to keep his rough cotton shirt from snagging on the blackberry vines.

After a small struggle he was through, and found himself in a long, low tunnel, dimly lit by fluorescent track lighting. Aldridge shut the metal door behind them, thumbed the print register, and keyed in a short sequence of numbers. A loud thump and click sounded as the heavy bolt sealed the door.

The tunnel seemed to be cut from solid rock, and Johnny found himself wondering how it had been accomplished. As if reading his mind, Aldridge said, "State of the art, government issue compressor drills. We scored three of them in a raid on a mining operation fifteen years ago. They didn't last long, but long enough for us to get through this rock." He motioned to the walls as they walked, scored with countless marks. "We moved all our critical operations down here – the place is hard to detect and harder to get to, and there's only two entrances." He grinned and clapped Johnny on the shoulder. "You should count yourself lucky, Perdue. Only a few of us have access to this bunker."

Main Control was a medium-size square room. It was dimly lit by the glow of a dozen computer terminals, none of which looked the same. Like most of the technology here, they were cobbled together; made from cannibalized parts that had been reworked and rewired for their current use, taken here and there in raids or salvaged from one of the many junkyards that bordered the larger metropolitan areas.

Most of the back wall was taken up by the most impressive display in the room - a large digital map showing the entire valley and surrounding area. It was incredibly detailed, and Johnny thought he'd like the opportunity to study it further, but he was being approached by a man and woman walking towards them, their faces lit by smiles.

The woman was tall and slender. She looked as if she was about sixty years old, but her face was radiant and shone with good health and vigor. The tiny wrinkles around her eyes were the only part of her face that matched her snow-white hair, which was piled on top of her head like a soft cloud, and held together with a long carved wooden pin.

The man was younger, perhaps Johnny's age, with long dishwater-blond hair in a ponytail. He had a scraggly beard to match, and a grin on his face. He held a clipboard which bulged with a random assortment of papers, but the thing Johnny noticed the most was the shirt he wore. It was a single-piece cotton job, with worn white lettering which read *'Fuck The Police'* in barely legible letters. Johnny couldn't help grinning at this – he'd never seen such outlandish attire, except maybe in old picture files.

"Welcome!" the woman said warmly, shaking Johnny's hand with both of her own. "Johnny? Of course, who else could you be? I'm Uma Peak, and this is Marshall Scott, one of our technicians. You had a good trip, I presume?"

"Great."

Johnny smiled and made eye contact, then let his eyes roam the room. Other than the four of them, there was only one other occupant; an older man with a long torso above short bowed legs, and a bald head rimmed with the graying remnants of his hair. He had his back to them and was working feverishly amid scattered stacks of paper, sitting at a small table to the left of the door.

". . . when we heard you were coming," Uma Peak was saying, her gray eyes flashing in the muted light. "Needless to say, it was a surprise. There isn't much new blood around here, as I'm sure you're quite aware. So how are things in Montana?"

"Just fine, ma'am," Johnny replied. The other man finally looked up from his work. He had a thin face and hooked nose which supported an ancient pair of bifocal eyeglasses. He removed these and thrust them into the breast pocket of his thin shirt, then began digging around in the haphazard stack of papers on his desk.

"Johnny, I'd like you to meet John Stark," Aldridge said. "He's our chief systems analyst and engineer, and most of the reason for the new grid technology. John, this is Johnny Perdue."

Stark's mouth thinned into what Johnny took to be an expression of greeting, and he nodded curtly. "Afternoon," he said in Johnny's general direction. "Scott, where the hell did you put those calibration reports? I can't find them anywhere."

The two of them began digging through piles of paper, leaving Johnny stuck with the Chairman and Ms. Peak. Something about the two of them, their easy camaraderie perhaps, made him feel that he stuck out like a sore thumb. He felt vaguely uncomfortable, and envied Scott and Stark their busied scurrying as they went about their jobs, intent only on the task at hand.

"So Jeremieah tells me that you want to learn the grid." Uma Peak laid a hand on Johnny's shoulder in an almost casual way, but Johnny could feel the strength flowing through her.

He cleared his throat. "Yeah . . . yes," he stammered. "I'd like to take it back to Montana. I mean . . . I think if the other compounds had this technology, it would go a long way towards . . . um . . . improving morale, and all that." He suddenly became aware that he needed fresh air. Blood filled his face, but she seemed not to notice.

"Yes, of course!" Her face lit as if from within. "Think what a boost it could be! It might be just the thing to get this resistance back on track! Heaven knows it couldn't hurt. I remember what it was like in years past, holed up underground year after year, never getting further than . . . how far, Mr. Perdue?

How big is the grid in Montana?"

For some reason Johnny felt embarrassed, and dropped his eyes. "Well, it's not *that* bad . . . maybe a mile or two."

She shook her head, clucking to herself. "Jeremieah, we've been taking this all for granted. Mr. Perdue is absolutely right! I don't know why we didn't think of it before. My stars! It's hard enough living like criminals, but . . . well, we never used to notice it, we were gone so much, always *doing* something. But these compounds have outgrown their original plans in the last ten years, and it's time we shared our blessings. It's no wonder we don't have any fresh ideas – it's impossible to be inspired when you feel like a rat in a cage."

Marshall Scott had apparently finished finding whatever he had been looking for and wandered over in time to hear the last of the conversation. "Speaking of fresh ideas," he said, "wasn't there mention of some miracle plug-drive?"

Johnny left with Aldridge a few minutes later, to look in on the compound's security 'brain', a conglomeration of ancient hard drives, personal computers, small laptops, and a few larger office models, all wired together in the room across from Control.

"How does it work?" Johnny was fascinated, running a hand over the plastic casing of one nearby machine.

"Good question," Jeremieah replied. "All the old protection grids worked by jamming the satellite signal. They would only give blanket false readings. Clouds mostly, for visual, and wind noise, or rain or what have you, for audio. That's the reason the grids have to be so small while taking up so much juice. They constantly had to be working, and because the images we used were so unsophisticated, we could never chance masking more than a few square miles.

"But Stark changed all that fifteen years ago," he continued. "He figured out how to tell when we were being sat-scanned, and so our grid only goes active when that happens. It saves a lot of power. The system runs on the assumption that we don't have to mask everything, but only specific elements that would give away our presence. Instead of producing blanket signals, our grid is constantly adjusting to real-time conditions; when we intercept the satellite signal, we send it back with a seamless string of images that perfectly match actual conditions in the area."

"How do you get the real-time data?"

"Another one of Stark's inventions; we call 'em spinners. They're multi-directional airborne sensors, constantly transmitting to the main brain, which synthesizes the false readings being sent back to the satellite."

"So you use your security feeds to create a digital composite of the entire valley, and that's what the satellite sees!" Johnny exclaimed. "That's brilliant!"

Aldridge smiled. "I'm impressed," he said. "You seem to have a pretty good grasp of this sort of thing. You think you'd like to work down there? They're always under-staffed, and seems to me you'd fit right in."

"Really? That would be great!"

Aldridge clapped him on the shoulder again, wearing his contagious grin. "Okay then. I'll talk to Stark for you."

The Chairman was as good as his word, and time passed quickly. Johnny settled into life at Compound West as if he'd been born there.

Allie Aldridge offered to help him set up his own hut in the trees of summer camp, but Johnny preferred to bed down in the woods. Summer was gone, at any rate, which meant people would be moving up-valley before too long. Besides, after that first night, he was always hopeful he would again wake to find Maia there . . .

But other than a few quick glimpses at dinner, he hadn't seen her since the night he arrived.

The Aldridges continued to look after his well-being, especially Allie, whose mothering instincts seemed to take over with regard to everyone younger than herself. This applied even to Johnny, and he accepted her knitted sweaters and steaming mugs of tea with a slightly embarrassed smile.

Darla, the Aldridges' oldest daughter, treated him with all the disdain that a pre-pubescent girl would have for an older brother, which was fine by Johnny. Mostly this entailed complete ignorance of his presence, to a ridiculous extreme. Sometimes, when they were all dining together, she would pretend she didn't hear him when he asked her to pass something his way, pointedly turning her back and conversing in an animated fashion with one of her giggly group of friends.

But it was the youngest girl, Karla, with which he eventually formed a strange kind of friendship. She was quiet and mouse-like, hiding behind her mother's skirts most of the time, her large brown doe eyes ever watchful of all that went on around her . . . but she seemed possessed of an intelligence beyond her years.

He'd spent the morning learning the intricacies of some of the instruments down in Control, which proved more challenging than anticipated. Frustrated, he knocked off early and walked back to the Aldridge's summer hut.

He borrowed a book from Allie — imagine something as ancient as a paperbound novel! — and headed off into the woods alone. He was scarcely twenty feet from the Aldridges' door, though, when a small sound made him turn.

Karla stood looking up at him bashfully, one small foot kicking at a twig on the ground. Allie stood smiling behind her, hands discolored from the wax she'd been using to make candles. "Karla wants to know if she could tag along with you," she said.

Johnny almost declined, thinking it somehow weird to be hanging around with an eight-year-old girl, but something in her expression made him relent. "I'm just going to go sit and read," he said, half hoping she would change her mind. "Nothing very interesting to do."

"That's okay," Karla said in a small voice, still looking at the ground. Johnny was surprised to hear her talk – in the weeks since he'd been here, he'd never heard her voice. "I won't bother you."

"You don't have to take her," Allie said, sensing Johnny's hesitance. "I'm actually surprised that she'd want to go with you. Normally she's very shy."

"No, it's okay." Johnny shrugged. "I'm not much for entertainment, though."

Karla was silent as a shadow as she followed Johnny along the forest path, and he soon all but forgot her presence. He found a nice grassy spot in the sun, overlooking the river, and flopped down to read the novel he'd borrowed. It was called 'Hearts of Gold', and was set in the early American West. He was soon engrossed in the characters and the story.

Every few minutes he looked up to make sure Karla hadn't gone anywhere, but she only sat playing by herself, picking dandelions and puffing the soft spores into the air, or winding strips of grass around her fingers only to immediately unwind them and put them carefully into a small pile. Sometimes she muttered to herself, with words Johnny could never quite make out, and once in a while there would be a sharp exhalation of breath as her mutterings found a louder voice. She sat like that all afternoon, seemingly content just to be near him, and Johnny found that he quite enjoyed her presence. Sometimes she smiled shyly at him when she caught him checking on her. Her face normally seemed so overly serious - eyes like shining coins above her small mouth, blond curls drooping around her chubby cheeks - that to see her smile was a golden thing, and he always smiled back.

A hundred pages and a few hours later, the afternoon began to darken. Johnny marked his page with a large piece of clover and pulled himself into a sitting position. Stretching his arms over his head, he looked to the west and saw a dark bank of clouds, swallowing the glow of the sun only to regurgitate it in shades of muted gray. The soft zephyr that had played along the riverbank all afternoon was beginning to turn to a steady wind, sweeping down the valley in increasing gusts, bringing a chill that got under his skin and made his bones ache a little. He shivered, wishing he hadn't left his jacket with his pack, in the corner of the Aldridge's hut.

Karla quit playing and scooted over beside him, burying her head in his chest. Surprised, he put an arm around her awkwardly, not knowing quite what to do or think. Her body was small and warm and seemed in that moment like that of a bird, vulnerable and fragile. Her breathing seemed shallow, and a little too fast.

She turned her eyes up to his face. "Will you be my brother?" She asked.

Again, that feeling of awkwardness. He cleared his throat. "I . . . um . . . " Before he could finish, she spoke again, pulling away into a more comfortable position. "It's cold," she said.

He nodded, relieved to have something as mundane as the weather to talk about. "It sure is," he said. "Maybe we should head on back to camp."

She didn't move, just sat there with her small plump arms around him, leaning her head softly on the shoulder of his knit shirt. Her breathing had slowed, and he was beginning to think she'd gone to sleep when she spoke again.

"This is happy," she said. "You can be my brother."

Johnny saw the spider, of the common garden variety, only a moment before she did. It was crawling along her leg, making its way around the various tears and holes of the patched blue tights she was wearing. He reached to brush it off without even thinking about it, and was caught completely unawares by an ear-piercing scream.

"What?!" He jumped to his feet, pulling the child with him, unaware until a moment later that he was shaking her. "What's wrong?"

She was utterly distraught; her face was pale, her eyes scrunched tightly, tears streaming from the corners. She began to sob uncontrollably, moving from one foot to the other as if trying to climb out of her body. "S-sp-sp-spider," she sobbed. "It was *on* me. I could *f-f-feeel* it."

Johnny didn't see how that was possible, since the spider hadn't been touching her skin, but this didn't seem the time to reason with a hysterical eight-year-old. "It's okay," he said instead. "The spider's gone now – look, no more spider."

She would not be consoled; she kept shifting from one leg to the other, moaning slightly, her eyes tightly shut.

"All right then," he said finally, with a sigh. "I'll carry you."

He lifted her, surprised at how light she was, and carried her like a baby, with her head over his shoulder.

By the time they were halfway back to camp, she'd calmed enough to get down, and she walked the rest of the way beside him, holding tightly to his hand. Dusk had announced itself in serious fashion, and the forest held the twilight like a lover, caressing the muted gray and green of the trees with the edge of the sighing wind.

As they struck the jut of path that would take them to summer camp, the first drops of rain spattered through the trees, sifting down through the boughs.

"We better hurry," Karla said in a loud whisper.

Johnny started at her tone, then laughed at the absurdity of it. "Why are you whispering?" he asked.

A tremor coursed through her small body. "There's bads in the woods," she said, no longer whispering, but speaking in a low voice, almost a monotone.

"Bats?" He frowned, thinking he must have misunderstood. Indeed, he'd seen a few of the flying rodents, but hadn't mentioned them for fear that they would scare her, and he didn't think she'd noticed them.

She laughed, a slightly hysterical sound that tinkled like crushed ice on the rain-spattered path and didn't seem at all to fit her mood. "Not bats, silly," she said in a normal tone of voice. "Nobody minds the bats." Dropping her voice to a whisper that bordered on tears, she added, "But I don't like the spiders. Or the mosquitoes, either. The bats are okay, but *I hate the spiders and the mosquitoes.*"

By the time they reached the front flap of the Aldridge's hut, however, she seemed to have forgotten all about her insect phobia, and ran to greet her mother, who'd poked her head out into the rainy dusk to greet them. Behind her, the low candlelight flickered against the woven walls, and Johnny could see Darla and her father sitting over big bowls of soup and buttered bread, laughing over their game of dice.

"How was she?" Allie gave her daughter a hug. "I was just going to come find you. We're eating here tonight, and you're welcome to join us."

"Thanks," Johnny said. "I think I will." He hesitated, then decided not to mention the spider, for fear of embarrassing Karla. "She was great. But I have to warn you – I think I've been named an honorary sibling."

"Fine by me," Allie said with a smile. "The more the merrier."

"That you, Perdue?" Jeremieah's voice boomed from inside the hut. "Come on in, man – we need another player."

8

The vibro-alarm, built into Daniel's bed, had been sending gradually increasing waves of electric vibration through his body for almost twenty minutes now, and they had moved past pleasant, through uncomfortable, and were now nearing annoying. He groaned and rolled over, his slim torso encountering the splayed arm of Neana, the female who'd shared last night with him. Like all the girls in Mephisto's harem, she was beautiful, quiet, and most of all compliant.

The soft down of her pubis was mostly obscured by the therma-sheet that lay rumpled over both of them, but this did not stop Daniel from running an inquiring finger along the small mound of her stomach, tracing a line down her thigh and under the sheet. She moved in her sleep and sighed, and Daniel felt himself growing aroused. He sat up, tried to put down the desire.

Something about this morning . . . what is it?

Another jolt from the vibro-alarm, a really good one this time. "Alarm off," he said, his voice a throaty croak.

A cultured female voice spoke from someplace in the vaulted wall above his head. "Alarm is in manual mode."

Of course it was. He'd set it that way the night before, specifically so he wouldn't miss his appointment with Grandfather.

This thought motivated him. He shook his foggy head and ran a hand through his black hair, rubbing sleep from his eyes, then slid his feet off the bed and sat on the edge. Another jolt from the alarm, and this time even the seemingly impervious Neana was affected, her long brown eyelashes fluttering quickly, blinking slowly three or four times before opening her eyes.

"Good morning, lover," she said, sitting up in bed, her straight brown hair falling in soft cascade over the tops of her breasts.

Daniel, annoyed by the thrumming of the bed, the impending meeting with Grandfather, and the fact that he couldn't sleep longer, pointedly turned away from her intimate tone and crossed the room in four quick strides. He entered a keypad sequence into the room's computer and the vibro-alarm stilled immediately.

"Are you angry, my lover?" Her voice was soft, almost plaintive, falling disappointed from her full lips like a drop of water into a pool.

He turned back to face her with a thin smile. "Of course not, Neana. I have a meeting I don't want to go to, that's all. I'd rather come back to bed with you."

Her mouth turned up in an innocent, beautiful smile. "I thought so."

"What?" he asked distractedly, looking for a clean shirt and not finding one.

She gestured at his penis, which wagged drunkenly at half-mast. "I thought so."

He laughed. "You're something, you know that? How do you manage to remain so . . ." he waved a hand, searching for the right word. " . . .so unaffected by your life?" He finished finally.

"I have no idea," she said with a shrug. "Life is beautiful, m'lord. We live in a palace that orbits the moon – what could be better?" She smiled coyly and patted the bed, her eyes teasing him. "Are you sure you wouldn't like to come back to bed? Just for a few minutes?"

Thirty minutes later, a rumpled Daniel hurried from his cubby, tucking his shirt into his brown polyzan pants as he went. He didn't look back at Neana, who'd already gone back to sleep on his bed. Tonight, perhaps there would be a different female . . . but perhaps not. He liked Neana; she was pleasant, and sharper than most of Grandfather's playthings. And her body . . .

He shook his head to rid it of the distraction, and was only partially successful.

He was late, and Grandfather would not be pleased. As he passed into the wide outside corridor, the endless view of the star-filled vacuum – which usually inspired in him a sense of awe – left him instead with a loose, reeling sensation in the pit of his stomach.

"Curtains."

The thick, translucent permaplast begin to grow more darkly tinted. After a moment, the view outside Mephisto Station, and with it the reminder of cold space which stretched away in all directions, was completely blocked. Daniel's stomach churned one last time, then subsided.

I should have eaten something.

A mechanic, so noted by the blue stripe on his uniform, passed Daniel going the other way. His shifting eyes were held down in subservience, his blocky face impassive as he walked past, his heavy boots thudding on the smooth corridor floor.

Daniel barely noticed him.

He stopped in front of a control terminal, set into a rounded alcove along the curved inner wall, and tapped the pad labeled 'Transport'.

The computer's cultured voice filled his ears. "Authorization required, level four."

He gave the code, shifting nervously from foot to foot as the console thought about the matter for a few seconds. Another worker walked by without a sideways glance, this a female with a ruddy face and dirt-brown hair cropped short and mostly covered by a drab green hat.

Lowest level worker. Genetically designed with emphasis on broad, strong girth and low intelligence.

He wondered absently what sort of errand she was on in this section of the station, where only a few visiting Elders and upper-echelon Mephisto crew had their quarters. Probably some menial repair. He gave her only a cursory glance before a panel beside the console slid aside, revealing a chamber lit with a milky green glow.

He stepped into the small chamber. "Engineering," he said. "Maximum allowable velocity."

⊷⊷《 ◌ ◆ ◌ 》⊶⊶

He could see in his mind's eye the layout of the station through which he wound on invisible rails – the vast hive of permaplast and steel, honeycombed with storage chambers and thousands of fully equipped crew quarters, though at the moment the station was only running at about twelve percent crew capacity. Theoretically, over four thousand people could comfortably live and work on the station at once, but now only a fraction of that number were housed here. He wondered why so few. But then, there were many unanswered questions.

What were the secrets of which Grandfather spoke? What is this future that he and his cohorts plan?

Daniel knew that the workings of the Parliament of Elders were subtle and broad and struck deeply into the affairs of all people on Earth. But since his meeting with Grandfather the previous week, he'd been wondering just how deep this connection was. And there was something else recently, as well – a nagging sense of something misplaced. It was a pervasive uneasiness; deep down, Daniel felt something inside himself shaking.

What am I to them? What is to be my purpose in the larger scheme? And the most frightening question: *How much information is being kept from me?*

The compartment slowed, which Daniel felt as a slight shift, though inertial buffers kept it from yawing too much. He knew he was deep in the heart of the station; even in this insulated chamber, he could feel and hear the deep rumbling grind of the massive centrifugal engines. He wondered why Grandfather chose to keep his personal quarters here of all places, behind the plugs and wires of the computer core. This had to be the darkest, most unglamorous hole on this decidedly streamlined and luxurious station.

Crazy old fool . . . probably makes him feel safe. As if he couldn't be gotten to, should someone want to.

These were reckless thoughts, and foolish. Daniel put them away immediately, thinking with a shudder how the old man divined his every emotion and intent with those hawk-like eyes. Lazaro Sol tolerated no weakness, especially not one as glaring as possible treachery.

The car stopped, the panel sliding sideways to reveal the gigantic machinery of the engines, towering above the tiny human figures below. Daniel stepped out onto the observation deck, which was made of interlocking hexagonal plates of two-inch grid steel. In this huge room, crisscrossed by catwalks, special-alloy piping, and conduit, the three main engines loomed, huge turbines that spun with a hum approaching a screaming roar, making conversation impossible.

This had been dealt with, however; every person who worked between the gleaming walls of this chamber was linked – all moved to the rhythms of the local Controller, who sat high in a small chamber on the side of the curving, polished opposite wall. Like the rest of the workers on the station, each of these engineers, specialists, and drones (including the Controller) had themselves been engineered to be best suited for their particular job.

Daniel knew this the way he knew everything else – it was all there somewhere, stuffed into his cranium, locked inside files in his mind.

But where did this information come from?

When he tried to recall his childhood, it seemed that there were memories – teachers, and school mostly, but no matter what, there had always been Grandfather.

Am I not more than the total of my memories?

With a sigh, he glanced once more at the Controller in his high booth, then turned down the dark hallway toward Grandfather's office.

"Try aiming higher this time." Johnny fitted another rock into his slingshot and handed it back to Karla. They were on the riverbank, among a stand of birch trees, their dusky white bark glinting with the passing glow of the mid-day sun. Small birds flitted between their half-nude branches.

After their afternoon walk, the day she had proclaimed solemnly that there were 'bads in the woods', he'd promised to teach her to use the slingshot, in hopes that it would bolster her self-esteem. So far she hadn't proven to be much use with it, but it was a nice distraction.

She let go towards the fat birch she'd been trying to hit for half an hour. The slingshot twanged in the autumn air, and she giggled as her shot went completely wild.

"What's so funny?" He regarded her with some amusement.

She shrugged her small shoulders and handed him the slingshot. "Put another one in it, Johnny."

"Here." He handed her the next rock, a jagged pebble the size of the end of his smallest finger. "If you're going to learn how to use this thing, you should know how to load it."

She took the rock carefully, as if it might hurt her somehow, and fitted it into the pad. "Like this," he said, steadying her arm. "Now . . . ready . . ." The shot was a narrow miss, which for some reason sent Karla off into another gale of abandoned laughter.

"That was better," he said with a smile. "Try it again."

The weeks had passed quickly and become a month, and then another, as autumn slid towards the mucky belly of winter at Compound West. Summer camp was struck during the third week after Johnny's arrival, and by the time the rains set in with a real vengeance, life had moved completely underground, into the main bunker system.

Johnny wasn't bothered by this at all – in contrast to the severe winters and year-round underground living in Montana, the worst rainstorms here seemed mild, and even beautiful in their own way. And there weren't many storms, mostly just a perpetual drizzle that seemed to permeate the air, wrapping the valley and the compound in a gray blanket that hung like cotton from the surrounding peaks and ridges.

He had remained close to the Aldridges, especially Allie, who treated him as a surrogate son, and Karla, who followed him everywhere if her mother would allow it. Allie respected Johnny's privacy and didn't let her daughter become too much of a burden, but still . . .

Johnny had never had any siblings, and he'd begun to develop quite an attachment to the little girl, with her drooping blond curls and chubby red cheeks. After the move underground, Johnny had allowed himself (with very little resistance) to be talked into rooming with the Aldridges in their earthen-walled quarters, where families shared low, spacious rooms, curtained off for privacy, in the honeycomb of interconnected bunkers. Since that time, he'd whiled away many a rainy afternoon playing dice or cards with Karla and Allie in the low aromatic glow of the spiced candles which lined the room. Sometimes Darla joined them, though most of the time the older girl was off playing with her own friends.

The rooms were cozy and clean, with a background of laughter and music and good smells, a mixture of earth and timbers and candles that Johnny soon began to associate with his new home.

Home.

It surprised him, that he could feel so comfortable around people he'd known such a short while. He hadn't gone out of his way to cultivate many close friendships – indeed, he spent many late afternoons and evenings roaming the shaded glens or rocky cliffs of the valley by himself – but he was well-liked by most of those around him, and they seemed to respect that his need for solitude was perhaps greater than their own.

When he wasn't alone, he spent most of his time with those few that he already considered family; mostly this meant the Aldridges and their close circle. This included Bud Arney, a jovial man of about sixty-five with a ring of snow-white hair around his large, shining bald head, frizzy white mutton-chop sideburns and long, drooping white eyebrows. He was always joking and laughing, and seemed to enjoy Johnny's company immensely. Abby Carmichle was another regular; a woman of about thirty, with short dark hair and a quiet manner, who oversaw the greenhouse where most of the Compound's food supplies were grown. Occasionally even Uma Peak would drop in for a cup of tea in the evening, and Johnny found a hypnotic pleasure in her vivacious self-assurance and sense of humor. She had stories that went way back, to her father and the beginnings of the resistance, and these Johnny absorbed as if they were precious nutrients for his mind.

His work in Control took up much of his time now, as well. Many mornings he would get the call that a spinner was down, and as the new guy, he'd get tapped to retrieve it. The six-sided multi-sensors that fed the grid computer their constant flow of information often got blown off course or hung up in trees or brush, and it could require some artful maneuvering to find them, even with the hand-held scanners John Stark had rigged for that very purpose. If they were close enough to camp, Karla would often tag along, and he found that she had remarkable knowledge of the valley and forest.

He caught strange moods from the youngest Aldridge, however; sometimes she said things that hinted at troubled thoughts. Often when he looked at her she would be staring into nowhere, her small, fat fists against her flushed cheeks, eyes drooping and glazed. He would have to say her name three or four times to get her attention, and when she finally broke from her silence, she would just sigh and say something like, "I hope the bads don't get you, Johnny."

The bads. When he asked her to explain, she didn't answer.

Marshall Scott, with whom he spent a good deal of time down in Control, was another of his friends. He reminded Johnny of his buddy in Montana, Dean Sullivan, who'd put together the information on the plug-drive he'd brought. Marshall had a sarcastic sense of humor, and the two of them had quite a few laughs at the expense of the stony-faced John Stark when the older man wasn't looking. Marshall privately referred to his boss as 'Stark the Shark', and Johnny, although he had great respect for Stark's mechanical and technological genius, couldn't help but laugh along.

Learning the advanced secrets of the protection grid was turning out to be more of a challenge than he had bargained for, and he began to rethink the idea of returning to Montana the following year, though he felt guilty about the *other* reasons he didn't want to go.

One was the sense of freedom he'd found in Compound West. Even during the rainy season, he was able to spend his afternoons hiking through the dense woods of the valley, seeking out new nooks and crannies amidst the withered blackberry bushes, stately stands of poplar, and dark green pines. This sense of freedom had lost none of its newness, and he craved it intensely. He didn't know if he could go back to a place where he'd be shut in again.

The second reason was Maia.

He hadn't spoken to her since the night they'd met; he'd seen her at the communal evening meal laughing and talking with her friends a time or two, but had been much too embarrassed to approach. And his work in Control kept him away from the rest of the compound most days.

But he couldn't get her out of his mind. Once or twice during the evening meal, he'd caught her looking at him, but she always turned away, pretending not to see him, before he could even advance a tentative smile.

He had asked Jeremieah Aldridge about her casually, hoping to elicit some sort of information.

"I really don't know her that well," he admitted. "As far as I can tell, she's kind of a loner. Spends a lot of time out in the woods by herself." He was chopping firewood with a short-handled axe, and now he hefted it, taking another crack at the knotty pine he was attempting to break up. "Dammit!" He muttered under his breath, as the axe bounced off the wood without making so much as a dent. "I think I'm getting a blister." He took a breather, turning to face Johnny as he wiped his hands on his rough wool shirt, his wide face ruddy in the cold air. "Why don't you just go talk to her? Women seem to like that."

A loner.

Maybe that was what was attractive about her. He had never met anyone who was more of a loner than himself, and he found that he was romanticizing her from a distance, even dreaming about her. He knew that it was a projection, and an unhealthy one at that, but he couldn't help it, and still he couldn't bring himself to take the Chairman's advice.

Then, one afternoon in early November, the decision was made for him.

It was lunchtime, but Johnny wasn't hungry. He borrowed another book from Allie – a hardbound science fiction novel this time, from the late twentieth century – and made his way out to the hill above the bunker entrances. Spreading out a blanket, he lay down and began to read.

The sun felt wonderful on his face, though there was a bite in the air, and after a while he found himself doing more daydreaming than reading. Across the grass-covered valley, the river was a silver ribbon, catching the cold afternoon sun and sparkling like a sheet of glass. In the distance he heard the shrieks of playing children whose mothers had deemed the day warm enough to let them out of doors.

He was startled by the sound of a breaking branch behind him, and turned to find that he was not alone.

"Hey, Perdue."

His stomach flipped over as he saw who it was.

"You mind if I sit down?" Her face was flushed by the cold, her large green eyes smiling down at him, her breath visible in the air. She was wearing a stocking cap and a dark green sweater, and he found her indescribably beautiful.

He swallowed hard. "Umm . . ."

She flopped down beside him without waiting for an invitation and handed him one of the two sweet rolls she'd been holding. "Here," she said. "Swiped these straight from the kitchen." The rolls were steaming and wrapped in a small towel, and he took his gratefully, glad for the diversion.

"So," she said, munching contentedly, "how do you like it here?"

"Here? On this hill?"

She laughed. "I meant here . . ." She made a vague motion to indicate everything around them. "In the compound."

He began to relax. "Oh. I like it a lot. The people are nice."

"Yeah. Everybody's pretty cool." She laughed. "Not that I would have anything to compare with. I've never been outside this valley."

He was surprised. "Never? Your whole life?"

"Nope."

"Wow. I don't know how you could live with yourself. That would drive me nuts. Even this place, as nice as it is . . . I have to remind myself that there's really nowhere else to go, or I get stir-crazy, even here."

She tucked the last bite of her roll into her mouth and chewed methodically, then swallowed and wiped her mouth with the arm of her sweater. "So, I'm . . . sorry we haven't hung out more," she said. "I know we said we would, after that first night, but . . ."

"I know," he said, nodding more vigorously than he had intended. "I've been busy, you've been busy . . ."

"Exactly! Yes, we've been busy. But . . ." Her gaze was warm. "Well, we shouldn't let that stop us. I wanted to tell you something."

He looked away, sure that his cheeks were burning. "And what might that be?"

She took a deep breath. "Well . . ." she began slowly, her hands twisting in her lap as if she couldn't decide how to proceed. "Now you have to understand, I haven't talked to people about this very much. Other than you, probably only Darby, and I think she just humors me. But I have a feeling that you might understand."

She took a deep breath. "I . . . I kind of see things. Auras, I guess you would call them, or energy patterns . . . I don't know. I see lights around plants, sometimes animals. Very rarely, I can see them around people as well."

Johnny was intrigued. "Really?" He hesitated. "What does it . . . what do they look like? The energy patterns, I mean."

She smiled, relieved. "You believe me? I *thought* you would!"

Johnny shrugged. "I don't have any reason *not* to believe you," he said. "I've always thought there must be more to the world than what I can see. Maybe you're tapping into some of that . . . whatever it is." He eyed her curiously. "You didn't answer my question. What do they look like?"

"Like balloons, made out of strings of light," she said, then hesitated. "Actually, it really depends. Sometimes it's stronger than others. During a full moon it's the strongest, or right after a rainstorm. For plants, anyway. With animals and people, it's much more random, at least the *when* of it. The who is pretty consistent."

"What do you mean?"

She looked at him solemnly. "I mean you, Perdue. Out of all the people in this compound, you're one of only two that I can see on a regular basis."

"Really?" Johnny didn't know what to say. "Who's the other one?" he ventured, after a bit.

"Your little pal Karla," she said. "But really, I've only seen hers a handful of times. Interesting that the two of you should become such friends." She took a deep breath. "Gods, d'you know how long I've been wanting to talk to someone about this stuff? I mean, someone who would really understand? I saw your aura the first night you got here, and that was why I followed you out to the river."

"You . . . *followed* me? You said you were just out for a walk."

Her face paled slightly. "I . . .is that okay? I'm sorry . . .I wanted to talk to you about it then, because I thought that we had this . . . *connection*, or something, but how do you begin that conversation? Hi, I'm Maia, and oh by the way, your aura is fascinating."

He laughed, visibly reducing her tension. "So, can you see it now? My 'energy pattern', or whatever?"

She looked at him for a moment, her eyes narrowed to green slits. "No." She shrugged. "Like I said, the when is pretty random."

"Oh." Johnny found that his heart was beating too fast. "Um . . . do you want to go for a walk, or something? It's a really nice day."

"Sure." She jumped to her feet in one long, easy movement, and he followed more slowly. "I can show you some great places that nobody else around here even knows about. Have you been down to the Mirror Pool yet?"

They spent the afternoon sitting on a flat rock above the Mirror Pool, just talking and getting to know one another. The conversation ranged to many topics, some of which Maia was more knowledgeable of than others. When he spoke of the resistance, his eyes flashed and his voice became full of reverent conviction. She became absorbed in the movements of his face, his strong mouth, the subtle clenching of his jaw, his words that tumbled out, now helter-skelter, now unwittingly articulate.

It took her a moment to realize that he had grown quiet, his voice falling to rest on the flat gray rock where they sat, herself in a loose lotus position, he with straight back and legs dangling over the side, reflected on the deep stillness of the Mirror Pool. A nutria waddled down the muddy bank on the other side of the water, where the current was swift and the reflections swirled in contrast to the placidity of the pool. The river rodent's nose disappeared into the foam of the moving water, and then it scurried into a barely visible hole under the muddy bank, only its rat-like tail visible, protruding from under a glut of roots.

Johnny was looking at her, a faint grin in his hazel eyes.

"What?" She was slightly embarrassed, realizing that he'd been waiting for a response to something he'd said.

"You haven't been listening at all, have you?" He looked away shyly and she realized that his feelings were hurt.

"I'm sorry," she said hastily. It had been the hypnotic timbre of his voice, mostly, that had lulled her, and she hadn't realized it was her turn to talk. "I was – I was just . . ."

He grinned, making eye contact again. He picked up a stray pebble and flicked it into the center of the pool. "You'll have to excuse me," he said. "I tend to ramble. And I haven't even smoked. Which reminds me . . ." He rooted in the pocket of his coat, pulled out a small wooden pipe, carved from a thick, seasoned cherry twig. It had been polished to a dark sheen, and she saw the green of the sativa that filled the bowl. He handed it to her, along with a small butane lighter.

"Twist my arm," she said with a laugh.

The afternoon melted into the sweet buzz of sativa and the chuckle of the river, the reflections in the Mirror Pool gaining in depth, moving with the changing rhythms of their perceptions. After they smoked, he'd stopped talking about the resistance; in fact, the conversation began to drift lazily, like the water itself.

Evening came early – before they knew it, the ridge had reared up to block the sun's light; clouds were descending from the peaks, floating in the stew of color mixed by the evening sky.

Maia had always been a cloud-watcher – for her, they became symbols, pulling apart like cotton, recombining like paint in water to form fleeting impressions, windows into other worlds.

"There!" she said, pointing at a particular cloud. The ridge above them had grown black, trees like sawteeth against the limbo of the twilit sky. "It's a ship. You see, there? The prow, the sail . . ."

Johnny laughed, and she thought he sounded relaxed, even delighted with their mutual discovery. "Yes!" he said. "I see it . . . if you look, you can even see the captain standing at the wheel."

"I don't see it."

"It's right there." He pointed, then moved nearer so she could follow the line of his arm.

"Oh, right." She realized suddenly how close they were; they were face to face, and she could feel the uncomfortable way that his body turned rigid, wanting to pull back, but wanting to be near her at the same time.

She withdrew slightly, putting a hand lightly on his arm. He was trembling under his thin cotton shirt.

"Johnny."

"Yes?" His voice was low, throaty, his eyes dark beneath the tangle of hair falling over his forehead.

"I wanted to . . ."

A weird buzzing sound cut her off, a whine they were both accustomed to hearing at times. A small, spinning orb, glinting in the muted light, flew over their heads. It hovered above the Mirror Pool for a moment, its tiny rotors whirring like a hummingbird's wings, then turned and began to move down the center of the narrow river. As it did, the dark shape of a bat suddenly materialized directly above it. Rodent and machine adjusted course at the same time and collided violently. The bat, one of the largest Johnny had seen in a while, recovered and disappeared into the darkness of the trees. The spinner, knocked from its course, fell with a plop into the water on the far side of the pool, where it proceeded to be washed downstream all of three feet before becoming wedged between two rocks.

"Holy shit! Did you see that?" Maia laughed, jumping to her feet.

He was already in motion, moving towards some small boulders twenty feet upstream that formed a helter-skelter path to the other side. As he made the jump from the last stone to the far bank, she heard the familiar crackle of static from his hand-com. It was John Stark, sounding harried. "Perdue, you out there?"

"Yeah, John."

"Number four is down, just south of the Mirror Pool. You copy?"

"I'm on it," Johnny answered. "But check your locator. It's actually pretty much in the Pool. It got creamed by a bat." He reached down and fished the spinner from the water.

"A *what*? Come again, Johnny?"

"You heard me. I watched it go down. There, I just shut it off." He depressed a tiny switch on the bottom of the spinner. "I'm gonna have to bring it in – it's got two . . . no, make that three cracked lenses, and the rotor is trashed."

A muttered oath from the other end, then: "All right. Get it down here as quick as you can."

Johnny pocketed the spinner and his hand-com and made his way back across the stream to Maia. "Sorry," he said with an apologetic shrug. "I guess I better run this over to Control. You want me to come back?"

"That's all right," she replied with a smile. "I have some bead-work to do. I'll catch up with you later."

"Is that a promise?" His eyes were wary and hopeful at the same time.

"That's a promise."

"All right. I'll see you later then." He waved and disappeared down the path. She thought she heard him humming for a minute or so, and then the sound of his passing was lost in the insistent calm of twilight.

She sighed and pulled her legs to her chest, wrapping her arms around them.

The rough hemp material felt good against her face as she rested her chin on her knees, and she let out a deep breath, trying to enjoy the approaching darkness like she would on any other night.

But tonight there were other thoughts. The feel of him so close to her . . . the wanting, the longing she was sure she'd seen in his eyes . . .and her own hesitation. She thought he might have been holding back to protect her, but that subject was a mystery as well.

After all, they'd spent very little time together; only a few hours, really, but those hours had been different from anything she might have expected. She'd been attracted to him because she could see his aura – an admittedly strange occurrence – and he had responded with interest and empathy. He hadn't ridiculed her or pretended to know what to think, but had rather extended a natural, open-minded curiosity.

She didn't need to see his aura to know that he was attracted to her, but unlike other boys she'd known, this young man had made no move. He hadn't tried to impress her with bravado or machismo; his questions revealed a curiosity about her that was as deep as hers for him, and his empathy seemed genuine.

She couldn't decide exactly how she felt about him. If he'd tried to kiss her, she wasn't at all sure she would have stopped him. But she hadn't felt any overwhelming urges, either.

She sighed, pushed her palms against the cool smoothness of the rock and got to her feet, dusting off her pants. Her head was beginning to hurt with too much thinking, and so she walked to relieve it, her breath frosty in the evening air.

10

This afternoon's lesson had been an unexpected change, and had left Daniel with a strange feeling in the pit of his stomach.

Grandfather had been up when he entered, standing at the back of the room, which was not customary for the old man these days – his failing health usually kept him in his chair. This afternoon, though, his face was darker than usual, as if more blood was seeping into those cold cells. He gave Daniel a look when he walked in, as if he were seeing something other than his grandson.

"Hello, Grandfather." Daniel sat in the red leather chair in front of the desk, avoiding the old man's eyes and letting his own adjust to the perpetual semi-darkness of this room.

Why does he always keep the lights so low?

"Ah, Daniel," Grandfather rumbled with a predatory smile. "Good afternoon."

Daniel wished that Grandfather would sit, but the old man remained standing, looming formidably behind the desk. "So, what have we learned so far?"

This was his style, Daniel had found – abrupt, as if trying to catch him off guard. He cleared his throat, thinking how to respond to this trick question.

"How do you mean?" He finally faltered, hating to answer a question by asking another, but unsure what the old man wanted from him.

"I mean, during these past three weeks." Grandfather spoke as if to a small child. "For example, what is your overall picture of what I've been telling you?"

Daniel took a deep breath and exhaled slowly through his nose. "I've been wondering what it all means," he answered after a bit. "And what part I am to play."

Grandfather nodded, seeming satisfied. He sat heavily in his chair, a small groan escaping his cracked lips, and gestured at the huge screen behind his desk, where a live satellite view showed the planet in repose. "Pick a continent," he said. "Any one at all."

"South America," Daniel said, off the top of his head.

"Excellent." Grandfather nodded, licking his lips. "That will do nicely." He tapped the control pad built into his desktop, and the image on the wall-screen slid smoothly to an enlarged view of the South American continent. "Now, pick any city."

Daniel obliged, picking a metropolis located on the western coastline.

"Switch to live view," Grandfather said to the computer. The digital recreation melted into a real-time satellite view of the city that Daniel had selected. The view revealed almost nothing except layered banks of gray clouds.

"Maybe I should pick a different city," Daniel said hesitantly. "We won't be able to see anything through those clouds."

Grandfather smiled. "Oh, but we will," he said. "In about thirty seconds, a microcamera swarm will be arriving above this city, and when it does, we'll see everything we want to."

"Microcamera swarm? What's that?" Daniel was intrigued.

"Fifty thousand invisible spies in the air," Grandfather replied loftily.

The screen beeped. "Swarm targeted," the computer said in a cultured female voice.

"Each camera is smaller than a molecule of oxygen," Grandfather continued, his fingers moving on the control pad. "And each is tuned to its own swarm. They work by selectively targeting any physical location – and they really *can* go almost anywhere. Each camera then broadcasts its own tiny view. The computer takes those fifty thousand views and synthesizes them into one three-dimensional picture."

The view on the screen had changed. It seemed to be directly inside the clouds. "The swarm is lowering," Grandfather said. "Just give it a minute."

Within a few seconds, the clouds had disappeared. The buildings, and the small, crawling cars that moved like ants between them, were obscured by a drifting haze of tropical rain, but the view was definitely one from below the clouds. "I've targeted the city center," Grandfather said. "The swarm is spread out above a half-mile radius, but we can target an area as small as, say, a person's hand."

"Amazing!"

"Select any area of the city that you can see," Grandfather said. His eyes held a certain nasty glint that had Daniel suddenly feeling reserved, cautious. He began to wonder what this game was – Grandfather's teachings definitely hadn't approached this level of hands-on before today.

"The square – right there in the middle," he said. "Just below the tallest building."

"Target plaza," Grandfather said.

Soon the large square was plainly visible, along with its entourage of cars and people. Shops lined both sides of the plaza, their colorful facades catching the rain-drenched light in swirls of tropical hues. People moved briskly up and down the sidewalks, some with umbrellas to ward off the heavy mist. Most were without extra rain protection – some even looked up, and Daniel caught their faces; brown faces, white faces, old faces as creased as Grandfather's. Others were like ghosts, moving out of range before he could catch a real look at them. He was amazed by the quality and resolution of the picture; a slight hitch in the video stream was the only thing that reminded him that this was in fact a computer simulation.

"So we're seeing that square, in that city . . . exactly as it is, right now?" He couldn't hide his fascination.

"Yes, that's right." Grandfather's voice had a greedy ring to it. "The swarm has targeted the square. Note how you can rotate the view, like so . . ." He touched a button, and the view shifted by a hundred eighty degrees. Daniel was now seeing the plaza from the opposite side. The swarm was so close that he could see details in the cracked cement. On a park bench opposite, a man sat reading a paper beneath a light-pole, which sputtered to life, only to blink off again.

And then, quite suddenly, the room was filled with sound. A murmur of traffic, the screech of tires, a sudden chorus of laughter from a nearby shop . . .the man on the bench looked up, shook out his paper with a rustling *snap!*, then bent again to read it. The light above his head blinked on again with a loud *buzz*, faltered twice, then regained its luminosity once more, this time apparently for good.

"Ah, there's the audio," Grandfather said with a look of satisfaction. "The swarm keys into local audio surveillance. The local audio is tied into the video signal from the swarm, but sometimes it takes a while for the system to figure it all out." He eyed Daniel shrewdly. "So . . . what do you think of this thing?"

Daniel was lost in a world of detail. Though his mind had absorbed and processed mountainous streams of data ever since he could remember, he'd never encountered anything that seemed so *real*. He was struck by a sudden longing, a need to touch this world with his fingertips . . . he brought himself out of it hurriedly, lest Grandfather notice his mental wanderings.

"Hmm, what was that? What do I think? It's . . . it's a brilliant piece of technology, sir."

"Yes, it is, isn't it?" Grandfather smiled. "I thought you'd like it. But our little game continues. You haven't seen anything yet." He leaned forward, looking more the predator than ever. "Daniel, I want you to pick out one person from those in the square – any person, it doesn't matter who."

An ominous feeling settled in Daniel's stomach as he surveyed the people in the square. A woman, crossing the street, seemed to look right at him, and he refrained from choosing her at the last moment.

"All right, that one. The man on the bench," he said finally, motioning to the man who still sat reading his paper.

"Very good." Grandfather's fingers worked the control pad, and the reading man loomed large on the huge screen, his paper obscuring his face. "I've targeted this man," Grandfather said. "Even if he moves, the swarm will key on him for as long as I tell it to." As he spoke, the man folded his paper, tucked it into a portable case, and got to his feet. He pulled his hat down a little tighter against the drizzle of rain and began moving along the row of shops, browsing the goods in the store windows.

Daniel could see every detail; the swarm must be right in the man's face! Incredible that he was being watched from hundreds of thousands of miles away without the slightest inkling as to his surveillance. He looked like a businessman, perhaps in his late fifties. Daniel could almost touch the shiny black polyzan of the man's hat, could almost feel the air that puffed from his slightly flared nostrils as he walked.

Grandfather's claw-like hands tapped out a security sequence on the screen.

"What are you doing now?" Daniel was curious.

"I'd just like to know who we're looking at." Grandfather's lips held a feral snarl, his eyes glinting coldly. "Ahhh . . . there we are."

Daniel raised his eyebrows. "You can do that?"

"Of course!" Grandfather laughed. "I forget, you haven't seen this technology before. Well, watch and be amazed." The computer had thrown up a block of data, superimposed over the image of the man they were watching. The data identified him as Juan Luca, age 51, among other various data; height, weight, medical and genetic histories.

Juan Luca, who by now was in a completely different section of the city, came to another bench and sat down. This bench, unlike the previous one, was partially covered by a hood of transparent permaplast, and a sign on the metal support post identified it as a bus stop.

Part of the swarm seemed to be inside the shelter with the man, and part outside. The reflection of the afternoon light from the clear surface kept appearing and disappearing; the computer was having a hard time tracking the disparate images sent from the swarm, but the feed was still amazingly lifelike. Daniel felt a sense of unreality wash through him as Juan Luca once more snapped his paper open and resumed reading as he waited, while the two of them greedily watched his every movement.

The sound, so lifelike while the man was in the city square, had faded to nothing, and Daniel commented on this. "Local audio has a hard time keeping up with a moving target," Grandfather said. "We should get the sound back in a minute or so, if he stays where he is."

"Why are we watching him?" Daniel asked, almost afraid to hear the answer.

"Because you picked him," Grandfather said. "And now you're going to exercise your power – it will teach you the truth about yourself."

An uneasy feeling twisted in Daniel's stomach, and he fought it down, clenching his jaw. After a moment, the feeling passed.

"What power?" He asked hollowly. "What truth?"

"As an Elder," Grandfather replied, his voice rising in a snarl, "you, Sol Daniel, will hold the power of life and death for all the people of our planet. You'll need to have the strength to exercise that power when it's required. You can think of this as a test."

"What are you going to do?" Daniel's mouth was suddenly dry, his stomach cramping painfully.

Grandfather smiled, baring his yellowed teeth. *"I'm* not going to do anything," he said. *"You,* my boy, get to have all the fun today. You are going to kill this man . . . with nothing but the touch of a button."

"But . . ." Daniel felt the blood draining from his face. "But . . .what has he done? Do you mean that we . . ."

"Not we," Grandfather corrected, ticking his index finger like a metronome in front of Daniel's face, then jabbing it forcefully at him. *"You,* Daniel. *You* are going to do it."

Daniel was baffled. "But why?"

Grandfather's face hardened, and Daniel immediately regretted the question. "I'm sorry, sir," he mumbled, head down. "But he hasn't done anything to either of us . . . has he?"

Grandfather's eyes were watchful. *"That is precisely the reason why you must do this thing."* The hard edge of his voice was barely obscured by his cultured tone. "We are impersonal judges – we are not on the same level as these . . . these *sheep!"* He gestured toward the screen contemptuously. The man in the black polyzan hat still sat, apparently waiting for his bus. *"That* is the lesson you will learn today. You have the right to do what you want. *Anything* you want. Always remember, it's *our* game! Those people down there . . . " he gestured vaguely at the screen, "are merely characters in our drama. *We* are the puppet-masters. Never forget that." The old man's creased face wore an intent, angry scowl, and he seemed to be breathing heavily. A cough racked his frame, shaking his torso, and Grandfather turned, hawked and spit into his glass. Daniel used the moment to compose himself, taking a deep, calming breath.

"How does it work?" He ventured after a moment. "I mean . . . how will we . . . how will he . . . die?"

Grandfather smiled broadly and sat back in his chair with a whine of servos. "Good to see that you're getting practical," he said. "Well, like every other citizen, this man is wired by microbotic sequencers; robotic cells, smaller actually than organic cells, but compatible with human DNA. You understand? The body treats them as organic."

"At any rate, each cell contains the entire blueprint for the circuits that are to be infused into the brain. They are administered by injection at birth, and within a few days, the sequencers have re-routed the subject's brain pattern. Not much, mind you, but just enough."

"Enough for what?"

"Enough to give us a level of control over any given person on the face of the planet. Electrically speaking, for example, it's not difficult to induce cardiac arrest in a person."

Daniel felt his face grow cold. "Is that what will happen to that man?"

Grandfather nodded. "Just as soon as you enter the right sequence. And we'll have a first-hand view."

It seemed that Grandfather was genuinely enjoying this little game, but for Daniel it held little appeal.

Do I have a choice in this? What will he do if I say no?

He took a deep breath.

"All right," he said, watching the man on the screen bat an insect away from his face. A strange feeling had come over him; a sense of pure and utter detachment. If Grandfather was going to force him to do this, then he would do it without feeling, whether he wanted to or not. "What's the sequence?"

Grandfather's face split into a hideous grin as he slid the remote pad across the desk.

When Daniel had keyed all but one of the numbers, he looked up again and saw that Juan Luca had risen from his seat and was boarding a bus. The swarm followed, a silent throng of invisible electronic eyes, as he took a seat at the front of the bus. Daniel could see only one other passenger, sitting next to the man – an elderly woman with white hair and listless, staring eyes. She kept muttering to herself – he divined this from watching her lips move, as it seemed that the audio had slipped away again.

Grandfather sat, eyes glued to the screen. He licked his lips, seeming to fairly come alive at the anticipation of what was about to happen. Daniel's eyes narrowed. He pressed the last of the sequence of numbers on the remote pad.

For a second he thought nothing was happening. But as he watched, the man's eyes grew large. He suddenly sat up very straight in his seat, clutching at his chest with both hands. The woman next to him seemed to notice nothing; her lips continued to move to the rhythm of some personal chant, and she never looked up as he slipped to the floor of the bus. His eyes remained half-open, glazed; a drop of saliva slid from the corner of his slack mouth. The color of his skin was seeping away as blood flowed into the core his body, in a final attempt to bring life back to the flesh . . .

But that life was leaving, and quickly.

The audio came on again suddenly; the rumbling of bus tires over pavement, the conversations of the passengers, and a sudden ripple in those conversations as those toward the rear of the bus realized that something out of the ordinary was happening. Someone voiced a concerned cry, and a young woman with dark skin entered into range of the microcamera swarm, which still targeted the dead man's body.

The woman was very beautiful, with straight dark hair tied in the back, and large breasts that hugged the folds of her dark-green blouse. Daniel found it odd, and a bit disturbing, that he should notice a woman's breasts at a time like this, but he became slightly aroused despite himself as he watched her bending down to shake the dead man's arms. Her blouse fell open to the prying eyes of the swarm, the soft crack of her cleavage briefly swallowing Daniel's attention.

He looked away, ashamed that he could have these thoughts as a man lay dying. Across from him, Grandfather was rapt, an ugly ecstasy written between the lines of his face. His lips moved, the tip of his tongue flicking against them as if he was trying to lap up the experience.

He's not looking at the woman, though. It's that man's death that's turning him on.

Grandfather turned to Daniel finally, his voice coming low, almost a whisper: "Do you see? Such will be your power as an Elder – to hand out life and death as you wish. You have passed the test, Daniel."

Despite what were – for Grandfather at least – words of encouragement, Daniel couldn't get over the feeling, or rather the vacuum of feeling, that had come over him as he keyed in the sequence that ended Juan Luca's life.

There *was* a kind of power that went along with such an action, and this was clearly the difficulty. Daniel didn't know if he *wanted* that sort of power, though Grandfather was obviously enamored by it.

But he couldn't convince himself that he *didn't* want it, either.

He was glad when the lesson was over. And there had been a surprising benefit. After he'd completed the old man's macabre lesson, Grandfather had given Daniel a gift – the use of a microcamera swarm.

"With the proper codes, you can operate it from your own quarters," the old man said with a benevolent smile. "Of course, I'm withholding the codes to do what you did to that man today – I can't have you wantonly killing innocent people, now can I?" His laughter at his own joke came like a series of dry, spurting coughs. He wiped his mouth, still chuckling. "You will, however, be able to access any and all information about anyone you care to spy on. I want you to think of the swarm as your eyes and ears. Explore the world that I am giving you, continue to learn, and new horizons will open up." He leaned forward conspiratorially. "There are even larger secrets, Daniel. Larger than both of us."

Daniel didn't care that he was denied the power to kill. It hadn't agreed with him, anyway. But the use of a microcamera swarm . . .well, that was different. His mind jumped at the new possibilities, and he was anxious to experiment in the privacy of his own quarters.

"We're through, then?"

"For today." The old man sat back in his chair. "I'm meeting with the Council. They're pleased by your impending initiation, Daniel, and they'll be interested in news of your training. You are performing well, my boy."

Daniel rose stiffly from the chair. "Thank you, Grandfather." He turned to go.

"Enjoy your gift," the old man said a tight smile.

"Thank you, sir. I will."

11

In a small conference room, high above Mephisto Station's engine chamber, thirteen black-robed Elders sat around a massive table. The tabletop seemed made of a single polished slab of black marble; in its center, inlaid in pearl, was one of the many esoteric symbols used by the Parliament of Elders, a pentagram within a circle.

Tinted permaplast windows gave on a view of the engines from above, rendering the workers as small as toy robots. This room was set into the wall above the huge engine compartment, across the way from the Controller's station, where the suited, wired Controller sat like an overgrown insect, holographic computer displays creating a terminal around him in midair. Occasionally, he reached out to make a change, and the hum of the engines would shift in pitch a moment later, reverberating even through the reinforced permaplast.

The engine room was busy, as usual; components, human and otherwise, ticked along like the inner workings of some giant clock. One or two of the Elders seemed interested in the mechanical workings of the station, watching the Controller or the workers below, but most sat silently or spoke together in hushed whispers.

Lazaro Sol occupied a spot at one end of the table, in his black padded chair, which had been moved here for the meeting. Randall stood just behind his right shoulder; small, impassive, and deadly. Four other Triad Agents were stationed at various positions around the room.

Lazaro felt tired; just dealing with the boy took everything out of him. He began to wonder if activating Daniel had been a mistake . . .but this was no time to second-guess himself. The entire Council waited for word of the clone's progress.

He cleared his throat. "If I could please have your attention," he said, his voice a low rumble. The few Elders who'd been standing at the window wandered over and took their seats. He waited just a moment, as the room grew quiet.

"Welcome, all of you," he began. "I trust everyone has had a pleasant experience, here on Mephisto?"

A few nods; mostly silence and the rapt stares of twenty-four hard black eyes.

"When will the clone be ready?" The voice was reedy and nasal, and came from Sol Marletta, a stooped old man with eyes that were too close together above a long, wrinkled nose.

"Ah, of course." Lazaro Sol allowed himself a small laugh. "We'll get right to the point. As you all no doubt know, the last attempt at Contact has failed, leaving us with only one remaining clone. As per our original plans in this case, I have activated the Daniel Protocol."

Nods from the assembled Elders, low murmurs of assent.

"We are planning to attempt Contact again at the time of the Spring Equinox," Lazaro continued, his voice rumbling in dissonant harmony with the cycling engines. "As this is more than four months away, I have no qualms in saying that the clone will, in fact, be ready. His program is holding strong. I am playing the role of Grandfather to him, according to the plan, filling his head with stories and secrets."

"But will it be enough?" This from Sol Detrius, directly to his left. Detrius was a man as large as Lazaro Sol, with heavy jowls and a ring of silver hair around his bald dome. He'd taken off his hood, and the lights gave his white head a silvery sheen. "It's all fine and good to give the clone a memory – it seems it's necessary, in fact – but will we be able to control him after he's been plugged in? Assuming, of course, that he survives being plugged in."

Lazaro smiled. "Once Contact is achieved, it will make little difference," he said. "He'll be more machine than organic at that point. Like any machine, he will require maintenance, but that is all; that is to say, he will survive Contact, but his personality won't. In the meantime, we can control him like we have always controlled people – with indirect fear and subtle pressure. His program has placed in him a strong fear of me, as well as respect for the Parliament and all our objectives. He will not be difficult."

Another voice floated above the table, this from Sol Ashbro, a thin Elder at the end of the table opposite Lazaro. "Is there anyone here who still thinks, like myself, that we should destroy this clone now? This is too much of a risk! I've said this from the beginning, and I haven't changed my opinion. We've thrown too much time at this project. Why can't we just use a computer, instead of this unpredictable . . . *thing*?" He spat the word venomously across the table.

Lazaro's patience was at its end. He glared at the man, but Ashbro simply gazed back at him, impassive as ever.

Lazaro Sol smiled grimly. "This vote has been cast," he said, in a voice of steel draped in silk. "Many, many years ago, as you'll all remember. Every bit of our research indicates that we need an *actual human mind* to comprehend and sort the amount of information in question, as well as to make predictions based on that information." He paused, gauging the reaction of the room. "I don't need to remind you of the stakes of this little game," he continued, voice lowered for emphasis. "This project *will* come to completion, and it *will* bring us total control."

Sol Ashbro was speaking again. "May I point out," he said calmly, "that the term 'total control' may be somewhat of a misnomer? Do we not already have control of this planet? Our societal machine is running quite nicely, I would say. The people are as content as we could hope for – why continue with such a risky project?"

Lazaro Sol slammed his hand down with a bang. "Enough!" he said sharply. "There is no risk in continuing the project through to the end. Either it will work, or it won't. If it doesn't fulfill our expectations, then we move on." His eyes glittered, hard knots beneath his wrinkled forehead. "Sol Ashbro may be right," he continued, letting his gaze sweep the entire table. "Perhaps we have spent too much time and energy on this project. But we are close, gentlemen. Very close. And if I am right about this clone . . .well, in a year the world will be a much different place. Imagine it! Perfect order, perfect precision . . .a global machine unlike anything ever accomplished."

Ashbro sat back in his chair, the muscles of his jaw rippling. Presently he smiled, tight-lipped, and tipped his head forward ever so slightly. "I will acquiesce," he said. "So long as my objections have been noted."

Lazaro Sol sat back slightly in his chair, content for the time being with this small victory. He smiled benevolently. "Very good," he said. "We will achieve Contact at the height of the vernal equinox. And the Great Work, begun so long ago, can move into its final phase."

Lazaro watched them leave, one at a time, like a group of ancient vultures, their black robes swishing as they slid out the door. The Triad Agents left with them, statuesque men in gray, like handsome dolls with hard dead eyes. Only Randall remained, standing at attention behind him.

Sol Detrius had remained as well, seated to his left, his large bulk resting comfortably in his own padded chair. When the door had vacuum-sealed behind the last of the departing crowd and it was just the three of them, he gave Lazaro a large grin and reached out with his right hand, grasping Lazaro's forearm in the ancient greeting. "Good to see you again, my friend," he said in a deep, rasping voice. "How long has it been?"

Lazaro allowed a smile for one of his oldest living companions. "Ten . . .no, twelve years? In Switzerland, if you remember. The last time I was on the planet. Before this. . . ." he coughed, his torso twisting painfully, and spat into a glass. His condition had taken a downward turn recently, and his body was paining him more than ever. He shrugged. "The doctors thought I would be healthier in a low-gravity atmosphere."

Detrius smiled. "Who wouldn't? I feel ten years younger every time I step into this tin can." His smile faded, and he looked at Lazaro with eyes that missed nothing. "So tell me, Lazaro. Do you really have as much faith in this project as you would lead us to believe?"

"Maybe not quite that much," Lazaro admitted. "But enough to continue to the end. I swear, the only reason we failed before is that the clones were given no sense of anything before we plugged them in. We have to remember what we're dealing with here. It's one thing to attempt a man-machine merge – but it's not just organic machinery we're dealing with. There's an ego there, a human psyche, a . . ." he was lost for words.

"A spiritual presence?"

Lazaro cocked an eyebrow. "Perhaps," he replied slowly. "Perhaps. But at the very least, we have to realize that people are not machines."

"Not yet," Detrius replied. "Not until after."

Lazaro allowed a thin smile to his lips. "Tell me, Detrius. Have you heard word of any trouble? And you know the kind I mean."

"Trouble? Ahh, you mean internal trouble. Well, there are always rumors, but I wouldn't worry – I think your ivory tower is safe for the time being." He frowned. "Why? Who do you suspect?"

Lazaro hesitated, then told him of his suspicions regarding Senator McElroy. Sol Detrius' frown deepened as he listened. After Lazaro had finished, he sat thoughtfully, his large head bowed.

"Well," he said, after a moment. "That is interesting. Yes, I know McElroy, though not well. Youngster, you know. Hasn't even finished his first term as Senator. Seems awfully green to be attempting something without help. But . . ." He hesitated.

"Out with it," Lazaro demanded, his eyes narrowing. "You know something."

"Well," Detrius said, "I know that Ashbro has been McElroy's personal sponsor for quite some time now. Putting him through his paces, you might say. Grooming him for advancement through the ranks."

Lazaro narrowed his eyes. "That could explain the Agent," he said. "Now, he shouldn't have access to one, but if he's being sponsored by Ashbro, well . . ."

"That's a whole different story."

"Indeed."

Sol Detrius placed his palms flat on the marble table. "Well, I'm with you, Lazaro," he said. "I believe you may be right about the potential of this project. I think it's worth following through, come hell or high water."

"Thank you, Detrius." Lazaro allowed a smile to his cracked lips, but he was still deep in thought. Suddenly, he felt very old and tired. He rose slowly to his feet, feeling the spasm of muscles in his back. He straightened, looking down at the other man. "Do me this favor, if you would. Keep your eyes and ears open – if you hear anything that seems important, let me know. There are limits to what I can learn from a quarter million miles away." He hesitated. "Our world hangs in the balance, Detrius. We shouldn't soon forget that."

Detrius smiled again, his large teeth gleaming in the low light. "Sooner or later, we will succeed, Lazaro," he said softly. "Of that I have no doubt."

"Here, give us a hand, would you, Perdue?" Jeremieah Aldridge's voice strained as he puffed cloudy breath into the cold, drizzling afternoon air. Johnny had been making a run for the lavatory, but his business was not as pressing as that of the Chairman and Bud Arney. He stopped to help.

Late autumn had arrived, and heavy rains had washed out one of the timbers that shored the kitchen bunker entrance, leaving a sagging mat of turf that dripped muddy water on the heads of anyone passing beneath.

The three of them soon got the new timber in place, heaving and puffing together with more than a few muffled profanities.

"Thanks, Perdue." Aldridge stepped back and wiped his hands on his pants. "I wasn't sure we were going to get it there before you came along."

Bud Arney clapped Johnny on the shoulder. "Who said you were good-for-nothing?" He said with a wink.

Johnny laughed. "Glad I could help," he said. "So you've got it from here?" They assured him that they did, and he set off again to finish his original business.

The valley was covered with thick gray clouds, hanging like damp curtains above the high ridges, and it was a bit cold, though not when compared to Montana.

The thick clouds *did* have their uses, though. The protection grid that kept the valley safe from overhead surveillance was rarely needed when the cloud cover was thick. Only bare peripheral readings were picked up and transmitted by the spinners, in case of low-flight recon plane, so Johnny wasn't needed as much in the Control bunker this week.

He was glad this was the case, as he would soon be on his way back to the warmth of the bunkers for a game of dice with Karla and Maia.

No amount of cloud cover could dampen his spirits these last weeks. After their afternoon spent by the river, he and Maia had begun to spend more time together, taking walks when it was nice or playing games when it wasn't. Karla often tagged along with them, and had taken to calling them her brother and sister to anyone who would listen.

Darla had tried to set her straight. "They're not your brother and sister, silly," she'd said with the superior air only a ten-year-old can muster. "I'm your only sister. Johnny and Maia are your *friends*."

Karla had put her head down, shaking her blond curls stubbornly. "I don't care what you say," she pouted. "Johnny's my brother, and Maia's my sister. Right, mommy?"

Allie, who had been working on re-stitching the hem of a pair of the Chairman's jeans, looked up absently, a needle in her mouth, her long brown hair haloed by the candle behind her. "Hm?" She took the needle out of her mouth. "Oh, sure honey. As long as these two are okay with that." She winked at Johnny and went back to her stitching.

Despite what Karla thought, Johnny's feelings toward Maia went well beyond the range of siblings. The truth was that she enchanted him. It was in her lilting voice; her laugh, like the soft music of water over stone; her quick, deep green eyes, so soft and yet impregnable in their depths; and the way she sometimes touched his arms with her soft fingers when she was trying to emphasize a point. All these things combined to exert a heady, suffocating pressure on Johnny's chest every time she was near.

He knew she liked him, but how far did those feelings extend? He wasn't sure, but he was in no hurry to press things. Spending time with her was good enough, at least for now.

"Five, ten, fifteen . . . " Karla's small voice was like a mantra as she painstakingly counted her score. The bunker was alive with the warm sounds of the winter-bound compound. Good smells came from beyond the curtain that separated the Aldridge's quarters from the rest of their bunker, drifting in with laughter and the occasional twang of a guitar.

"I win!" she announced, looking up at Johnny and Maia, who formed the other two-thirds of their small circle. Maia clapped her hands lightly. "Good for you!" She said, then looked over at Johnny. "How was the weather out there, Perdue?"

Johnny shrugged. "About what you would expect. Cold, but it's mostly stopped raining."

"God!" She stretched her arms above her head, stifling a yawn, then dropped her hands heavily into her lap. "I'm going stir-crazy," she said. "Do you want to get out of here?"

"I'm game if you are," Johnny said, getting to his feet. He stretched and yawned, wondering at the drowsy lethargy that seemed to have overtaken him recently.

It had been weeks since he'd really thought about anything other than his immediate surroundings; in fact, though he hated to admit it, he'd been thinking a lot about Maia. He hadn't spent a moment reflecting on the Resistance, or Montana Compound, or any of his friends there, since . . . how long *had* it been? It seemed that he had always lived here, at Compound West.

The recognition of this lethargy aroused an inner alarm, but it was a quiet voice, easily put aside. The Resistance would wait, but a walk with Maia was something else entirely.

They left Karla with her mother, over loud and wailing protests, and walked out into the chill afternoon air, heading up the valley. The cloud cover was thick and shifting, but for the moment the rain had abated, leaving the ground soggy.

"So, has anyone told you about the Winter Celebration?" Maia asked as they walked slowly.

"Scott mentioned it." Johnny broke a small twig off a dead spruce as they passed it, chewed on it absently. "When is it again?"

"Right after the winter solstice," she replied. "You'll love it, I'm sure. A whole week of bonfires and beer and games and music – it's quite a tradition. Every year, we all pitch in and try to outdo the year before. Last year they . . ." she paused. "Oh, shit. Don't look up."

Of course, Johnny did the exact opposite. They were passing the uppermost of the five concealed bunker entrances, and a few people were milling there, under cover of a stand of pines. Johnny recognized one of them as Will Matthews, a young man he'd met once or twice in the kitchen bunker. Matthews' deceptively mild eyes watched them pass with an ill-disguised expression of dislike. When he caught Johnny's eyes on his, he looked away quickly, feigning conversation with another young man who stood nearby.

"What was *that* all about?" Johnny asked when they were out of earshot.

Maia shook her head with a mild look of distaste. "Will Matthews," she said. "He's had some weird crush on me since we were both ten, and he's never quite got the point that I'm not interested." She laughed. "It probably really yanks him to see me out walking with the new guy."

"Well, it's not like he has anything to worry about," Johnny said, then immediately regretted it.

She stopped walking, turned to look at him in mild surprise. "What does *that* mean?" She asked with a quizzical expression.

He shook his head, embarrassed. "Nothing."

"Oh, no, Perdue," she said, shaking her head vigorously. "You're not getting off that easy. I think it does mean something." She appraised him shrewdly. "You know, Johnny, I'm starting to wonder about you."

"Yeah?" He was surprised. "In what way?" They had resumed walking, the sound of their footsteps muffled by the moist earth. The scent of pine needles was strong, adding a pungency to the crisp air.

"Well," she said slowly, "you obviously like me. I'm beginning to wonder why you haven't made a move."

Her face was intent, sincere. Her eyes seemed to be mining some precious commodity from the depths of his brain, and suddenly he couldn't think. He felt his ears blossoming into red roses; his heart hammered in his chest, and his throat went very dry. "Well . . . I . . . uh . . ." he sputtered, trying to come up with something to say. "I mean, I didn't want . . ."

They were under a copse of fragrant juniper, out of sight of the compound, and she was suddenly very close to him. Her moist breath was warm, her reddened cheeks like flames. "You didn't want . . . what?" she asked softly, tracing the tips of her fingers down his upper arm and letting them linger there. "This?" She reached up suddenly and kissed him, her eyes partly shut, her lips moist and full.

Something exploded in Johnny's mind, and then he was kissing her back; the two of them were entwined, lips meshed, bodies groping. She was incredibly warm and soft, and seemed to melt into him as if she'd always belonged there. He kissed her more deeply, abandoning himself to the wet softness of her lips, the way her body pressed against his, pulling her against himself . . .

"Wait!" She pulled her mouth away from his, her face flushed, breathing heavily. He realized that his hands were inside the back of her shirt, feeling the silk smoothness of her skin. "Not here!"

He laughed; a little hysterically, he thought. "Sorry," he mumbled. "I mean . . ."

"You apologize too much, Johnny," she said, looking directly in his eyes. "I'm not a bit sorry. But it's too cold to get naked here, and that's what we were about to do . . . wasn't it?" Again, she seemed no less than sincere.

"Well . . . I suppose . . . if you want . . ." Once again, she had caught him off guard. He felt the fool, a puppet whose strings were connected to something deep in her oceanic green eyes.

"Come on!" she said. "I know somewhere we can go." She grabbed his hand, pulling him back onto the path.

"Where are we going?" His heart was tripping, threatening to explode out of his chest.

She laughed. "Oh, I know a place. Just trust m—"

A scream tore through the drenched afternoon like a projectile, fading into wailing echoes. Johnny felt something inside himself turn to stone and sink. He knew that scream – he'd heard it once before, on an afternoon not long ago.

"Karla!" he gasped. "Oh my God, that was Karla!"

Another scream pierced the air, and he began to run towards it. Maia was right behind him, ducking under a broken limb, dodging a root, leaping over a moss-covered stump.

"Are you sure it's her?" she panted, following Johnny around the end of a fallen pine. They were getting closer to the river, and Karla too; they could hear sobbing now, a choked wailing punctuated by a howling yell that raised Johnny's hackles. He didn't answer, but he was sure.

They broke into a clearing and saw her, lying on the soaked grassy earth by the river. She was huddled in a fetal position, kneeling; but her hands waved convulsively over her head, as if she was trying to bat something away.

Johnny sensed danger, though he could see nothing out of the ordinary. "Stay back," he warned, instinctively wanting to protect Maia, then darted forward, keeping low. He didn't know what to expect. Had she been shot? Maybe she'd merely tripped and twisted her ankle. He didn't see any blood, and she was obviously alive, though hysterical.

"Karla!" His voice was low as he approached, but forceful enough for her to hear.

"Johnny! Johnny!" Her voice was tremulous and broke off with a whine, but she recognized him. That was good.

He was moving at a run, was almost there . . .and then he saw what she was screaming about.

"Are those *mosquitoes*?" Maia had ignored Johnny's suggestion and was right behind him. Now they both stopped, stymied. Dozens of dark brown bodies swarmed over Karla's head, arms, and hands. By the look of them, they were indeed mosquitoes, but there was something conspicuously odd about them . . . their color, for one thing. They were darker than any mosquitoes Johnny had ever seen. And something about they way they were swarming, burrowing into her hair, seemingly oblivious to her hands, which batted at them frantically.

In a moment, Johnny and Maia were upon her. Johnny killed fifteen or twenty of them at once with one hand, and Maia smashed another twenty, leaving long red smears down Karla's cheeks and on her hands. The insects were stirred up by the intrusion on their meal, and their whine cut Johnny's ears like a tiny buzz-saw.

"Jesus!" Maia exclaimed, out of breath, clapping her hands together in mid-air. Three dark, mangled bodies dropped to the grass, and a fourth hung suspended, glued to the edge of her palm with a large spot of dark-red blood. She flicked it off with her other hand. "What the fuck kind of mosquitoes are *these*?"

"We've got to get her into the bunkers!" Johnny said. "Karla! Are you all right?!"

Karla was shivering violently. Her face was a mass of bites, which were mounding on her skin. Some of them were beginning to turn purple.

"Christ!" he muttered, under his breath. "Grab her arms, would you? I'll get the legs." He felt a crawling sensation on his left hand, looked and saw one of the mosquitoes sitting on his middle knuckle. He felt a tiny pinch as it began to bite him, but it soon disappeared as he smashed it into a smear of red.

"Come on!" He grabbed Karla by the heels of her leather moccasins. Maia already held her arms. Together, they moved quickly. She was quite light, and soon they had her into the trees. The high-pitched whine had dissipated;

looking around wildly, Johnny saw none of the bugs.

"Did any of them get you?" He was backing through the trees, and had to keep looking over his shoulder to avoid running into any of them.

"No, I don't think so . . . shit!" Maia tripped over a small branch and swerved violently, nearly dropping their blond-haired cargo. "Sorry!"

They were on the dirt path that meandered through the upper meadow, away from the river and back toward the compound. Johnny looked down at Karla's face and was alarmed by what he saw. She was moaning; a thin froth of spittle wagged from her lower lip, bubbling down onto her chin. The mosquito bites were large; some of them were as big around as acorns and stuck out from the left side of her face and neck, which had been bitten the worst. She appeared to be unconscious.

"Were those mosquitoes?" Maia blew a strand of hair off her nose. "I've never seen *anything* like that!"

Worried, Johnny didn't answer. It was the beginning of December, for Christ's sake! The summer's batch of mosquitoes should've all died out by this time of year. But there *had* been something strange about those bugs . . . if they were mosquitoes, they were a different strain than any he'd seen.

They reached the upper bunker entrances, startling a group of people, including Will Matthews and his friends, who'd been tossing their bone-handled knives at a target they'd carved from a thin slab of oak and nailed to a tree.

"What's going on?" Will asked, immediately dropping his game and falling in line with the crowd of stragglers who had been caught up in Johnny and Maia's wake.

"She's hurt!" Johnny said. "Run ahead and get the doctor. And let Allie know, too."

"Right!" Will trotted ahead of the group, his long arms swinging at his sides. "I'll get the doctor," he said, seeming happy to delegate. "Thad, you go tell Jeremieah what's up. I think he's with Uma. Jerry, see if you can find Allie."

Just then, Johnny spied Allie Aldridge, materializing from the trees ahead. She was looking around absently. She her hands on her hips, looking towards the river. "Karla!" she called. "I know you're out here, you little rascal." She put her hands to her mouth, forming a crude megaphone, and was just getting ready to call out again when she spotted the small procession hurrying towards her. For a moment she gazed at them with a bemused expression on her face, but as they got closer her look changed to one of horror.

"Karla!" she screamed, breaking into a run. Her skirt and her long, dark hair flew out behind her, sucked into the wake of her frantic lunge towards her daughter, whose body was now a limp, dead weight between Johnny and Maia.

As she came up, Johnny stumbled, going to one knee in the mud. Karla's body hit the dirt with a thud, and she moaned once. Her right eye fluttered open for a second. "Johnny," she whispered. "The bads, Johnny . . . Johnny!" Her good eye rolled up into her head so that all he could see was a bloodshot sliver of white. The eyelid fluttered twice and closed tightly. Her breath began to come in ragged gasps, with a high-pitched wheezing sound that made Johnny ache.

"Karla!" Allie was upon them, bending over her daughter, wailing. "Oh, Karla, Karla . . ." she sobbed. She looked up at Maia, who had dropped Karla's arms and was breathing heavily. *"What happened?"* She asked, her voice only one click away from hysterical. "Was she with you two?"

Maia was at an utter loss for words. She shook her head, her face distraught. Johnny thought she looked as if she might cry. "We found her," he offered, laying his hand on Allie's arm. "She was by the river – we think it was mosquitoes."

"Mosquitoes!" Allie looked back and forth between the two of them with an unbelieving, uncomprehending stare, then back at her daughter. She began to cry, large blubbering sobs that tore out whatever was left of Johnny's heart. "Mosquitoes did *this?!*"

Johnny was spared having to answer the question by the arrival of Chairman Aldridge and Doctor Tinney, who shouldered their way through the crowd brusquely. "Coming through . . . mind yourself . . . dammit, man, *move!!*" The Chairman's large shoulders leveraged the last of the gawking onlookers out of the way, clearing a path for Ralph Tinney, a spindly man with wispy hair and large, worried eyes which appeared even larger behind his old-fashioned spectacles. He carried an antique black doctor's bag, which he clutched to his chest as he followed the Chairman into the middle of the circle of people.

"All right, all right," he said, his voice breaking. "Let the poor girl breathe, if she can. Goodness knows she doesn't need all you folks standing here staring at her. That's right – give her some room . . ." He knelt beside Karla, who was shuddering violently. Her face had turned an unhealthy shade of blue, highlighted by the bruising purple bites across the left side of her face and neck.

His practiced hands moved over her with quick efficiency, touching the surface of her skin, checking the bruises. He held a listening instrument to her chest, then nodded once, curtly. "She's breathing okay for the time being," he said. "And her heart sounds good." He snapped open his case, pulled out a small vial and dipped a syringe into it. "I'm giving her a shot to stop the swelling, and then we need to get her inside where I can run some tests. All right . . ." he snapped a finger against the syringe, then deftly pumped the clear liquid into Karla's arm. She moaned once as the needle sank home, and her eyelid fluttered again, but she remained unconscious. "There. That ought to help. Come on – let's get her inside."

Twilight had pooled like a viscous liquid in the valley, the high ridges holding back what heat and light the sun tried to provide. In the kitchen bunker, the normal sounds of the evening meal had taken on a subdued quality. The news about Karla Aldridge's mishap by the river had spread through the compound, and more than one mother was keeping a close watch on her brood. No one really believed that mosquitoes had caused the problem, but whatever was out there was scary enough to worry about.

The bunker where Dr. Tinney kept his instruments was small and crowded, and smelled of sweat and fear. Karla lay on a bed in the corner, breathing in ragged gasps. Once in a while her small body arched slightly, taking in a great gulp of air with a wrenching wheeze before collapsing back to its inert position, her eyelids fluttering. She hadn't regained consciousness since they'd brought her in.

The doctor sat at a small table in the corner, in a pool of soft light thrown by a battery-operated lamp. He muttered to himself occasionally, but other than that he'd said only a few words. He was studying a sample of her blood through an old microscope. He kept murmuring to himself, but Johnny had no real idea yet what his professional opinion would be.

Allie's eyes were red from an afternoon of crying, but now she sat mute at the head of Karla's bed, stroking her daughter's blond locks absently, only the autonomous act of her own breathing seeming to keep her going.

Jeremieah sat in the corner to Johnny's right on a rickety wooden chair, his head in his hands. Aldridge raised his head and looked at Johnny. "Are you absolutely sure it was *mosquitoes?*" he asked again, for at least the tenth time. "I mean, there are some weird bugs in the woods, no doubt, but I've never seen a mosquito that packed that kind of bite."

Johnny nodded, lips tight. "I know. I know. But I told you, they didn't look like normal mosquitoes. They were bigger and darker and . . . meaner." He felt that his explanation was lacking, and it was frustrating. "Maybe I could go back out there," he added hopefully, grasping at any solution. "I mean, we killed probably a hundred of them. There's got to be a few dead ones out on the riverbank."

Aldridge's eyes were pale, ghostlike as he looked at Johnny with a solemn expression. He shook his head slowly. "No," he said. "Maybe in the daylight, but if there's something out there that can do this . . ." he gestured limply at his daughter, " . . . then we shouldn't take any chances. Besides, finding dead insect bodies in a field of grass?" He let the absurdity of the idea hang in the air, and Johnny knew he was right. It would be the proverbial needle in the haystack.

"Those were not by any means ordinary mosquitoes." The voice came from Doctor Tinney, who now turned to face the room, blinking, owl-like. "If they were mosquitoes at all. Whatever they were, they were created by human beings."

"What?!" Johnny was incredulous. "Listen, doc, I know what I saw. They were mosquitoes . . . or at least that's what they looked like."

The doctor smiled, a tight, forced expression. "I have no doubt you're telling the truth, Mr. Perdue. But if they were mosquitoes, then they were altered in some way that is far beyond any genetic manipulation I've ever seen. If they were ordinary mosquitoes, they wouldn't be alive in the first place. I'm sure you've noticed that it's winter?"

"But . . ."

"It's certainly possible," Jeremieah interjected. "We haven't had access to any new technology in a long time. I'm sure there's all sorts of heinous experiments taking place. But if that's so, then where did they come from?"

"I don't know." Doctor Tinney took a deep breath and let it out in a long sigh. "But we might want to find out."

Allie spoke now, a low, husky whisper that crept into Johnny's gut and hardened into a knot. "What did you find, Doctor? In her blood, I mean. How do you know these . . . " her hands gestured in the air, desperately trying to make sense out of something that was obviously more than any mother could bear, " . . . *mosquitoes*, or whatever they are, were genetically manipulated?"

"There are artificial elements in her blood," the doctor replied. "I don't have the tools to examine those elements the way I would like, but I think these bugs were doctored to deliver some sort of payload."

"A biological weapon?" Aldridge looked at Doctor Tinney, a forlorn expression on his weary face. "Is that what you're telling me? My daughter has been infected by some secret government weapon?"

The doctor looked from Johnny, to Jeremieah and Allie, and back again. "I don't know," he said, with an attempt at a professional smile which was only ghastly. "We're just going to have to keep a tight watch. I'll run new tests every few hours. She's young and strong. We just have to hope that her immune system can fight this thing off – whatever it is."

Maia was sitting just inside the bunker entrance on a pile of blankets, staring out into the blue-black night. The rain had started up again, a heavy drizzle, and an occasional gust spattered her face with moisture, but she didn't seem to know or care. She seemed to sense Johnny's presence before he said anything and turned toward him, her eyes large and more serious than Johnny had ever seen them.

"Hey, Perdue." Her voice was heavy, drugged by the events of the afternoon. She rose to her feet and they embraced. He held her close, smelling the faint odors of woodsmoke and raindrops that lingered in her hair. Her body trembled, and he knew she was crying.

"Hey," he said in a low voice, desperate to absorb at least some of her pain. "It's not – it's not your fault . . ." but he too began to cry quietly, a well of fear and confusion that sprung from his eyes and trickled down his cheeks.

He knew that what they were feeling was the same. No matter that it wasn't their fault – they both felt the same guilt. They had been caught up in each other to the exclusion of everything else, and Karla had come looking for them. It was as simple as that.

"If only . . . we couldn't have known . . . oh God . . . " She began to sob all over again.

He held her until their tears had subsided, until their fears had begun to turn to something else, then held her at arm's length. "Now listen to me," he said forcefully. "Neither one of us is to blame for what happened out there. We have to get that through our skulls if we're going to be any use to Karla." He hesitated, not sure how much of what he had heard from Doctor Tinney was supposed to stay confidential. "They weren't normal mosquitoes," he blurted out finally, and told her what the doctor had found.

She listened with wide eyes, hardly breathing.

"You know, I wondered about that," she said, when he had finished. "It didn't seem right, mosquitoes out there in the dead of winter."

"And did you notice how they looked?" Johnny asked. "Besides being way too big, they looked . . .I don't know, different somehow."

"So where do you think they came from?"

The question brought him up short. "I don't know." He flopped down on the mound of blankets she'd been sitting on. "Maybe they've mutated. Or maybe someone's been experimenting on them . . .you know, genetic manipulation."

She sat down and laid her hand on his forearm. Her touch was light and her hands were warm, and even in these circumstances the emotional attraction that he felt for her was as inevitable as the gravitational pull of one celestial body for another. He laid his head on her shoulder and she pulled him near, and for a while, warmth and closeness blotted out the day's horror and became fitful, restless dreams.

The truck's wheel spins lazily in the glaring light of blast-gun fire. The guns thump and sizzle, creating loud crackling bursts that sound like static from a dead radio. They're all here – his mother, his father, and the other man and woman.

He wants to help them, but they can't hear him. His father's contorted, frightened face moves in slow motion as he screams at the other man that it's useless, they have to leave now!, goddammit . . .

He knows the chopper is there; he can feel it coming up over the old barn, which in the dream is a bright shade of red. A feeling pervades this dream, of hopelessness, and regret, and loss, and Johnny is trapped. There's the chopper, like a huge slavering locust, and now it's eating the barn; it's eating everything, a giant hungry machine with steel jaws that screech and bang, metal on metal, tearing, ripping . . .

"Interesting."

Johnny turns and sees a man standing beside him. The man's face is wide and he is smiling, but it is his eyes that catch Johnny's attention. They seem to be too large for the face, or maybe it's that they're so full of light – they are a shifting collage of colors, and Johnny cannot take his own eyes from them.

The landscape has changed – the only thing left is the machine and the remains of the barn, timbers shredded to mere toothpicks. The two of them are standing on flat, hard-packed earth.

Johnny is suddenly aware of himself, aware that this is a dream . . .and that this is not the first time he has seen this man.

"What's interesting?" The words come out sounding tinny and odd, and very loud. Everything around him vibrates in slow motion, and he is terrified by the sudden realization that everything is so, so real – as real as any place he has ever been.

The man makes a gesture, sweeping the scene with his right arm. "All of this. It's different than before. Usually a recurring dream stays the same from one time to the next, with only minor changes over the long term. But then, I'm here and that's probably affecting you."

"Who are you?" The giant clacking insect-machine has finished with the ruined barn and turns to face the two of them, glowering from sightless glass eyes, hovering with a beating of its insect-rotor.

"You don't know me," the man says. "But strangely enough, I know the young woman sleeping next to you, which is probably why I'm in your dream. I am .. .look out!"

The gnashing insect-thing, which looks more and more alive - even aware – is coming closer, lashing out with pincers as long as a man is tall. "What is this thing?" Johnny asks, jumping out of the way. The panic he feels is perfectly real.

The man chuckles. "I'm sure I don't know," he says. "This is your dream."

"Perdue!" The voice was a hissed whisper. "Maia! Hey, you two, wake up."

Johnny blinked painfully into the glare of an electric lantern. Maia stirred beside him, the warmth of her body reluctantly retreating from his as she sat up, squinting into the dancing shadows. Johnny almost didn't recognize the woman holding the lantern; Uma Peak's hair was not in its accustomed tower upon the top of her small head, hanging instead in soft gray waves past her shoulders.

It seemed to be the dead of night. Outside, the rain had stopped and a restless breeze blew holes in the cloud cover, through which peeked the reticent light of a thumbnail moon. The breeze was cold, and Johnny shivered, pulling one of the blankets around himself and holding it tightly.

"What is it?" he asked, his voice hoarse.

"Karla's awake," Uma replied. "She wants to see both of you." She helped Johnny to his feet with hands that were surprisingly strong, and Johnny in turn helped Maia to hers.

"She's awake?"

Johnny, pessimist that he was, was afraid for the hopefulness in Maia's voice, but he said nothing, only followed Uma Peak down the hall.

The damp earth around them seemed dead and cold, the smell like oozing putrescence. No incense burned to mask it; no good odors of food, or the normal friendly sounds that went with life in the compound. The people were all asleep, most likely dreaming uneasily of mutant insects or other nasty things.

Dreaming . . . mutant insects . . . nasty things . . .

A sudden memory passed through him, hitching his movement in mid-stride. *Was I having a dream?*

It seemed imperative that he remember, but it was gone like a stalk of dead grass in a winter's wind. He shivered, and felt Maia's hand tighten over his. He was very glad for her right now; glad that at least they could go through this together.

The hospice quarters were exactly as Johnny had left them a few hours before. The doctor was leaning over Karla's small frame, checking her pulse, but he straightened as they entered, moving away and allowing Allie Aldridge access to sit by her daughter's head again. Jeremieah sat on the opposite side of the bed against the wall. His face was puffy, his eyes red. His normal ruddy cheerfulness had been replaced with a fatigue that seemed to have all but knocked him over. He was absently stroking Karla's right hand, and didn't seem to register the three people who had just entered the room.

Karla was indeed awake, as Uma had said, but the sight of her brought a whispered moan from Maia's lips. "Oh God, Johnny . . ."

Johnny bit his lip, not wanting to look, but not wanting to look away either. Karla's one open eye had locked on him as soon as he entered, and what Johnny saw there was a terrible, hurting sadness.

The entire left side of her face and neck was a grotesque lump; the mosquito bites seemed to be one giant infected sore. The skin was red and cracked, and oozing with a viscous, semi-opaque pus which Allie was carefully wiping with a cold compress. Johnny didn't know how she could stand to sit there, watching her daughter in what was obviously hellish agony. A glossy sheen of sweat stood out on the parts of Karla's face which were unaffected by the bites, and the skin there was a pallid, sickly gray color. Her golden curls were a darkened, sticky mat that clung to the sides of her face.

Her mouth, twisted and swollen on the left side like the rest of her face, now moved, the cracked lips trembling with a mighty effort. But only a small, crackling sigh escaped them. Allie leaned over her daughter. "Don't try to talk, sweetie," she said, and Johnny was mightily impressed by the calm that seemed to have replaced her earlier hysteria. "It's okay, honey. You don't have to say anything."

But Karla was looking past her at Johnny, who now stood awkwardly frozen in the center of the room. "J . . . Johnny . . . " she gasped, the words forcing themselves with superhuman effort from her lips. She was trying to sit up now, but Jeremieah held her arm, gently forcing her back to her pillow. Allie took a small medicine dropper, filled with water, and wet Karla's lips with it. She turned to Johnny. "I think she wants you," she said pointedly, with a subtle motion of her eyes that Johnny should come toward the bed.

Speechless, trembling inside, Johnny advanced and knelt by the bed, laying a hand lightly on Karla's arm, which seemed so vulnerable and bird-like suddenly. Maia followed and stood behind him, her hand on the back of his neck.

"Karla," he said in a low voice. "I'm so sorry, Karla."

Her one good eye held an alien light as she seemed to stare through him. He felt that her very soul, always troubled before, was reaching toward him through untold pain, as if the act of speaking, or even of regaining consciousness, had been one of sheer will. "Johnny," she said again in a ragged whisper, licking her swollen lips painfully. "The bads, Johnny. They're here. They're in my head now."

"What? Karla, what are you . . . "

"They're coming for you, Johnny. They're up in the sky . . . have to run . . . "

Allie turned her face up toward Johnny, and despite her composure he could see terrible pain there. "What is she talking about?" she asked in a low, urgent voice. "She keeps talking like that – about the bads. What are the bads?"

Johnny shook his head mutely. Karla coughed twice, a hoarse, vulgar sound that made Johnny's skin crawl. A thin froth of red-tinged spittle came from her mouth and stained her lower lip. She took three large gulps of air. "I see them, Johnny," she said, her voice wheezing. "They're trying to find us, Johnny. Don't let them find us. I'll be okay, Johnny. I'll be all right. But don't let them catch you. Johnny . . ." her voice broke off and she coughed again with that horrible retching sound that seemed much too large and guttural to come from her tiny frame. With a groan, she turned her face away, further exposing the horrific, purpling sores on the side of her face. Her eyelids fluttered and then closed, and her gasping breath seemed to smooth out, her tiny chest rising and falling with some semblance of normal rhythm.

She had gone to sleep.

13

Two months had passed since Simon DaLuge had activated the final clone with the updated program, and ever since then he'd been on edge. His nerves were shot, in fact; his emotions swung from wild elation to terrible paranoia and back again. The thing that concerned him most was the thought that something would go wrong with the clone that might give away his involvement; some glitch or manifestation of the 'extra' code he'd inserted.

Even though Senator McElroy had seemed confident and unconcerned about their covert meeting, DaLuge knew that what he'd done would amount to treason in the eyes of Lazaro Sol . . . and there was always the possibility that he had somehow been observed. He'd swept for microcameras, of course, but he knew that for every means of detection there was an equal and opposite means of avoiding that detection.

And, if he was suspected of any sort of treason, he knew Lazaro Sol would be monitoring him.

Fortunately, he wasn't subject to the kind of intrusive monitoring and manipulation that the Elders and their networks perpetrated on the unfortunate City dwellers – if he were wired with microbotic sequencers like the rest of society, his elevated brain activity would be considerably compromised, and no one wanted that, least of all DaLuge himself. That was why everything must go smoothly from here on out – he'd had a promise from Senator McElroy of a retirement that seemed like paradise to him, and it was this dream on which everything now rode.

He'd been young once, and idealistic; a brilliant and gifted scientist who'd turned heads at NYIT from the time he arrived there, the day after his eighteenth birthday. His professors at the New York Institute of Technology had been amazed by his ideas, and his natural gifts for everything from chemistry and bio-physics to complex computer design. He'd won the NetLink Design Award during his second year, for virtual reality adaptions to NetLink technology that significantly heightened the degree of user interface potential, allowing common civilians access to virtual worlds online. The invention had revolutionized NetLink, had indeed shaken the electronic world to its core. In fact, his designs were still those upon which NetLink based their current virtual reality interface nodes, some three-and-a-half decades later.

He had reveled in all of it, as any young star would do. He'd been invited to the most posh and exotic parties, had discussed philosophy and physics with the brightest minds in the country. He had bedded dozens of beautiful women, caroused with the best and the brightest that the elite school had to offer. He had been so full of himself, in fact, that when the day arrived that was to change his life forever, he'd had no chance to resist.

It was the last day of winter term in his third year at NYIT. He'd gone to the computer lab alone after classes to put the finishing touches on his quarterly project, a relatively simple graphics program. A few minor tweaks, nothing really important. He wasn't too impressed with the program, actually; it wasn't his best work, but then one couldn't be a genius *all* the time, now could one?

The lab was empty, with the exception of an elderly, stooped janitor whose shuffling steps echoed from the far end of the room, across the rows of monitor stations where the golden rays of afternoon sun filtered through banks of windows, highlighting dust motes that hung suspended in the still air.

He bent over his work, focused on finishing while it was still early enough to go out. He was almost there – one more minor change and he could save his work and go.

A sound made him look up. The room was empty; the janitor had gone.

Thinking it must have been the sound of the door that he'd heard, he went back to his work. Another sound, the soft slip of a leather shoe on tile, was accompanied by a brown smear of movement from the corner of one eye. He looked up again.

"Simon DaLuge." The voice held no question.

"Yes? Who are you?"

The speaker was a man of some indistinct age between fifty and eighty, with cold, hawk-like eyes and a shock of peppered gray hair. He was dressed in a business suit, over which he wore a long brown overcoat. Simon realized after a moment of observation that it was the man's face that made his age inscrutable. Though he looked distinguished (he might have been one of DaLuge's own professors), his face was smooth, showing no age spots and very few wrinkles, except around his eyes, where deep crow's feet made him seem all the more cold and remote.

"I represent a certain agency that requires your services."

A quickening sensation in his chest. "What agency?"

The man's smooth face hardened into a smile. "Unfortunately, I can't disclose that at this time. Should you accept our proposal, of course . . . well, your security clearance would rise significantly."

DaLuge felt a sudden surge of adrenaline. "I'm listening."

"May I?" The man's eyebrows arched as he pointed to a plastic chair nearby.

Simon, already nervous, had to suppress a laugh he was quite sure would have turned into a hysterical screech. In light of the man's stealthy arrival and obvious secrecy, his asking for permission to sit down seemed absurdly out of place.

"Of course," he replied, waving a hand in a nervous gesture. "Whatever you wish." Regaining a bit of his composure, and remembering his own high standing within his social circle, he took a deep breath and looked intently at the man's face. "What do you want from me? Are you with the government?"

The man pulled a flat handheld screen from somewhere inside his overcoat and sat down, crossing his legs in a comfortable fashion and sitting back in his chair. He tapped the screen to activate it.

"Simon DaLuge," he said. "Born ten-twelve-2036 . . . raised by a single mother . . . standout in all academic fields from grade one forward . . .National Scholastic Award Champion for grades eight thru thirteen . . . no, wait . . ." he lifted his eyebrows, and his gaze drifted up to meet Simon's. "What happened to grade eleven?"

"I came down with mononucleosis for three months." Simon shifted uncomfortably in his seat, tapping his right foot nervously on the tile floor. Hearing a synopsis of his life, read so casually from a government file, had a sobering effect on him.

The man nodded and went back to reading. " . . . heavily recruited by all of the top ten technology institutions, as well as Harvard, Yale, Oxford . . . developed groundbreaking VR interface . . . youngest programmer ever to win the NetLink Design Award. Very impressive, mister DaLuge."

"Thank you."

The man tapped the screenpad until it went dark, then tucked it into a jacket pocket. "However, none of it means a thing without what I am about to tell you." He sat forward in his chair. "You're different, Simon. You've known that all your life. What you don't know is *how* different you are."

Simon felt a cold empty sensation in the pit of his stomach. "What do you mean?"

The man's voice softened. "Didn't you ever wonder," he said slowly, "why you were so far ahead of everyone else your whole life? What takes others months to understand, you comprehend in minutes."

DaLuge began to feel defensive, uncomfortable with the way this conversation was going. "People are different," he said with a shrug. "There's a whole spectrum of individual characteristics. I'm not the smartest person in the world."

The man's face slowly broke into a broad smile. "That's true," he said, nodding emphatically. "Very true. But let's not mince words here. You know as well as I that you *have* lived a charmed life. Your name adorns an entire building on this very campus, and you've yet to graduate! So let me ask you, Mr. DaLuge - to what do you attribute your unbelievable success?"

Simon sat back in his chair, more uncomfortable than ever. A thrill of fear began to work its way into his gut, alarm bells sounding. Something was going on here, and he didn't like it one bit.

"What do you want from me?" he asked again, thankful that his voice sounded calm.

"Only what is rightfully ours," the man replied. "You owe us, Simon."

"I don't even know your name, much less whom you represent!" His voice was on the verge of cracking, and he fought for control. "What do you mean, that I owe you?!"

"I mean that your very brain is different from those of anyone else that you know," the man said. "You were selected before your birth to become that which, I must say, you've done quite a job of becoming."

Simon was infuriated. He felt the blood rising in his cheeks, and yet when he replied it was with a tremor in his voice. "I worked my ass off to become what I am."

The man said nothing in reply, only nodded and smiled as he allowed the import of his words to truly sink in.

When Simon spoke again, it was in a subdued, careful voice. "So . . . I'm a product of genetic manipulation," he said slowly. "A clone? Is that what you're saying?"

"You?" The man gave a short laugh. "Oh, you're one of a kind, Simon, never fear on that score. But measures *were* taken to ensure a high synaptic density in your brain. And, more importantly, you weren't wired."

"Wired?"

"You were never inoculated. Everyone in our society is inoculated with microbotic sequencers at birth – but not you. Don't you find that strange?" The man's voice had taken on an almost intimate tone that had a strange lulling effect on Simon. He shook it off angrily.

"What the hell are microbotic sequencers?" His mind was jumping ahead to all the possible answers to that question, and he didn't like any of them.

"I'm sure you're acquainted with microbotic research?"

"Of course." The man was of course referring to a branch of robotics developed for making microscopic machines, usually for surgical techniques and curing disease. "But what type of sequencers?"

"You'll have to pardon the term. I suppose it's not very clear. The sequencers are tiny machines, each composed of simple circuits that can conduct an electric current. But each of them also contains an instruction program that keeps it in contact with all the other three hundred thousand or so sequencers that have been injected. They make their way to the brain and use gray matter to form a type of antennae, allowing an interface with outside transmitters – all, of course, without the knowledge of the person who's been wired. The wires don't show up on EKG scans or X-rays. The sequencers themselves are too small to be detected unless you actually went looking for them, and once they've done their work, they disappear entirely." He stopped, tipped his head to one side. "Well, of course it's not difficult, you see – the procedure is instituted at birth. Who would suspect?"

Simon DaLuge sat back in his chair very slowly. He felt as if he'd been punched in the stomach. A ringing sound arose in his right ear, and he slowly clenched and unclenched the muscles of his jaw to rid himself of it. He felt the color draining from his face, and this time he didn't fight very hard for control.

"My God," he whispered, as the implications began to really sink in. He knew that what the man said was very likely true; at any rate, it was certainly possible. The lab seemed foreign suddenly, and all he wanted was to be anywhere else. The waxy light of the sun seemed to cast a pall into the harsh stillness.

The man looked at him intently. "There is no God," he said. "Or rather, if there is, then it is us. I represent the highest order on the planet, Mr. DaLuge – the question is, do you want to become a part of that order?"

Simon's head was reeling. He took deep gulps of air, trying to calm himself. "Why are you telling me this?" A sudden question struck him, his damned scientific curiosity in the midst of a storm of new information.

"What do they do?" he asked impulsively.

The man seemed almost surprised, then genuinely amused. "Oh, you mean the wires? It's not as invasive as you might think. You have to understand the role of government these days, my friend. People are willing to sacrifice a lot to perpetuate their way of life, especially in our enlightened era. Originally, the wires were simple location and identification tags." He shrugged. "But the sequencers have evolved – our understanding of the science has grown. Within five years, the wires will allow citizens direct access to NetLink – people will be literally plugged in to the system. They will be able to issue commands to any NetLink computer terminal by power of thought, or possibly by specific small facial or hand movements – say, like blinking an eye."

DaLuge was speechless for a moment. "But how?" he blurted finally, almost stuttering. "How are you going to allow people – Christ, you're talking about direct communication with machines! The people will know! How could you explain that sort of thing? Evolution? The human brain just suddenly learned to communicate with the computer brain? It's absurd!" His voice had risen, was cutting almost hysterically through the quiet of the room.

"You'd be surprised what people will believe," the man said, again seeming genuinely amused. "But there is a much simpler way. It can be explained that the hardware itself is reading their thoughts – and that's not too far from the truth. People place a lot of trust in machines, my friend." He smiled coldly. "A *lot* of trust. And soon, that trust will reach an even higher level. Wait and see."

DaLuge steeled himself against the horrific inevitability of what the man was saying. "And if I refuse? If I go to the authorities with what you've told me? What then?" He mustered every ounce of bravado that resided in his rangy frame, but he knew it was a bluff as he was saying it, and the man in the brown overcoat wasn't buying it.

The man laughed, a broad smile seeping through his face. "An amusing idea. Who do you think these *authorities* get their authority from, Simon? I beg you not to test the seriousness of my claims. The Elders will think nothing of applying extra . . . ah . . . *pressure*, should you resist." The man sighed and sat forward on the edge of his seat. "Believe me, I appreciate the emotions you are feeling. Moral outrage, horror, even grief. And I do apologize; I know only too well the shock you are experiencing . . . not that it will be much help to you. Once, I sat where you are now sitting, faced with a similar choice. And before long I came to the same conclusion you will come to."

"Which is?" Simon's breath was a flittering ghost in his chest. His heart seemed to knock against his eardrums.

"Which is this – that it's really not a choice." He gave a small bow. "And now I bid you farewell. You have tonight."

The man in the brown overcoat turned on his heel and left the room, his leather shoes slip-slapping on the eggshell-colored tile. In a moment he was gone, the door closing softly behind him.

⚜

The familiar droning hum of Lab One brought Simon back to the present. He sighed and scratched his scalp, trying to remember exactly what he'd been doing when this reverie had caught him off-guard. Lately he'd fallen victim to more absent-mindedness than he liked.

It didn't help that the entire motherboard had needed to be taken apart and rewired to a higher resistance. The glowering mainframe, which covered a full third of the circular wall of Lab One's core, was a gigantic piece of technology, and it had taken the better part of sixty days to accomplish. But it was done now; the Project was back underway, and this time, he was sure it would work. He only hoped Lazaro Sol's move to activate the clone so early had not been rash.

He looked down at the glowing blue screen, which showed a schematic of the re-worked imaging generators. The task of synchronizing them with the wired suit – the one he'd designed for the Supercontroller to wear during Contact and beyond - had given him nothing but trouble from the top, and he was fairly certain they were responsible the deaths of those three boys, the three who'd preceded Daniel . . .

No. Not boys. Clones.

They were machinery, nothing more. He could not afford to think of them as human.

A wry, bitter smile twisted his lips.

How long have I been thinking this way? How many sacrifices have I made?

And the larger question, looming like a monolith, smashing through all the others . . .

Did I really have a choice?

After the man in the brown overcoat had left him in the lab, he'd gone home, but his condo had seemed horribly small and claustrophobic. Pulling on his overcoat and hat, he'd set out alone, at first walking the campus, and then the suburban hills in the surrounding areas.

He walked all night, hands buried deep in his pockets, with no care for the chill breeze that set in after midnight, or the gray blanket of clouds that followed a few hours later, blowing in abruptly and pulling a spectral pall over everything; he walked through residential neighborhoods, past sleeping, clean white and cream crackerbox houses, with their differently colored trim that was supposed to make them unique but seemed only to accentuate their sameness.

He seemed unable to think clearly, which was a disturbing sensation for him; he'd always had his mind, and the thought that it might not belong to him was profoundly unsettling. His thoughts kept circling back to the last thing the man had said to him.

It's not really a choice. You have tonight.

And it was those last three words that said it all, wasn't it? What he thought about it meant very little.

In the first light of dawn, he came to a place that held pleasant memories for him; a park, only a few miles from the campus where he'd spent the last three years, filled with green grass and shapely hedges, tall elms and oaks. The trees seemed ghostly and dead, the breeze whistling rather that sighing through their creaking limbs and bringing a shiver to Simon's spine. Still, the green of the grass soothed him, and he made his way to the center of the park, where the flagstone pathway circled a whitewashed concrete fountain.

Around the perimeter of the small courtyard were wooden benches, and he mindlessly took a seat on one of these now, staring off through the fountain's meager trickle towards the skyline. He had no idea how long he'd been sitting there when he became aware of another person who had taken a seat at the other end of the long wooden bench. Glancing over, he gave a start. It was the man who'd accosted him in his lab yesterday, dressed exactly the same, down to the long brown overcoat.

The man smiled at him with only his lips; his eyes remained cold and distant and seemed to be fixed on an indistinct point somewhere over Simon's left shoulder. "Good morning, Simon."

Simon was speechless for a moment, then angry. He controlled the anger, which gave way to a sort of numb shock. "What? What do you *want* from me?"

The man gestured over Simon's shoulder, where the city skyline rose in pristine permaplast and steel, catching and reflecting the early morning sun; the shining fangs of God, dripping with the poison of industrial perfection.

"A beautiful sight, no?"

Simon shrugged but didn't reply.

"Did you know that this city was planned out over four hundred years ago?" the man continued. "It was, and remains, the brainchild of the Parliament of Elders."

Simon knew he was being baited. He glowered at the man, flaring his nostrils and narrowing his eyes. But try as he might, he couldn't resist. His curiosity was too great. "The Elders again," he said. "You mentioned them before. Who are they?"

The man smiled again, and it seemed this time he was genuinely amused. "Ah," he said. "Yes, that is the question, isn't it? But in order to find the answer, you'll have to come with me."

"Come with you? You mean now?"

The man spread his hands, palms upward toward the sky. "When better?"

"But that's insane!" Simon protested. "What am I to tell the school? And my friends? Not to mention . . . "

"They're not like you," the man said coldly, cutting him off. "Not even remotely. You will learn the depth of that truth soon enough, Simon. As for the school, leave that to us."

"What will you do?"

"As far as they're concerned, you will cease to exist sometime tomorrow evening," the man said. "There will be some sort of accident . . . positive identification will be made . . . that will be that." He wiped his hands together briskly, then opened them and smiled. "No fuss, no muss."

"So that's it? I'm dead, just like that?" Simon was angry; his hands had clenched into fists.

"No . . . not dead. Only your social self will cease." The man laughed lightly. "You should be thankful, Simon! You're much more likely to become a legend if you die young. Stick around and you'll just be one more old man, growing fat and losing your edge."

Simon tried to think, but everything was a haze. "Say I come with you," he said finally. "Just suppose I do it. Where will we go?"

The man had risen to his feet, and now pulled a pair of tight leather gloves from somewhere in his overcoat, slipping them almost elegantly over his fingers. "Sorry, old chum," he said with a grimace. "That's classified." He stood, looking down at the young scientist for a moment, almost sorrowfully. "I told you yesterday," he said softly, "and I can see by your expression that the truth has finally found its way in. *You never really had a choice.*"

He turned and walked slowly toward the edge of the park, where DaLuge saw that a long, sleek black car had pulled to curb and sat, engine tuned down to an idling hum. When the man was twenty yards away he turned and looked back at Simon, who still sat rigid on the bench, his ears ringing, all sense of reality fading like the memory of a pleasant dream that had turned into . . . well, whatever this nightmare was.

"They're waiting," the man called softly. "Are you coming, or will there need to be additional pressure?"

With a great shuddering sigh, Simon got numbly to his feet, felt them begin to move as if on their own toward where the man waited. The open door of the car was like a cave that held both intrigue and horror, and his heart thudded faster in his chest the closer he got.

The man in the brown overcoat ushered him to the curb with a thin smile. "Don't worry, Simon," he said. "You've always belonged to us."

"Doctor DaLuge?" the voice crackled through his hand-com unit, and he became aware that it was the second or third time he'd been addressed. "Doctor DaLuge, come back. Are you there?" The end of the sentence was swallowed by a short burst of static.

He keyed the small unit. "Yes? DaLuge here – who's this?"

"It's Wheeler, sir. Level three."

Simon sighed, prepared for the worst. "What is it this time, Wheeler?"

"I apologize for interrupting your work, sir – normally I wouldn't, of course, but . . . well, we've found them."

"Found whom?" Simon's voice was sharp.

"The bugs, sir."

"The bugs? You mean the mosquitoes?" Well, this *was* unexpected. He'd never hoped to get them back, had written them off and forgotten all about them. "How'd you find them?"

"Well, that's why I'm calling you, sir." Wheeler's voice betrayed a hesitancy for which Simon suddenly found he'd lost all patience.

"Well, spit it out, man! How did you locate those bugs?"

"They seem to have . . . *infected* someone, sir. I thought . . .well, when you can spare a few minutes, you might want to come take a look for yourself."

DaLuge leaned back in his chair with a frustrated sigh, putting his index fingers to his temples and rubbing in slow circles to alleviate the tension that was building in his head. This did not bode well. If those mosquitoes had found their way to an urban area, then Lazaro Sol would have to be notified, and that was precisely what Simon didn't want.

"All right, Wheeler, goddamn you," he said into the hand-com, not hiding his frustration. "Just sit tight. I'll be up there within an hour."

"Thank you for getting here so quickly, sir," Wheeler said, rushing his words. "I really hate to bother you at a time like this . . . I know you're very busy, and all . . . "

"Save it." DaLuge's voice was flat as he strode into the room. "What've you got for me?"

"Well, er . . . ah, here we are." Wheeler tapped a small display screen next to the room's main console, bringing up a relief map of the Clifftop facility. "Now this is us, of course. Don't need to tell you that. But if you widen the view a little . . ."

He double-tapped the screen, and the view zoomed out to show an area four or five times the size of the original.

" . . . and go southeast about a hundred fifty miles . . . ah, there it is. The signal you see on the screen is being produced by a functioning transceiver unit. Our mosquitoes found a target."

On the electronic map, a red blip pulsed on and off. It was centered in an area of low mountains.

"Can we get a better fix on that signal?" DaLuge asked. "The way it looks, it could be coming from anywhere in a hundred-and-fifty-square-mile area."

Wheeler's face was a grimace. "Sorry, Doctor DaLuge," he said. "This is the best we can do. The signal is very weak." He hesitated for a moment. "Sir? Who do you suppose they infected? I mean, that's hundreds of miles from anywhere. Nobody lives out there . . . do they?"

DaLuge was having the same thought. Who indeed?

"Is there any possibility that those bugs infected an animal?" he asked curtly. "A deer, maybe? Or a dog – something with a similar heat pattern to a human. Those bugs were definitely unfinished. They could've malfunctioned."

Wheeler hesitated again, obviously not wanting to contradict his boss. "Well," he said after a bit, "I suppose it's . . . well, anything's *possible*, but . . . we've got the bugs' heat recognition pretty well dialed in. We haven't had one that would bite anything but human flesh for a long time. Now, granted, the microbotics were unfinished, which is probably why the signal is so distorted and weak –

the transceiver probably didn't form properly, which means that whoever – or whatever – was infected is definitely going to know something is up. Their body is most likely rejecting the sequencers, or at least trying to. I think it very likely that whoever it is might not live through the experience."

DaLuge sighed and rubbed a hand over his mouth as if it might rid him of the responsibility of having to deal with this mess. Lazaro Sol would have to be contacted, which angered him – there should be no reason to bring more scrutiny down on his head. This should be a routine matter, but . . .

If there were human beings in those hills, then they were most definitely *not* wired citizens. According to Wheeler, the infection had taken place nearly twenty-four hours earlier, and the signal hadn't moved at all since then.

He came to a quick decision, sitting forward in his chair. "I want you to keep a close eye on this one," he said, fixing Wheeler with a steely gaze. "Let me know if anything happens – and I do mean anything. Understood? This is priority one until I tell you otherwise. And I want you to transfer all relevant data to my office as soon as possible."

"Yes, sir." Wheeler seemed overjoyed by the prospect of such a simple task, and relieved to have the responsibility lifted from his shoulders. "No problem, Doctor DaLuge. You'll have it by lunch."

DaLuge's lips thinned into an artificial smile. "One hour, Wheeler," he said. "You'll have it for me in one hour."

Two days had passed.

Maia's face, normally vivacious, was drawn and pale from lack of sleep and concern for Karla. "If there was only something we could do," she sighed, laying a king and stealing the discard pile. She absently arranged the cards in her hand, looking over them at Johnny. "Can I tell you something, Perdue?"

"What is it?"

"Well, you know that you and Karla are the only two people I can . . . you know, see, right?"

"Yeah, I remember."

"Her . . . " Maia took a slow breath. "Her aura's changing, Johnny. I mean, she always seemed very unique to me, psychically. She gave off very interesting vibrations."

"So what's different now?"

Maia hesitated as if she didn't want to continue. "Well," she said finally, "I can't see her all the time, you know, but when I do . . . well, her energy has grown very cloudy, I guess you could say. Cloudy and dark. When I see her it's like through a dark cloud." She stopped with a hollow laugh. "I guess that's redundant. What I'm trying to say is that I've seen the same thing in plants . . . old trees especially."

"Right before they die?" Johnny's voice held an edge that he recognized as a frustrated defense mechanism. He hesitated, trying to soften his tone. "I mean . . . I don't know what I mean. Christ, Maia! It really seems messed up that we can't do anything about it." He sighed and ran a hand through his mop of black hair, which felt greasy and unkempt. He realized that he hadn't bathed in three or four days, and wondered distractedly if he was repulsive to her.

But she had put her cards down, and now scooted over beside him and laid her head on his shoulder. If the layer of grime on his clothes bothered her, she didn't let on, and Johnny could see that she was also in no immaculate state. The tracks of her tears on her stained cheeks were readily visible, and she hadn't bothered to wash them off.

Johnny found it strange that he should be thinking these thoughts, given the circumstances.

Who cares about romance in the face of this?

But he knew that he cared, and cared desperately. If anything, this tragedy had drawn the two of them closer to each other. They'd been nearly inseparable for the last two days, and if it hadn't been such a nightmare, it might have seemed a dream come true.

His hand-com unit beeped suddenly, and he thumbed the receiver. "Yeah?"

"Johnny? This is Allie. I . . . " he could hear her voice stretching, straining; a thin filament, threatening to snap. "I've been awake for almost sixty hours. Could you come sit with Kar for an hour or so? Jeremieah will be back before too long, I think. I have to get some sleep."

"Absolutely," Johnny got to his feet. "I'm on my way." He looked down at Maia. "Why don't you stay here and sleep, too?" He wished that he could stay and do just that himself, nestled on her bed in the corner of the small, comfortable room, but shook the image from his tired mind. "I'll be back in an hour and join you."

"Okay." Her smile was forced, but he sensed strong feeling in her, reaching for him. He leaned over and kissed her hair. "I'll be back," he said, then left before the urge to stay became impossible to resist.

"I'm sorry, Johnny, but I can't even think," Allie said as he entered. Her eyes were withdrawn; she seemed like something hunted. "If I don't rest I'm going to lose it. I try to sleep in the chair but it's not comfortable, and there's no room on the floor."

"Where's Tinney?" Johnny looked past Allie to Karla's still, pale form, which seemed tiny and lost among mounds of blankets, damp cloths and pillows.

"He went over to Control." Her voice was a fatigued murmur. "Stark called, said he had to talk to him. The doc left in a hurry." She leaned over and kissed Karla's fingers. *"Bye, honey,"* she whispered. *"I'll be back in a little while. Johnny's here to take care of you now. Okay?"*

Karla did not respond, but one of her fingers twitched, and a low moan escaped her throat.

"Stark?" Johnny frowned. "Wonder what that's all about?"

"Don't know." Allie was already moving to the door, slowly but with purpose, heading up the hall towards the one thing her body simply could no longer do without. "I sure wish there was someplace closer to sleep than my quarters. It's a quarter-mile hike, and I don't think it's a very nice day."

"You could probably sleep for a while up in Maia's room," Johnny said. The poor woman looked like she might simply drop dead on her feet if she didn't lie down soon.

"I might just do that. Which room is it?"

"Fourth hovel on the right,"

This elicited a half-hearted grin. "You've been a good friend, Johnny. I really appreciate you helping out."

"No problem. Just go get some rest."

She nodded with a sad smile and moved away, the sound of her feet a weary shuffle on the packed dirt floor of the tunnel.

He had a sudden pang of guilt as he realized that he hadn't talked to Stark or Scott in more than two days. They would have been expecting him for his shift yesterday afternoon, and he hadn't even called them on the radio to let them know he wasn't coming.

They would understand, of course, but still he didn't like to shirk duty. Not calling was irresponsible.

He looked over at Karla and winced as he got a clear view. It didn't get any easier to look at, no matter how he tried to prepare himself. The purple-red lumps on the left side of her face and neck seemed strangely set, almost as if her pretty, girlish face had been re-shaped, mutated somehow in a way that looked like something other than normal swelling. The area between her left ear and shoulder was a fleshy mass that had stopped swelling – but Doctor Tinney had told him that it wasn't responding to the anti-inflammatory drugs either, which he administered faithfully every few hours. Where her left eye had been, there was now only a tiny line of shadow. The right one remained closed almost all of the time, rolling feverishly in its socket as she hovered somewhere just below consciousness in a place that was not quite a coma.

"I'll be perfectly frank, young man," the doctor had said, pushing his glasses up into his frizz of wispy brown hair. "I've never seen anything like this. I'll do what I can to control the swelling and infection, but we're dealing with something for which I've seen no medical precedent. I really can't say what will happen."

The rest of her body seemed changed as well, somehow; she had a sunken look about her. He could almost see her veins through her skin, which was pallid and waxy. Her blond curls, once bouncy and with a mind of their own, lay flat and tangled on a pillow, which would have to be changed soon – it was encrusted with the milky yellow secretion from the multitude of bites, which were still infected and oozing. Her mouth was twisted on the left side with the effects of her condition, giving her a downturned expression of sadness that was almost unbearable to look at.

He looked away, thinking that he ought to call Control to report in, if only to uphold some sense of normalcy and duty. Besides, he was curious what Doctor Tinney could want to talk to Stark about. Could it have to do with a cure for Karla?

His hand-com beeped suddenly, making him jump. Before he could answer it, the Chairman's voice crackled through, sounding frantic.

"Everyone listen up! We need total radio silence as of right now. Everyone shut your hand units down and get under cover. We are going to shut off the power, so light candles and get ready for the lights to go out. This will happen in one minute. Extinguish all fires other than candles, that means no smoke outside where it can be seen. I repeat, fires out. If you see anyone outside, get them in immediately. This is not a drill! Repeat, not a drill. We are at condition invisible. That's condition invisible. This will be the last communication. Radios off! Over and out."

The radio crackled and went silent. In the bed beside him, Karla gave a low, distressed sound.

With a convulsive movement, Johnny clicked the unit on his belt into the 'off' position, his adrenaline spiking. He reached for the emergency cache of candles, set on a shelf on the wall to his left. His grip was unsteady, and he dropped the heavy wax candles. Two of them broke into large chunks of yellow on the floor. He picked up three that hadn't broken and lit them with trembling fingers, setting them on the shelf and on the doctor's small desk. His heart was beating hard, but he realized with extreme irritation that he could do nothing but stay exactly where he was. The thought of leaving Karla alone, even for a minute, seemed utterly irresponsible.

On the other hand, Maia might not have had her radio on – someone should warn her. He got up and paced the room, debating on whether to go. Cursing himself, he cast a final look toward Karla and sprinted down the hallway, arriving at the store-room to find Maia sitting up, knitting by the light of a small battery-powered lamp. Allie lay asleep, one arm flung out over the edge of Maia's bed. Maia stared at him in consternation. "What's wrong?"

"Can you sit with Karla? I have to find Jeremieah. Something's going on. And we need to light some candles." He found a few and lit them, placing them in the low candle-trays that lined the room.

Maia's eyes were scared. "What's going on, Johnny?"

"I don't know, but I have to find out. Come on! Karla's all by herself."

Maia followed him up the hall to find Doctor Tinney and Aldridge just arriving. Jeremieah was wrestling a bulky piece of equipment which sported an antenna and a small dish. Johnny recognized it as a mini grid shield, a small portable device for jamming radio signals or masking electronic signatures.

"I – I didn't mean to leave her alone, Jeremieah. I was just . . . " He couldn't stop himself from apologizing, but trailed off as he saw the look on Jeremieah's face. "What's going on?"

"We may have been marked." Aldridge's iron-gray head swayed in the lamplight. "Help me with this, would you, Perdue?" He was attempting to set up the unit next to Karla's bed.

"There's . . . there's some kind of signal," the doctor said, wringing his hands in agitation. "Karla's giving off some sort of . . . of . . . *radio* signal!"

"A signal?" Johnny snapped open one of the unit's leg-stands and braced it against the wall. "I don't understand."

"Like a homing device." Jeremieah's voice was weak. "That's what Stark says. They've been having all sorts of trouble with frequency distortions or . . . or something like that. I'm not a technician. At first they thought it was just the wind, but then Scott ran some sort of scan and found a signal, originating from within the valley."

"It all fits in," the doctor said morosely. He removed his glasses and rubbed his eyes with fatigue. "The 'foreign elements' I found in her blood. It must be some sort of micro-technology. Whatever it is, it's creating a radio signal that can be traced."

"Where's the blasted switch?" Aldridge ran his hands over the gauges and dials spread askew below the battery housing.

"Just to the right of where your hand is." Johnny pointed it out. "I've used one of these before. They're great for ground transports. Wish they could make 'em with smaller batteries, though."

"Is that thing ready?" Maia's voice twanged in the tenseness of the still room. "I mean, not to be rude, but let's turn it the hell on already."

The shield unit gave a low hum that permeated the room. Johnny tweaked the selector switch to 'radio' and set it on automatic search. "It will take about thirty seconds to isolate the frequency and jam it," he said. His voice was hushed, which he found absurd suddenly. It wasn't as if anyone could hear them.

But the thought that they might have been detected hung heavy in all their minds. The room was intensely quiet as they waited, hardly daring to breathe. There were no sounds but the squelching whine of the scrambling unit as it cycled through sets of frequencies.

After what seemed an eternity, the machine gave a low 'beep' and ceased making any sound at all.

"Well, there you go," Johnny said, heaving a large sigh. "That should at least buy us some time. We . . . "

"*Shhhh!*" Maia hissed suddenly. Her eyes were closed. Her face was contorted with concentration, and she seemed to be listening. Her eyes fluttered open and assessed them all with frightened clarity. "Do you hear that?" she whispered. "There's a sound . . . it's not . . . natural. I . . . oh, can't you hear it?"

And then they all heard it at once, a low thudding vibration that seemed distinctly out of place against the backdrop of their valley. Johnny felt the sound in some indistinct place below his breastbone – a clattering resonance that seemed to be growing louder. He looked at Jeremieah, whose eyes held a repulsive kind of fright.

"What is it?" Maia broke the silence.

"Choppers," Aldridge whispered. He looked like a wax statue of himself suddenly. "Civil Enforcement helicopters." He closed his eyes, seeming to muster all of his strength. "We have to go topside and seal all the tunnel exits. I saw at least three of them open when I came in here."

"I'll go with you," Johnny said. The clattering rhythm of the choppers had drawn a little closer, and now it seemed as if the vibration was coming up from the ground itself.

Aldridge moved down the tunnel at a pace which belied his obvious exhaustion, and Johnny was impressed with a strong sense of why this man was the unacknowledged leader of this band of people. His daughter lay ill and possibly dying only yards behind him, and still he moved with forceful purpose. Johnny lengthened his strides to keep up.

They burst into stale gray light, the remains of a sunny day gone sour as old milk. The wind whipped the tops of the trees, not gale force but much more than a breeze. The air made a sound like a giant moaning in its sleep as it funneled down the valley, and underneath it was the ominous sound of the choppers, moving closer.

Johnny found himself amazed at the level of preparedness exhibited by the compound folk. They had sprung from a near-dormant state into full alert in under ten minutes. Not a single soul was visible on the hillside or in the meadow; in fact, there was no sign at all of human presence here with the exception of the bunker entrances.

Each bunker entrance was well-placed for concealment in the event of just this kind of emergency – some of them were sunk below the roots of fallen trees, while others were hidden by some of the large boulders that dotted the hillside. Three of them were already covered, their thermal camouflage screens pulled down hastily.

The two of them worked quickly, out of breath from the effort. They moved across the face of the hillside, pulling the emergency screens across each of the bunker entrances, arranging random bits of foliage to camouflage the screens. The choppers were louder and nearer, working their way up the valley, or perhaps coming up just the other side of the ridge. The insectile sound brought back Johnny's recurring dream, and he paused for a moment, scanning the near horizon for any sign of them.

Suddenly, a movement. He squinted across the field of blowing trees, his heart sticking in his throat. "I see 'em!" he shouted. "We have to get under cover!"

Ducking low and keeping to the line of boulders at the bottom of the low hill, they scrambled for the tree-line. The sound was un-muffled now; there were no overgrown ridges to channel the ratcheting rumble, which boomed over the river and chattered through the whipping grass. The two of them slid under the protective overhang of a low juniper just as two choppers came around the last bend and into full view.

Aldridge was fishing in the pocket of his jacket. "Here," he said grimly, looking out through the boughs as he jerked out a folded thermal sheet. "Maybe this will bust up their scans a little." The two of them hunched on the ground and pulled the sheet over themselves.

Johnny edged out a little to get a better look as the chopper came down the valley. It was huge – even bigger than the ones he had seen, in real life and in pictures. It was a dark metallic shade of green and had three rotors, which made a deafening clatter, roaring even through the high wind.

"I was wrong," Jeremieah hissed in his ear. "They're not CEC. Wrong color and too many rotors. I don't know where they're from."

"The wind is helping," Johnny replied, pointing. "Lucky for us. See, they're leaving. They didn't see shit."

It appeared that he was right. The choppers weren't turning around, but just kept clattering down the valley. After a few minutes the sound had ceased, fading into the wind like a nightmare that disappears with the light of morning. Johnny pulled the thermal sheet from over his head and stood up, brushing against the pungent juniper boughs. He took a deep, relieved breath.

"Damn," he said shakily, suddenly wanting nothing more than to be back inside with Maia. "Damn. I hope we never get that close again."

He took a deep breath and started to say something else, but stopped when he looked at Jeremieah. The Chairman's large body, normally so imposing, was crumpled against the bole of the juniper, his head in his hands. His whole body shook, and Johnny realized with surprise that he was crying.

Aldridge raised his head, his eyes wet and red. His expression was one Johnny hoped he'd never see on a grown man again. It was a kind of wretched hopelessness, the look of a fighting man who knows that he's beat but will never quit.

"We're sitting ducks," Aldridge said quietly. He closed his eyes and leaned his head against the tree trunk. "It's all over, Perdue. You know that, don't you? They were looking for the source of that signal, and just because the weather's bad today doesn't mean they won't come back tomorrow, or in two days, or a week, and just clean us right the hell out."

Johnny swallowed hard, trying not to listen. "Don't say that," he protested weakly. "I mean, there's got to be something we can do. Right? Come on, Jeremieah, let's go inside. It's cold out here."

Later that night, an emergency Council meeting was called, deep in the bunker system that housed Control. The room was specifically for conferences, and was bisected by a long oak table. The table had a shiny, oily finish that reflected the candle-light dully onto the grim, tense faces of those surrounding it. Debate had been raging for nearly half an hour now, and they seemed nowhere nearer any answers.

" . . . transmitter could be only part of the package," Marshall Scott was saying. "Maybe it's just a homing beacon for them to come find whoever or whatever has been infected. Which means, depending on how important this . . . experiment, or whatever, is to them, they might very well be coming back."

"I think that goes without saying," responded Uma Peak. "We have to begin to think of alternatives."

"Alternatives?" Stark's face pulled together in a scowl. "That can mean only one thing, and I'd like to know what you think you're going to do with three hundred people in the middle of winter. If you're suggesting we leave, then I'd like to know in advance where we're going that will be more defensible than this valley."

"Relax, John." She raised her hands with a weary, defensive smile. "All I'm saying is that we need to think about this from every angle. Do you have any ideas?"

Stark nodded. "We can expand our security perimeter," he said. "We could give ourselves quite a bit of extra heads-up time to work with. Put the whole compound on high alert for a while. We should have escape routes planned, of course, and maybe cache some stuff further up-valley in case of the worst. But I don't think it's feasible to move everyone right now. Even if they come back, they can't cover every square inch of these mountains on foot, and if we don't give them anything to look at from the air, we might just be okay."

"Well, I don't see how Karla can be moved, anyway." Johnny said. "If we're going to figure out how to help her, we need every ounce of medical technology we have, and that's all right here at the compound."

"So what are we looking at?" Bud Arney's usually jovial face was sober. "Winter underground? No power? No fires? We can do that. We survived a hell of a lot worse back in the day."

"We can't say for sure just yet," Aldridge answered. "But I think it's best that everyone be put on alert. And I think that yes, everyone stays underground, at least for a while. We just can't afford to take any chances."

"We need a twenty-four hour live watch," Stark said, fingers drumming. "We can run eight-hour shifts: me, Scott, and Perdue. Can't take a chance putting the system on auto-pilot all night. Something might sneak through."

"We're going to have to cut non-essential power as well," said Marshall Scott. "Especially if we're going to boost security. Running with the lights on, we'd be open to electronic signature scans from further away than we can detect. They might see us before we saw them." He looked around, his scraggly bearded face seeming out of place wearing a serious expression. "It's cat and mouse," he said after a moment. "And we're the mouse."

"We've got plenty of candles and quite a few battery and gas-powered lanterns," Arney said. "I inventoried 'em not three weeks ago. If we're mice, then we're well-prepared mice. We'll do fine. I just hope the young folk don't get too antsy."

"What the hell." Johnny grinned sourly. "The way it's raining, there's nothing to do, anyway."

"If we're through, then?" Uma rose to her feet. "I want you all to get some rest. Tomorrow is important. Tomorrow and all the other tomorrows behind it. We need to be in top shape if we're going to stay ready."

The meeting was adjourned; bodies shuffled to their feet, rough clothing rustling as chairs were pushed under the table and people grabbed their coats. As Johnny was heading toward the door, thoughts of Maia and sleep foremost in his mind, Marshall Scott approached with a grin on his freckled face.

"Hey, Perdue," he said. "We were just drawing straws for the first night shift. Here's yours." He handed Johnny a slim stalk of grass about three inches long.

"Great." Johnny raised an eyebrow. "Let me guess: this is the short one?"

Scott grinned and slapped him on the shoulder. "See you in eight hours, Perdue. I'll tell Maia where you went." He pulled his lined denim jacket tight and disappeared up the corridor.

Johnny sighed and walked the opposite direction down the hall, toward the small white door marked 'Control'.

15

Lazaro Sol coughed twice, his large frame heaving with the effort. His lungs felt burnt today, as if not all the oxygen he inhaled was getting where it needed to go. He spat into his water cup. Nothing today, and yet there *was* something there, rattling in his chest.

Less than four months remained until he could discard this ragged shell. One hundred seven days, to be precise, and then everything would be different. For Lazaro Sol, certainly, as rancid age would be transformed to glorious youth. It wouldn't be the first time he'd undergone the procedure, certainly – in his four hundred plus years, he'd inhabited at least half a dozen bodies. But it would be the first time he would be given such a beautiful, unused body, and the mind that went with it. Ah, that mind – he had yet to see it in action, as he kept the clone inundated with sexual temptation, drowsed by that most wondrous drug, Elepro, and distracted by expensive toys . . . but he sensed it waiting to break through, just the same.

Waiting to be inhabited by Lazaro Sol.

The servos in his chair whined as he turned to face the large screen behind his desk. His planet hung there, a floating blue jewel, a prize waiting to be won.

And we will win.

He and the Elders had waited for centuries. They had planned. They had prepared. And in four months, when Daniel achieved Contact, victory would be fairly in hand.

He sighed, leaning back in his chair. Strange how even in these most pressured times, he felt so strongly the need to rest. Closing his eyes, he reached into the depths of his robe and retrieved a small silver flask. Uncapping it with a single twist, he slurped a healthy draught of its contents, grimacing with pleasure at the cold salty taste. A rush of adrenaline surged through him, making him feel light. Presently his head cleared and he felt strong again, though he knew the feeling would pass soon enough.

The small screen on his desktop gave a mellow *ping* behind him and he swiveled to face it. "Yes?"

The screen was on audio only, and now a familiar voice came through. "DaLuge here, sir. I regret having to bring this to your attention, but we have a little situation down here."

Lazaro listened as DaLuge outlined the mosquito problem, tapping his long, cracked fingernails on the faux-marble desk.

"I'm very sorry to bother you with this," DaLuge concluded, "but I thought it might be a security threat, considering how close they are. As far as I know, there shouldn't be anyone living in those mountains, but we're fairly certain the infected party is human."

"Couldn't you contact the local CEC, tell them there are . . . oh, I don't know . . . refugees to rescue, or something like that?" Lazaro asked patiently. "Or Clifftop Security? They could take one chopper over the area and probably take care of everything in the space of an afternoon."

"They took out two," DaLuge replied. His voice sounded tired. "It's very mountainous country, sir – lots of hills and windy conditions. They were out there for hours and didn't see a thing, other than a couple of deer. As far as the CEC, I thought of that too, but there's going to be a lot of questions if they find the person who was infected. Those sequencers are definitely not in working order. A competent specialist might be able to detect them."

Lazaro Sol narrowed his eyes. "You're a good man, Simon," he said with a nod. "You were right to contact me. Anyone living off the grid is to be dealt with properly, especially given their proximity to Clifftop. Where there's one human, there's bound to be more, and for all we know, they could be terrorists. They could know about Clifftop and be planning to sabotage our work." He paused, thinking. "That's probably not the case, but it's good to know they're out there, whoever they are. And they might be of some use to us."

"Right. So what should we do?"

"How soon can you get a good lock on their actual position?"

DaLuge grimaced. "It could be tough. Four, maybe five days using standard detection methods. I don't know. We tried running a satellite scan but we haven't seen anything, or found any human heat signatures, anywhere near where the signal's originating. And it keeps fading in and out, which we haven't figured out yet. One minute it's strong, the next it's completely gone, only to come back again a half hour later. I was about to assign a team with a microcam swarm, but it's still going to take some time."

Lazaro had a sudden thought. "Transmit everything you've got to me here," he said, smiling at his own idea. "I've got someone on board who might enjoy this task."

DaLuge seemed surprised. "Are you sure? I mean, it should be a fairly routine thing, time spent aside. I only notified you because it seemed like a security issue. We can handle it down here."

"I'm sure you could, but I have something in mind. I'll update you on an hourly basis, if you want to keep your team apprised," Lazaro said. "How's the re-wiring coming, by the way? We haven't spoken in a week or two."

"Just finished." DaLuge scrubbed a hand across his face. "We should be conducting preliminary tests within a day or two."

"Good. Ready by Equinox?"

The scientist laughed. "Do I have a choice?"

Lazaro smiled, but there was ice there. "Not at all, my good friend."

"Then yes, it will be done. I only hope your clone can handle it. How is he, by the way?"

"Coming along nicely." Lazaro's tone was clipped. "Don't worry about the clone. You just handle your end of things."

"Thank you, sir. DaLuge out." The screen fuzzed gray, then turned a deep mellow shade of blue. Lazaro tapped it off, sat back with his fingers steepled beneath his jowls, and began to think.

Since he'd given the clone access to a microcamera swarm, Daniel had been holed up in his quarters, obsessively watching the activities of the planet's people through the vicarious medium of his invisible eyes. For the first few days Lazaro had checked in on the boy's activities regularly, watching whatever he was viewing on either of the two screens in his office while the other simultaneously showed the surveillance feed from the camera that was hidden high in the corner of Daniel's small room. This allowed him to monitor what the boy was looking at as well as his reaction to it.

Evidently the Elepro was doing its job; although Daniel possessed the finest brain in all the known universe, he had failed to ask the most elementary questions, such was why he had been given access to such a powerful surveillance tool in the first place. Lazaro had a strong temptation to reduce the dosage of the suppressant medication, but resisted. The time would come soon enough when Daniel would have to be weaned in preparation for Contact; in the meantime, that powerful mind was reason enough to consider the clone a threat until the plan was complete.

Lazaro knew the boy wondered about himself, Elepro or not; he wondered what anyone might in his place: what the Elders were planning for him, and what was to be his place in the hierarchy. He could see the questions there, lurking deep in Daniel's eyes, trying to swim to the surface but pulled back by the predestination of his programming in combination with his drug regimen.

This was unavoidable.

Human beings, especially those, like the boy, who had a strong dose of the Elders' ancient bloodline running through their veins, were highly volatile, emotional creatures. And emotional creatures have a tendency to question, though they may never vocalize those questions.

Daniel never had.

As Lazaro Sol had predicted, Daniel immediately began to use the swarm to satisfy his burning sexual lust. This was also part of his programming – if the clone was busy in pursuit of pleasure, he'd be less likely to meddle where he didn't belong.

Lazaro had watched him closely for a day or two, just to make sure Daniel didn't get any crazy or mutinous ideas, but - at least at first - the clone's voyeurism had been unswerving and intense. It was made even more so by the fact that Daniel was experiencing the swarm images while wearing sophisticated VR gear; to his senses, he was wherever the swarm was, experiencing the space they inhabited, complete with sound. And, although he'd grown too old for sexual pursuits himself long ago, Lazaro found himself fascinated by Daniel's seemingly unending appetite. Daniel often brought in two or three girls from the harem to pleasure him as he watched the deviant escapades of unsuspecting humans.

Strangely enough, though, after only a few days the boy had turned from sexual interests to other things. He seemed to have become bored by his exploits much too quickly, and had grown far too fascinated recently by the less developed side of human society; the rat culture which grew in the 'rim yards', the refuse dumps on the edges of each metropolis which would eventually become paved-over landfill - parking lots, malls, stadiums.

This sudden shift was something Lazaro found mildly worrisome – the boy needed structured distraction if he was to keep that amazing mind busy while simultaneously preparing it for Contact.

This was something to which he'd given a lot of thought recently.

These months leading up to the event had set Lazaro Sol to speculation. The reason he'd activated the clone early in the first place was because his gut told him that Daniel needed to have a set of memories before Contact. And not only pre-programmed memories, though the program was a nice (and necessary) first step.

Lazaro believed that it had been this lack of real, evolving memories – the only kind which can become the 'ego-self' – that had in large part kept the first three clones from achieving successful Contact.

This new development with DaLuge's renegade mosquitoes would be the perfect project for Daniel – something to keep his mind busy for a while, making new connections. That mind would eventually be assimilated by Lazaro Sol, of course – this was a foregone conclusion, and Lazaro wished heartily that the transfer could occur immediately . . . but it would have to wait until after Contact was successfully achieved. There was far too much risk in trying it before, not to mention the intrigues that went along with his plot. The Elders, even the Twelve, knew nothing as yet of his plans to inhabit the Supercontroller's body.

His own body was dangerously old; any resistance on the clone's part could foul the transfer and his soul could be lost, his essence trapped in the murky void inhabiting the space between two minds. And there *would* be resistance if he attempted the transfer now – that was the danger of the clone's extremely potent brain. No matter what precautions they took, that mind was sure to try and protect itself. No – better to wait until Daniel had completely accepted the protocol program. Afterwards, the transfer could be made while he was in a deep, controlled hypno-sleep, monitored from within by the very system he was plugged into.

Lazaro took out his flask and drained it, then, with a sudden sharp movement, flung it across the room. It hit the wall and bounced off harmlessly, only to smash into an antique Chinese vase on a small pedestal in the corner. The remains of the vase toppled, shards of pottery tinkling to the carpeted floor.

He sat frozen for a moment, then shook his head and guffawed loudly.

Where in seven hells did that come from?

Stress. It had to be.

He could employ patience when he had to, but he hated uncertainty. He wanted this thing over with, and to hell with everything else, especially this wretched body. It dragged him down, made it hard to think. Tests had confirmed that his synaptic activity was declining along with the rest of him, although at a slower rate.

There was one good thing, and for this he congratulated himself. He'd purposely set the boy up with the virtual reality technology so that Daniel's motor memory control would be ingrained before the consciousness transfer – the swarm, as well as many other suitably interfaced computer programs, could be manipulated by subtle body movements. Why bother having to learn such a tricky system when he could let Daniel learn it? The memories would be assimilated by the consciousness of Lazaro Sol, as would all of the experiences Daniel gleaned during his short period of personal existence aboard Mephisto.

This was an area in which he had some limited experience. He'd assimilated others before; it was the only way to pass an Elder's consciousness from one body to another. The best ones, like the former inhabitant of the body he now possessed, were those with great physical strength and unblemished minds which could be bent to their new master's ends. But the memories of those whose bodies he'd assumed were always there, in the back of his mind. They were like trophies he took through the years, from one body to the next. He had 'ghost memories' of things he knew had never happened to him, events experienced by others whose personalities he'd absorbed when he'd taken over their bodies.

These things could be useful later. The knowledge of how to handle the swarm, for example, would be something Lazaro Sol could use after he assimilated the boy's supple young mind – the swarm, along with many other sources of surveillance and information, would be like his eyes and ears at that point, and it wouldn't hurt to have some residual knowledge. Lazaro himself had very little experience with such things.

Thinking of this gave him another idea, and he inhaled sharply with its force, only to go into a long fit of spasmodic coughing.

When he had his unruly lungs back under control, he took out a new flask and drained it, breathing as deeply as he could. He sat back in his chair, stunned by his own genius.

If the boy were to learn advanced clone control . . .

The Controllers - like the one in Mephisto's engine room - worked with virtual reality technology much like that which Daniel was currently using, and the techniques were not so different from one another in either concept or application.

That sort of ingrained knowledge could be priceless!

As soon as Contact was achieved, the clone would for all practical purposes take over the operational controls of the planet, plugged in to virtually every computer system in the world. If, as with the swarm, Daniel's motor memory for Control techniques could be ingrained before Lazaro Sol took possession of his body, then so much the better when it came time to exercise his power.

Not that Lazaro Sol doubted his own abilities to master anything he wanted – especially in that young, souped-up body. But it was still worth some thought. It could give the Elders an edge they desperately needed. The Great Work was years behind – everything should have been completely in place by now, and yet there were still so many unknown factors.

A voice of warning resonated from somewhere in the depths of his centuries of experience.

Don't trust anyone too far . . . not even yourself.

If he went ahead with this plan and allowed Daniel to learn the Controller's art, the boy would have to be monitored even more closely. More drugs might be needed – the urge to question must be avoided or suppressed at all costs, and Daniel's powerful mind made him a threat.

Lazaro knew he would be riding a fine line, but his gut told him it could be done.

If it can be done, then I'm the one to do it.

16

The shoddy little man, wearing only a faded pair of pants and taped plastic slaps which passed for shoes, made his way through endless piles of refuse - metal, composted dirt, glass. He was unaware of the thousands of tiny eyes watching him, threading their coded electrical relays between the very molecules of the earth's atmosphere to a waiting satellite, which instantaneously relayed those signals to Mephisto Station's computer core where they could be re-shaped into translatable data.

This data appeared as a fully three-dimensional moving image on the lenses of Daniel's virtual reality goggles.

The shoddy little man paused, looking around. His upturned nose sniffed at the air, and then, quickly, he disappeared under the large hanging lip created by a jutting sheet of rusted metal. Daniel debated on sending the swarm in after him, just to see where he was going, but he knew he'd probably find nothing more interesting than a couple of scruffy junkers sitting around a fire eating rat-meat. There was no audio here either, and the swarm didn't transmit as clearly from dark places. He pulled the camera cloud up to reconnaissance position, just over four thousand feet, and let it hover while he debated his next move.

These places . . . these *rim yards* . . . fascinated him. They were the downside of Grandfather's 'perfect' societies, the domain of the outcast, those for whom survival was the only work.

He'd been studying them for two days now. The rim yard currently on his monitor was in the outskirts of a city somewhere on the Asian continent, but it could have been anywhere. They all looked the same.

The various metropoli, massive standing waves of buildings and lights and technology, all had bustling industrial centers which sprawled for many square miles before giving out into the urban and sub-urban sectors, where grew schools and shopping centers and perfect box houses with immaculate lawns that looked like a green and gray patchwork quilt from this height. But on the outskirts of each city, beyond the eyes of those who traversed the highways every day within only a few miles of them, were always the rim yards and the rat culture that went with them.

Once in a while, if the swarm was high enough, he could see the remains of old roads, running unevenly for a few miles before disappearing into nothingness, or the bones of an old town, burnt and twisted buildings in abject disrepair from more than half a century of disuse.

He wondered if Grandfather knew the sorts of things he looked at with the swarm. For the first few days he had amused himself by peeking into the most private lives of anyone and everyone on the globe, watching their actions when they believed themselves to be alone. He watched them in their houses, in their bathrooms, in their bedrooms, feeling a heady sense of power at his own omniscience.

But after only a few days of this, he began to find it all incredibly boring. The planet over, people's lives were basically all the *same*. He could find almost no real variation, other than in their strange instinctual ability to find more and better ways of sexually pleasing themselves and each other. But after these escapades, after he'd sent the girls away, after the warm buzz of orgasm decayed and left him simultaneously exhausted and restless, the same desperate boredom would set in as he sent the swarm to city after city, hoping in vain to find someone whose life would be interesting enough to care about.

For a while, he wondered if he might be able to use the swarm to spy on the Elders themselves, to find out more about their plans and where he might fit in. He'd had a hard time lately shaking that strange feeling he had about them. There was something about all that Grandfather was teaching him . . . something, even, about *himself* . . .

Something that didn't fit.

What is it?

He didn't know. A certain restlessness was building, a conviction that vital information was being withheld from him. And, when he tried to think back, to compare this feeling with past experience, he began to see that there were holes in his memory, as well.

For instance, though he remembered thousands of 'lessons' with Grandfather, and almost any given 'fact' that he'd ever memorized, he could recall almost nothing about his own childhood other than his lessons. Had he really lived here, on Mephisto Station, his whole life? His memories, his time-based sense of continuity and logic said yes, but the *context* seemed all wrong.

He seemed to remember having visited many sites on Earth – the Great Pyramids in old Egypt, the Grand Canyon on the North American Continent – but he couldn't say when, or who he was with. Sometimes it seemed that he'd only really been alive a very short while, and this feeling was cumbersome and unwieldy.

It seemed strange to him, after spending days studying Earth-bound humans, that he had no real companions. Neana and a few of the other girls came closest to this, but they could hardly be called friends, much less intellectual equals. Why had he never formed real friendships? And why now should he suddenly be concerned with this? His motivation, his one goal, his every ambition, had always been to fulfill his destiny within the Parliament. Why should that suddenly change?

Grandfather had said he was to be initiated as a full Elder in just three months. But if that was the case, why then was so much information on the very subject of the Elders being withheld? He felt that he was being used – that he was a tiny piece in a very large puzzle of which his knowledge was almost nonexistent.

But though he desperately wanted answers, it was just too risky to chance using the swarm to spy on the Elders. He would have to find a better way. No matter that Grandfather always spoke to him with such a glittering mask of parental affection, worn uneasily over his heavy jowls; no matter that the old man veritably fawned over him, treating him like some sort of exotic pet. He couldn't chance it. Better to lay low, to go along with whatever came until he had enough information to act on his own behalf.

But something was definitely not right.

He pulled off his headgear, sighed and rubbed his eyes.

I need a break.

He checked the time and saw that he'd been at it now for three straight hours. He was just thinking of calling the chef and having something brought up – maybe a roasted chicken with cream sauce and broiled vegetables – when the screen on his wall emitted a low beep and the picture shifted to a glowering image of Grandfather, red rheumy eyes set in deep shadowed pockets. The old man was not looking well these days.

He began to speak with no preliminaries, his voice an unwelcome rumble. "Daniel. Come and see me, my boy. I've got an assignment for you. Something I think you might enjoy."

17

Johnny awoke to the squelching whine of the grid shield. The band had been shifting again, trying to cover the signal emanating from Karla's body. He sat up, rubbing his eyes and trying to think about the details of the dream he'd been having. It seemed terribly important that he remember, that he make sense of it; but with waking, the dream faded quickly and was gone.

The shield whined again, the band readout clicking back and forth, shifting to match the rogue signal. It was an uphill fight. Even with the most recent modifications, Marshall Scott had told Johnny privately, they couldn't be sure that the signal wasn't getting through.

"The micro-technology is very sophisticated," he said. "The signal keeps modifying itself in response to the shield. I'd bet that if someone out there is looking for that signal, they're finding it at least part of the time."

The extra shifts in Control, especially the graveyard shift Johnny worked three times a week, were grueling. Often, like today, he would sit with Karla while he wasn't on shift, inevitably falling asleep for a while in the chair by her bed. It was uncomfortable at best, but with people in and out all the time, there was just no room on the floor. He could have gone to his quarters or Maia's, and sometimes did, but mostly he was reluctant to leave Karla's side.

It had been two weeks now, and her condition seemed stable, which was about the only silver lining anyone could find. She did not appear to be on the verge of death, though her body continued to show distinctive signs of the changes taking place within it. But when Johnny asked Dr. Tinney how long Karla's body could withstand this weird infection, or whatever it was, the doc only shook his head sadly and looked away.

Karla had remained on the bed in the corner of the small hospice quarters, where the entire Aldridge family now fairly lived. They moved to and fro in shifts like frightened ghosts, trying to stay out of the doctor's way as he monitored and experimented and postulated. Allie, her pale, small features stamped with gritty resolve, was constantly at her daughter's side, bathing her swollen face or murmuring to her in soothing undertones. Jeremieah paced the halls outside, drinking enormous amounts of strong hot tea, checking in on Karla every couple of hours between those administrative tasks which he simply could not avoid. Uma Peak, always a bastion of strength, rose to the occasion, taking over most of Jeremieah Aldridge's duties.

Johnny was disturbed by the change that had overcome all of those closest to him. While the entire compound had been hit hard, it was the Aldridges and those closest to them who had born the brunt of the tragedy. This was Johnny's entire social circle, and so it had been a difficult week.

In the small bed where she'd become a fixture, Karla's hair had become a ghostly shade of its former rambunctiously golden self. Her left cheek and neck, where the bites had been, no longer festered and oozed; what had been swollen, infected flesh ten days before now seemed to be a solid fleshy mass, a mutation of almost half her face.

Her tiny lips were perpetually pulled down into a grimacing frown. Her left eye remained a slit, and although no one had said anything, to Johnny the slit seemed to be closing. He wondered morbidly if she would ever see the sky again.

The entire compound was in a weird state of calm, strangled paranoia. Even though the shield generator was up and running, which should assure escape from satellite detection, most people didn't venture outside unless they had to. When they did, they stayed under the trees or in the shadows, hopping like scared rabbits from rock to rock before diving into their burrows. Faces were grim, expressions tense.

Food and supplies had been cached at three strategic points within half a day's walk from the compound. In the case of exposure or attack, escape routes had been plotted, and compound members had been drilling three nights a week so they would know what to do in this eventuality.

The best part of Johnny Perdue's life these days was Maia, who sat in another chair by the foot of Karla's bed, knees clasped to her chest tightly, rocking slowly. She caught his gaze and smiled, and he looked away, unnerved by her presence though they had been nearly inseparable for the last week.

He wondered idly what she might be thinking.

Compound power had been off for nearly a week, and since conservation of supplies was a must, even candles were rationed. Days were stifling dullness sharpened by an almost unbearably heightened sense of danger. Nights were worse if you couldn't sleep. From her quarters, Maia had heard more than one voice raised in frustration as family members lashed out at one another.

The Winter Celebration had been canceled with the exception of the annual feast, which would be held in the large kitchen bunker and a few surrounding storerooms, with games and singing to follow. No one talked about it, but everyone knew it would be at best a half-hearted attempt at joviality.

Going outside had not been expressly forbidden, but anything unnecessary - a stroll in the woods up-valley, for example - would be frowned upon. Really, the weather was generally disagreeable enough that most of the people would have stayed inside anyway, even without the new risk of detection. But with candle rationing, lighting was bad and any attempt at entertainment or games ended with fatigued eye muscles, made worse by the closeness of the quarters.

Maia, however, was very good at not being noticed, and she'd found a few occasions to slip outside for a while. Escaping the damp, suffocating winter quarters for time in the forest was something she did every winter, and now these trips took on new meaning. No matter the weather, she needed air, and she needed time for the forest to heal her. She was exhausted, not only in body but in spirit and mind.

And now there was Johnny to reckon with, as well, and he was a handful.

Beautiful, tormented Johnny Perdue, with his coal-black hair and intelligent eyes; so unsure of himself, so hesitant. She wondered if he had any idea how she adored him. His act was one of intelligent toughness, but with her he was vulnerable, almost childlike. She loved the way his eyes clouded over as he turned inward, seemingly out of touch, only later to repeat word for word her conversation when she accused him of drifting off. He seemed simultaneously to notice everything, and to be impossibly and perpetually distracted.

She'd been surprised by her romantic attraction to him, completely unprepared. But she liked him enormously, anyway, and she was comfortable enough with herself to trust her liking of him – of all those in the compound, it was Johnny who most understood her eccentricities. He had a faraway look in his eye a great deal of the time himself. Her feeling was that it was a great craving for adventure and travel from which he suffered . . . and indeed he did suffer from it. She had no such craving herself, but she would travel with Johnny, if it came to that. She wasn't opposed to it. They'd be good together, roaming the country . . .

But this was foolish speculation. The compound was in trouble, and Maia felt, along with everyone else, the looming threat of imminent extinction. It was wearying.

She looked at Johnny, who had fallen asleep earlier in his chair by the head of Karla's bed. He was awake now, and she smiled at him. He smiled back, but ducked his head in an embarrassed way as if he felt that he didn't qualify for such a look from her.

"Hey," she said. "Do you want to get out of here?"

His brows knotted in a mild frown. "It's still light out," he said. "You know we shouldn't go out during the daylight."

She sighed, stood up and stretched. "I want to go out now," she said. "I need some air. And so do you, Johnny. We're not doing anyone any good rotting away underground."

"There are rules," he said lamely. "We're not supposed to go out unless it's an emergency."

She sighed and sat down, crossing her arms over her chest. "Well, I don't care. The protection grid's working, isn't it? We're safe from satellite scans, and I don't hear any choppers. Besides, we can stay under the trees. I looked outside earlier, and it's really nice today. There might even be snow up-valley. Definitely on the peaks."

"I have to stay with Karla," he replied, though she could tell that he wanted to go. "We can't leave her alone."

Doctor Tinney walked into the room with a shuffling gait, wiping his hands together nervously, as was his habit. "Oh, hello," he said. "Here, I'll just get my papers and go." He moved to the table that held his small array of tools, including his microscope and a rack of diagnostic equipment. "I can work down the hall as well as here."

"We, I mean I, was just leaving." Maia rose to her feet and shot Johnny a meaningful glance.

Doctor Tinney removed his thick oval spectacles and polished them on the tail of his shirt. He smiled uncertainly. "I'd be happy to keep an eye on Karla if you'd like a break," he said.

"Are you sure?" Johnny asked, uncertain as always.

"I'm here anyway," the doctor replied. "I'm sure it will be fine." He replaced his glasses on the tip of his nose and blinked owlishly. "I'll come get you if anything changes."

Johnny got up slowly, his backside tingling and numb from sitting for so long. He stamped his booted foot on the floor to get the circulation going. "Thanks," he said. "I'll be back before too long."

"You know, there's more than choppers and satellites that can spot us," Johnny said as they struck the up-valley trail just above Control.

The afternoon was a bit breezy, but unseasonably warm, and he began to feel thankful they'd chosen to bend the rules a bit. Still, he felt compelled to speak of the dangers. "There are spy planes that can take pictures from miles up. We'd never spot 'em if they were up there."

"They use digital photography, don't they? So the shield grid should take care of it." She paused halfway up a muddy embankment and turned, hand on her hip. She looked like a goddess there, with that determined look in her eyes and the firm set of her chin. She was so confident, and yet so unconscious of herself, and these were qualities he admired and coveted. He'd always been shy, slow to speak his mind. He wondered if she knew how he was in awe of her, how he thought of her all the time, how being with her had made this whole painful week a little less excruciating.

"That's pretty impressive," he said with a bit of a grin. "I didn't know you were up on spy technology."

"Hmm.   Well, you shouldn't underestimate me.   I'm not completely uninformed."

The forest was starkly beautiful in the winter sunshine, damp but not soggy, and the air was fresh and crisp. They kept moving, talking in low tones, both glad to be out. The trail had flattened out and widened enough that they could walk side by side, and so they did, moving generally uphill. She slipped her arm through his.

About a mile up-valley from the compound, they both stopped in unison as they came around a bend in the path.

"Wow!" Johnny exclaimed. The view was spectacular – below them the rambling upper valley stretched under cloud-littered skies; patches of dead blackberries, impassable thickets, the bare arms of oaks waiting for their spring coat to come in. And the roar of the river, eternal and unforgiving.

"Yeah." She smiled. "I like it here."

Johnny un-shouldered his pack and looked around. They were under cover of an overhanging ledge which protruded from the hillside, a natural shelter. The boughs of three gnarled willows dipped and swayed over the edge, shielding them from prying eyes. The backpack had popped open, and Maia laughed when she saw what was inside.

"Come prepared for anything, did we?" She pulled out the thin blanket that was stuffed into the top of the pack and dug to see what was underneath it. "Backwoods fuel cells, extra matches . . . thermal rain gear?" She shot him an inquisitive look. "How long do you think we're gonna be out here, Perdue?"

He forced a smile. "Just habit," he said. "Besides, if we're caught out in the open when those choppers come back, you'll be thanking me for bringing all this stuff. It could save your life."

She shook out the blanket on the pine-needle-covered earth. A small brown mouse scurried away with an indignant squeak and popped out of sight down a hole at the base of the overhang.

Johnny began to feel a mixture of discomfort and anticipation as she sat on the blanket and crossed her legs. She looked up at him with her almond-shaped eyes, those green depths that were so alive, so inviting. "Well, are you going to sit?"

"Sure." She was so soft, so immediate . . . as he sat, he caught her scent, warm and organic. He knew if he looked at her he would have to have her, right then and there, and this impulse alarmed and attracted him simultaneously. He felt his pulse rate going up, his heart throbbing loudly in his ears. Looking out at the opposing ridge wall, now blazing with reflected light from the setting sun, he remembered the last time they'd been alone in the forest, on a similar day . . . had it been only two weeks ago? On that day, they had been close to consummating their relationship, but their passion had been rudely aborted. Was it that memory that plagued him now?

"What's wrong, Johnny?" She seemed almost amused, but her voice held tenderness too, as if she knew his discomfort but would humor him for the time being. She scooted next to him, and her hip brushed against his. She smiled warmly, her eyes reflecting empathy.

"Don't be afraid."

Her voice was low, almost husky. Her breath touched his ear like a feather, distending his body as if it was a wire, humming with too much electricity. And still he resisted, though he didn't know why.

She laid her head on his shoulder, the soft insistent pressure of her breast heavy on his arm. "Relax, Perdue," she whispered. "You're way too tense." She ran her hand under his shirt, tracing the muscles of his stomach with the tips of her fingers. He stifled a gasp.

This is unbearable!

"Maia . . . " He began in a choking whisper, but the words weren't there. His jaw worked, but no sound came.

"Don't talk, Perdue," she said gently.

He kissed her.

It was a forceful kiss, as if something inside him that had been chained up for a long time had suddenly broken free. That *something*, whatever it was, needed her as fundamentally as a body needs water. There was nothing between them suddenly, as she unbuttoned his shirt and pulled it free, her hands stroking his naked skin. They drank from each other with abandon, running their tongues over each other's lips, probing as if they could reach the other's soul through the communion of bodily fluids. So complete was this abandon, this rapture, that he barely noticed when their clothes came off. She pulled him down on top of her, gasping as he entered her.

This act seemed second nature, as if they'd been doing it all their lives, and the friction that created the physical pleasure was only a small part of this exchange. Her eyes were open, locked on his, their union swirling toward climax; they seemed melded together, mind, soul and body, by a force infinitely stronger than either of them. The moment seemed to last an eternity as Johnny observed, with riveting detail, every facet of the experience; light through the branches of the swaying willows, motes of dust playing in the air, and *her* . . . her breasts, her hair, her eyes.

But when it was over, their bodies fallen apart like two spent fighters after a brutal match, it seemed their encounter had been far too brief. The sense of doom and failure that had dominated Johnny's mind for the last week was beaten back . . . but he knew the respite was temporary.

She sat up, her skin luminescent in the fading light, red-gold hair cascading across her white shoulders. He ran a hand lightly along her arm. She was staring out, down the slight incline toward the direction of the river. Her face was wrinkled in a mild frown.

"What is it?" He sat up, looking. "I don't see anything."

She shaded her eyes with her hand, took a deep breath, then shook her head. "It was probably nothing," she said.

But her eyes remained troubled.

During the entire hike back to the compound, Johnny couldn't shake the feeling that something was wrong; the hackles on the back of his neck kept going up, as if . . . as if . . .

As if we were being watched.

Paranoid thoughts, and useless. They made their way to the quiet darkness of Maia's quarters. Johnny was exhausted – too many late nights recently, and too much stress. He stripped off his shirt and lay on the softness of Maia's bed, allowing himself to sink into the comforting folds of the blankets with a weary sigh.

She'd remained quiet on the walk back, and now he watched her move around the shadowed confines of the candle-lit room, curious as to her thoughts.

After straightening up, she got undressed and slid under the blankets next to him. He put his arms around her and they lay in the semi-light of one candle, feeling each others' warmth, feeding from it. After a while, the candle guttered and went out, leaving the room in utter blackness.

"Maia?" he barely whispered from the edge of sleep.

Her breathing was deep and she made no reply. The words he was about to say, so important only a moment before, tumbled from his mind, falling apart like unconnected pieces of a puzzle; a house of cards coming down, giving way to the void of the dream world.

18

It took Daniel most of two weeks to locate the source of the renegade signal that Grandfather had asked him to track down. He was surprised by the amount of time involved in the search; he was used to sending the swarm to specific destinations almost instantaneously. But it had turned out to be his most interesting period of observation yet, and well worth the time.

He'd had hundreds of square miles to cover, and so he set the swarm on a roaming pattern and just sat back to watch, taking mental note of all he saw. It was hypnotic, to just let his remote eyes caress all of that land. Swooping up and down, over mountain ridges, into wooded valleys, up and out above the vast, unpopulated landscape, he began to see the land in a different way.

The silence, for one thing, was unusual. All of that area, and not a single audio feed. He wasn't used to such silence, especially accompanied by the visual effect of being, for all practical purposes, out beyond the reach of Grandfather's systems in country that was still very wild.

He took his assignment seriously, to be sure; always looking, scanning with his eyes as well as the thermal technology built into the swarm's capabilities. But he enjoyed himself, too. And the experience seemed to be having a clearing effect on his mind.

For the first twelve days, he saw nothing that even resembled human beings, though he scanned hundreds of square miles.

And then he got lucky.

He'd had a feeling all day that he was close to success. The weather in that part of the world had cleared up, making the swarm more efficient and visibility much better.

He'd come over the lip of a high cliff to find a spectacular view of a waterfall, directly below him. Following it down, feeling almost giddy from the three-dimensional perception of a four hundred foot drop, he saw that in fact it was *two* waterfalls. The first, higher falls cascaded into a deep pool about three-quarters of the way down; from there, the water tumbled the rest of the way to the valley floor, churning through a gauntlet of sharp, glistening rocks.

Reasoning that a water source would be a universal need, he set the swarm to follow the river. From there, it didn't take long.

It was movement that attracted him, coming from the slope of the valley wall, among the trees; a young man and woman who appeared quite intent upon each other. They lay stomach to stomach, arms and legs entwined.

It was so unexpected that at first Daniel didn't know what to do. He moved the swarm closer, curious.

The man had shoulder-length black hair and wore only a pair of pants, which seemed made of some coarse fabric. Unexpectedly aroused, Daniel moved the swarm to get a better view of the woman. His lust had jumped to the fore with no warning whatsoever; he'd almost forgotten about his assignment, and the fact that he had most likely completed it.

As she came into view, he was transfixed; she was a goddess, this woman! He became aware that he was holding his breath, and let it out in a shuddering sigh. Such beauty he had never seen! But what was it about her? Not her physical form, surely, though she was indeed beautiful. No, it was something else, something . . .

Something new.

She seemed so wild, so unabashedly free . . .

It's like she's from a different world.

He moved the swarm so close that he was practically on top of them, able to take in every detail of this magnificent creature. Her hair was red-gold and hung about her pixie-like face in waves and ringlets. Her eyes were green and seemed to carry great intelligence, above a small, slightly upturned nose. Her limbs were slender, with beautiful hands and long, graceful fingers that caressed the cheek of the man she seemed so enthralled with. As he watched, she sat up, pulled her blouse over her head and tossed it aside.

Her skin was living silk – suddenly Daniel wanted nothing more than to simply run one finger over that warm, smooth body. Unable to look away, he watched as she pulled her lover down on top of her. Her face was ecstatic; eyes closed, she seemed to reach for the heavens.

The silence gave the scene a translucent, surreal beauty that seemed somehow tragic. In Daniel's mind, a new thing had appeared with awful suddenness, like a black cloud rising from the horizon to blot out the sun. A terrible loneliness welled up in him, a force that made him gasp and shiver, as if the temperature had suddenly dropped twenty degrees.

He felt a surprising sensation, one for which he had no frame of reference; a mind-rending confusion of tumbling thoughts, completely irrational. It took him a minute to deduce that he was dealing with jealousy. This caught him completely broadside, and he nearly laughed out loud. It was unprecedented, and ridiculous! In the first few days with the swarm, he'd done almost nothing but search out people engaged in sex, simply to watch. It had been impersonal, if arousing, but he'd always felt appropriately distant. So why this sudden personal interest?

The lovers had reversed their positions. The red-haired woman's breasts swayed hypnotically as her man reached to caress them. Daniel observed her silent groan of pleasure and felt an intense and very quick rush of blood to his groin. Her eyes were half-open, eyelids fluttering, cheeks ruddy. She bent down and pressed herself against the dark-haired young man, whispering something in his ear. He tensed and pulled her tightly to him; then, as if in slow motion, their bodies shuddered and arched together.

Daniel watched with clenched jaw, simultaneously aroused and angry as the unreasoning specter of jealousy descended upon him once again. An intense and unwelcome frustration sank into him, a terrible feeling of loneliness for which he had no antidote. Nowhere in his memory was there record of this anguish.

It seemed they lay for a long, long time in post-coital embrace before slowly, reluctantly pulling apart. Their bodies were flushed but satisfied, their eyes heavy-lidded with afterglow.

Suddenly, the woman sat up and narrowed her eyes, looking in the direction of Daniel's point of view. She said something to the man, and he too shaded his eyes and looked. It seemed they were looking directly at him! He shivered violently with this perception, though he knew it to be false, and pulled the swarm back a hundred feet or so with instinctual swiftness. His head was pounding, his arousal gone without satiation, his stomach fluttering.

He took a few deep breaths to calm himself, reminding himself of who and where he was, and that he still had a job to do. These two obviously lived here in the forest and would most likely lead him to the source of the signal.

He resolved to wait and follow them when they left.

He didn't have to wait long. After only a few minutes, they got to their feet and put on their clothes. They both slipped on jackets and stepped out from under the rocky overhang. The man turned his face up briefly toward the lowering sky as if looking for something, then they moved under the trees and began walking downhill along a dim, narrow path. Daniel followed closely, wishing for the first time that he had an audio feed so he could listen to their conversation.

They took their time, walking hand in hand, doing what lovers do on afternoon walks. Daniel found it strange that human ritual should be the same in the wilderness as in the controlled cities, but their behavior seemed not altogether different from many people he'd watched. There was *something* different about them, though – they seemed to enjoy each other and the day in a way that made Daniel a little angry.

Or jealous.

And there it was again, that emotion he'd always known of but never felt until today. Something about *her,* specifically – he'd watched many women but had never observed one who seemed so self-aware and so free at the same time. Everything about her was hypnotic – the swing of her hair, the way she walked, her flashing eyes. He felt a stirring for her that was only partly sensual, and that great gulf, that pit of loneliness, threatened to open up and swallow him again.

It was almost as if he knew her from some past life, some former time that was nothing but the hint of a memory now. He closed his eyes, trying to blot out this irrational and wholly unhelpful thought, then remembered that while he was wearing VR equipment, the images were sent directly to his optic nerve, bypassing autonomous eye control. He couldn't shut them out.

He sighed and focused on detaching himself from what he was watching, with some success. The lovers had followed their forest path out into a flat, grassy clearing that was more like a low plain. The river wound slowly through this grassland, meandering down the valley at a leisurely pace. Daniel suddenly wondered very much what it would sound like there, with no artificial life support, no rumble of engines, no radios. How did these people live?

The two moved quickly now that they were out of the trees, keeping to the most shadowed spots almost as if they were aware they were being watched. That was impossible, of course, but that superstitious quiver shot through Daniel's stomach again as he remembered how she had seemed to look right at him. But she *hadn't* looked at him – he was imagining things.

It must be a day for irrationality.

Suddenly they seemed to disappear into the low hillside. Daniel instantly triangulated their position and zoomed on it, only to find the mouth of a small cave or tunnel. An indistinct figure, dimly lit from someplace inside (he didn't believe it to be either of the two he had followed – it looked like an older man) was reaching up and pulling down some sort of screen or cover that soon shut off the tunnel mouth completely.

Daniel was impressed – even with infrared overlays, he would never have guessed the tunnel was there, but for the fact that he'd just watched two people disappear into it. For ten or fifteen minutes he let the swarm roam over the hillside, periodically pulling back and checking the landscape to get his bearings.

There were definitely people here, and far more than just a few, though how many he could not yet say. He caught them in the fading twilight as shadows mostly, scurrying between a few different tunnel openings, all as artfully concealed as the first one.

As the natural light went, he turned up the infrared. The effect was to render the darkness a searing shade of green; it was annoying, to say the least, but necessary, and effective. He thought about sending the swarm inside one of the tunnels . . . maybe the tunnel where the red-haired woman had gone? She was sure to be in there somewhere. Just to see her face again would be sublime, worth any amount of trouble.

He shook his head, irritated.

Irrational thoughts again.

Instead of sending the swarm into the tunnels, he shut off the infrared and brought his remote eyes up to a thousand feet. He recorded his position one more time just for good measure; then, sitting back on deep cushions, he ripped the VR helmet off with an almost violent movement, dropping it to the floor. How long had he watched them? An hour? Two? His back ached, and he put his hands over his head and stretched. Something in the side of his neck popped with a *crunch,* and he felt a little better, a little looser.

There was something soothing about his familiar, sterile surroundings. He absorbed the smooth permaplast fixtures, the round molded corners, the soft flickering glow of the digital clock and the wall-screen, which still showed a two-dimensional infrared view of a particular valley on the North American continent as seen from a quarter-mile in the air.

He would have to tell Grandfather now that he had completed the assignment, a fact which he suddenly wasn't so sure he liked. He wanted time – time to study the culture of these people, whoever they were. What sort of person dared to live outside the lines, to hide from the world government which controlled the lives of everyone on the planet?

It would definitely be more interesting than anything he could find in the cities.

Maybe I could put off telling him about it.

The thought was not without allure, but then again . . .

What if I'm being watched, right now?

In fact, now that he thought about it, he became almost certain that his room was bugged. It had to be. Either that, or they could simply be monitoring his own video feeds directly, seeing exactly what he was seeing. After all, Grandfather was Security Chief of the entire planet. He would certainly keep tabs of things here on Mephisto. Daniel sighed and got to his feet, pacing the room slowly, getting his blood moving.

He debated about calling for Neana or one of the other girls, just to have some company, but he wasn't in the mood for a romp, and he couldn't imagine having the conversation he desired with any of them. He knew he should report his findings, but still he stalled.

Finally he pulled on a shirt and stalked out of the room. A cloud born of equal parts boredom, uncertainty, and dread was growing in his mind like a dark three-petaled flower. There was something wrong on Mephisto! And not only here, but down there, on the planet, as well. Why could he not grasp what it was? For all of his education, he felt inadequate, and incomplete. He looked for the source of this feeling and realized that it was *information* that he required, specifically information about himself, and it was the lack of this commodity that had produced his frustration. It struck him as odd that he should have to ask someone else about his own life, but as he thought back over his childhood, it seemed some very important things were missing.

For example, although he could execute perfect recall for hundreds, even thousands of specific lessons going all the way back to his earliest memories, he couldn't remember the face or name of a single one of his teachers. There *had* been teachers . . . hadn't there? Of course there had been, otherwise how could he have learned? But they were faceless shadows, ghosts with generic voices, overlapping in his memory like successive waves in a pool.

Now that he thought of it, he couldn't recall a time in his life when there *hadn't* been daily lessons, and found it odd that it had taken him this long to find it odd. In the stories he'd read as a child, and in those he read sometimes for entertainment even now, people had a childhood; they weren't brought up in a rotating tin can, in orbit around a satellite rock, waited on by fawning women ready and willing to perform at his command like exotic trained pets. His life seemed suddenly absurd.

As he walked the outer rim corridors aimlessly, lights dimmed so that he could see the deep, starlit void of space falling away beyond the barriers of the station, he felt suddenly, intuitively, that a storm was brewing on the horizon – something large and lurking, an entity event with deep roots, intrinsically connected with the path of his own life. He closed his eyes, trying to fight the feeling, but it intensified. A dreadful certainty possessed him suddenly, an indescribable pull toward a very specific destiny . . .

A destiny in which he had become unrecognizable to himself.

This thought startled him. It smacked of the prophetic, but what did he know of prophesy? He was, if anything, a scholar – it had always been his talent to absorb and process large amounts of information, but his knowledge of mysticism was limited to the words left behind by those whom history had deemed mystics. Those words were in the databanks of Mephisto; therefore, they were known to Daniel. But this impression just now had gone beyond rhetorical knowledge. He had *felt* something: a thought, or omen, whose cosmic parameters were not comprehensible to him. It was a frightening sensation, and he resumed walking, eager to be rid of it, whatever it was.

An hour and a half later he returned to his quarters and flopped on his bed, exhausted and covered with perspiration but not feeling much better. He'd spent the last while in the fitness room, running along the virtual shore of a virtual ocean intended to add aesthetic value to his workout. But it had served only to make him more forlorn.

When was the last time I saw a real ocean?

A memory surfaced, of a starlit walk along an actual shoreline . . . but when, exactly, had that been? And who else had been there? These missing details maddened him, and he tossed in his bed, unable to rest.

Finally he could take it no more. He got out of bed and went to the low-backed cushion chair that he used for his virtual forays. He donned his gear, thinking that perhaps he could find something interesting enough to take his mind from the vision of the red-haired woman in the forest. For a moment he considered sending the swarm back to her valley, but the thought of all that infrared, and the fact that it would be nearly impossible to really see anything, held him back.

He had just activated the swarm when a red light in the upper right corner of his vision informed him that he was receiving a local transmission. He pulled off the VR gear and told the computer to accept the incoming call.

Grandfather's face was smiling, a grotesque thing to behold. His eyes glittered as he beheld his young spawn. "Well done, Daniel," he said in his rumbling voice. "You've completed your assignment."

Daniel hesitated only a second before replying. "Yes, sir. I would have notified you already, but I wanted to wait until I had located the actual source of the signal. It won't be that difficult – I'll do it as soon as there's local daylight."

"Never mind that," Grandfather replied with a subtle, dismissive gesture. "You've become quite adept with the swarm, which is good. But I was thinking of giving you another assignment, another . . . challenge."

Daniel felt his face tense and fought to control it. For some reason, the thought of not going back to that valley tomorrow and continuing to observe the people there, especially the red-haired woman, seemed unfair and nearly unbearable. His tone of voice was chosen carefully as he replied. "I'd like to continue to observe the people I found, if you don't mind."

Grandfather's expression darkened slightly. "Oh? Why is that?"

Daniel hesitated. "They . . . fascinate me," he said after a moment, knowing it was a lame response but unable to come up with anything better. "It's an interesting little sub-culture - they're unlike anyone else I've seen."

Grandfather's eyes narrowed for a moment, then slowly his face broadened into a forced smile. "Where you wish to take your swarm on your own time is up to you," he said. "But I want you to report to the engineering room at zero-seven hundred tomorrow. You are to begin a new course of study."

"What kind of study, Grandfather?" Though disappointed, Daniel's mind leapt at the possibility of new knowledge. Maybe here would lie a clue to what was in store for him! Maybe finally he could piece it all together.

Grandfather smiled more widely, a nearly impossible feat. "Tomorrow," he said. "Don't be late."

19

Simon DaLuge was finally satisfied with the re-worked motherboard.

All circuitry had been gone over with a fine-toothed comb, all connections tested and re-tested. With only two months and change remaining, all preliminary simulations and projections showed that they were right on track. The compiling rate of the mainframe was up by almost thirty percent, the computer's memory nodes had been re-fitted with new organic relay switches, and the rate of data extraction from local databanks was unprecedented. In other words, the best, fastest, and most completely integrated computer in the world was coming together beneath his fingertips.

Even better, he was no longer losing sleep over his acceptance of McElroy's offer. If Lazaro Sol suspected anything, he'd had plenty of time to do something about it, but nothing had happened, and this led Simon to believe that he was probably safe.

Yes, everything was coming together nicely . . . except for one small problem, and Simon DaLuge *had* lost a lot of sleep trying to solve this one.

The imaging generator programs - along with their attendant hardware components - were key to the entire issue of organic/machine meshing, and they were giving him fits. He was almost certain that the deaths of the three previous clones had been at least partially due to the tiny bit of delay between the information they were receiving and the mainframe's ability to synthesize the appropriate corresponding images. This could possibly have led to a feedback loop of such high frequency as to drive a human mind beyond the brink of sanity; indeed, instinct told him that this was exactly what had happened, though he couldn't prove it.

The screen gave a mellow 'ping' and Wheeler's large face appeared. As usual, he appeared nervous and slightly disoriented, which wasn't too much of a surprise. Since the day they'd lost that batch of bugs, Wheeler hadn't exactly been in DaLuge's good graces, and his department was paying for their mistake.

"Good afternoon, sir."

"What is it, Wheeler?" DaLuge purposefully avoided making eye contact with the man, instead shuffling an irrelevant stack of printouts that happened to be lying on the corner of his desk.

"We've done the prelim work on that surveillance case, and there's something I thought you might want to take a look at."

"Well? What is it, man?"

"An interesting mutation in the subject, sir. We've been filtering the swarm transmission for a while now and we're getting a pretty good look. They're underground, you know, and it took a while . . . "

"Yes, yes, don't make excuses. What sort of mutation?" DaLuge caught the man's gaze through the screen, his own eyes narrowed.

Wheeler shifted uncomfortably. "Well, it's hard to tell, sir. Would you like me to transmit the shots to you now so you can take a look? It would only be two-dimensional, of course, but . . . "

DaLuge heaved a sigh and pushed back in his chair, forcefully interrupting the other man's apologetics.

"No," he said, standing up and running a hand through his unruly hair. "No, I could use a break anyhow. I'll come take a look."

In the corner of the Level 3 laboratory room, a makeshift station had been set up to monitor the encampment in the forest. It comprised three digichrome monitors, in front of which sat a technician whose name he didn't know. The man was intent on his screens and didn't look up at DaLuge's approach.

Wheeler's horse-like face seemed pallid and rubbery, his large lips forced into the semblance of a smile. "Thank you for coming, sir," he said, nervously rubbing his palms together. "I'd like you to meet crew tech Sneed – he's been monitoring the situation for us all morning."

The man at the monitors looked up for the first time, nodded and extended a hand. "Pleased to meet you, sir," he said as he shook Simon's hand. He gestured to the screens. "Some interesting things happening down there."

"Would you like to sit down, sir?" Wheeler asked, dragging over a light permaplast chair. "Or maybe you want to stand."

DaLuge accepted the chair without comment, pulling it close to the trio of monitors. "What've you got, Sneed?"

Sneed tapped the control pad on his console and the view on monitor three moved in a little. "Well, the most interesting thing from my point of view is the fact that we're getting nothing on satellite scans. Obviously there are people there, a fairly large group from what we can tell, but I've got four satellites on this to compensate for angle and cloud cover and even when we have a clear shot, we get no view of any activity at all . . . as you can see here."

"Some sort of cloaking technology," DaLuge muttered.

"And fairly impressive, if I might add," Sneed said. "Look at the detail there. If we were relying on satellite view alone we'd never have found them. I'm not a surveillance guy, but to me it looks as if they've found some way of transmitting a digital image that covers up their entire valley – how, I couldn't really say, but . . . "

"Like you said," DaLuge interrupted, closing his eyes and rubbing his face vigorously with one hand, "Like you said, it's all very interesting, and no doubt the appropriate people will be quite surprised at the level of technology. But what about the mosquitoes?"

"Right." Sneed turned to monitor one, tapping it with the nub of pencil that seemed like a sixth finger on his left hand. "The swarms don't work as well in artificial light," he said. "I'm running a filter to clean up the image, but right now what we have is this."

The monitor showed what looked like a bed in the corner of a small room. On the bed lay a pre-pubescent female child; next to her sat a woman, and a rack which held some sort of mechanical apparatus.

Even with the grainy image, it was easy to see that something was very wrong with the child. The left side of her face was distended and dark; her left eye was puffed to the point of almost disappearing into her face. Her neck, too, was swollen so that it seemed her shoulder sloped right up to the vague cauliflowered hole that was her ear.

"*Jesus,*" DaLuge muttered. "How did *that* happen?" He turned, caught the expression on Wheeler's face. With disgust, he realized that the horror he saw there didn't come from what Wheeler was viewing; rather, from the certain knowledge that he didn't have the answers his boss needed.

"I . . . well . . . " Wheeler sputtered, nervously wringing his hands. "I mean, those bugs were unfinished prototypes, sir! We always knew that if they infected anyone, the results would be unpredictable. Obviously, there's been a mutation of some type . . . "

DaLuge shook his head, held up a hand. "Thank you for your blinding insight." He turned back to the monitors.

"Sir, if I may . . . " Sneed was digging through a pile of printouts. "Here we go." He spread one out on the table. "Now, I wasn't on the project when the bugs escaped, but I've been looking at the data. That particular batch was designed to do exactly what it did – isolate human targets outside city perimeters and establish a radio signal. That about right?"

DaLuge nodded. "Go on."

"Well, like you said, the bugs weren't ready when they escaped – they hadn't been tested, and the sequencer programs had yet to be fully integrated into their DNA. In other words – and this is the real kicker – they shouldn't have been able to deliver their payload in the first place. Which leaves the really interesting question of how the sequencers managed to set up signal generation at all."

DaLuge frowned. "Are you saying what I think you're saying?"

Sneed licked his lips and smiled nervously. "Well, that depends," he said. "It's only a theory, and without time to run more scenarios it's hard to say. But I think we may be looking at an adaptation in the micro-sequencers that occurred in the bugs *before* they infected their target . . . "

"Which would explain the mutations we're looking at," DaLuge said, eyes narrowed. "But those sequencers should not have been able to adapt at all."

"Sir," Wheeler's voice was pleading. "Sir, I assure you we had no way of knowing this would happen. My team cannot be held resp . . . "

"Shut up, Wheeler." Simon's patience had finally reached its end. He pushed his chair back abruptly as he stood up, and it tipped over with a muted bang. "Sneed, you're doing a fine job. I want you to keep on this thing. If the technology actually *has* adapted on its own . . . well, then it might be worth our time."

"Thank you, sir. I will."

"I'm also promoting you to department head. Wheeler, you're off the project. See that all relevant information is transferred to Sneed here. When you're done with that, report to Psych for re-evaluation and new orders." DaLuge gave the man a thin smile. "That is all. Have a productive day, gentlemen."

20

Daniel sat high in the Controller's booth, a fly on the wall of Mephisto Station's gigantic engine room. The centrifugal engines whined and powered down as they completed their cycle, and he relaxed a little, allowing his team a moment before the next cycle would require his attention. In front of him, a three-dimensional control board was projected over the transparent permaplast window, an interactive holograph responsive to the refractive shield of the helmet. With the helmet on, he could see and manipulate the board by using the thermal gloves he was wearing, as well as view the crew below him through the window.

Controllers, he was finding, had great flexibility in the use of their teams. Right now the board was set up in standard mode, controlling six teams of four drones, each team identifiable by differently colored uniforms.

'Very good', a voice floated into his mind. *'But do not allow your attention to drift. On the next cycle, I want you to attempt to change the main motor housing. And this time let us avoid any casualties.'*

The Controller was a small, thin bald man with enormous eyes under a wide forehead which seemed to go up forever. Daniel didn't like him very much, but he had to admit that without this strange little man's help, he probably would have lost a great deal of workers by now.

The incident the Controller was referring to had happened on the second day of Daniel's apprenticeship, when he'd accidentally killed two workers by sending them to repair a shorted electrical node without first locking out access. Another drone, following his commands, had accessed an electrical system which Daniel hadn't known about, and the first two drones were fried in a second when the node came on, blowing them both over the metal railing, where they plunged to the decking fifty feet below. On that occasion the Controller hadn't been quick enough, and Daniel had been severely reprimanded.

The Controller sat now in a chair off to one side, wearing a version of the same helmet that sat upon Daniel's head, its net of heavy cables feeding up through cable supports before spreading to fifteen or twenty different terminals throughout the engine compartment. The Controller's helmet was connected to Daniel's as well, allowing him to maintain theoretical control even while handing the reins to Daniel during his instruction.

Experiencing the life of a Controller had been mind-opening for Daniel, a challenge much more suited to his adept brain than simple topographical searches. He'd thrown himself into this new work wholeheartedly, eager for any distraction, anything to keep him from thinking of his uncertain future – of that *thing* on the horizon, the cloud that blotted out his vision. He was changed; that he knew, and this new knowledge was an abstract thing. Since finding that group of refugees in the wilderness, he'd felt there was a new part of himself, a part that *needed*, that longed for something with qualities he could not pinpoint.

He'd visited their valley nearly every evening in the weeks since finding them, always trying to find a way to watch *her,* to follow her, to see who she was. But the members of the valley complex seemed wary of being outside, even during those daylight hours that coincided with Daniel's evenings. He wasn't sure he'd caught even a glimpse of her since that first night.

It didn't matter.

Her face was burned so clearly into his mind that he knew he'd never forget her if he lived a thousand years. At night before he fell asleep he saw her behind his closed eyelids, and try as he might, he could not clear her from his mind.

Irrationality had gained a foothold, and he beheld it, fascinated, from the part of himself that only observed. He wondered if Grandfather knew of this new thing, this sliver of darkness that had worked itself deep into his grandson. How would it affect him later, when he would be called upon to fulfill his duty to the Elders? Less than a hundred days remained until his initiation . . . and he still had no idea what *that* might entail. Whatever it was, it seemed intrinsically connected to that *thing* that he felt, that quickening inside himself. At night, behind visions of the red-haired goddess, behind dark curtains of loneliness that threatened to overwhelm him, a cold light shone from deep in his mind, illuminating what would be, throwing ghastly light upon—

What? What is it?

But he couldn't grasp what it was, this thing, and so instead he focused on the immediate challenges of learning the Controller's art. He supposed he should be grateful to Grandfather for allowing him to learn these new skills, but he trusted the old man's motives less with each passing day. What could possibly be the old man's reasoning? And would these skills somehow play into Daniel's role as an Elder?

He couldn't see how it fit.

Information, information, why was there not enough information? He realized suddenly that he knew almost nothing about the Elders themselves, with the exception of what Grandfather had told him . . . but how much could he trust that information? It seemed that vital pieces were missing, and his sense of being a pawn in a game he didn't understand became deeper, more jaded.

'I'm sure you see the problem you are about to have.'

The Controller's voice, electronically implanted into his brain, jolted him back to the moment and the twenty-four 'level three' workers under the umbrella of his Controller's command. Below him, two groups of four workers each were about to clash because he'd forgotten to clear their commands from the previous cycle. The second group, dressed in yellow, carried the new motor housing, and they were confused because the first group, with green uniforms, hadn't taken the old one apart yet.

'*You must remember that each drone or group will always revert to the last command you gave them,*' the voice came again. '*I've told you this before. You are responsible for many interconnected lines of command – it's important to see them all, and to do so you must concentrate. You must learn to foresee possible complications, and for this you must be able to do many things at once. Remember that Controlled work crews are only more efficient than fully automated systems to the degree that each Controller is the consummate master of his art.*'

Daniel sat back in frustration, pulling his hands from the thermal gloves as the Controller took over, smoothly rectifying the situation with a few deft strokes. Daniel was glad for the backup; this time, disaster was averted. The first group below them, a unit of green uniforms, began making preparations to take the housing apart at the beginning of the next cycle; the second group set the housing down and began a rudimentary inspection of its many ports and connections.

'*If in doubt,*' the floating voice came once again, '*you can always give a static order to one or more groups. This is done to keep them contained in a small area for a given amount of time so that other groups may move freely. There, now I've returned control to your station.*'

Daniel thrust his hands back into the gloves and reached out for the holographic board. Redoubling his efforts, he pushed all other thoughts from his mind and concentrated on the rhythms of his crew. Red group to deck four to grease the outside bearings, check . . . blue group inspecting the power couplings on deck one, check . . .

'*When I tell you to, I want you to split your yellow group. This is the next step in your instruction.*'

"Splitting groups?" Daniel asked. "Can you do that?"

There was a hint of pride in the Controller's voice. '*I've heard of Controllers who have successfully manipulated crews of two hundred or more, but that is a degree of artistry that few obtain. I personally could manage up to one hundred workers individually if required, though groups seem more efficient for most procedures. But you're a long way from that, my young friend. Without the proper training, which it seems apparent you are not to receive, the best you can hope for is a rudimentary understanding. So let's see how you do with splitting one group for now.*'

Recalling instantly everything he'd learned about programming the holographic board, Daniel set about splitting the controls for his yellow group.

'*Remember that you are only implanting suggestions,*' the voice came again, and Daniel narrowed his eyes at the intrusion. '*These drones have been predisposed to respond to your suggestions, which makes them seem almost automated, but they are yet flawed, individual organic units. They are not robots. You must be attuned to them as fellow creatures if you are to guide them in their work.*'

"Why are you telling me this?" Daniel asked.

'*Because understanding the way the technology works is the subtlety of the art. All Controllers must learn this. You need to know that when you give what you perceive as an electronically issued command, what the worker receives is a highly disguised subliminal suggestion. As I was saying, these workers are well-bred and trained, and so they rarely do other than that which you order them to do. But it is possible, and if that time comes, you must be aware of the psychological factors involved so that you know how to respond, to maintain order.*' A pause, like a mental sigh. '*I see you have reprogrammed the board for the split. Very well done.*'

For the rest of the three-hour session, Daniel succeeded in blocking out all thoughts, and by the time he gave up the helmet and took the lift back to his quarters, he had achieved an adequate degree of control over his split team.

21

Lazaro Sol was about to do what he did best; he was going to solve a problem, and the solution would have to be as ingenious as it was dangerous.

He'd been watching Daniel closely since he'd given the boy over to learning the Controller's art, and he was disturbed by some of the things he saw. The clone seemed preoccupied much of the time lately, spending hours during his off-time obsessively scanning that insignificant and pitiful group of misfits he'd found in the woods.

What is he looking for?

Lazaro Sol had spoken with DaLuge only that morning, and the situation was well in hand, from a security perspective. The group appeared to pose no real threat – probably some leftover band from the Peak Rebellion or one of the other malcontent groups who'd appeared on the North American continent all those years ago. They were being monitored, of course, and when the time was right, they would be assimilated or exterminated - quietly, of course, and without media attention if possible.

So what does he find so interesting there?

He'd begun more regular monitoring of Daniel's scans, but time pressures permitted only limited observance, and he still didn't know what the boy was looking for in that valley.

Not that it really mattered; the key was the knowledge that the boy was borderline obsessive, which, though helpful in some ways, could create complications in others if not properly dealt with. Some of this he had expected; after all, he'd given Daniel addictive tendencies as a control mechanism, and for the most part they had worked wonderfully. But there was a fine line between addiction and obsession. Obsessive behavior could lead to violent or even suicidal tendencies, either of which were a serious threat to the security of the project. The boy's behavior, even omitting his perusal of that far-away valley, had been agitated lately – his heart rate was up, and so was his synaptic activity.

But there was another, bigger problem.

The clone had been disposing of one of his medications; his daily dose of Elepro, to be precise. Remote scans had picked up the lack of the drug in his system, and Lazaro had confirmed it through infrared analysis of video taken during Daniel's bedtime ritual, when he was supposed to take all his medications.

This presented a terrible logistical problem. He couldn't confront the boy about it – that would be far too straightforward. After all, what sort of legitimate business would a grandfather be about, drugging his own grandson without his knowledge? But neither could the boy be allowed to continue without medication. The project depended on his predictability, and his rationality. Paranoia did not fit well with the picture, and without Elepro in his system, it was likely Daniel would become more unbalanced.

What a dilemma!

If Daniel knew he'd been drugged, he was likely to be very suspicious. Lazaro Sol could only imagine what questions the boy's paranoid mind was coming up with, and the lack of the drug would only enhance this agitation. His method of disposing of the Elepro capsules every night, under cover of darkness, suggested that he knew of the possibility that his room was monitored.

If Daniel didn't know, then things would be much easier – he could say that he'd noticed his grandson's recent agitation, and did he know that this was a side effect of certain vitamin deficiencies common to space-bound individuals? Had he been taking all his pills?

But this was an unlikely scenario – Daniel was too smart for that.

Our own fault. We made him that way.

The real question was whether or not the boy would say anything about what he suspected. His gut told him that this was a low-likelihood possibility, but it was possible. In any event, the key was to find out how much Daniel knew, or suspected, and then bring up the issue of the medication in an obscure and non-threatening way.

And, if conditions were right . . .

The germ of an idea had been flowering in his ancient mind, and depending on the conversation he'd have with the boy later today, there might just be another way – a way to use Daniel's own curiosity to occupy his time until the moment came when he could be sedated and hooked to DaLuge's machine.

And then, after Contact . . .

Oh, that young mind! That unsoiled specimen!

The thought, when it came, filled him with a giddy sense of expectation that was in direct proportion to the towering wall of fears that moved unceasingly toward him recently.

His body, quite frankly, was going to hell, and more quickly than he'd thought.

Damn this project! And damn waiting!

If not for the necessity of waiting, he could have already been walking around in a new body. There were hundreds of them, frozen in suspended animation bays in the sub-basements of Clifftop, waiting to be inhabited. But there were dangers, apparently, which only the priests understood, and his request had been unequivocally denied.

He hated himself for the trepidation he felt at the thought of the priests, with their cold eyes and leathery skin. After all, he'd been through the procedure before, had withstood the shock of leaving an old body and entering a new one, had felt the resistance as the person's kan-ya, their essential being, was compelled to move or be absorbed. He'd survived, and thrived, more than once.

And after this time, maybe I won't have to do it again.

But immediate concerns were what they were. He must *continue* to survive, and he was as vulnerable as he'd ever been. Again he cursed this old mantle, damned its aging corpuscles and hardened arteries, its stiffened joints and dead, befouled lungs which wheezed and gasped all the time now.

I must survive!

This thought had a strength all its own; a strength he was glad of, and proud of. How easy it would be to stop, to simply lay down and die. But not Lazaro Sol. He was strong, in mind if not in body . . . and soon, this strength would be compounded by an unfathomable exponent. The mind of a god, and youth and strength to go with it - all would be his, and soon enough.

22

Kingdoms rise and fall; mountains thrust from heaving earth, burning the sky with clouds of smoke and steam. Time bends and turns back on itself, and Daniel is the only constant. He is the hub, the center of the vision, radiating wires like spokes to all things, all people, all events . . .

But the people run screaming . . . run screaming, from . . .

Why? Why do they run from me?

She's there too, the red-haired goddess, but she turns away, shaking her head slowly as she covers her face.

She's disappointed in me!

It's torture, horrible torture, why does it hurt so . . . ?

Daniel's eyes snapped open, fixed on the digital clock readout, glowing mellow red, 0543 hours. The room was dark and still, and only his quick breathing told him that he was in fact awake. He'd been dreaming again, intense and chaotic visions that frightened him with their vividness. In the week since he'd stopped taking the white pills marked with the small 'e', he'd been visited nightly, beset by these terrible visions; maddening flights of fantasy for which he had no frame of reference.

He had only stopped taking the one type of pill, the little one with the 'e' on it. He couldn't have said exactly *why* he'd stopped taking them – he just felt that he didn't want them anymore. He certainly knew enough to *pretend* to take them each night, along with all of his other various supplements and medications. He put them in his mouth, between his cheek and gum, then gulped down copious amounts of water along with the rest of the pills.

Later, though, when the lights had gone out and he was in bed, he would use some motion of his body, like turning over, to spit the vile thing out and grind it to dust beneath his pillow.

But without the medication, the visions came.

He'd accessed Mephisto Station's vast library, in hopes of finding something relevant. He looked under 'sleep disorders' first, moving over page after page before encountering 'dreams' – a word that he'd heard before, certainly, but never in this context.

Dreaming.

The word had an exciting taste on his tongue, but his stomach turned over uneasily.

Why did I never dream before now?

Surely it was not a coincidence that his visions had begun the very first night that he hadn't taken the 'e' vitamin – but was it a vitamin? If so, why the dramatic effect on his psyche?

He'd found another word, not too far below 'dreams' – that word was 'drugs'.

Is that it? Are they drugging me?

And if that was the case, what of the other five pills he took every night? What would happen if he stopped taking them all? He didn't dare. His system of getting rid of only one pill per night was dangerous enough.

The lack of the drug - if that was what it was - had had multiple effects. Besides his newfound dreams, questions came in constant waves during his waking moments, a heady barrage that seemed to float up with perpetually increasing strength. The thought of his upcoming initiation into the Elders filled him with a fear that seemed more immediate, more terrifying than any emotion he'd yet experienced.

Was this another effect of the drug, or rather the lack of it? It seemed strange, this paranoia. Only a month before, he'd felt good about the initiation, even looking forward to it. What had changed?

The gaps in his mind continued to widen daily, and it was a maddening sensation. That splinter of missing information tore deeper, laying waste to his nights. When he wasn't dreaming, it kept him awake, as it was doing now. How could he know so much, his mind filled with orderly rows and columns of information about everything from global economics and geography to advanced mathematics, and yet be completely uninformed about dreams, which apparently were a normal part of human experience? What else had been hidden from him?

I'm nearly twenty years old . . . why am I only asking these questions now?

He hadn't been called to Grandfather's office in recent days, for which he was grateful. He didn't know if he'd be able to keep his fear at bay if he had to be in the same room with the old buzzard. Instead, he'd been sharpening his skills as a Controller, learning advanced techniques from the large-headed man in the booth above the Station's engine room.

He'd gotten quite a few looks from the Controller lately, glances that belied uncertainty in the man's carefully guarded words of praise when Daniel did something well, which was almost all the time now. He hadn't made a serious mistake in more than a week, and he felt his mind sharpened to new levels of responsiveness as he attuned himself to the Controller's ways.

He could *feel* them now, his team of workers – he could read their responses individually by the lights representing them on the holographic control board;

he could adjust instantaneously, subtly changing program context to align the worker drones' will to his own. His teams were now almost as efficient as the resident Controller's, which probably explained the large-headed man's new attitude. He acted almost deferential to Daniel now, an abrupt about-face from the beginning of his training, only a few weeks earlier.

Daniel sensed that the man's attitude was due to nervousness about the possibility of his being replaced as Controller, but instinctively he knew that this was not to be so. Grandfather's actions lately regarding his grandson had been forming a pattern, and Daniel knew that his time in the Control booth was short. He couldn't have explained this to anyone, but he knew. As soon as he had accomplished whatever Grandfather wanted from him, he would be given some new task.

First the swarm, then the art of the Controller . . . almost as if I'm being groomed for something. Or distracted from something. What's next?

"Lights." The fluorescent lights came on, filling his room with stark shadows. He squinted into the unwelcome glare, gave himself a moment to adjust. "Lights down thirty percent." Slipping from under his sheets, he went to the VR setup, which had gone largely unused during recent weeks. He flicked a switch and it hummed to life.

Donning the helmet and goggles, he took a moment to re-set his mind for swarm control – so much different than the Controller's art, and yet there were striking similarities – and went through the procedure to activate his swarm. The screen pulsed with blue light, distorted through the VR goggles. "Activate swarm, code Daniel Contact Alpha Three."

The screen went blank. The computer's voice came, inhuman with its cultured inflection. "Inoperative code sequence," it said, then: "Would you like to try again, Daniel?"

He frowned, tapped the VR unit as if it were somehow responsible for the malfunction. "Yes." He repeated the code with a strident tone, hoping illogically that if he raised his voice the problem would be solved.

There was another pause, as if the computer was loathe to tell him the news. "Inoperative code sequence," it said again after a moment. "Would you . . . " the screen beeped and went blank, and Grandfather's face appeared, ancient and looking more haggard than ever.

"Hello, my boy," the face rasped. "Don't . . . " Grandfather turned sideways and began to cough violently. He appeared to be convulsing.

"Grandfather! Are you . . . "

" . . . don't bother answering back," the face continued, then coughed once more and spit into something off screen. Grandfather wiped a red sheen from his lips with the back of his hand. "This is a recording, programmed to come on when you try to access your swarm. Obviously you've done that, so I'll just say that I've locked you out . . . for now. We haven't spoken much this last week, and I've begun to miss our little conversations. At any rate, I'd like to speak with you in person, so please call my private line any time you like and we'll arrange it. Oh, and Daniel – your progress as a Controller has been nothing short of astounding. You've gone far beyond what I'd hoped for you." Grandfather smiled, an expression that almost seemed to be actual paternal pride peeking through his crinkled flesh . . . but Daniel knew enough not to trust it.

He's playing me. His pride comes from his self-congratulatory feelings about how well he thinks he's doing it.

He narrowed his eyes at the image, which had frozen and receded into the upper left corner of the screen. The right side now contained a menu for options to repeat, save, or delete. Daniel chose the latter, noticing as he did how his jaw clenched.

Have I been found out? Do they know I've been palming my meds?

The question pulsed with the beat of his heart, and he took a deep breath to calm his fear. What other reason could Grandfather have for cutting off his swarm access, for 'calling him in', so to speak? Rationality forced him to remember that there were other workable scenarios, but an alarm screamed in his mind, drowning rational thought.

After a moment he sat back on the low cushion. Pulling the helmet from his face, he leaned back and closed his eyes. Darkness swam, brightening into flooding vision, and then there she was, inescapable - red-gold hair floating on water, face upturned to his, eyes beckoning. Her mouth was so sensuous, so alive...

In his fantasy, they were one flesh; minds locked in patterns of eternity, beings entwined, mouth to mouth, breast to breast, pure as water . . .

He opened his eyes slowly. The digital clock readout said 0557.

He wanted to sob, to scream, to tell someone what he was feeling, but there was no one to listen. Only a moment he'd closed his eyes, no more, and still the visions would not stop. Waking or dreaming, she would never quit haunting him until he could see her, talk to her, ask her who he was.

She knows. She knows what I need. She can tell me who I am.

It didn't matter that there was no one to listen, because she knew who he was, and she would listen. Of this he was more than sure.

Unable to sleep, he stepped into the lavatory for a fast shower, then dressed and walked out into the long corridor that stretched along the station's outer rim. He moved slowly, the curving panes of transparent permaplast opening on a view of the looming moon below.

He stopped, stood with hands behind his back, looking down on the pocked surface, his exhausted mind slowing to the mundane for a change, thinking what needed to be done in the coming day.

Damn Grandfather!

Hatred for the old man welled in him, taking him by surprise. Grinding his teeth, he forced the feeling away, focusing instead on the path of a small shuttle moving across his field of vision, its red con-light blinking clockwork intervals. It moved slowly from right to left, glinting in the reflected light from the moon. By the time it was obscured by the curve of the turning Station, Daniel's thoughts were once again under control.

Hate, love, or indifference aside, he would have to go see the old man today. The thought hung like a cancer in his breast, shortening his breath, and he began to walk again, faster. A few drones moved down the hall, their flat, expressionless faces looking only forward, bodies moving like sluggish animals toward whichever quadrant of the station housed their work areas.

I'm one of them – nothing but a drone, groomed to do a job.

This unwelcome thought frightened him, and he shivered, wrapping his arms around his chest as he walked.

I'm one of them, that's true. But I am changing. I am becoming something else, but I have to play along for now. I must remain strong, and vigilant, and when I see my chance I must take it.

For a brief moment, the storm-clouds in his mind seemed to part, and he saw things clearly. The vision of the event-entity in time – a massive convergence of energies beyond his, or anyone's, control - hovered just beyond his vision, shimmering like a jewel behind a net of water, and he reached for it, but it retreated.

But he was calm now. He felt strong.

He stepped into the lift. "Engine room," he said. His own voice sounded good in his ears, and he clung to this new confidence as if it might actually stay for a while.

"Maximum allowable velocity."

23

Lazaro Sol's desk-screen *pinged* twice, indicating someone waiting on the other side of the airlock that served as the entrance to his quarters.

"Yes?"

"It's me, sir. You wanted to see me." The clone's voice crackled smoothly from a small speaker hidden beneath the desk.

Something different, perhaps, about that voice . . . ? Perhaps not.

"Of course, my boy! Come in, come in!"

Too much! He'll know!

Lazaro kicked himself mentally. It wouldn't do to underestimate Daniel - he couldn't simply play the affable Grandfather today. Not after what he'd seen recently.

The familiar click and hiss of the airlock, and the heavy door emerged an inch from where it lay flush with the wall. Another click, and Daniel's face appeared, with Agent Randall behind him. The Agent re-sealed the airlock, securing it from the outside, and Lazaro Sol was alone with his 'grandson'.

"Hello, Grandfather."

The clone's voice was casual, fluid . . . more so than Lazaro Sol would have thought possible, given Daniel's state of mind lately.

Is it possible I've made a mistake?

But he'd clearly caught Daniel on vid-feed, getting rid of the Elepro. The clone must be in a state of profound fear, and yet he showed so little!

Lazaro found himself a little awed, and somewhat prideful, at the authenticity of Daniel's act. It seemed almost a pity that this boy's talents would be wasted, that he must be assimilated . . . but only almost. Still, what a pupil he would've been, had Lazaro Sol been able to teach him fully!

He allowed himself a congenial smile. "Good day, Daniel. Sit down, my boy." Perhaps the Grandfather figure would play after all.

One convincing act deserves another.

Daniel slipped into the oversized red leather chair opposite Lazaro's desk, running a finger over the rough texture of the wood of the arm-rests. When he spoke, Lazaro thought he detected a hint of the strain that must be there, but it was well-masked by subtle overtones.

"Why did you cut off my swarm access?"

Right to the point . . . but the question reveals his obsession.

He decided to counter with a question on a different tack. "How are you feeling lately, Daniel? I've noticed that you seem . . . concerned, or bothered, lately. Is there anything I can do to help?"

He saw the instant of fright on Daniel's face, the dilation of his pupils, and realized his blunder before he even finished the sentence.

Gods of Hell! I haven't seen the boy in more than two weeks! He'll know how closely I've been watching him!

He continued speaking smoothly in an attempt to cover his mistake. "What I mean to say is this: the Controller mentioned during his last report that you seemed agitated recently, and distracted . . . at least sometimes. Not so?"

Daniel stared at him from the dark pits of eyes that had become suddenly calm. Lazaro Sol's first emotion was to recoil from those eyes, but he resisted, gave Daniel his best grandfatherly smile instead.

"You said I'd surpassed your every expectation in that department," Daniel said coolly after a moment, then added lightly, in a tone that wasn't quite mocking enough to call out, " . . . not so, Grandfather?"

"Indeed," Lazaro responded smoothly, the beginnings of anger left unexpressed somewhere behind his cheekbones. "I was only passing along a comment. The Controller said that while you are quite proficient at the board, you've seemed . . . *preoccupied* . . . during your breaks. He was concerned that you might not be taking all of your vitamins. This sort of behavior can be a symptom of certain deficiencies in the metabolism, especially in space-bound individuals."

There, I've done it. It's out now - let's see what he does with it.

He watched the boy closely, looking for a reaction, but Daniel's face registered nothing . . . or was that a slight change of color in his cheeks?

The boy shifted in his chair and smiled. "I'm taking all my vitamins," he said. "As to the Controller, I will tell him personally, as soon as we're through here, that he has nothing to fear. If you must know, I probably seem preoccupied because I *am* preoccupied . . . but only with the demands of learning the Controller's art, which is incredibly complicated . . . but I'm sure I don't have to tell *you* that."

Oh, the impudence of this brat!

Lazaro stilled a tremble of his cracked lower lip that was equal parts amusement and annoyance. He decided to bait the boy a little more.

Abruptly he leaned back in his chair, servos whining in surprised protest. "I apologize for cutting off your swarm access," he said in a warm tone. "I must admit that it was personal as much as anything. I've missed your company recently."

The look of relief which flickered across the clone's face told him exactly what he wanted to know, and he congratulated himself internally.

Whatever he's obsessed with is in the valley at the other end of that video feed.

And there was something else, as well.

He doesn't believe I called him here for personal reasons, and it doesn't matter to him one bit.

This thought left a cold residue in his gut, a deep chill with roots he couldn't trace. He made an instantaneous decision to employ the course of action he'd been contemplating earlier.

"There was another reason, too," he said. "For calling you in here, I mean." He leaned forward intently, forcing the boy to focus on his words, allowing them to gestate on the tip of his tongue, growing larger in the pregnant pause . . . and when he dropped them it was with all the calculated force of a bomb.

"I want you to go to the surface," Lazaro said. "To one of our bases there, the Clifftop facility. This thing with these guerillas in the woods has gotten out of hand. We think they may be planning some drastic action. I want you to take charge of the operation from Clifftop, to contain the situation in my stead, as it were. I . . . " he paused, coughed for effect, whining and rasping with the effort, then cleared his throat, a wretched sound in the quietness of the office.

"I haven't been feeling too well lately, you see," he continued. "My medical advisors tell me that a trip to the surface wouldn't be advisable until I'm more . . . well, more myself. But this is something you can handle easily, especially with your recent training. It'll most likely be a routine mop-up, anyway. I can't imagine those people will be prepared for the likes of what's coming down on them." He allowed himself a dry chuckle, masking the intensity with which he studied Daniel's reaction.

He wasn't disappointed. It gave him some smug satisfaction to see the way the strong feelings suddenly showed themselves on the boy's face. And still, after only a moment, Daniel fought his face back under control, only a widening of the eyes registering his surprise.

"You . . . you want *me* to go to the surface? And . . . "

"Yes, yes," Lazaro responded, "and take charge of the security action that's being planned against these terrorists. Now . . . "

"Terrorists? How so?" Daniel's eyes narrowed. "I didn't see any evidence of weapons, or training facilities, or even much machinery of any type. How . . . ?"

Lazaro decided to go a little further out on his limb – it seemed solid enough for the time being, and it was most certainly diverting Daniel's attention. He could see the boy's exquisite mind rolling with the new information, getting a handle on it. And that was exactly what he wanted – the clone needed to feel hope, a sense of order and purpose.

"We've detected evidence of biological technology as well as some micro-technology," he said, knowing this to be only a partial truth.

Close enough, though. It will hold up, If he bothers to check up on it.

"These discoveries," he continued hastily, "prompt us to believe that these people might be dangerous, if they have even the least of hostile intentions. The lack of any apparent defense systems only makes them seem more suspicious – it's possible they have a secret hidden base somewhere nearby, or an underground laboratory to develop chemical or biological weapons. At any rate, we can't know for sure without going in, can we?"

"But . . . but they seem so . . . harmless!" Daniel blurted, unable to contain himself. Lazaro Sol narrowed his eyes as he honed in on what he'd been looking for.

Well, well, well . . . .he certainly is attached to something there.

For the first time it occurred to him that it was probably a woman, and he couldn't keep himself from smiling as he responded.

"They *could* be harmless," he said. "Or they *could* be a link in a massive terrorist organization. The key to good security is not to leave it to chance."

Daniel pursed his lips, studied him coldly through half-lidded eyes.

This boy has no fear of me whatsoever.

He felt suddenly, profoundly thankful that he only needed to occupy Daniel for another seventy days. Even that was proving to be much more of a challenge than he'd suspected.

"All right," Daniel said abruptly, his features smoothing into something resembling a collected smile. He tipped his head deferentially. "I would be honored to go in your stead, Grandfather. When will I leave?"

"Eight days," Lazaro replied, thankful that the conversation had moved to more concrete footing. "Randall will accompany you, and facilitate all the necessary arrangements for your journey and mission."

"Yes, sir. Is that all?"

"For now," he replied, studying the boy. He wondered if he'd gone too far. It was risky business, letting the clone out of his immediate presence during this critical time . . . but Randall was a trustworthy Agent, and distraction was absolutely what Daniel needed if he was to be maneuvered into final position.

He leaned back, appraising the boy, hands folded over his chest. "I'll apprise you further in a few days. And of course you'll need medical clearance . . . all the proper forms, a checkup by the station physician, you know . . . " He waved a hand casually, noting the way Daniel's face stiffened at the mention of a medical appointment. " . . . all the standard procedures. Nothing too extraordinary, I'm sure."

"Very good, sir." Daniel hesitated. "And, the swarm . . . ?"

Lazaro waved a hand in grandfatherly good humor. "Reinstated, of course," he said. "Use it at your leisure."

Daniel nodded, a look of palpable relief flitting across his delicate features before disappearing. "Thank you, Grandfather. And my Controller training? Will I continue?"

"At your discretion for the next eight days," Lazaro replied. "But I'm going to send you all the relevant data, and I'd like you to spend some time going over your mission before you leave."

"Of course. And thank you, again . . . sir." Daniel hesitated, clearing his throat, then stood up awkwardly. "If you don't mind, I'm expected in the Controller booth for my morning lesson. I'll begin preparing for the surface mission tonight."

"Excellent." Lazaro grinned broadly. "Ah, Daniel, you don't know how excited I am for you! You'll make a fine Elder someday. A fine Elder, indeed. The Council will be pleased."

"Thank you, Grandfather." Daniel nodded formally as he moved to the door. Lazaro released the airlock with a hidden switch, and the massive steel door hissed from its frame.

"Send Randall in here," Lazaro called after him. "He and I have some business to discuss."

⌐ ⟵ ⟪ ⊃ ◈ ⊂ ⟫ ⟶ ⌐

Going to the surface!

The thought played back on all frequencies across Daniel's overloaded mind. It was all he could do to remain upright on the walk back to the engine room. It had taken a supreme effort to hide what he felt from Grandfather, and even so he wasn't sure the old man wasn't simply playing games with him.

The idea of his taking charge of any serious security action was a joke; this had been his first thought when Grandfather told him of his upcoming trip. He didn't have the experience, for one thing. Training he did have, in tactics and strategy . . . but he knew how serious Grandfather was about his position as Security Chief, and he wouldn't send Daniel to do this job if it was really as important as he claimed.

So what was the true motive, then? It seemed obvious that no matter what Grandfather said, the ragtag group living in that valley did not present any serious security risk.

At a certain point in the conversation, Daniel had had something of an epiphany. He didn't know how he knew what he knew, but some part of his mind was suddenly certain of a new fact - one that fundamentally changed his perception of his own position in the scheme of things.

It had happened when Grandfather said that he'd noticed Daniel's preoccupation as of late. The old man had recognized his mistake immediately, had tried to cover it up, but too late. That calculating something in Daniel's mind had latched onto Grandfather's mistake and given him a new piece of data, a calculation in a matter of less than a second. Grandfather had been spying on him, that much was sure, but he wanted to hide this fact, rather than confronting Daniel about it . . . therefore . . . therefore . . .

They need me!

Whatever his position, whatever Grandfather wanted from him, he would not be harmed or killed. Manipulated, yes, maybe even drugged. But he couldn't be touched. The way Grandfather catered to him, lied to him, manipulated him with such obvious techniques . . . these were ways to treat that which is a resource, not an expendable commodity.

His mind, ever sharpening since he'd stopped taking the little white 'e' pills, presented to him the notion, solidifying into fact, that he was at the mercy of a conspiracy whose complexities he could not begin to fathom. Strangely, the sheer obviousness of the fact, after months of speculation and fear, was almost a relief.

So I am needed, then . . . but for what?

No assumption was safe.

He stepped through the door at the end of the corridor, stopped as he viewed the gargantuan engine compartment, stretching a hundred feet up and fifty down. The booming rumble of the centrifugal engines was an overwhelming vibration, humming through his core. He leaned on the rail for a moment, closing his eyes against vertigo.

And behind the darkness of his eyelids, he saw her face again; eyes wide, lips moving.

The event-entity, whatever it was, loomed in the dim future, a vortex that threatened his very sanity . . . but now *she* was there too; her face, her voice, soothing his fractured nerves.

Abruptly he opened his eyes, widening them intentionally so they wouldn't close of their own accord, simply to see her face.

Going to the surface . . .

He smiled, his gaze directed inward, still seeing her in his mind.

There must be a way. I have to find her, talk to her. She can help me make sense of it all. I know she can!

This thought propelled him forward along the steel catwalk, toward the lift that would take him up to the Control booth.

"You're doing *what?!*" Simon DaLuge could not believe his ears, and the question jumped from his mouth before he had time to censor himself. Normally he would have been worried about Lazaro Sol's reaction, but the sheer seeming stupidity of what his boss was planning had short-circuited his own control mechanisms.

Lazaro Sol's seamed, haggard face peered in glowing digichrome from the screen at DaLuge's main laboratory workstation. "You heard me correctly, Simon," he rasped.

"But why? I . . . "

"The boy is becoming . . . well, stir-crazy, I guess you'd say. He's gone off the Elepro . . . "

"What!?"

"Let me finish!" Lazaro's seamed face reddened with exertion. "He's showing signs of curiosities that I am not going to be able to satisfy from here. However, one of these curiosities seems to be a certain young woman from that bunch your mosquitoes found in the woods. And, if the situation can be leveraged into enough of a distraction, it could have more than one beneficial effect."

DaLuge, now that he had calmed down, began to see a certain logic to the plan. He nodded grudgingly, biting down lightly on his lower lip. "Hmm. Distraction, yes. I see where you're going. But are you certain . . . ?"

"If we can just keep him occupied for the next couple of months," Lazaro interrupted, his voice patronizing, "then we're home free. Any sort of passion – anything he can become desperate about, anything he can care about - will only bend him more to our cause . . . and it will strengthen his personality, a further buffer against the shock of Contact. Isn't this what we need? Oh, I forgot – we never quite agreed on that, did we?"

DaLuge's mind was working ahead, processing the possibilities. "Hmm? No, not completely, sir, but that ship sailed the day we activated him. There's no going back now, so I daresay that what you are suggesting may be our best course of action. But what about the medication? You said he's off the Elepro? How did that happen?"

"He's become somewhat paranoid," Lazaro replied. "I don't know if the dosage wasn't high enough to begin with, but he's been getting rid of the pills at night. In fact, I was going to ask what you thought about getting him back on them. Maybe we could use a routine pre-flight medical checkup to . . . "

DaLuge shook his head emphatically, and Lazaro trailed off in mid-sentence. "You don't think it will work?"

"I'm sorry, sir. But he was on a fairly high dose to begin with, and if that wasn't enough, then I'm not quite sure what to do. A lesser dose now might temper his curiosity a bit, given his upcoming change of venue, but I doubt it. And any larger dose than what he was already on would render him less than efficient – we'd risk turning him into a zombie . . . so to speak. And that could hurt us at Contact. Anything less than full consciousness and we might as well have never bothered activating him early in the first place."

"Indeed." Lazaro's voice was contemplative. He didn't speak for almost a full minute, instead leaning back with eyes closed. DaLuge began to wonder if he'd gone to sleep.

Finally he spoke, eyes still closed, his voice rough with fatigue. "It will have to be distraction, then. We'll have just under sixty days from the time he arrives at Clifftop. We must put off this little 'security action' as long as possible. I'll come up with a schedule – every minute of his time must be accounted for. Randall can keep proximity surveillance and I'll monitor his work from here. We'll eat up as much time as possible before we let him go in with his team, and then . . . well, if I'm right, then the woman will be more leverage than we need to occupy him until Contact."

"Yes, sir." DaLuge hesitated, then: "I'm only curious, sir. This woman . . . who is she?"

Lazaro's laugh rumbled through the screen. "A hot little redheaded number," he said. "Most of the time he's spent observing that group, he's either been watching her or looking for her. An unhealthy obsession, no doubt, but we can use it. All's fair in love and war, am I right, Simon?"

DaLuge smiled sardonically. "Of course."

"Good. Then you'll see him in eight days. And Simon . . . when he gets there, I want him treated as a fully initiated Elder. Make him feel good, let him tour the facility . . . with the obvious exceptions, of course. I want him to feel privileged and secure. Maybe that will help take the edge off his suspicions."

"The old smoke screen," DaLuge muttered, jotting down his instructions on a nearby scrap of paper.

"Damn straight." Lazaro Sol coughed; a dry, retching sound, slightly distorted by the com connection. He dabbed at his forehead with a folded white handkerchief and took a sip of water. "Are we clear, Simon? I want this handled with utmost delicacy."

As if I don't have enough on my plate already.

"Clear, sir. Oh, and one more thing, if you don't mind. When we do send him in with his team, we need to preserve the little girl. Some of my people are very interested . . . "

"Who? What little girl?" Lazaro frowned and coughed again.

"The source of the signal," DaLuge replied with more patience than he felt. "The little girl that was infected by our mosquitoes. I'd like to have her here for observation. Also," he added, almost as an afterthought, "it might be worth our while to keep their head engineer alive. Seems like he's the one responsible for the majority of the shielding technology that's been giving us fits. He could be helpful."

"Oh . . . well, I don't see why not. It'll give you and Daniel something to discuss. Use the time to let him build trust in you. That's going to be important in the end, you know. Someone's going to have to strap him into your machine."

"Don't remind me." DaLuge's voice was flat and slightly annoyed. "Sir, I must say again, just for the record, that I really feel we're leaving too much to chance. I . . . "

"Don't waste my time crying over spilt milk," Lazaro growled. "As you put it just moments ago, that ship has sailed. And whether you see it or not, this was the only way to get the job done. So we're just going to buckle down and make sure it happens. Understood?"

DaLuge smiled, tight-lipped. "Of course."

"Good." Lazaro took another sip of water, licked his cracked lips. "How are things going, by the way. Are we ready to go?"

"We will be." DaLuge smiled easily, but the imaging generators were still giving him fits. And though he hated to admit it, he really didn't know if the solution was anywhere near at hand. Contact could be attempted with the machine in its current state, of course, but he was almost positive that, fully conscious or not, Daniel would fry if he didn't find a way to eliminate that microsecond of delay.

"No problems, then?" The old man seemed suspicious, fishing for signs of weakness. "We have enough to worry about without the hardware going haywire."

DaLuge waved a hand in an airy, dismissive fashion, but his chest felt tight. "A few minor glitches, a handful of tests left to run . . . nothing we can't handle. The mental stability of the clone will be a far more precarious thing."

"Well, we know how we're handling that, now don't we?"

"Yes, sir."

"All right. Get back to work, Simon. Oh, and Simon?"

"Yes?"

"Merry Christmas."

"Thank you, s . . . " DaLuge started to reply, but Lazaro Sol had cut the connection with his usual dramatic abruptness. DaLuge leaned forward over his desk with a mighty sigh and rubbed his face vigorously with both hands.

24

The annual Winter Celebration had come and gone, and January had arrived, all with little fanfare. The mood around the compound was still the same; grim, and growing more so by the day.

Maia awakened early one morning a month or so after solstice, pulled on her clothes and hat. Leaving Johnny snoring on the pallet they shared, she made her way out into the cold, refreshing morning air.

Rain had fallen overnight; heavy drops glimmered on the tall grass like mercury. A few birds were out, a sparrow and some friends, flitting between the bare branches of a nearby oak and conversing in subdued chirps. The tall, stately firs that composed most of the valley's tree population reached up toward the low blanket of clouds, a small breeze wagging their upper boughs.

She swung out on a familiar trail, warming to the day, the fresh air stimulating her thoughts. No one else was out yet, and she had the forest all to herself.

Johnny had come back from the council meeting the previous evening to find her sitting with Allie, talking beside Karla's bed in Doctor Tinney's quarters. He'd seemed preoccupied with something or other, but he'd told her that the ban on outdoor activities had been lifted, at least on cloudy days, and this news had gone quite a ways towards making her feel better. Not that she hadn't been outside at all during the ban, but knowing it was allowed made it a little less strenuous. And it *would* be nice to go for a walk with Johnny. The last time they'd been in the woods together had been very romantic, but she knew Johnny had wrestled with his conscience after the fact.

"We're not above the rules, you know," he'd told her with that concerned, vaguely troubled look in his dark eyes; it was this same look that made him so adorable. "What if we'd've been spotted?"

She hadn't given him an answer . . . but she knew he'd needed that forbidden rendezvous even more than her.

Their relationship had changed with the addition of sexual intimacy. She'd expected this, of course, but she hadn't been at all prepared for how intensely she wanted to be with him now. She'd always been the aloof one, needing nothing for completeness, wanting only her sun-drenched forest bowers, the smell of the earth, and the waving ferns to inspire her.

But Johnny made her want something more.

She'd caught herself thinking on more than one occasion of a future with him, and this made her nervous. Part of it was his moody temperament; he scared her sometimes, the way he went inside himself. His eyes would get a look that was distant and somehow cold, and then he would seem to be somewhere far, far away.

But part of it was something else, something indefinable; a growing feeling that her world was about to change. She knew this had to do with Karla's mysterious condition and the paranoia in the compound, but lately it seemed more than that.

All her life, she'd seen things differently from other people. All her life, she'd been party to a kind of sixth sense, and now it was as if that sense – that part of her that kept track of everything – was picking up hints from her subconscious and sounding some vague alarm, which she heard clearly but couldn't put in context. It was frustrating, and there was really no one to talk to about it. After all, *everyone* was feeling the tension.

Maybe that's all it is – just normal tension.

She laughed out loud at this thought – as if the situation was anything resembling normal!

What scared her most, nagging at her mind, was the near-certain feeling that she and Johnny would somehow be wrenched apart. It seemed to her that they were navigating an uncharted sea, at the mercy of winds and currents over which they had not a whit of control.

And there was something else too . . . an idea that had been growing in her mind for a few weeks now. She hadn't found the courage to share it with anyone just yet, not even Johnny. But that subconscious 'thing' ticking away in her mind told her that it just might work.

Maybe I can help Karla.

The small, inert body in Doctor Tinney's quarters continued to simply lie there and breathe, though not well. Apparently a small amount of fluid had begun to collect in her lungs, which rendered every breath a labor.

"I can't honestly say how much time she has," the Doctor had told Maia and Allie in a grim tone, only the night before. "I'm giving her meds for the congestion, but I may have to pump her lungs if those don't help. And I really don't know how well that would work with the equipment I have."

Karla's death was a possibility they'd all come to accept. Allie's reaction to the doctor's grim news was an expression of resolve that didn't hide the pain she was feeling. She only nodded and said: "Well, we already knew we needed a miracle. I guess we still do."

Maia knew there were some who quietly believed Karla's death would be a blessing, and she could see the logic in this view. The girl was in a seemingly impenetrable coma – death might be the only release she had left. At the very least, it would mean that the radio signal being generated by her body would cease to be a threat . . .

Maybe I can help her.

The idea continued to blossom like a flower in her mind.

She reached the river's edge and knelt on the wet grass of the bank. She leaned down, scooped a double handful of water and splashed it on her face, rubbing her eyes and cheeks vigorously, then ran her wet hands through her hair, loving the way the coldness made her instantly more awake.

Maybe I can help her.

The thought wouldn't go away, and she resolved to talk about it with Johnny over breakfast. She pulled her wool cap down tight and headed toward the bunkers.

Johnny sat up with a start, his eyes fluttering, struggling to stay open. *What just happened?*

A dream, surely, but . . .

What kind of dream was that?

A memory swam by, just out of reach, of a broad, smiling face . . .

Who is he?

He reached for Maia, but the pallet they shared was cold with her absence. He tried to remember more as he dressed, shivering into jeans and jacket and pulling on two pairs of socks, but he was distracted by his rumbling stomach. The remnants of the dream dissipated like fog in the morning sun as he pulled up his hood, ducking through the blanket that served as a door to their cubby.

The outside bunker entrance was open to the waxing dawnlight, and by the color of the iron sky as he blinked and yawned into the open air, he judged it to be about seven or so.

"Hi hon."

He turned and there she was, coming up the path. He was surprised, but couldn't help smiling. As always, she appeared radiant and full of the morning.

"Hello, beautiful," he said. "Where were you?"

"Woke up early and went for a walk." Her eyes were bright.

"Yeah?" He smiled and hugged her close, smelling the sweetness of her hair, the musk of her body. "You hungry?"

"I could eat." She kissed him on the corner of his mouth, her breath warm and fresh, then took his arm. "And I wanted to talk to you about something."

They made their way along the nape of the hill towards the kitchen bunker, where a few people milled about, eyes half-closed, squinting and blinking in the early morning light.

"What a bunch of gollums," Johnny laughed.

"What?" She looked puzzled.

"Sorry," he said. "It was in a book I read once." He gestured at the idling group. "They haven't seen the light of day in a while."

"Oh." She pushed her hands deep into the pockets of her jacket and looked skyward. "It's nice to be out, for sure."

He grinned a sly grin. "Yeah, you haven't been out at all, have you? Not even once."

She smiled demurely but didn't say anything, and they walked to breakfast in silence, arm in arm. As they rounded the large boulder to the left of the kitchen bunker entrance, he made an overly dramatic bow and gestured with one outstretched palm at the large doorway, where a few early birds stood eating from steaming plates. "After you, m'lady."

She rolled her eyes and mock slapped his face as she went in. "You're a damn weirdo, Perdue."

◦∙◦←‹‹‹− þ−⟡−þ−›››→◦∙◦

"So what did you want to talk about?" Johnny spooned up a large bite of spicy potato hash, savoring the heat in his mouth. His stomach gurgled appreciatively.

She toyed with her food, pushing it back and forth on her plate. "Well . . . I have an idea. It's . . . it's something I've been thinking about for a while, but I don't know if it will work. What do you think the weather will be like today?"

"Huh?" He was completely confused now, but curious and listening just the same.

"I mean, is it going to stay cloudy all day? Could we take a hike?"

Johnny was simultaneously confused and intrigued. "I would love to, but why? I thought you said you wanted to help Karla."

"I do," she replied. Her eyes danced. "But there's something I have to do first. Are you in or not?"

He grinned. "You're going either way, aren't you?"

"Of course."

"Then I'm in." He got to his feet. "I don't have to be in Control until midnight, so we can get back and see Karla tonight for a while before I go on shift."

"Sure. But we better get going. It'll take us a couple of hours to get there."

"Where?" He followed her outside.

"Up-valley," she said, taking his hand. "All the way to the Falls."

25

The only sounds were the muffled slap of moccasins on dirt and the occasional lonely cry of a hawk or crow. The undergrowth became less the higher they climbed, the composition of the ground more rocky, with large boulders looming between sparse, dark trees. It gave the feeling of space, and of sacredness. A deep quiet seemed to have come over the two of them.

They had been walking for nearly an hour. At first they'd talked, mostly of nothing at all, but now they'd been silent for half an hour or more, and the silence had grown until it was an almost tangible thing, an entity that demanded respect. So, when Maia started to speak, he was ready to listen, though her voice was barely a murmur.

"I don't know if it will help Karla or not," she began, "but sometimes in the forest, I can . . . well, I *have* before, anyway . . . oh, shit." She stopped for a moment, her brow wrinkled in concentration. "One time about eight years ago," she began again, taking a new track, "I brought a flower back to life. It was wilting away and I . . . just *felt* it, you know? I knew I could do it, and I *did*. I felt it weakening, but then somehow I just . . . *focused* myself on it."

"What kind of flower?" Johnny was intrigued.

"A water lily," she said. "One of those big white ones, you know? The stalk had been bent and partially crushed. But I saw it; you know, its aura, and I was able to . . . *add* my strength to it, kind of. I gave it a boost, I guess. And it lived! For months afterward I went to visit it. I couldn't believe I'd been part of something like that." She sighed. "I forgot about it for a long time, but the other day I got to thinking. I don't know if it will work in Karla's case, but maybe if I'm clear enough, if my purpose is strong, then . . . well, who knows? Maybe I could do the same for her. I mean, it's worth a try, right?" She seemed wary, as if wondering whether he would take her seriously.

"Has it happened again since that first time?"

She shook her head. "I've never tried to heal anything else, if that's what you mean, but I can sometimes touch the auras of plants. And . . . " her gaze broke from his. "On the night I met you, I did the same thing to you. While you were sleeping."

"What?!" Incredulity broke like a wave on the shore of disbelief. "What are you talking about?"

"Right before you woke up, I . . . touched your aura, I guess. You have to understand that I was pretty blown away by the fact that I could see it at all. I guess I just wanted to test my . . . what's wrong, Johnny?"

He had stopped walking and turned to face her, his head cocked to one side and a perplexed look on his face. "You know," he said. "That's kind of odd, but . . . I wonder if you had something to do with it."

"With what?"

"Right before you woke me up that night," he said in a low voice, "I had a dream. A recurring dream, the one of my parents that I told you about."

"I remember." It was Maia's turn at piqued curiosity.

"But it was *different* that time," he said. "There was a man. He spoke to me."

"What did he say?"

"That I wasn't dreaming." Johnny's face was a mask of concentration. "Damn! I can't remember any more than that." He sighed.

"It's all right," she said. "You'll remember if you're supposed to. Don't waste your energy." She massaged his shoulder. "Do you want to keep walking? We're more than halfway there."

"All right." He wagged his head from side to side as if that might jog his memory. "It's just so weird. I wonder if it means something."

She didn't answer, but slipped ahead again, guiding him through the woods, silent as a ghost. The trees were growing thinner, and the churning of the waterfall had become a distant audible roar.

They came out of the trees onto a wide escarpment of smooth, weathered rock; a mesa-like tabletop formation, its surface broken only by the few solitary blades of grass that had somehow managed to find a foothold in the cracks. Beyond the lip of the precipice to his left, Johnny could see the silhouetted tops of the tall, swaying pines as they rose steeply with the opposing ridge. They were at the far upper end of the valley now, which was very narrow here, its sides much steeper, choked with deadwood and tumbled boulders and the rushing roar of water, which echoed its way up to their ears.

The Falls was fully visible from here; a wide ribbon of undulating silver, broken only by black knives of jutting rock below, which shattered the falling water into rainbow flumes of spreading mist. Johnny could see now that there were really two waterfalls – three quarters of the way down, a wide basin caught the foaming, churning river, holding and calming it before allowing it to continue the plunge to the valley floor. In its entirety, he suspected the falls was most of four hundred feet high, though it was hard to tell from this height.

They walked to the lip of the precipice and he peered over, his stomach feeling unaccountably nervous. Idly, he kicked a fist-sized rock over the edge. Down, down it tumbled, clinking once on the cliff face below before bouncing out and over tumbled boulders and fallen trees to disappear in the brush below.

Far below and to their left, perhaps three-quarters of a mile downstream, the river became broad and ponderous, as if the water had spent its energy in the drop and was content to rest awhile before moving on. Johnny forgot himself for a moment, looking back and forth, fascinated by the natural symmetry.

As he turned to say something about it, he noticed with a start that Maia had disappeared. His breath hitched in his throat and he had a moment of blind, panicky fear, thinking she might have fallen while his back was turned . . . but this didn't last long.

Her smiling, freckled face appeared suddenly, seeming to pop directly from the rocky ground, some twenty feet away near the edge of the precipice. She yelled something that he couldn't catch over the roar of the Falls and the whipping wind, but he understood her impatient gesture and hurried toward her.

She was in a wide fissure, a crack in the surface of the rocky cliff-top. The tumbled rocks in the throat of the crack formed an almost natural staircase, and he had no trouble making his way down to where she was. She grinned and grabbed his hand without a word, leading him further down and to their right. After a moment, they cleared the edge of the fissure and Johnny was surprised to find there was a ledge along the face of the cliff, really a path, wide enough for the two of them to walk single file. He also noticed that the cliff itself was cut inward; soon they would be under its lip, unable to see the plateau from which they had just descended.

The ledge slanted conveniently downward along the face of the cliff – indeed, now that he was walking on it, it was obvious to Johnny that the ledge path had been constructed this way intentionally. He wondered who might have done such a thing. Surely not Maia, or any of the folk from Compound West. Could it have been native people, in times before this part of the world was colonized by the white man? It was certainly easy to imagine; this place seemed nearly as old as time itself.

A short hike brought them down to a narrow, sloped plain, tucked into the upper end of the valley below the Upper Falls. Scrub oaks and hardy blue spruce dotted the limited landscape, along with a few straggling bushes and the spiky green blades of some tough grass that had found a foothold here. A few dead, blackened trees, evidence of some long-ago fire, extended their twisted and charred limbs at strange angles toward the sky. In one of these snags, a small hawk sat like a statue, only a tic of its head giving away its presence.

He could see why she'd brought him here, and why she seemed so rapt. The small plain was a hidden refuge, suspended above the valley floor but out of sight from the cliff above. Perhaps fifty yards from where they now stood, and slightly above them, the behemoth Upper Falls plunged into the basin pool which they'd seen from above, and Maia walked that way now, beckoning him to follow.

As they approached, he saw that the pool itself was flanked by a sheer wall of slick black stone on the left and a steep, impassable ridge, covered with scrub brush, on the right. A hundred feet downstream, the land began to slope at an impossible angle to the valley floor, a hundred feet or more below and probably most of a quarter mile away. The drop between was choked with blackberry vines and thorny bushes, which acted as a natural barrier; there was no way down to the valley floor from here. In fact, Johnny noticed, the sloped ledge path was the only route in or out of this place.

The thought filled him with mixed emotions. He was excited to be with Maia in such an exotic place, but part of him trusted no one and no situation . . . and no situation had ever been more tailor-made for disaster.

He put away his paranoia impatiently, reminding himself that the chance of anything going wrong out here was extremely small.

But still . . .

"Strange place," he muttered to himself.

"This place is very special to me," she said, putting her mouth right next to his ear and raising her voice to be heard over the deafening crash of the Falls. Her eyes were shiny, her face flushed. "Just stay close to me and you'll be fine."

She'd obviously been here before; she knew just where to go, flitting between bunches of grass and avoiding the low, marshy spots in favor of higher, drier ground. Twice as Johnny followed her he found himself only a shoe's width from slippery mud, and once he might have tripped over a large rock had she not somehow known and steadied him with a hand at precisely the right instant.

Their pace had slowed somewhat, but they were still moving generally toward the rippling pool beneath the Upper Falls. The crush of water rendered conversation unintelligible at best, so after a couple of lame attempts, they fell silent, simply walking hand in hand. Johnny found himself in an exquisite state of mind – he was completely content and yet completely taken by the volatility of his environment. Every sense was sharpened, every movement rendered somehow surreal and dramatic.

The pool proved to be quite a bit larger than it had appeared from above. Its edges were lined with an apron of sand. Here, directly below the massive onslaught of the churning water, the air itself seemed made of something different; something frothy, vibrating through a million tons of solid rock to catch the two of them in this moment. Even if he could have been heard, Johnny wouldn't have spoken, not for anything in the world.

Maia, too, seemed afflicted; her face was suffused with an otherworldly glow, her eyes wild and shining. She looked at him and said something that he couldn't hear. He shook his head, cupping a hand behind his ear to let her know that he hadn't understood.

She reached for him, pulling him close, and they were in each other's arms.

Their caresses seemed a phenomenon as natural, beautiful and moving as the waterfall, which echoed a thundering backdrop for their embrace. They were probably only there for a few minutes, but to Johnny it was an eternity. Finally she pulled away, planting a hand squarely on his chest. He tried to kiss her again, but she remained firm.

"Wait," she mouthed over the roar of falling water. Motioning for him to follow, she began picking her way around the right side of the pool, again staying on high ground to avoid the sticky, wet sand. As they approached the base of the falls, Johnny craned his neck back as far as it could go, straining to see the upper lip. From directly below, it seemed impossibly immense. Where the crush of water struck the pool, it foamed and churned, spitting spray which formed tenuous, shifting rainbow patterns that floated above their heads. Flecks of foam and mist fell on his head and shoulders, dampening his hair.

Maia walked confidently, hopping precisely from boulder to boulder, avoiding the wettest, slickest ones. Johnny got the impression that she was as sure-footed as a mountain goat and was only doing this for his benefit, but he didn't mind.

She made the base of the steep slope, on the right side of the falls, and now he could see a faint path there. It cut steeply upward to a small rocky basin, right next to the sliding curtain of the falls. The roar of the water was deafening, and Johnny kept getting spray in his eyes, but it had now become apparent that she was intent on a specific destination.

She made it to the edge of the rocky basin, then suddenly side-stepped and disappeared behind the edge of the sheet of falling water, only to immediately stick her head back out. Once again Johnny could hear nothing, but she reached out a glistening arm and beckoned him. He saw the foothold she had used, and managed to slide behind the curtain of falling water without getting completely soaked.

As soon as he was behind the waterfall itself, the noise dropped to less than half its former level. His ears popped a couple of times, and he shook out a headful of water droplets which sprayed the clay wall to his right. When he'd gotten a step or two further in and given his eyes a moment to adjust, he found that the wall slanted away in that direction, leaving a usable space perhaps fifteen or twenty feet long. The smooth clay ceiling was perhaps ten or twelve feet overhead, curving up toward the perpetually shifting wall of sparkling water.

Johnny realized their vulnerability here even more than out on that enclosed plateau; one misstep and either of them would fall through that curtain, most likely to drown under a few million gallons of plummeting water. He made a note of this and stepped further toward the wall, careful of his footing.

He soon forgot his fears, however – the floor seemed much drier than he would have guessed, and in general the space seemed very comfortable. Once again it appeared that Maia knew her way around. After his eyes had fully adjusted, he spotted her at the back of the cave, kneeling beside a dark object, which turned out to be a piece of heavy burlap. She unwrapped this carefully, exposing a small clay jar.

"You like it?" Her voice sounded strange to his ears after hearing nothing but the crash of water for the last fifteen minutes.

She offered him the jar, and he took it, turning it in his hands with admiration.

"Did you make this?"

She nodded. "What do you think?"

"It's great." His attention was drawn to a series of figures, scratched into the clay. He looked closely and saw the outlines of a bird, a deer, a bear, and a spider. Interspersed with these was a repeating symbol that he took to be a mushroom. The figures were simply but elegantly drawn with long curving strokes, and like the jar itself, were beautiful, though crude.

The contents of the jar were held in place by a large cork. Johnny was assailed with a sudden suspicion. He shook it and was met with a dry, rattling sound.

"What's inside?" He handed it back to her.

She smiled, but didn't answer. Once again she took his hand, leading him to the back of the cave. She dropped to a cross-legged sitting position and motioned for him to join her.

She set the jar off to one side and reached further into the slanted recess formed by the cave's back wall, extracting a handful of twigs, leaves, and small branches which she piled on the dry earthen floor between them. Then she proceeded to unroll the burlap all the way. Johnny could now see that it was an old potato sack with the words 'Clifton Farms' written on it in ancient, faded reds and blues. She reached deep inside it and pulled out a small pouch which, when opened, contained flint and steel.

She immediately set to work building her small fire, and Johnny leaned back against the wall to watch. He was interested to see if she could actually do it – he recognized her tools, of course, but he knew how hard it was to build a fire this way. Had he been a betting man, though, he would have liked her chances – the flint and steel were worn down to nubs, and looked as though they belonged in her strong, slender fingers.

Before a minute had passed, a flickering tongue of flame had caught, and within another half-minute they had a perfectly serviceable, though compact, campfire.

"I'm impressed." He raised an eyebrow. "When did you bring in all that tinder?"

She squatted, fanning the flames until they jumped up, sending flickering, distorted shadows to play on the walls and the curved ceiling. She shrugged. "Last time I was here."

"Who showed you this place?"

She smiled and tossed another handful of fuel onto the fire, which by now was crackling merrily. Johnny found that he was comfortable to the point of drowsiness, and sat up a little straighter, blinking his eyes like an owl to regain his attentive state of mind.

Maia laughed lightly, but still didn't answer his question. Johnny decided not to push.

"So," he said. "You never told me what was in the jar."

She relaxed back into a sitting position and removed the cork. An acrid, bitter smell wafted from the jar for a moment; Maia wrinkled her nose and handed it to Johnny. He tilted it so that he could use the light of the fire to peer inside.

"If you really want to understand the forest," she said in a solemn tone, "you have to eat the mushroom."

A curious sensation came over Johnny. He'd heard of hallucinogenic mushrooms, of course, but had no experience himself, or even a frame of reference.

"What will it do to me?"

She smiled, took the jar back from him and tipped the contents into her hand. The dried mushrooms looked like crushed reedy fibers, mixed with powder and a few caps. She stirred through the pile with a finger, then picked out a cap and ate it slowly. She extended her hand, and Johnny uncertainly followed suit, grimacing at the acrid, bitter taste. Maia picked another small bit from her palm and began chewing, with no change of expression save a small grin when she saw the look on his face.

"I know," she said. "They taste like shit."

The mushrooms were gone; the fire had burned down to glowing coals. The two of them sat together, their backs to the clay wall. Maia's body was warm next to his, and comfortable, and Johnny was beginning to feel a little sleepy. He wondered if it was an effect of the mushroom. Most likely not – Maia had said that it usually took most of an hour to feel anything, and it had barely been half an hour. He attributed his tiredness to the long hike and the hypnotic, muted noise of the falls.

"I like it here," he said. Then, as an afterthought: "You never told me how you found this place."

"I don't know," she said. "It was here to be discovered, wasn't it? I'm actually surprised nobody else beat me to it."

"No one else knows about it?"

"Not that I know of. I don't think anyone would be that interested, honestly." She looked at him, eyes large and glistening, lips curved in a smile. "We should go outside."

He noticed a brightness to her eyes, a flush in her cheeks. He wondered if the mushrooms were taking effect, but somehow time had slipped sideways while he was considering the possibility, and she was halfway out of the cave before he knew it, maneuvering nimbly along the slick path behind the waterfall.

He followed her without really thinking, and they blinked out into in the overcast afternoon, which seemed far brighter than it should be.

The boom and rush of the falls was overpowering, a static grind in the back of his cranial cavity, a sonic assault that almost hurt, but somehow washed his psyche clean instead. Maia stood next to him, transfixed, her hair back and blowing, droplets of spray ringing her face, looking up at the crush of water that plummeted endlessly into the pool.

A moment later and she was gone again, and he had to turn to follow her progress as she navigated the treacherous path back around the pool.

Something was definitely happening.

Everywhere, color and sound vibrated, interchangeable spirals looping behind his eyes. He had a hard time focusing on where he was going –

What time is it, anyway?

– or what he was doing. Every time he focused on something, it demanded his full attention. A group of boulders morphed into a pack of dwarves and back again to solid stone in the space of a glance. A giddy sensation filled his stomach, not entirely pleasant, and the sharp caw of a crow bladed the scene like an aural razor. Perception fell useless at his feet.

Not knowing how he'd got there, he found himself on the desolate plain near the dead stump of tree that he'd seen. The twisted, gnarled branches were ancient claws that beckoned and twisted in a wind that wasn't there. The hawk was gone; in its place sat a huge albino raven with blood for eyes and shifting, restless wings. It eyed him balefully and gave a call, a *screeeee!* that tailed away eerily, echoing down the canyon.

Maia sat beneath the twisted tree. Her eyes were closed, the ghost of a smile playing across her lips. Her head was thrown back, her arms held loosely at her sides, palms up. Her mouth moved silently with words he couldn't guess.

She was the picture of radiant femininity, materializing before him as a goddess, a preternatural queen of the forest whose soul lived in the trees and verdant earth.

He shook his head to clear it, but only succeeded in shaking out a few brightly colored stars that whirred and whizzed in front of his eyes before shooting off into the ether.

"Maia?" his voice was a thick liquid

thickquid?

that spilled into the brightly colored air. She seemed not to notice him. Her eyes rolled behind closed lids, her voice a breath he couldn't quite hear. He turned slowly, around and around, ingesting awe from every sparkling quadrant. High above, the Falls was a slow-motion curtain, rippling and unchanging; below, the valley spread like an enchanted land from time immemorial, a forgotten kingdom of magic.

Time slowed, ticked to a stop, then dissolved completely.

From the corner of his eye, he caught a movement, sliding sideways just beyond his peripheral vision. He reeled towards it, and saw

otherness

something he'd never seen before. Somewhere to his left, red hair moved in a phantom breeze and her frightened, white face came towards him in stop-motion. As if through a tunnel, her voice came, faint and familiar,

"Johnny! Run, Johnny!"

but he was captivated suddenly, hypnotized by the source of the movement he'd just seen. Two shaggy black creatures crouched before him, limbs contorted at odd angles. Their heads were huge on their necks, their bodies parallel to the ground.

Am I hallucinating?

The creatures' eyes were huge and spellbinding in their wide, smooth white faces. A sudden rush dropped Johnny in his tracks. He felt himself being lifted, light as a feather. A flying blackness surrounded him, and an insectile chirping, a skittering sound like dead leaves blown over smooth rock.

Consciousness faltered.

26

At the very top of the waterfall, atop a large boulder by the water's edge, a man of average height and build sat cross-legged. Shoulder-length black hair framed a wide face, with prominent nose and cheekbones. Muscular arms hung loosely at his sides, thick fingers resting on the rock. Three hundred feet down, the Upper Falls crashed into the calm of the pool before making the plunge to the valley below.

But Milos wasn't here for the view.

His eyes were closed as he listened, becoming attuned to the sound of the water, letting himself mingle with it. He caught the rhythm he was listening for and allowed his mind to uncoil a bit, moving with the rushing water. His concentration deepened; his brow furrowed as he applied his art, allowing his consciousness to slip over the edge. It was a technique he'd used many times before, sitting on this very rock, whenever he wanted information about the group of people living in the valley below.

He had helped their founding members in a time of great need, though the people who lived there now would have no idea of these things. It had been more than sixty years, and none of those he had known was still alive. He was sure that if any memory of him lived in the compound, it was only as story and myth.

He was used to being forgotten; in fact, there was even one person who knew him and yet could not remember him at all.

He'd seen her the first time, there by the pool at the base of the falls, more than ten years prior. He'd intentionally perceived her energy body, and with great surprise found that she was a natural seer. She had ingested the seer's fungus just before he began to observe her, and he was astounded at the natural way she used it to move her perceptions, as if sorcery was in her blood.

He had approached her without a second thought. Coincidence; omen; one and the same. He knew the spirit had pointed the girl out to him, and he knew what he had to do. He'd descended the hidden path to the base of the falls and waited until twilight, when his dreaming energy would be the strongest. Then, hiding behind a patch of scrub brush, he allowed his dreaming consciousness to rise in the shape of a great bird that glided down upon the girl, overtaking her as she was preparing to climb the path up the cliff.

He'd landed in front of her and transformed his dreaming body into a semblance of his own powerful frame, causing her to gasp in alarm and drop her small pack. She shook with fear as she looked at him, her mouth open, face pale.

He immediately pinpointed her energy body's secondary perception points, which were still glowing from the seer's fungus, and bundled them with his attention until they were attuned to him. This was easy for him, and he did it automatically and with little effort; it was the same technique he used to isolate individuals in the dreaming fields. Unfortunately, it had the side effect in most instances of rendering the memory of the experience unavailable to the person, but that was unavoidable, and in this case, hopefully temporary.

The girl stopped shaking immediately, looking up at him quietly as he told her who he was and why she interested him. "You must trust me," he said kindly. "Walk with me to that stand of brush and you'll see what I mean."

She did as he said without hesitation or complaint, and had been more curious than aghast at finding his inert body lying behind the brush. Awakening from his vision, he'd taken her with him and for three days he'd outlined for her the complexities of the seer's way, beginning a tutelage that had continued ever since.

But even now, more than ten years later, the girl still could not consciously remember him, or his lessons, unless she was with him.

It was imperative that she be made to remember.

If Martuk was right, the girl was the key; the one female sorcerer for whom the two of them had waited, year upon unending year. When he'd brought her in, Martuk's ancient eyes had lit up, resonant with a deep glow. He'd spent a full two minutes examining her with his secondary perception, watching the pulse of her luminous body while she fidgeted and chewed her lip.

There was no doubt that she was a born sorcerer. Even Martuk was impressed with her natural, though undeveloped, skills. She could travel with the wind or the clouds at will, transporting her dreaming body with precision. She'd also learned some basic shapeshifting skills, but seemed uncomfortable using them, preferring her own body or the freedom of astral travel.

But though they'd tried everything to give her the gift of her own powers, she was hopelessly cut off from them when she was not in their direct presence. Without the sorcerers to exert energetic pressure, all memories of these extraordinary events faded as quickly as a dream, and she always returned to her life without any real idea of who she was or where she'd been.

They could not convince her to stay with them. She said over and over - very stoically – that if she could not remember them on her own, then she didn't want to leave her life behind, for she had no trouble remembering her 'normal' life when she was with them. She would miss her family, she said with genuine affection, and could not simply disappear without explanation.

Milos did not press the matter – if she knew the real reason they wanted her to stay, the pressure would simply be too much. It was natural that it take time; in Milos' own case it had taken nearly twenty years, and he'd seen it take longer. And so they waited with sorcerers' patience, though time was running out with astounding speed.

If worst came to worst, he knew they'd simply have to take her against her will and explain the real crux of the issue as best they could. But maybe it wouldn't come to that. Maybe next time she would remember.

His dreaming consciousness moved freely with the water now, drifting down, listening for her. He could always *feel* her when she came to the falls. This place had something of an effect on her secondary perceptions, and it was here that she was closest to remembering.

He knew she was here now, somewhere below.

His consciousness hovered above the pool, the vision coming stronger as he applied the force of his considerable will to solidifying it. Something caught his attention suddenly; a foreign element. He stopped moving, focused on the place . . . there! The wall of brush at the bottom of the cliff, near the base of the falls. Something was hiding there, and not using only the blackberries for cover. To the naked eye it would be nearly invisible, whatever it was, but he could sense it, just the same.

Intrigued and alarmed, he allowed his consciousness to drift closer with an eddy of water and saw that there were two of them, whatever they were. He did not try to see their physical forms, knowing this to be impossible, instead focusing on their luminous bodies. With great patience he allowed his concentration to sharpen until—

He was so surprised by what he saw that he nearly lost control of his secondary attention. Only a great act of will kept the vision from collapsing. The energy bodies of the two creatures were similar to a human's, but with marked differences which to Milos' trained perceptions meant a highly evolved consciousness with a great degree of psychic control. These creatures definitely did not suffer from the strange lack of psychic perception present in most humans, and he withdrew a bit so that they would not sense his presence.

What are they? And what are they doing here?

He was no stranger to mysteries either great or small, but he'd never seen anything like these creatures. They were not human, but they were very similar from an energetic point of view. What they looked like was harder to say; they were shielding themselves somehow so they were very nearly invisible. They seemed to be focusing on something downstream.

He detected a shift in one of them that told him he might have been noticed, and let his consciousness slide deeper into the river, moving with the water for a moment to camouflage his presence. After a few moments, he rose into the spray of the falls and studied them from a distance, trying to determine how they were accomplishing their shielding.

Their energy bodies were like oblong glowing orbs, their secondary perception points bundled much closer to the surface than in humans, which meant a greater degree of awareness, perhaps even rivaling his own powers. They seemed to have found the correct alignment to shield their physical bodies from light, rendering them mostly invisible, but he sensed that it was taking a great deal of energy to accomplish this. And something else, as well . . . a pulse, like a heart beating. The two beings were connected, not only to each other, but to something else; faint luminous lines left their energy bodies, seeming to disappear into the base of the cliff below the falls.

They began to move, focusing on something further down on the plain. Milos suddenly remembered who he was looking for, and let himself go with the water, propelling further across the spray-soaked pool, looking uneasily for what the creatures were focusing on, hoping it wasn't what he thought.

But there she was, she and the young man she'd been running around with, the two of them only a hundred yards from the two advancing creatures. It was easy to see that they'd both recently eaten the fungus, which was most likely not a good thing. They'd be very slow to react, especially since the creatures could not be seen by normal methods.

His mind coiled like a whip, pulling his consciousness up the Falls and snapping him awake on top of the boulder with such swiftness that he had to steady himself with both hands to avoid falling physically over the edge. Even with all the energy at his disposal, it would be a challenge to survive the beating he'd receive from the jagged rocks on the way down.

He inhaled sharply and sprang to his feet, climbing quickly down from the boulder and moving along the tree-lined drop to his left. There was no time for the path. He flung himself out, over the edge, head first. His fingers found the top of the young pine he'd been aiming for; the tree gave with his weight and he shifted focus, finding a sturdy limb on a scrub pine some fifty feet down the slope. Using the sway of the tree he clung to, he propelled himself at the limb, pulling himself with every ounce of psychic strength at his disposal.

He caught it with both hands, swung all the way around it like a gymnast might do, and launched himself at a flat boulder down and to his right. He landed unsteadily on the rock and risked a moment to look down, but he couldn't see what was going on through the trees.

Jumping from the top of the rock, he struck the shale slope, sliding with the rocks, dust spuming into the air. Another hundred feet, and he struck the lower end of the hidden path that led to the bottom. His feet thumped the earth as he sprinted down in galloping leaps, sliding precariously, avoiding roots and loose rocks by a mere breath.

The path emerged only a few feet from where he'd spotted the two beings, and he burst out beside the pool where his dreaming body had been only moments before, spray from the falls wetting his face and hair. He wiped the moisture from his eyes, looking around desperately. He couldn't see the two creatures except as indistinct shadows, and didn't have the time to stop and perceive their energy bodies. They were almost on top of Maia and her boyfriend now, and Milos went into a full sprint towards them, his sandals slapping the ground.

Maia sat sprawled on the ground behind the young man, her eyes wide, frozen in terror.

The young man's face was blank, his eyes like saucers. He was being manipulated by the two creatures, no doubt about it. He was in another world, completely unaware of the dark-haired man who suddenly came charging from nowhere.

"Maia!" She turned towards him, uncomprehending at first. "Get back!"

With incredible slowness she turned her head again, looked at her boyfriend, then back at him. Some degree of recognition dawned on her face, and her mouth opened, closed, then opened again. He jumped between the girl and her boyfriend, keeping the creatures in view, or at least trying to determine what they were doing, but they showed not the slightest interest in either Maia or himself. They were more visible now, but when he looked directly at them they still seemed mostly distortions of light and shadow. He thought he caught a glimpse of a huge eye, black and probing . . . and then they were gone.

He felt more than saw them leave. The luminous lines of energy he'd seen seemed to vibrate and tighten, pulling them a hundred yards in a flash, back towards the tangle of blackberries at the base of the Falls, where he'd first seen them hiding.

And Maia's boyfriend was gone, too.

The only sound was the crash of the Falls. On a nearby snag, a hawk perched, eyeing the situation carefully. Maia's face was pale. Sudden realization dawned, and she frowned.

"M . . . Milos?" her voice was tentative. "But . . . *oh* God. I know you, don't I? Why didn't I remember before?"

"You always say that," he replied. He was breathing deeply, bent over with hands on his knees; the trip down the steep slope had taken a lot of energy.

"What happened to Johnny?" Her face wore a puzzled frown.

For a moment he was taken aback with her matter-of-fact question, but then he remembered the seer's fungus. It, along with his presence, was altering her perceptions to such a degree that the whole thing must seem incredibly abstract. Best to take advantage of it while it lasted, before she realized that Johnny just might be gone for good.

"Come on," he said. "We have a lot to do. You must remember, Maia. You must focus all of your strength, and this time you must remember."

"Johnny! Johnny! Over here!" Maia's laughing face appeared from behind the bush where she had apparently been hiding. He took a step towards her and she seemed to retreat, or maybe she just ducked back behind the thick screen of waxy, triangular leaves. It was hard to see; the light seemed to shift and bend, and the sounds around him had a hollow overtone. "Come and find me . . . " Her voice floated on the wind, seeming to entwine itself with the very air.

Where am I? How did I get here?

The massive onslaught of the Falls loomed in slow motion above him; or rather, a waterfall loomed . . . but not the waterfall. It couldn't be. There were too many trees here, too much foliage. And the sky – the sky was the wrong color, a deep bruised purple that seemed to undulate and ripple.

"Perdue! Where are you?" Her voice was full of love and laughter, and he wanted to follow it, to abandon all thought and plunge into . . . .

Dreaming. Hallucinating. This can't be real.

His mind seemed frozen, detached. Thought was impossible.

The mushrooms . . .

This thought, bearing the seeds of real memory, jolted him for a moment and the vision shifted and changed. He was flying, only a few leftover ribbons of color traces fading behind his eyelids to accompany a feeling of moving at tremendous speed, hurtling through an inky void.

What is happening to me?

His mind seemed to be thawing out. The rushing feeling slowed by degrees and became the feeling of moving, still through darkness but at a slower speed. Sounds came to him; the slap of feet on earth (his own?), the trickling of water, and another sound, a swishing like dry leaves crackling on stone. That sound came and went, growing louder and then trailing off.

Am I still hallucinating? Where's Maia?

He began to wonder, vaguely at first and then with growing trepidation, how long the mushroom experience was supposed to last. He had no time-sense; he'd been catapulted into some nether-realm where linear thought had all the substance of smoke.

Are my eyes open?

No way to tell, though he could feel himself blinking. Vague distorted shapes in leftover light strained against his eyeballs, but there was nothing solid, nothing real.

A sudden ceasing of motion; everything swirled to a stop. No sounds except that of his own heart, its liquid squelching disproportionately loud in his ears. He took a deep breath and heard that too, and with it came the smell of earth.

Another sound broke the silence then; an eerie ululating, clicking sound that seemed almost musical, though if it was music it was being played much too fast to be picked up. The sound dilated and floated, first coming from ahead, then behind.

Suddenly, he experienced a sharp pain on his neck, directly below and behind his right ear, like the bite of an insect. He moved his hand to slap at it, but his hand seemed to have disintegrated in the meantime.

A bright spot of light bloomed in the distance, then came closer. He blinked a few times and the light became the golden light of late afternoon, a beautiful sunny day in a place he knew well.

He sat up and looked around. He was on the sloping hill above the line of bunkers, in the valley compound. Around him, tall green grass wavered elegantly in the sighing breeze. Below, children played and shouted, their laughter echoing all around. To his right, maybe twenty or thirty feet away, Maia sat cross-legged with her back turned partially toward him. She was carefully braiding together the stalks of some tiny white and blue flowers to make a crown; she seemed peaceful and content, her eyes shiny and full of laughter as she saw him and smiled.

"Johnny! Johnny!"

He turned, gasping past the lump in his throat as a small form bounded up through the grass, golden curls bouncing. Karla's face was that of a cherub; eight-year-old perfection in shining eyes and flushed red cheeks. He began to sob uncontrollably as she fell with childish abandon into his waiting embrace.

"Baby, what's wrong?" Maia's face was the picture of concern as she came toward him, her long skirt swishing musically as she walked. He couldn't answer, but pulled her close, felt the realness of both of them, their hair, their smells, their solid flesh in his grasp.

He took a deep breath and wiped his eyes, let go of them, and they pulled back, questions written on their faces.

"Sorry," he mumbled, then: "Is it over?"

"Is what over, Johnny?"

Karla's voice, so sweet and innocent, unleashed another flood of emotion in him, and he got to his feet, swaying drunkenly.

"Johnny?" Maia sounded concerned. She laid a hand on his arm.

He began to shake his head, slowly and then with jaw-clenching vigor.

"No." He breathed. "No!" Louder.

He raised a hand toward them, palm out, almost a warding gesture. "This isn't real! It's not summer, we're not here . . . none of this is happening, don't you see?" he grasped his face with both hands, squeezed his own head like it was a rotten fruit he could burst. "I have to wake up. Have to wake up!!"

"Johnny, I don't understand," Karla's voice was tiny and hurt. "Johnny, don't you want to see me?" But already her face was fading, morphing into something hideous.

"IT'S NOT REAL!!!!!!!" He screamed with every ounce of himself. "NOT REAL! NOT REAL! NOT REAL!!!!"

But he was screaming into a moving black void, his thoughts dropping frozen from the tip of his brain.

Have to wake up . . .

27

Milos' hovel is quiet; the green-checked curtain has been pulled back to let in the silvery light of morning. All is stillness, within and without. A single bird trills, somewhere outside, and Maia moves toward the door automatically. She seems to remember that sound . . .

The bird whistles again, a chortling that gives her a feeling of great serenity. She moves through the door, almost floating, into the outdoor light. She can't tell what time it is; she can't see the sun, though she strains to do so. The light is of an indistinct quality, silver-edged and loose. The very air seems to be oozing this particular light, lending a surreal quality to everything around her.

She remembers this place distinctly now, and with great fondness; in fact, she is amazed that she hasn't remembered more before now. The view is fantastic; mountains all around, some higher and topped with snow, some lower that give on gentler slopes. Rocky promontories, tumbledown boulders, saw-edge ridges .. . but here, in front of Milos' humble home, are mostly just plants, trees and grass. A deer bounds across her field of vision and is gone, and in its wake comes that bird's call again.

The sound stirs a physical sensation in her abdomen, a wistful longing that draws her with no volition of her own. To her right is a low hillock, scattered with foot-sized rocks and a few larger boulders. She's sat there on a few evenings and watched the sunset with Milos, as he's strained to explain to her the intricacies of the sorcerer's way.

"The basic art of the sorcerer is knowledge of how to move," he would say. "To move your energetic self using water, or clouds, or fire . . . these are the oldest, most accepted ways. But I've found the sunset, the very light of twilight itself can be a powerful tool in dislodging the dreaming body. Using light itself – that is a way of great purity, and hence great danger, but I've seen no one with your natural gift in this area. It's unfortunate that you don't take this gift more seriously."

She remembers the entire conversation now as one chunk of information, a complete unit that arises like a bubble from the depths of altered memory. She examines it curiously, feeling that this bubble might lead to more bubbles.

What else do I know?

Chirr-UP! Chirr-UP!

The cry of the bird is more forceful now, drowning out everything else. It actually seems to be coming from inside her own ears.

The small hill is covered with lush grass, and on the top of the largest boulder sits a magnificent bird. It is pure white, almost albino, with silver-edged feathers that gleam and shimmer in the weird light. It might have been a raven except for its exceptional size, and the fact that its cry is completely different from any raven Maia has ever seen.

Entranced, she moves toward it, seeming to float up the short, steep hill. The bird eyes her with calm reserve. It's stopped making that noise, and now it stares at her, through her . . . it seems to be probing her very mind. She doesn't know how she knows this . . . something about a specific rush of thoughts over which she has no control.

The bird is controlling my thoughts!

She feels a defense rise to this probing that she doesn't even know she possesses, an instinctive wall rising from somewhere within her, shutting off any outflow of thought, feeling or information. She finds herself very calmly thinking about tiny details of a jacket she has been planning to embroider for Johnny. Red crisscross stitching on the sides, green on the back. She hasn't even told him about it yet. She smiles as she imagines his reaction to her gift. He'll like it – of that she is sure.

But Johnny is gone.

This thought is out of place here, and she pushes it away.

The bird seems to have stopped trying to do anything to her; in fact, the more she looks, the more it seems just an ordinary bird. Preposterous to think it could have done what she'd thought it was doing, probing her mind like that.

She takes her gaze from the bird and looks around again. The morning seems the same, the lower valleys soaked in mist, the peaks strutting through, pushing toward the bright blue sky.

"That was a good job with the bird."

The voice is Milos's, warm and good-humored and at the same time mysteriously direct. He is leaning against a scraggly tree nearby whose twisted, branched trunk forms a perfect seat. He leans his back against the rough bark, folds his arms casually across his chest.

"I would've intervened, but you handled it quite nicely."

She frowns. "But I don't understand," she says slowly. "Was that a bird? What was it doing to me?"

His gaze is level. "You know it wasn't. That's why you reacted as I taught you."

"What did you teach me?"

He shakes his head very slowly, a smile of amused disbelief on his face.

"To disassociate when met by an unknown dreaming entity," he says. "You obviously know this, Maia. You detach yourself to avoid entanglement, just as you did a moment ago. That bird was after your energy. She's a sly one, but she's no match for you." He peers at her shrewdly, eyes narrowed. "You may not remember the occasion, but you've met her before."

There is a sound right next to Maia's ear like that of a branch cracking, and she suddenly has a realization, like a light exploding somewhere behind her eyes. "Yes, yes . . . in the dreaming fields!" She gasps, inundated with the force of sudden remembering. She looks at him hesitantly. "We're dreaming right now, aren't we?"

That eerie familiarity is back; echoes of past dreams, his voice in her ear . . . it is a haunting déjà vu. A warmth floods her belly and creeps upward, loosening the mortar that has crusted around this forgotten pool of memories. She gasps as she looks around. Everything is changing, except for the hilltop where they sit, she upon her boulder, and Milos upon his crooked tree.

His eyes are pools of light. The expression on his face is neither sorrow nor joy, but instead a strange intense knowing, a look that says he apprehends what he sees directly and without judgment. He nudges her attention to the valley below with a slight movement of his head, a gesture she knows well.

How many of my dreams has he invaded? How well he must know me!

Something amazing is happening. In the valley below, a strange mist is collecting, pooling like some viscous liquid, swirling with eerie light and crackling with subdued energy. She can hear the crackling with some facility that is not normal hearing – the sound seems to be inside her abdomen, focused at a point around her navel.

The viscous mist is arranging itself into lines, concentric circles flowing into one another. The mountains around them have disappeared, and now only the valley remains, and they at their vantage point. She looks over at Milos but he seems lost in watching the scene unfolding below them.

"What is it?" She asks.

"The dreaming fields," he says without moving his lips. "But you already knew that, didn't you?"

"Any sign of them yet?" Allie Aldridge tried to keep her voice hopeful, but it was getting more difficult with each passing day.

Her husband's large frame filled the doorway, blocking out the light from the hallway.

"Not yet." His tone was despondent.

She swallowed hard and looked down, ran a hand across Karla's sallow cheek. As always, she hoped for movement, or any sign of life, but there was none. Her daughter was immobile; her body didn't move at all except for the nearly imperceptible, shallow breaths which her lungs dragged in autonomously.

Even if Johnny and Maia were found, there was no longer any doubt that Karla was dying. It was only a matter of time.

Jeremieah came in, pulled up the absent doctor's chair and straddled it. He hooked his arms around the chair's creaky wooden back and looked down at his meaty hands, absently picking some dead skin from a thumb. "We found Johnny's slingshot," he said.

A fresh raft of tears broke through her defenses and she began to cry silently, tears trickling down to plop on her tattered sweater. Jeremieah only looked at her, his eyes distant.

Of everything that had happened, it was the depth of his despair that made her feel the worst. Before, when there had been trouble – and there had always been plenty of trouble – he'd always been the one to put a hopeful spin on things, to see a way through when things looked bad.

But the ponderous dying of his youngest child had taken the life from him; had broken the hope in his eyes that had always been a beacon for her. It was a frightening transformation. He'd become someone she hardly knew in the space of just over a month. She looked away, concentrated on a small bug that was crawling on a nearby shoring timber. The bug stopped, moved one way, then the other, and disappeared into a crack in the porous surface of the treated earth wall.

Seeming to sense her need, Jeremieah reached a hand across Karla's skinny chest and touched her arm.

"Hey," he said. "It's only been three days. We could find them yet."

She shook her head, splattering more tears. Almost violently she reached up, smeared the wetness from her eyes and blew her nose into a sodden handkerchief.

"You know it's not that," she said in a strangled voice. "Well, it is that, but not *only* that." She started to say something else, then shook her head and closed her mouth tight, drawing her lips into a hard line. When her voice came again, it was in a cracked, forced whisper. *"Why is this happening to us?"*

He could only shake his head, the light in his eyes again moving to a beat she couldn't fathom, his mind spinning out in an orbit she couldn't touch. He withdrew his hand.

"We're going to try again tonight," he said. "They've *got* to be in this valley somewhere. I mean, Perdue wouldn't just disappear like that unless something was really wrong. Maybe one of 'em got hurt somewhere and the other one's standing guard. If the weather cooperates we're going to try spinners at higher altitude, modified with thermal scanners. John thinks we'll find 'em."

The hope in his voice was false, and she knew it.

"Don't lie to me, Jeremieah," she said in small voice. "I know you better than that."

He leaned forward over the rickety back of the chair, resting his chin on his gnarled hands. He looked out at her from puffed, rheumy red eyes, and she realized that he'd been crying too. He shook his head in mute despondency, the muscles of his lantern jaw working without sound, creating defined shadows in the dim light.

"I just don't know where they could be," he husked, and now all the false hope was gone. "We've been over the whole valley with spinners more times than you could count, and we're not getting *anything*. Johnny had a hand-com unit on him when they left, or at least we presume he did. He usually carried one, and the one he always used is missing. So not only should they be able to contact us, but we should also be able to pick up the homing signal from the hand-com. But it's nowhere in this valley, or else it's not turned on." He shook his head. "It doesn't make sense."

"None of this makes sense. *Nothing* for the last month has made any kind of sense!" The desperation, the anger she'd been holding back for so long made a try for the surface with some success. Her face became red, nostrils flared. "Goddamit, Jeremieah!"

He looked at her with something like surprise. She was angry, and now that the feeling had hold of her, it wouldn't go away without being expressed. "Why the hell is this *happening* to us?" She was nearly screaming, her voice high and breaking.

Again, he could only shake his head.

She looked down at her hands, balled into tight little white-knuckled fists, shaking with suppressed rage. She wanted to take those hands and wring the neck of whoever was responsible for her daughter's condition, but there was no way to exact revenge, or restitution, or even to know who that person might be.

She thought of Johnny, whose vigil at Karla's bedside had been second in intensity only to her own, and Maia, who'd made a wreath of pine boughs for Winter Celebration and had brought it down 'to spruce up the room a little bit.' The wreath still hung behind her on the wall in a painfully non-festive way, but she hadn't had the heart to take it down when the Celebration was over. Now, it might just be the last thing she had to remember Maia by; cheerful Maia, who always smiled at everyone and who'd been a true friend to her, and to Karla.

Instead of making her weep, these thoughts seemed to give her strength. She became calm again by degrees, beating down the horror little by little, until it only lived in a small, cramped space inside her stomach.

She took a deep breath and tried on a little smile. "Well," she said, "at least we're still alive, right? That's something."

He just looked at her, and then past her, as if his thoughts were following that bug she'd seen, down a crack and into some healing oblivion.

Marshall Scott leaned back from his console, stretched his hands over his head and sighed loudly. It had been a long three days since Maia and Johnny had disappeared, and in that time he'd slept a total of maybe five or six hours. He let his arms drop with a thump and rubbed his eyes hard with both hands, trying to blink himself back to the chore at hand.

Where can they be?

He reached for the half-full cup of lukewarm tea next to his keyboard, sipped it absently.

Running normal spinner routes had proven on the first day to be an exercise in futility. So, on the second day, they'd assigned every one of the devices to look for the lost couple, hoping for at least a glimpse of *something . . .*

Thirty-odd hours, and still nothing.

They'd been hopeful for a time, when Will Matthews found Johnny's slingshot on a rock beside one of the up-valley forest trails . . . but no one could remember the last time they'd seen Johnny with it. It could easily have been there for a month.

After that, the search parties concentrated on the upper valley, but the steep terrain and debris-choked gullies made for difficult going. And, as team after team returned with no news, hope seemed to be giving way to quiet desperation and even anger.

"Idiots," John Stark had growled, in a moment of frustration the night before. "We give 'em permission to take a little walk in the woods, and they wander off to never-never land." The look on his face belied his anger, though; he was just as worried as everyone else.

Ever the pragmatist, Stark had pulled back all but the normal array of spinners the night before. "We just don't have the power," he'd explained to Scott quietly. "We need to get back to normal recon and surveillance to conserve energy."

Scott had begged a single spinner to continue the search. "Just let me keep looking for a while," he'd said, and Stark hadn't had the heart to say no. And so that was what he'd been doing for the last eighteen hours – searching every nook and cranny of the valley.

The spinner was modified for thermal imaging, and for the first six hours his heart jumped every time he saw a red thermal smear . . . but the readings were only birds, or deer. One time he saw a bear, down in the lower valley, and a big one at that. On an average day he might have asked someone, maybe Johnny, to go check it out with him just for the hell of it, because bears didn't come around much and they were interesting to see.

But today was not an average day.

Dead people don't give off thermal readings.

He pushed this thought away and kept searching, methodically, relentlessly. The last six hours had been spent combing the area around the waterfall and just below. Right now his spinner sat vibrating quietly on bank of the river, three miles up-valley, not far below the falls. He switched the spinner to regular camera and got a close-up view of wet, stringy blades of grass, out of focus and with dark spots that might have been mud.

Where could they be?

He stretched his arms one last time and twisted his neck, producing a loud series of popping sounds.

"Jesus, Marsh." Stark's voice was a mutter from beyond a toppling pile of printouts on one of the rusty terminals. "Keep that up, and one of these days you're going to break that skinny neck of yours."

Marshall knew this was an attempt at levity and gave a courtesy guffaw as he punched the sequence to activate the spinner. John Stark's thin, balding head poked up over the pile. "You want some coffee?"

Marshall turned toward him as he finished the now-cold cup of tea. "Sure," he said. "Here's my . . . "

He stopped at the look on John's face, turning quickly to face the monitor. The spinner had gained a little altitude and was hovering right above the river. And, after eighteen solid hours of searching, Marshall Scott was completely unprepared for what he saw.

She walked slowly along the riverbank, seemingly unconcerned with anything at all. There was no audio feed from the spinner, but he could've sworn she was humming to herself. He reached for his keyboard with wilting hands to find that Stark had flung himself around the partition and taken control of the spinner, moving it with deft clicks, closer to the shambling figure.

It was definitely Maia, looking none the worse for wear; in fact, she seemed perfectly composed. Her clothes were clean with the exception of a smudge of dirt on the knee of her jeans. Her hair was pulled back and her eyes seemed clear. She turned and saw the spinner. For a moment she seemed hesitant, as if she'd never seen one before, but as recognition dawned she smiled and raised a hand tentatively in a wave.

Scott and Stark looked numbly at each other.

"I wonder where Perdue is," Scott mumbled, sitting down heavily in his chair. *"Jesus!"*

Stark was already on his radio. The Chairman's voice came back within three seconds, his tension hardly masked by the crackle of static. "Aldridge here. What is it?"

"Get somebody up to the big meadow below the falls," Stark said. "We've spotted one of our wayward children."

"Only one? Which one?"

"It's Maia," Stark said. "She looks like she's okay, but we need to check her right away. She looks a little . . . too untouched . . . if you know what I mean."

A pause, then: "One is better than none, I guess. I'll go get her myself. Aldridge out."

"Stark out." He turned, dropped the radio absent-mindedly into a basket of surveillance charts, and sat down heavily.

Maia was lost in childish fantasy, walking in dreamlike peace through the forest which had always been her home. Everything was radiant, though the sun's light was thin and silvery when it mustered enough strength to break through the slate of clouds. The pine forest was dark and mysterious between patches of deciduous trees. Their bare branches spoke of winter, and death, but her mind was leaping instead to the lush possibilities of the coming spring. In the back of her mind, she heard her mother's voice, singing an old song full of words whose meanings she didn't know . . . but their lilting poetry gave birth to delightful pictures in her mind.

The voice of her mother is the only voice. All other sound comes from directly around her; in an eddy near the bank of the river, a bubble rises silently to the surface, and she hears an exquisite pop as its tiny existence burgeons and disappears in one fleeting instant. A woodpecker strikes the trunk of a nearby oak tree; once, twice, three times, its' rhythmic rat-tat-tat pinging hollow and perfect in her ears. A twisted oak leaf detaches from a crooked branch with a small cracking sound and holds her in fascinated wonder, sliding back and forth on its way to the ground, twirling end over end . . .

When she saw the spinner it took her a moment to figure out what it was. It seemed out of place here, a relic from another dimension.

Recognition dawned slowly.

I need to walk downstream if I want to get back to the compound.

Her mother's voice now seemed the relic - a beacon from another world.

When did I last hear my mother's voice?

She felt faint suddenly, and sat down right where she was on the wet grass. She was still sitting there thirty minutes later when Jeremieah Aldridge and Will Matthews arrived, panting, red-faced, and out of breath. When they asked her about Johnny, she just looked at them blankly. It took her a good share of the walk back to the compound to even remember that she'd ever known a Johnny Perdue, and for an hour or more she could only recall him in vague generalities. Her mind seemed unable or unwilling to think in linear mode, and so she stopped trying to remember and just walked, absorbing every detail of the forest around her.

By the time they made it back to the compound, it was late afternoon. The last of the day's cold sunlight rendered the valley in long shadows, and she shivered as she pulled her sweater tight.

They came around the last corner above the meadow, where the trail headed away from the river, and the force of memory finally caught up with her. They were very near the place where she and Johnny had found Karla, screaming and covered with

huge mutant bugs

mosquitoes, and now it was coming back. His face, his eyes, his voice boiled into her head with force enough to make her gasp.

"What is it?" Will Matthews' voice was tinged with concern. His hands were strong as each clasped one of her arms to keep her from swooning. "Jeremieah, we gotta get her inside."

As the two of them helped direct her unsteady limbs toward the kitchen bunker, now only a few hundred feet away, she recalled with perfect clarity every moment spent with Johnny. She remembered the reason they'd gone for their walk in the first place, remembered sitting behind the waterfall, remembered eating the mushrooms . . .

But that was where it stopped.

It was as if her mind was on a line, a leash which had reached its maximum length. Scattered, disjointed memories lay just beyond her reach. She could almost see them there, lying broken and unorganized on the floor, waiting to be picked up and put together like a puzzle . . . but she couldn't muster the energy.

Something happened to Johnny.

Her mind ached with the strain of trying to remember.

They were at the kitchen bunker door, now moving inside. Warmth and good smells and the glow of candles inundated her senses. Bread, yes, and Diana Russell's brown gravy . . . coffee and anise seed tea . . . and most of all the smell and feel of a room full of familiar people. Bodies crowded around her, too close suddenly, and again she felt that she might faint.

"Back!" It was Uma Peak's voice, strident and insistent. "Give her some room."

Someone brought a thick blanket and wrapped it around her shoulders; a man's large hands placed a steaming bowl of potato chowder under her nose; someone else brought a mug of tea, also hot and steaming. The people around her grew quieter little by little until the only sound was a nervous cough from somewhere on the edge of the room.

She took a hesitant bite of the soup, felt spicy warmth beginning to thaw her. She swallowed, chased the soup with tea.

"Maia . . . " Uma Peak sat next to her on the bench, a mottled hand resting protectively on her shoulder. The older woman's face was filled with concern.

"Something happened to Johnny," Maia blurted, the words finally coming on their own. "He . . . we . . . I mean, I can't . . . "

Her mouth seemed filled with molasses. Someone handed her a clean handkerchief, and it took her a moment to realize that she'd begun to cry, the tears filling her eyes and dripping down her cheeks. She blew her nose loudly and sat back, then took another spoonful of soup. She hadn't realized how hungry she was until now, but as the hot chowder continued to warm her she felt a little better, so she continued to eat, ignoring the uneasiness her statement had wrought.

The tension in the air was obvious. People huddled in knots around the rough oak tables, clenched fists wielding mugs of coffee and tea like weapons that might keep their helplessness at bay. Whispers and low mutterings sounded as they digested her words.

Something happened to Johnny.

The words had knocked the collective wind out of the room.

"What happened, Maia? What happened to Johnny?" Uma Peak's voice was tender and soothing, but her voice carried the static undercurrent of the room's energy, reflecting the tension of everyone there.

Maia closed her eyes, trying to bring the memory into focus. "We . . . went . . . up-valley." The words were like rusting chunks of metal, clanging from her lips. "I . . . " She hesitated. "Well, we . . . " She shook her head as the memories swam behind her eyes. "The waterfall," she blurted. "We went to the waterfall. And then . . . "

She remembered it in linear order, finally, but hesitated.

The mushrooms. I was going to try to heal Karla.

Would anyone understand if she told them the real reason she'd taken the fungus? They'd think her irresponsible, or crazy, or both. She was aware of eye contact and muttered conversation behind and around her. John Stark was one of those talking, his voice low.

"Is Karla still . . . is she . . . " her voice still didn't want to obey her. "How long have I been gone?" she asked finally.

"Three days." Uma Peak rose from the table. "You've been gone for three days, Maia. Karla is still . . . alive, if that's what you were going to ask. But . . . " she let her voice trail off, sending a troubled sideways glance at Jeremieah Aldridge, who hadn't seemed to notice where the conversation had gone. His head was bent toward John Stark, who was earnestly holding forth in a low voice.

The Chairman and Stark stopped talking, looked up abruptly as they noticed Uma's and Maia's eyes turning towards them.

"I know what you're thinking," Maia said, surprised at the strength she'd suddenly found in her voice. "I'm not bugged."

John Stark's eyes spoke of his wariness. "I'm sure it's fine," he said in his best soothing voice, which was not very soothing at all.

A sudden commotion at the door, and Maia heard Darby's voice. "Where is she? My God! Maia! Maia!"

"Over here," she called, feeling a sudden burst of warmth in her breast at the concern she heard in her best friend's voice. The crowd parted to let her in.

"Maia! Where have you been? And don't tell me you went camping again." Darby approached her at the table, fear and concern written on her face. As she saw that Maia was all right, she burst into tears and threw her arms around her friend's shoulders, pulling her into a trembling embrace. For the moment, all else was lost as they clung to each other.

Darby pulled back, wiping her face roughly with the backs of both hands. "You scared the shit out of me," she said, her laugh choked by emotion. She looked around the room. "Where's Perdue?"

All conversation died again as everyone looked expectantly at Maia. She pushed her bowl of soup back very carefully, not taking her eyes from it, as if this single-pointed consciousness could help to buffer the reality of what she had to say next. "Something . . . happened to Johnny," she said, her voice trembling. "I . . . " She shook her head in exhaustion. "I don't know. We . . . " she lowered her head into her hands, unable to think clearly.

More whispers, and gentle hands shook her shoulders.

"Maia." It was Uma Peak. "Maia, I'm going to have Darby take you to your room. Why don't you get some sleep, and we'll talk about this tomorrow."

She nodded mutely, tears again brimming in her eyes, distorting her vision and turning everything to smears of color and shadow. Darby took her shoulder with hands that felt like they might not let go and helped her to her feet, pulling the wool blanket tight around her shoulders.

The silence in the room was pregnant as they stepped out into the twilight, feet finding the familiar path back to the bunker where the two of them had shared winter quarters for the last six or seven years. When they got there, Darby helped her into bed and then lit a few candles. Their light flickered around the corners of the room as she tidied up, folding Maia's clothes and hanging up her coat.

"Maia." Her voice was low. She finished what she was doing and turned to her friend. "Maia, what happened to Johnny?"

But Maia was snoring softly, her face peaceful and serene.

28

Creak-thump.

"You've doubled back." The old woman's eyes are crinkled and inquisitive, her hair a loose white cloud around her shriveled head. She is tamping her pipe; he can smell the warm scent of fresh tobacco. *"Have you learned anything yet? No? I can see you're confused. But this is to be expected - you're not quite all here, you see."*

She waits, as if for a reply, but he only stares at her stupidly. After a moment she nods, as if at some inner voice, and continues.

"You're confused because you're dreaming from the position of Johnny-that-was. This makes your experience brand new again, as if it hadn't already happened." She smiles warmly at him. *"This is the work of the double, which is a feat all by itself, but I won't confuse you further by delving into that now. We'll just say that for our purposes, you're doing fine so far."*

She lights her pipe and squints at him through a haze of sweet-smelling smoke. The desert is quiet in the star-bright night, and he is quiet within it, as if speaking will dispel this vision. And surely, it must be a vision ... mustn't it? But the smell of oil in the ancient pine railing, the creaking of her chair, the moon rising above the sawtooth horizon, the scent of tobacco, even the feel of his own body – these things are real! As real as anything.

"Where am I?" He finally asks, knowing it's a stupid question.

"This is just a juncture," she says with a knowing smile. *"A connecting point in time-space, to put it very crudely. Or you could think of it as a checkpoint. But like I said, you're doing fine. I ... "* she trails off and looks out at the gloomy wasteland, shading her eyes with one gnarled hand.

"I must say," she says, sitting up a bit straighter, an amused glint in her eyes, *"I don't remember inviting anyone to dinner. So who do you suppose that might be?"*

A dark figure has disengaged itself from the shadows of the cacti and is approaching at a walk. The figure appears to be a man, very tall and thin, dressed the way Johnny supposes a local peasant might dress. He wears no hat, and his lank, dark hair hangs around his face. His eyes are blue and diamond-bright, and Johnny catches his breath when he sees the look in those eyes; a look of power tempered by curiosity, of boldness matched with respect. His smile is wide, his long teeth flashing in the moonlight as he approaches the porch, his steps cautious but sure.

"Hello!" He says brightly, and takes a long, sweeping bow, his eyes never leaving those of the old woman in the rocking chair. "Might it be permitted to make an introduction?"

Creak-thump.

The rocker comes down a final time and the ancient being pretending to sit there (he knows she's pretending, somehow, as if he's seen this all before) sits forward and peers down at the newcomer.

"No introductions needed," she says. Her eyes are narrowed, but there is a mischievous glint there. "Welcome, Martuk. And might I add that you're quite a bit early. Always before, you've dropped by at a . . . well, shall we say, a different point in the story?" She chuckles. "Now what could this mean? Perhaps there is hope for our young friend here, after all." She motions to Johnny.

Martuk raises his eyebrows and wiggles them in a comical fashion, baring his teeth in a horse-like exaggerated smile.

"I must say, this place is amazing." He gestures at the desert around them, the mountains, the glowing full moon peeking from behind the clouds. "All of it. The detail, the perfection of fixation . . . I gave my hat to a young man I met over yonder hill who claimed to live in a local village. Can you imagine?" He laughs easily. "But I'll be damned if I've been here before. I certainly think I might remember it. But then . . . " he looks at her shrewdly, again over-exaggerating his expression, like the world's most sincere ham actor.

" . . . But then, I guess I know how this works. You're going to tell me that it's only the first time for me, aren't you? You probably exist in more dimensions than I could even count, much less keep track of. I am, after all, naught but a humble traveler. And this one—" he levels a finger at Johnny, "this one, I can see now, has been here many, many times. I wonder . . . "

"I'm wondering the same thing," says the wrinkled old woman. She begins to rock again, very slowly, creak-thump, creak-thump. The glint has not left her eye.

"I'm thinking there has been a ripple. Very interesting. Very, very interesting. I shall have to divert more energy to studying this phenomenon." She takes a deep breath and sighs. "I'm sorry, gentlemen, but for now I must ask that you take your leave."

She waves a hand, and—

⋇

When corporeality came, Johnny stared with numb surprise.

In the distance, the spires of the double pine rose protectively over the lower side of the compound. To his right the river oozed by with deceptive complacency, running high from recent rainfall. Low, threatening clouds sulked overhead, spitting bits of rain which his body seemed too numb to feel, though he was shivering violently.

Blink.

Everything was dazzlingly bright and colorful, which seemed wrong given the nature of local meteorological phenomena. It was a gray day, and cold, and yet he couldn't get over the color and crispness of his otherwise normal perceptions.

He knew this place well – he was just on the high side of the Knob, where he and Maia had come together many times. Yes, and there was the grove of poplars, between himself and the river, their dull green leaves glistening with an intensity that caught his attention and left him feeling out of breath.

Not real! Not real! Not real!

Agony, this limbo. It shot through him like a spike, skewering him to this moment *(not real!)* which he knew only existed in his own mind.

For a long time he simply stood there, numb and unbelieving. Finally, as the light began to seep from the day, he oriented himself towards where the compound should be and began to walk.

The Council was all there in the meeting-room below the Control bunker, nervous fingers tapping cups, faces gaunt and strained. The smell of coffee was burnt and rancid and seemed to add an element of acidity to the way most of them were feeling. The single bank of fluorescent lights overhead sputtered and popped, casting pallid shadows across nervous faces.

"Well, we can't just throw her out on her ear," said Bud Arney, his normally jolly face looking wrinkled and serious, jowls quivering indignantly.

Murmurs of assent sounded from around the table. "Nobody is saying we should do that." John Stark's voice held an edge of frustration. "But the simple fact is, we just can't know where she's been, or who's had access to her."

"She's done this before, do you remember?" Uma Peak's small face looked more ancient than usual, the wrinkles unsmoothed, her hair fallen from its perennial tower to sit tiredly on her shoulders. "When she was younger. I remember that everyone thought . . . "

"We all thought she'd gone AWOL, that time," Stark said impatiently. "It turned out she was off camping somewhere. But that was a different time. We didn't have anywhere near as critical a situation then, and there was no one else involved. Regardless of where Maia has been, we're still missing Perdue, and I'll bet anything they weren't just off on a camping trip. Johnny knew better than that – besides, he had a shift to fill that night. He would have made arrangements if he was going to be gone overnight, not to mention three days."

"Maybe she'll remember after she gets some rest," Uma said. "We should at least give her that much courtesy."

"All I know," Stark went on, his voice hollow, "is that she didn't look like she'd been camping, and she didn't look like she'd been hurt . . . at least not physically. She sure as hell was out of it when you guys brought her in, not to mention Johnny not being with her. She can't remember what happened, which fits . . . "

"We all know what the pattern fits," Jeremieah said, raising his voice for the first time. "People gone missing who come back without all their memories intact. It fits with old rumors about CEC practices. But you have to remember one thing – if they're looking for us, they already know a great deal about where to find us. Why would they kidnap . . . "

"Information," Stark interrupted. "They might've wanted to know what they were up against. Let's assume they've found us, but can't get effective satellite reconnaissance due to our jamming. They might want some information before they come in and clean us out. Which is why we can't afford to take chances. We obviously can't turn Maia out, but we do need to isolate her until we have a better idea . . . "

"Isolate her? What do you mean?" Bud Arney's voice reflected his distaste at the idea.

Stark leaned forward across the table, his hands knit together so tightly that they were beginning to turn white.

"Look," he said with tight-lipped evenness, "we never saw those mosquitoes coming. It never entered any of our minds that such a thing was even possible, let alone that anyone would do it. Well, for whatever reason, call it bad luck or whatever, we got hit. And now..." He paused and took two deep breaths, fighting for control. His jaw clenched, then slowly loosened, nostrils flaring slightly. He blinked a couple of times, then his face hardened again as he continued. "Now, you have to hear me out. We have to run some more extensive tests on Maia, and we have to start tonight. We've got to make sure she hasn't been bugged, or drugged, or otherwise tampered with. Do you all understand?"

"You make her sound like a piece of equipment, John," said Bud Arney. His chair creaked as he shifted his bulk.

"Christl! What is *wrong* with you people?! We've got a goddamn *emergency situation* here!" Stark's self-control was all but gone. He was half out of his chair, his upper body strained as he leaned out over the table, slamming his palm on the table. "Now look! I'm as rational as the next guy, but we've got a man missing and a girl who's apparently lost half her marbles, who wanders back into camp looking like she'd been at a goddamn picnic for three days! We've got a security nightmare because we can't tell if we've been spotted, or by whom, or from which direction an attack will come . . . if one comes at all! And if it doesn't come tomorrow, or next week, then maybe next month, or in the middle of summer when we least expect it. Well, I for one am going to expect it, goddammit! We need to step up evacuation drills, we need round-the-clock

watch, and by all means I am going to run every imaginable test on that girl, tonight if possible, and I don't care if it means that her hair turns blue and falls out!"

The table was shocked into complete silence. No one moved a muscle or even blinked for several moments, and then everyone began talking at once. John Stark held up a hand, a look of tortuous pain overriding his seamed face. For a moment he looked as if he might say something else, but as the clamor in the room thickened, he threw his hands up and stormed out, pulling his jacket from the peg by the door as he went.

Uma Peak nudged Doctor Tinney, sitting to her left. "Ralph," she said in a low voice, "I want you to follow him. He's probably going to Control or to Maia's room, and I think he's serious about running those tests. You and I both know he won't do anything to hurt Maia - I'm sure he was just blowing off steam, but you should be there to help him if he decides to start in the middle of the night. Try to keep him at Control until Jeremieah and I can get there. Tell him you want to help him formulate his tests."

Dr. Tinney blinked owlishly, twice, as if surprised by her request, then said, also in low tone: "Well, it won't be a lie. I do want to help, if there's to be any testing done." He pushed his chair back quietly and slid out of the room without anyone really noticing.

When he was gone, Uma cleared her throat and rose from her chair, summoning all the respect she could command with that slowly dignified movement. She held up a hand, and the room fell to uncomfortable silence.

"Now, you all know John Stark as well as I," she began, and as the clamor rose up again she held her hand even higher. "Listen!" she said, her voice sharp now, and commanding.

"If we resort to the invasive procedures of our enemies," ventured Abby Carmichle, her voice hesitant, "then we are no better than them. If we lose respect for our own, then we lose respect for ourselves. Maia is like a sister to us, or a daughter. She has obviously been through something terrible, and the least we can do is wait until she's well enough to okay the tests herself. It's all that any of us would ask, don't you think?"

Heads nodded; eyes connected; voices murmured yes.

Uma Peak took a deep breath. "You are right, of course," she said. "But so is John Stark. None of you have the responsibility that he has, of keeping this compound as free and safe as possible. I know for a fact that he takes much of what has happened here recently as a personal matter – he feels responsible for Karla's tragedy as well as Johnny's disappearance. Now, we don't know what happened to Maia, but he's right about one thing. We desperately need to find out. And if that means starting some tests tonight, then I personally am voting that we allow it. I will be there myself to make sure nothing invasive is done. Doctor Tinney and John himself both assured me this afternoon that there are several procedures that involve nothing worse than a few electrical sensors loosely taped to the skin.”

She stopped and surveyed the table, accosting every set of eyes, one by one. They seemed more relaxed, more open to what she had to say. She sighed wearily and sat down, knitting her hands together on the table.

“Maia’s already been asleep for five hours,” she said, “and she’s not showing any signs of waking up soon. Depending on the degree of her shock, she may sleep for a day or even longer, and I don’t have to tell any of you that speed is important on this thing. If there are people looking for us and they’ve managed to kidnap her . . . well, that brings up other points which need some thought, but first I believe we need to vote. Assuming Jeremieah, myself and Doctor Tinney are there to moderate John’s enthusiasm, do we allow testing to begin tonight? Raise a hand for a yes vote.” Uma raised her own right hand to shoulder level, then looked around the room, waiting.

Their hesitation was evident, but one at a time all the other hands in the room went up.

Uma Peak sighed and shook her head. “I know this is a hard time for all of us,” she said. “And I thank you all for making a difficult decision. Now, I’d like to talk about a few other things while we’re all here. One, it seems that we must accept the state of emergency we’re in. I’d like a vote on stepping up evacuation drills, and also one on beginning thorough weapons training and practice for a few key people. If we’re attacked we’ll need to fight, and that means a good inventory on all weapons stores. I don’t believe we have enough guns for every able-bodied adult, but those that we have should be inspected for usability and cleaned thoroughly. Any objections to this?”

Their faces had become grim, mouths uniformly taut, turned down at the corners. She could see that the month of desperation had taken its toll on all of them, but that desperation seemed now to be turning to determination.

“If no one objects, then I’d like to personally take on weapons duty,” said Jeremieah Aldridge. “I’ll be starting the inventory tonight if anyone wants to help.”

“I’ll help,” said Will Matthews.

“Me too,” said Bud Arney.

“Good, good,” she nodded. “Then that takes care of . . . ”

A sound invaded the room, the pounding of feet from the hall outside. Marshall Scott entered running, eyes wild, hair wilder and coming out of its habitual fuzzy ponytail. This might have been funny if not for the extraordinary circumstances, and so every person in the room held their breath as Scott bent over to get his. Every ear strained as he puffed and wheezed, trying to get the words out. The few seconds it took to execute this maneuver might as well have been forever.

"What . . . ?" Uma began to say.

"Down-valley," he panted. "P . . . Perdue. We got Perdue. He's a mile down-valley by the river. Got a confirmed visual but no thermals, weird enough. John says . . . "

The rest of what he said was lost as the room exploded into action; hands reached for coats and hats and the whole group plunged out into the hall as one, heading for the surface, and maybe an answer.

When they approached him, they seemed cartoonish and weird, like characters in a dream, though he recognized them all. Uma Peak, with her toppling tower of white hair, led the way. John Stark was right behind, thin face stretched into a tight white grimace. Marshall Scott was with them too, and Bud Arney, puffing and blowing from the effort of moving his large frame so quickly.

Their questions buzzed around his head like an angry and disoriented swarm of bees, and he could barely process it all, much less come up with answers. Numbness pulled him deeper inside himself, and the whole group fell into an uneasy silence as they approached the kitchen bunker. Johnny began to shiver violently, his teeth locked in a dissonant chatter, and nearly fell.

"Here, let me help." A friendly voice, that of Abby Carmichle, and a heavy wool blanket was draped over his shoulders.

"Th-thank you," he mumbled. How to tell her – any of them? – that it wasn't the cold outside making his teeth to chatter, but rather the frost that was creeping in where the personage of Johnny Perdue should be.

They got him inside and seated comfortably at one of the long oak tables that lined the room, a steaming cup of hot anise seed tea in front of him. His shivering had stopped and he felt a little more comfortable, but still there were acres of space between his ears, where his mind had only recently been. He shook his head and closed his eyes, wishing he could express something to these good people who obviously cared so much about him, but he felt blank and empty.

Not real!

Finally he looked up. "Where's Maia?" he asked, his voice low. "Is she all right?"

Aldridge and Stark exchanged a covert glance. "Uh . . . yeah, Johnny," Stark said after a moment. "She's fine. She'll be happy to see you, no doubt."

Johnny slumped back in his chair, again drifting somewhere beyond their reach. "That's good," he mumbled, closing his eyes. "That's good."

A long buzzing sound filled him, a whooshing that sucked him through an endless void, and when he next remembered himself, he was in the forest.

A huge raven with shimmering white feathers perched on a nearby branch, regarding him severely. Overhead, the moon floated between rags of stratus, watching balefully.

Not real.

29

The vibro-alarm had barely begun its gentle waking cycle when Daniel rose from his bed. His feet hit the ground, catlike, and he was dressed in a matter of seconds.

He was ready – for what, he didn't know, but he'd barely slept all night. Every time he closed his eyes, the nexus was there to greet him, looming, pulsing, ripping his mind. He knew it was coming, this event-entity, or at least thought he knew; a confluence of events bigger than history itself.

And I'm at the center of it all.

This quasi-knowledge was maddening; and even more maddening was the fact that he had no idea what any of it meant. It seemed to smack of the portentous, and mystical, and he felt unprepared to deal with either subject.

He took a deep breath and stopped in front of the mirror for a final look at himself. His face, boyish and round, caught him almost by surprise. His flesh was young, but what was inside had hardened. The experience of being a Controller, especially, had changed and matured him.

He straightened his silver singlet, smoothing his dark hair.

Ready or not, Earth, here I come.

He smiled, allowing himself a moment of blissful fantasy.

A walk down the beach . . . her hand in mine . . . the ocean, perfect backdrop for romance . . .

Thinking of *her* caused him to bite his lip suddenly, as he was reminded of his upcoming mission and what it would entail.

Whatever happens, she must survive.

Grim resolve gripped him, and with a last glance in the mirror, he stooped, picked up the single garment bag he'd packed, and left the room without looking back.

The shuttle launch bay was empty when he got there, save for two workers dressed in drab olive-green. Daniel ignored them and walked directly to shuttle bay nineteen, where the craft waited that would take himself and Agent Randall to the surface.

He popped the vacuum-sealed side door and peered inside, noting with satisfaction that his VR gear and swarm control unit had been neatly packed and delivered, per his instructions of the night before. He slung his bag onto the cushioned seat nearest the door.

"Daniel."

Grandfather's gravelly voice could not be mistaken, though Daniel's back was turned. He stiffened despite himself, but with an act of will quickly slipped into his 'acquiescent grandson' persona.

Nothing can go wrong! I must go to the surface!

He turned around slowly, with a smile he allowed all the way into his eyes. "Hello, Grandfather. I didn't expect to see you this morning. Is everything all right?"

Grandfather laughed, a little too loudly, and Daniel was relieved to see that the old man was having to fake it just as hard as he was. "Not be here? To see my only grandson off on what could be a great adventure? You underestimate me, my boy! I wouldn't miss it!"

Daniel relaxed a little when he understood that plans for his trip to Earth had not been changed, and even smiled cordially at Randall, who'd appeared like a wraith in the shadow of Lazaro Sol's black-cowled figure.

"You have everything you need, then?"

"Yes, Grandfather."

"Good, good. Now, listen . . . you'll be working with a man named DaLuge - Simon DaLuge - and also with General Kirkland, one of our most trusted military commanders. I've instructed them to take good care of you and treat you with the same respect they would show me. If you need anything – anything at all, you hear? – you get ahold of me and I'll make sure it happens."

Daniel had to contain a derisive laugh at hearing the old man go on like this, and just barely did so by faking a sneeze.

Why is he trying so hard to be so caring? What's he covering up? He's definitely glad to see me go – I'm sure of that. Only grandson, indeed.

"Thank you, Grandfather." He looked at Randall. "Are you ready?"

The small gray man smiled a demure grin that was somehow shark-like. "Always, young sir," he said, and gestured toward the shuttlecraft's open door with a repulsively gallant motion. "After you."

Daniel boarded the craft, suddenly very, very bothered by something that had just occurred to him, as he was saying good-bye..

Only Grandson. His only grandson. But . . . what of my parents? Who were they?

Randall was saying something, but Daniel barely registered that the Agent was speaking at all. His mind was far away, absorbed in thought, as the bay door began to slide open, revealing the moon and the star-studded void beyond. The most disturbing question of all loomed dark and ominous in his mind.

Why in all hells am I only just now wondering about all this?

Nothing could have prepared him for the ride that followed.

The shuttle crept from behind the moon and he caught his first real-time glimpse of Earth, hanging bejeweled in space like a giant blue bubble. His breath stuck in his throat, and a wild feeling possessed him, momentarily eclipsing his distress and confusion. He had to breathe deeply to contain himself, and noticed Randall looking at him with a sidelong stare.

In order to cover his emotional reaction, he engaged the pilot in meaningless conversation. "Make this run often, do you?"

The pilot was a large man with a shock of bright red hair and an embroidered orange crest on the front of his smart silver-gold singlet, denoting his credentials. He turned to look back over his shoulder and did a double-take, as if he wasn't used to being addressed by his passengers.

"Talkin' to me, were ya?" He grinned good-naturedly. "Yeah, I do this run at least three times a week. Lot of supplies coming up here. Not too many people, though."

"How long does it take?"

"What, the ride down? Not long. Forty-five minutes, maybe. Take a few minutes to get docked, once we're down. Should be a nice easy ride, though. What about you, sport? How long since you been down there?" He gestured at the planet in the viewscreen.

"Me? I . . . " Daniel broke off his reply as he realized that for some reason, he didn't want to admit that in fact he couldn't remember.

"Might I point out, sir," Randall said, "that your lap belt is loose. Perhaps you would like to adjust it." The Agent's tone was easy, but there was a hard glint in his eye.

"Uh . . . yes, thank you."

Daniel adjusted his belt, grateful for the distraction . . . and aware of something else, as well.

He did that on purpose. No one is to know who I am . . . or was. He was trying to distract the pilot so he wouldn't ask me any more personal questions.

The distress, and its companion, confusion, were back again, with the central, over-riding question at the bottom of all the other questions.

Who am I? Who am I REALLY?

"Might get a little bumpy," the red-haired pilot intoned. "We'll be entering the atmosphere in a minute."

He'd barely gotten the words out when the small craft shuddered and pitched hard. Daniel's stomach lurched, and he grasped the handle built into the panel next to his seat.

The pilot laughed and whooped as the craft righted itself and began to burn through the atmosphere.

"What a ride! I never get tired of it."

Daniel was surprised at the feeling he'd gotten when the craft swayed, and now took a moment to examine it. It wasn't panic, or even fear, but rather a giddy sort of elation; a surprise at being truly alive.

He breathed deeply, imagining he could taste the fresh air outside, though he knew the shuttle's life support system to be completely closed and self-sufficient.

The planet grew larger by the minute, the sunlight brighter as it refracted through the upper atmosphere, now miles above them. All sense of Earth's being a ball in space was lost as the landscape (real land!) loomed ever nearer, the horizon a bluish-white arc at the edge of sight. The craft shuddered again, and Daniel noticed that the temperature inside the craft, though regulated, had risen at least a degree or two.

"Almost there," the pilot shouted over his shoulder. "Only a couple minutes now."

A few wisps of cloud shot past, then more striated, puffy masses, and within moments, they were through the cloud cover and coming in fast over a gray, choppy sea that seemed to fly away behind them at an incredible speed.

Daniel strained his neck to look, captured by the novelty, the freshness, of what he was seeing. For a moment, he spied only water in every direction, but then, distant but fast approaching, a gray-blue line began to grow on the horizon. Soon he could see that this was land; a long stretch of cliffs, and a series of ridges beyond them, stretching inland further than he could see.

He was spellbound by the rugged beauty of the land. Some of the cliff-faces dropped sheer into the crashing ocean below, while others descended more gently to pristine white beaches, stretching away to the north. Directly ahead, and apparently their destination, a massive complex of structures rose pristine from the top of the cliff.

As the craft slowed and banked to land, coming in low, Daniel heard the huge breakers below, crashing into the rock and sending up gouts of spray. A moment later, visibility was broken by a three-walled concrete enclosure with a landing pad in the middle. The engines whined as the pilot cut the thrust for landing, then gently set their craft down in the center of the pad.

"Welcome to Clifftop, gentlemen," he said. He un-snapped his restraint, thick fingers dancing over the control touch-pad as he keyed in the shutdown sequence. The whine of the engines cycled down to a low hum.

The door opened with a whoosh, and Randall rose to his feet, snapping his gray felt hat onto his head.

"Follow me," he said to Daniel, in a voice that brooked no reproach. "Leave your things. They'll be delivered to your new quarters shortly."

Daniel did as he was told. As he descended the few steps to the slick concrete pad, all his senses prickled at the unfamiliar, all-consuming reality of the world around him.

Such a dazzle to the senses! As they walked from the enclosed landing area into the clear morning air, he nearly swooned at the sight of the ocean, the intricacy of the clouds as they rode, swift and silent, on the cool salt wind blowing in across the waves.

Real wind on my face!

He felt like weeping.

"I believe they are waiting for you, sir."

Randall's voice was just short of sounding impatient, and Daniel realized he'd stopped and was simply staring at everything; the clouds, the trees that ringed the fortress, the sky.

He cleared his throat and willed himself back to the moment.

Can't let down my guard. They're watching me. I have to act as expected.

He cleared his throat. "Sorry," he said slowly. "A bit of vertigo, or jet-lag, or what have you. I guess it's been a while since I've been off the Station. Just getting my 'earth legs', you might say." He tried a laugh at his little joke, but it sounded false and awkward.

A hint of a smile graced Randall's sardonic features. "When you're ready then, young master."

They'd walked only a few more paces down the wide walkway – expertly paved with smooth, rust-colored cobblestones - before the sound of voices reached them, coming from somewhere near the herculean front entrance of the mammoth main building. Daniel couldn't help staring at it; it was a gigantic structure, built in grand nineteenth-century gothic style, with huge stone columns flanking the wide, imposing main doors.

Two men in white lab coats were walking toward them, speaking in low tones. The shorter, and younger, of the two held a bustling clipboard and was hurriedly taking notes of what the older man was saying, barely looking up as he walked.

The older man had an unruly mop of wispy, sandy-gray hair and a hawk-like nose, thin lips and widely spaced, piercingly intelligent eyes. Old fashioned spectacles rode his brow haphazardly. When they were only a few meters away, he looked up and his gaze locked with Daniel's, seeming to assess him in the space of a moment, then flicked to the gray-suited Agent beside him, his thin lips stretching into a forced smile.

"Agent Randall! It's good to see you again. And this must be Daniel, I presume? Welcome to Clifftop, sir, and may I say we're quite happy to have you. My companion is Mr. Sneed, my personal assistant, also in charge of one of our laboratories here. I'm Simon DaLuge, head of research operations.

I've worked closely with your grandfather on many projects, and he's asked me to work with you, to show you around and make you feel comfortable. Any questions you have, you come to me."

A dozen questions jumped instantly to Daniel's lips, but he bit them back with a forced smile of his own. "Thank you, Dr. DaLuge. I'm sure I'll be quite comfortable here."

"If you would be so kind . . . " Randall's voice was smooth as oiled wood. "I'm sure the young master would like to inspect his lodgings."

"Of course!" DaLuge smiled, revealing uneven teeth that were beginning to yellow. "I have the information right here . . . " He dug in one of the many pockets of his white lab coat and produced a crumpled sheet of paper. "Block 13, suite 10. Right across the lawn there and to the right. The living quarters are right past the apple trees." He gestured at a small grove of trees, a double line that roughly marked the spot where the front section of the main building ended.

The grounds seemed exotic, almost opulent to Daniel, and he continued to absorb everything around him as they walked across the lawn.

Huge stone columns supported the massive façade of the building, and no expense had been spared in the immaculate landscaping of the property. Roses of unnatural size and beauty bloomed next to a fountain shaped like a naked woman, from whose mouth and breasts trickled water that had been treated to shimmer and sparkle unnaturally in the afternoon light. Stone walkways wound through mazes of ivy trellises and trimmed hedges shaped like abstract, almost grotesque geometrical images.

DaLuge accompanied them, strolling along with hands behind his back, acting for all the world like a nonchalant tour guide.

"The trees are one of my projects," he was saying. "Normally apple trees wouldn't grow this close to the ocean; the weather is simply much too cold and volatile. These trees were enhanced genetically, and I chose to use them because they make an excellent wind break; and, I must add that the smell is heavenly, even when they're not in bloom. I think you'll appreciate it, once you see where you're staying."

Within moments, DaLuge's words were proven true, as their feet found a winding stone path through the apple trees. The smell was indeed heavenly, and Daniel had to carefully monitor himself to keep from grinning like a stupid kid at the sensual assault. Great golden apples weighted the rustling branches, and he had to wonder at the absurdity of ripe apples this early in the year.

The path broke into a wide lawn, immaculately manicured and hemmed in on the far side by a thick, towering hedge. To the left was the yawn of space beyond the cliff's edge and the roar of the ocean; to the right, a low line of three or four comfortable-looking condominiums, each with a small brick courtyard facing west. Along the line of the cliff was a low brick wall covered with climbing ivy, atop which were ceramic pots filled with flowers, their small colorful buds swinging in the gusting breeze.

"Ah! Here we are," DaLuge exclaimed, coming to a halt on the chipped flagstone of the second condominium's patio. He entered a quick key sequence on the reader, and the large glass door slid silently to the right, revealing a posh studio.

Daniel entered, relieved to be stationary for a bit. He hoped they would all leave soon, so he could be alone with his thoughts. The beginnings of a headache ghosted through back-alley circuits in his over-stimulated brain, and suddenly he felt tired, though he knew his day had only just begun.

My God!

Only an hour previous, he'd stood in the shuttle bay, looking out at black space from the orbit of the moon, a quarter of a million miles from where he now stood. The sheer distance involved was staggering, but this was not what was bothering him.

"Daniel?" DaLuge's voice held concern that sounded genuine, but seemed somehow wrong. "Are you feeling all right?"

A finely beaded sweat had broken out on his forehead, but he held control of his voice, forcing a smile. "Fine. I think I'm space-lagged, that's all. Perhaps I could rest for an hour before continuing the tour? And a bite to eat might be nice, as well."

"Of course!" DaLuge's smile was too broad, and this did not escape Daniel's attention. "If you need anything, use the com unit by the bed. Ask for Martine; she's the concierge responsible for this section. If you want to explore the grounds, feel free. If you use the inside door, it will take you to all of our guest facilities. Come on, Mr. Sneed – we have work to do."

The two of them left, and Daniel flopped on the bed, ignoring Randall, who'd taken a post just outside the patio door. His gray felt hat spun idly through his fingers.

Daniel closed his eyes, squeezed them shut for a full two minutes, trying to wish the Agent away, but when he looked again, Randall was still there, watching him from the corners of his flat eyes.

"You don't have to stay here, you know." Daniel could not keep the edge from his tone. "I'll be perfectly fine by myself. I think I might take a nap in a while. I've been rather busy lately, and I think I must be tired from the flight." He knew this excuse was lame, but blundered on anyhow. "I have nothing on the schedule today, correct? Nothing until tomorrow morning?"

"General Kirkland would like to have dinner with you this evening at 1900 hours local," Randall said, his expression inscrutable. "It would be a good thing." He hesitated, then added, "If you feel up to it, of course."

"Of course."

"Very well, then." Randall placed his hat tightly on his head and pulled it snug with a practiced flair. "I'll be here at 1850 hours. You have all the usual amenities at your disposal, and your VR gear should be delivered soon. A good afternoon to you." He left silently, and Daniel heaved a huge sigh of relief.

When he was certain he was alone, he rose and walked out on the patio, wanting nothing more than to look at the ocean and breathe the fresh sea air. The wind rose to meet him, blowing a dusting of leaves across the flagstone. In the distance, scudding clouds scuffed the blue horizon, and closer in, a whirl of gulls screeched and cawed, one or another occasionally landing on the low brick wall and eyeing him hungrily.

He closed his eyes and drew deep breaths, allowing himself the joy of the moment despite the mounting turbulence within him. The boom of the surf at the foot of the cliff, hundreds of feet below, was like a balm for his senses.

I'm really here!

This self-manifestation was pure joy, and he let it take him for now. Let the chips fall where they may. A vision passed before his inner eye, of red-blond hair and shining eyes. She smiled serenely at him.

I love you, Daniel.

She was his destiny. She must survive.

30

Maia sat alone in the greenhouse, listening to the slight breeze that played listlessly in the trees outside. Her thoughts were scattered, and she felt alone and psychically bruised.

At least the tests had stopped; that was something she could be thankful for. After she'd returned from her mysterious three-day absence, she'd felt like a science experiment for a few days, what with the endless barrage of skin samples and psychological tests. It was maddening, and frustrating, especially with everything else that was going on.

Not that she blamed anyone. She understood why Stark had felt the tests necessary. The mood in the compound was beyond tense – emotions ran high everywhere, and there was every reason for full precaution to be taken.

It didn't help that she couldn't remember where she'd been, or what had happened to Johnny. How to explain these absences . . . or the fact that this was not the first time? Before now, she'd never even considered the need for an explanation, even for herself . . . and for the first time, she was beginning to wonder why.

She'd been naïve, that much was obvious. *Something* had definitely happened to her, and to Johnny.

Were we together those entire three days?

She didn't think so, but she was sure of nothing.

Why can't I remember?

She remembered taking him to the Falls. That day had felt sacred to her, every detail crystal clear in her memory, up until they went into the cave. At that point in her memory, after they'd eaten the mushrooms, everything went kind of swimmy; vague images cracked like shards of broken mirrors, pieces that didn't fit.

She sat back and sighed. Taking off her wool cap, she ran her hands through her mop of wavy hair and rubbed the backs of her eyelids until spheres of light popped on her retinae.

The worst of it was what had happened to Johnny.

He was back in the camp, which was a relief . . . but something was wrong with him. He seemed broken somehow - an eternal vacuum seemed to expand from somewhere behind the lights of his eyes. His skin seemed the wrong color – pale, almost translucent, his features hollow. He never seemed to eat, or to sleep either, at least not when she was near him, which didn't seem to be very often anymore.

When he could muster up the energy to communicate, it seemed to cost him a great effort. His face would contort in seeming exquisite pain as he tried to get out a sentence or two, mostly simple responses to her gentle questions.

His body seemed wrong, too. When she tried to embrace him he seemed weirdly rigid, and his skin was icy cold.

And she couldn't see him anymore, either, the way she'd been able to before. Or rather, what she did see was meaningless to her. If forced to try to explain it, she would have said that before, she could see his aura, but now it was as if he were *all* aura. When she tried to see him in that way, there was nothing but a smoking, rose-colored darkness that eluded her attempts at visualization.

Whatever the case, it didn't seem to be a simple psychological problem. Something was very, fundamentally *wrong* with Johnny Perdue.

Even the tests which Stark and Scott administered had confirmed this.

For one thing, they couldn't seem to get any accurate readings of his vital signs. His core body temperature seemed to fluctuate between literally zero degrees and something over a hundred fifty. His heart rate, too, was extremely erratic, to the point where there had been times when it seemed to disappear completely for a few minutes at a time.

At first they'd been convinced that there was a problem with the equipment, but when further tests eliminated this possibility, it became a source of much speculation and tension. Everyone was baffled, including Doctor Tinney. Out of earshot of the others, and especially Johnny, he'd confided to Maia that it was the most unusual thing he'd ever heard of, including the very strange case of Karla Aldridge.

Thinking of Karla was no help, and Maia roughly pulled on her cap and stood up. She needed to get outside, into the air.

The afternoon showed a hint of sun as she blinked into it, and the sulking breeze brought earthy smells that reminded her of the coming spring. Normally this would have made her smile, but the good feelings that wanted to come somehow got mixed up with thoughts of Karla, and Johnny, and all the other things she wouldn't be able to enjoy this spring.

She burst into tears, unable to control the sudden onslaught of sadness. It was the worst feeling she'd ever experienced; equal parts loneliness, vulnerability and helplessness, it consumed her completely.

Abby Carmichle, walking up the trail with a wheelbarrow load of fertilizer, heard her and called out in concern.

"Maia! What's wrong?"

Maia couldn't answer. She shook her head, trying to say she was sorry, that she would be okay, but those words weren't true and wouldn't come out anyway. Instead she broke and ran like a child, weeping openly and wildly into the welcome oblivion of the forest pathways.

Mindless, her feet picked their way along seldom-used trails, higher along the ridge than anyone normally traveled. All sound of human contact faded away, and she found herself alone, the only sounds the padding of her sandals on the path.

After fifteen minutes of walking, she came to a place she knew well, though she hadn't been there in years. It was a high, level ledge that overlooked the valley above the compound. A natural bench of stone protruded from an ancient boulder, and she flopped down, exhausted and glad to be sitting.

Dark, silent deciduous trees hemmed her on both sides; on a level with her eyes, a lone hawk floated above the green valley, riding into the beat of the wind. She watched it waiting there, nearly motionless, for nearly a full minute, and then the bird spotted some movement – perhaps a mouse far below – and plummeted in a deep, silent dive, out of her field of vision.

Along the incline of the opposing ridge, shadows of clouds moved inexorably, deepening the sense of rich greenness that this place always seemed to exude.

She took a deep, cleansing breath, feeling almost relaxed, then exhaled slowly, relishing the air, clean and cold on her neck and face. A shaky sense of perspective returned, incomplete but welcome.

It will be all right.

The words soothed her, though she didn't believe them.

She remembered suddenly that she'd had a reason to go to the falls with Johnny that day, a reason for eating the mushrooms. There had been a plan, hadn't there? She'd been preparing to see Karla, to . . .

To try and heal her? You're crazy, Maia. You know that, don't you? Who do you think you are? A magician? She needs medicine, not voodoo.

These unwelcome thoughts angered her, and she gritted her teeth, trying to summon the feeling that she could make a difference for Karla. She reminded herself that once she had healed a swamp lily, had reached out to it and brought it from crushed death back to health and fullness with only the force of her attention.

Closing her eyes, she visualized a mantra and repeated it internally, until her breathing had returned to normal and the fist of stone around her heart had loosened its hold.

> *I am a child of the universe.*
> *I am a being of light.*
> *The power of light is the power of love.*
> *The power of love is the power of life.*
> *Life is the essence of the universe.*
> *I am a child of the universe.*

She didn't know where the words came from,
(Milos)
but she repeated them stoically, again and again, and with their repetition she gradually returned to the state of inner watchfulness and clarity she'd been seeking.

She sat that way for an hour or more, simply *being*, letting the afternoon soak through her, shades of sunlight and shadow dappling fern and bracken, smells both divine and pungent wafting on soothing swells of breeze.

When she felt more like herself, she rose without premeditation and set off, back to the compound, with resolution in her step and conviction in her heart.

She would try to help Karla.

She waited until after dinner was over and made her way back to the tunnel complex. Pushing aside the blanket that was pinned across the door to Karla's room, she stooped and entered.

The smell hit her like it always did; the cloistering, sterile odor of impending death. She wrinkled her nose against it and pushed away all negative thoughts.

I'm here for one reason. I can't forget that.

In the corner, the small monitor showing Karla's vital signs beeped relentlessly, one tick after the next, as her heart pushed blood through the channels of her body. She was on a respirator now, an ancient, hideous thing Dr. Tinney had unearthed from the deep piles of parts and electrical bracken in one of the 'bone rooms' – the store-rooms where John Stark stored all the equipment and pieces of equipment that weren't immediately needed. The respirator stood at the foot of Karla's bed like a mad sentry to the netherworld, dials protruding like devils' horns, tubes like whips encircling the bed. The sucking whine of the thing was a sound that Maia knew might soon drive her mad.

Next to the bed, the squelching buzz of the grid shield continued to make sure no one received the rogue radio signal being generated by Karla's shrunken, limp body.

"Oh, hi Maia." Allie's voice was low from the hammock chair she perpetually occupied now, at the head of her daughter's bed. "How are you, dear?"

"I suppose I'm all right." Maia looked around, noting the doctor's absence for the first time. "Tinney's not in?"

"He left a while ago, for dinner. I don't blame him for getting out – things are pretty steady here. Karla's breathing a little better today, thank God. Yesterday I thought she might not survive the week." The resignation in Allie's voice chilled Maia.

Karla's not going to make it and everyone knows it. They've all given up, even her mother.

Allie gestured absent-mindedly at a rickety folding chair. "Won't you sit with me for a while?"

The two of them spoke amiably for a few minutes, and Maia got the sense that Allie found her company cathartic. She seemed to need to talk, and Maia let her do just that until an inner sense of urgency reminded her of the reason she'd come down here in the first place.

She laid her hand gently on the other woman's forearm. "Allie," she said, "you need to get out of here. Diana made a great stew tonight, and there's a lot left. You should go eat. See a few people. Like you said, things are pretty steady here. I can sit with Karla until you get back."

Allie hesitated, and Maia saw her gaze turn reluctantly from her daughter's inert form to the doorway. "Well . . . " she said, "I *have* been meaning to go up for dinner one of these nights. I won't be gone long, you understand, just an hour or so . . . "

"Go along," Maia said with a smile. "Everything will be fine here. And there's Dr. Tinney's hand-com if anything happens." She gestured at the small radio on the corner of the doctor's cluttered desk space.

"Well . . . " Allie's voice was reluctant, but she was smiling. "I suppose it will be all right. Let me just get my shawl."

Maia waited until Allie had been gone for a few minutes, then walked silently to the door and peered out, checking the hallway.

A few rag-lamps burned in their sconces on the walls, illuminating the hall with ghost-light and sending greasy smoke out the front bunker entrance. She heard muffled coughing and low conversation from two or three of the other rooms in the section, but no one seemed to be out and about. Really, the only people likely to come down here tonight were the doctor, the Aldridges, and Johnny.

She knew that Jeremieah Aldridge was working with John Stark tonight, going over the camp's limited firearm supply, checking and labeling. They would be at it all night, she knew; it was high priority right now. They had to get all the weapons inspected and distributed to the various stockpile points in the valley where people were to go in the event of trouble, and with Johnny out of commission, Control was hurting for bodies.

The doctor was known for his long jaw – he was probably sitting around the fire with Bud Arney this very moment, getting drunk on Bud's private stash of homemade corn hooch and regaling whoever would listen with old war stories.

Maia thought she could count on Allie being gone for at least three-quarters of an hour. And Johnny . . . well, who knew where he might turn up? Either way, he wasn't likely to come down here.

She returned to Karla's bedside and laid a hand on the little girl's face. A pang of sadness threatened to envelop her as she noted how much her little friend had changed. Karla's once-chubby, rosy-cheeked face was pale and wan, skin shrunken around bruised eyes, except for the left side, where her skin was distended and leathery, and an unnatural shade of purple. Her body was stick-thin, her breathing raspy and labored.

With a mountainous effort Maia shook off the sadness, returning her mind to her task.

I am a child of the universe. I am a being of light.

She took Karla's hand and focused her energy on *seeing* Karla in the way that only she knew how, relaxing her eyes and letting her body take over. As her resolution grew, the room lost clarity, and only she and the girl remained.

She perceived Karla's aura suddenly, a pulsing, red-veined balloon of thundercloud black. As she did, a blinding pain coursed through her, a white-bright terror that shook her focus. She bore down harder, ignoring her terror, intent on one thing

healing

and one thing only. She pushed out with all her psychic energy, and perceived a cord of silver light, snaking from her abdomen and pumping life into Karla's body. The two of them were joined suddenly, and the force of the psychic experience jarred Maia so that again she nearly lost her focus.

The power of light is the power of love.

Maia held on with all her inner strength as the melding deepened. She began to *feel* Karla, to perceive her inner dreamworld. Torrid visions raced behind her eyelids, jagged remnants of eons in nightmarish worlds, an eternity of white-hot pain. A vision manifested, and she knew she was sharing Karla's experience directly.

She saw the room they were in from a place somewhere above their heads. The small space was fractured with hell-light, distorted and congealed in a red-orange forever moment. She saw herself just as she was at this moment, holding the girl's hand, eyes rolled up in her head. But the vision locked into terrible, slow motion, sliding by interminably. As she watched herself, she saw a fly that had landed on her arm begin to move. Each beat of its iridescent wings lasted an eternity, and minutes passed before it gained flight, moving with such breathtaking slowness that it appeared to be simply hanging in midair. She experienced it with excruciating, vivid detail; the sound that the fly's wings made was grotesque and rasping. It nauseated her.

A mind-numbing sound blasted awareness, and something in her screamed and tried in vain to cover her ears against the skirling reverberations. A few moments passed and the sound dissipated. She was vaguely aware that it had been the buzzing of the grid shield that she'd heard, but it was distorted and much, *much* too loud.

Suddenly, it was *all* too much. She let go of Karla's hand and fell to the floor, gasping, all focus lost. Echoes pounded through her head, and the seeping darkness that was Karla's aura filled her mind. Red-dim images clung to her, pulling her in, and it took all of her inner control just to breathe.

The world returned to itself slowly. The dull thudding in her skull dissipated and left her with a ringing headache. She felt drained, disoriented. A sob shook her body, convulsing her.

How can one person stand so much pain and still be alive?

She had shared Karla's awareness, and saw now how awful it was. The girl lived in perpetual slow motion, acutely aware of the world around her in full, excruciating detail. Maia shuddered at the memory. And she'd only shared the experience for a matter of seconds.

How many eons have passed in her mind?

Living in that eternity of awareness would drive the most rational mind to madness.

And she's only a little girl!

Maia suddenly understood Johnny's passion when he raged about the Government and the Establishment. This was *horrible*. It was beyond bad and into the realm of pure evil.

And she knew now that she could do nothing about it.

For the second time today, she broke down and cried, huge uncontrollable sobs that wracked her body and left her limp and spent.

Life is the essence of the universe.

The words had lost their meaning. Nothing could quell this pain. She would have bolted from the room if it wouldn't have meant leaving Karla alone. It took all of her willpower to remain seated beside the bed.

Gradually the force of her crying subsided, and she was left feeling completely empty, husked out and washed clean by her tears.

When Allie returned, half an hour later, Maia was composed. She'd tied her hair back and washed her face in the basin, and sat beside the bed holding Karla's hand. She managed a smile as Allie came into the room, and was happy to see that Allie looked better, too.

"You were right, Maia," she said. "That stew was *good.*"

31

A long ridge of windows, halfway up the side of the sprawling Clifftop complex, caught the afternoon sun's full glare, reflecting it back at an unseeing ocean. Overhead, gulls wheeled in the brisk sea breeze, calling to one another and looking for a morsel from any of the few technicians, scientists, or other off-duty personnel who might be out for a walk and inclined to share some bread or a cookie.

In the near distance, the surf pounded at the foot of the four-hundred foot cliff that was this establishment's namesake, but this sound could not be heard inside the room with the ridged windows.

"Sir? If we could just go over this topographical display once more, we could . . . Sir?"

Daniel tore his gaze away from the scene outside. It seemed too surreal, anyway – the tinted permaplast gave the windblown afternoon a dark cast that didn't do justice to what it would feel like to be out in it. Now that was something he wouldn't mind investing some time in.

But it wasn't to be.

Earlier, the thought had crossed his mind to steal a car this afternoon – to just leave, to go find a place to walk on the beach by himself . . . but this, of course, was out of the question. He could afford no slip-ups if he was going to find out what was going on here; he must act exactly as was expected of him.

Give them no reason to suspect anything.

He cleared his throat, looking around the table at the motley group assembled there.

"Yes, Mr. Sneed? You were saying?"

Sneed shuffled the stack of printouts in his hand, feathered one across the table to Daniel. "The topography of the valley in question," he said. "If you look . . . "

"I'm quite aware of the valley in question," Daniel said, his voice tired. "I'm the one who found it in the first place, remember? Now, I've spent some time looking it over, and I'm still not convinced of the validity of this mission! Where is the proof that these people are a terrorist faction at all? They seem hardly able to do more than maintain their meager existence. I know what my grandfather believes, and of course the General here agrees, but is there really reason for all of this . . . " He waved a hand vaguely in the air, trying to find the right word. " . . . this incessant *briefing*? This 'mission' is, what do you call it

. . . a cakewalk. I could take one good Controller team in there and have the place cleaned out by dinnertime tonight."

Simon DaLuge, sitting further down the table, noticed the look of silent alarm that crossed the General's face at Daniel's mention of his Controller status. The military used Control teams, of course, but Daniel seemed a bit of a wild card – he didn't look like a Controller, for one thing, and the General had good reason to be concerned. The way things were made to appear to him, this whole operation seemed questionable – Lazaro Sol's bratty grandson put in charge of something he wasn't qualified for – and a Controller, to boot? The whole thing smacked of nepotism.   The thought amused him.

You have to hand it to the old buzzard.

Lazaro Sol had everybody snowed. The boy believed he was here to complete this mission, after which he was to be initiated as a full Elder. The General believed that a legitimate terrorist faction had been found in the wild, little more than a hundred miles from this hub of classified activity.

Neither knew that they were pawns in a much larger game.

General Kirkland cleared his throat. "Sir . . . " he said, addressing Daniel with all the respect due a full Elder – despite his misgivings, he would never dare go against orders that came all the way down from Planetary Security - "
. . . sir, if you don't mind my saying so, there are simply other considerations. The faction in question . . . "

"You mean this group of campers?" Daniel said coldly, looking him in the eye as he said it. "Let's not play games, Mr. Kirkland."

Mister Kirkland?

Somewhere in the back of DaLuge's mind, a silent alarm went off.

He knows too much. And he's getting cocky.

"Of course you're right, Daniel," he interjected smoothly, sitting forward with a smile, hoping he could mediate between Daniel and the five-star General the boy had just insulted. "But regardless of the terminology, these 'campers', as you call them, have technology that renders satellite scans useless. You know as well as I that the Organization would like a chance to study this technology – if it's possible we've overlooked one group, then how many others might be out there? You are of course aware that these orders came directly from your grandfather?"

"Grandfather plays his own games," Daniel said. "He . . . " He stopped abruptly, bit his lower lip, hard, as if holding back a flood of bad feeling.

DaLuge had a sudden moment of clarity.

The program didn't entirely take. He hates his 'grandfather' too much to be healthy. And Lazaro Sol knows it, too - that's why the boy is here.

Out loud, DaLuge continued, keeping his voice soft, non-threatening: "There are other concerns, as well, Daniel. Certain of our micro-technologies have fallen into the wrong hands. This presents a security risk, in and of itself."

"The mosquito infection, you mean?" Daniel's tone was cold. "The microbotic sequencers? Have you seen the vid-feed, man? These miserable people can't even construct a way to help the poor girl, much less learn the secrets of the technology!"

"This has gone on long enough!" The General rose halfway from his chair, pounding his fist on the table. "We have our orders, dammit! It's not up to us to question. Not even you, Sir," he said, addressing Daniel. "Not even if the orders came directly from your grandfather. I would think you might be trying to prove your worth to him, and to this Organization, instead of . . . of . . . "

DaLuge caught the edge of frustration in the General's voice, tensed himself to intervene, but Daniel spoke first, his eyes steely and reserved.

"I apologize, General," he said in a low tone. "You're right that it's not my place to question. Grandfather saw fit to put me in charge of this mission, and I'll do it to the best of my abilities. But you above all should understand the value in counsel." He paused, seemed to assess Kirkland, eyes slightly narrowed. "I trust I've not offended you? We'll need to work together, you and I, to co-ordinate the details of this mission."

The General, who had been poised like a hawk above the table, relaxed visibly, drawing a deep breath. His heavy features smoothed out.

"You have not offended me, Sir," he said. "And I'm pleased to cooperate with you on this assignment." He sighed. "And, if I were to state my opinion frankly, son . . . well, I, like you, might not think this mission deserves the priority it's received. But our job is to act on the information we've been given, not to ask questions or state opinions."

"Quite right," Daniel said gravely. He turned to the white-coated Sneed. "You were speaking of topography?"

The meeting began to proceed on schedule, and DaLuge watched, wheels spinning in his mind.

The boy suspects something. That whole display was a sham – he knows the futility of trying to change the mind of anyone here. He was trying to gain information! Otherwise, why the sudden change in mood? If only we could get him back on the Elepro . . .

He sat back, taking in the meeting, watching Daniel carefully. He hoped Lazaro Sol was right when he'd said that Daniel's personal interest in the forest compound could distract him for another month. If not . . .

Without the drugs, this boy could be dangerous.

Staring at the sunset from the windows of his quarters, Daniel felt nervous; unsatisfied. From a military standpoint, the meeting this afternoon had gone well. All the pieces were in place; the General's squadrons were on alert and undergoing daily training exercises in preparation for what promised to be a routine maneuver. These military units would be complemented by Daniel's Controller team, a relatively small squad of forty grunts with which he'd be working over the next few weeks. He'd drilled them twice already, and they were a tight team.

No, there were no problems with the plan. In fact, it was ridiculously simple.

The Controller team would move in and take out any initial resistance. They would be followed by the overwhelming force of Kirkland's special-ops military teams, who would seal the valley and take control of all target technologies, including the mysterious shielding technology and the unfortunate little girl who'd been attacked by the mosquitoes.

The problem, for Daniel, was one of incessant questions and few answers. He'd tried to rock the boat a little at the meeting, to punch holes in the smooth fabric of the operation to see what sort of light would shine through . . . but he felt it had been a largely unsuccessful maneuver.

Simon DaLuge, now – there was a mystery. What were his motives? He seemed above this place, somehow, like a person convinced that he's living someone else's dream, and is just waiting to wake up. And yet DaLuge was, without a doubt, the brains behind nearly all the scientific marvels currently brewing in Clifftop's many laboratories. Daniel didn't know how many levels Clifftop had. He had access to 'official' blueprints, of course, and he'd seen all six of the laboratory levels that showed on those diagrams . . . but he knew that didn't mean much.

Since arriving at the complex, his questions had only multiplied. He didn't trust anything about this place, nor any person in it. Everything he saw pointed to a scheme of which no one seemed to know the whole – of course, this was a secret installation, and as such, information would obviously be on a need-to-know basis . . .

And this, of course, was the real problem. It was his need to know that was twisting him, feeding on his fear and isolation, filling him with devout paranoia that came to call with disturbing regularity. On Mephisto, he'd been overjoyed at the thought of leaving. He'd felt that going to the surface would be exactly what he needed. Although his schedule here was regular, the workings of his day like those of a clock, he felt more isolated than ever.

His function here was clear, and he performed it perfectly, but only because it was so easy. Too easy, in fact. Secretaries and technicians, scientists and military personnel – the day-to-day workings of Clifftop spun like cogs in perpetual perfection. Things seemed much faster here – his entire day was a schedule, served up and devoured like meat by those around him. A drill here, a meal there, the meeting of an important dignitary after lunch, the looking-over of the latest microswarm shots from the forest compound.

Even though his assignment was an easy one, Daniel knew it to be nothing but a front. It had to be – a distraction, something to keep him busy until . . .

Until what? My initiation?

Every time he thought of the mysterious ceremony to which Grandfather had alluded for the past several months, he felt an unwelcome tug of fear.

What are they going to do to me?

He could feel the answers to his questions, lurking in every humming, brightly lit laboratory, but he couldn't get to any of them. He was cut entirely off from any source of real, usable information.

It was maddening.

He tried to start casual conversations with everyone he met, thinking someone would surely know *something*, that they might perhaps part with some tidbit of information he could use . . . but the people here seemed inclined to tight lips when the subject was anything not directly related to their field of work.

He'd gone out into the air, had walked the concrete path along the top of the cliff on a few different nights, but this could not even serve to clear his head. No matter where he went, the eyes of Grandfather's pet Agent followed him, thwarting his efforts to feel free. Randall was good at staying in the background, but his ominous presence always seemed to chase Daniel back to his quarters, where he would usually toss and turn on his bed until his mind wore itself out and he could sleep.

His early-morning dreams were becoming more and more violent and surreal, and the thought had crossed his mind that he should think about requesting more of the white 'e' pills, just to see if they would help.

But this wasn't an option. It would mean admitting that he hadn't been taking the medication, and this would bring up too many questions. Whatever his fears, the answers were here – he could feel them, lurking behind everything.

But for now, there were only more questions.

She will understand. She will have the answers.

The red-haired woman; his only solace. He used as much free time as possible watching her, which wasn't ever enough. At times, it was a few days between his 'visits' to her forest home, but he always returned. He would find her sitting on the bank of the small river, or wandering the forest paths, usually alone. She was nearly always alone now, which he noted with deep, indulgent satisfaction. The young man she'd been with when he first found her seemed no longer a part of her life.

She was a vision he couldn't shake; the sorceress behind his eyes, keeping him from getting to sleep at night . . . but she was there in the morning too, chasing away those other, more disturbing visions as he awoke. Thinking of her was all that kept him from madness. He didn't know why she haunted him so, but she seemed somehow connected to the unknown purpose that had brought him to this place.

And now, with so little time left, a new plan was taking shape in his mind, a plan that he knew to be madness . . .

But then, madness lay in every direction.

She will understand. She can help me. And when she sees me, she will know, too.

Late at night, in the solitude of his quarters, only this thought gave him hope.

32

Control was a mess.

Marshall Scott observed this with a sigh as he backed through the door with two steaming mugs, one for himself, one for Perdue.

The usual state of this room – one of comfortable clutter – had begun to murk towards chaos. Readouts fell forgotten, slipping behind desks crammed with three-day-old sandwich rinds and crusted coffee-cups, chewed nubs of pencils, and pieces of broken components that should have been repaired days ago.

Unfortunately, there just wasn't time anymore for everything that needed doing. With only himself and Stark to man the place, and increasingly stressful conditions in the compound, it was all they could do just to maintain normal security.

Things had only gotten more confusing since Johnny's return.

He didn't know where he'd been. He didn't know where Maia had been. He spoke in half-sentences; rags of words that dripped in contorted mumbles from his lips and made no sense. He seemed half asleep most of the time.

"Here ya go, Perdue." Scott set the mug on the wooden desk-top next to Johnny's white, nerveless fingers. "Hot as shit and black as hell."

Johnny wouldn't drink the coffee, of course. He'd just sit there in the corner, staring through everything around him, warming his hands on the mug, letting the steam try to thaw some of the numbness. His eyes, frosted and opening inward to some unthinkable void, moved for a moment, and he mouthed a word: *"Thanks."*

Scott nodded absently. "Oh sure. Anytime, Johnny." His voice had taken on a bitter, sarcastic edge, but he didn't care.

Damn them both!

Why'd they have to leave, to go and put themselves in danger like that?

Totally idiotic, that's what I think.

He sighed, closed his eyes for a moment to let the negative feelings wash away. Bad enough that all this could happen at once. No use getting mad at your friends . . .

But it *was* hard not to notice the raft of shit that had floated into Compound West around the same time as Johnny Perdue. They hadn't had a single security breach since Marshall had been working in Control - almost nine years now. No CEC patrols or choppers had ever found their valley in more than twenty-five years. So why now?

Useless to speculate.

"You all right, Perdue?"

He knew it was a pointless question. Perdue was gone; the ghost was back. There he sat, thin hands wrapped around his mug, face buried in steam, his body rocking slightly. Scott sighed and tapped his console, then leaned over and fired up his hard drive. The ancient machine whirred to life and his screen beeped as green letters flashed boot codes.

With a final glance at Johnny, he set about his daily tasks.

Johnny watched his friend, knowing in some disconnected way that Scott was worried about him. He wished he could say or do something to ease the tension, but too much was going on within himself; too many fragments of thoughts bulleted through the fog of his mind, too many visions sparked in the dreaming ether. Hallucination made the world around him crawl – most of the time it was all he could do to remember where he was.

Marshall's head bobbed up and down as he checked readouts and ticked off routine security points on his clipboard. The air moved slowly around him, dust motes whirling. Light refracted from the cracked computer screen, splitting Johnny's vision. He shook his head and was vaguely aware that his head wasn't there.

A hum permeated his senses, and the smell of ozone suddenly assaulted his sleeping nostrils. For just a moment he was *himself* again, all Johnny, all the time . . .

He'd risen from the chair without knowing it. The hum was coming from Marshall's computer, on a shelf beneath Marshall's low table-desk. It fixated him, drawing him in.

Scott continued to mutter to himself, bent over his clipboard. He didn't see that Johnny had set down his cup and risen; he didn't see his friend moving toward him, almost gliding, eyes empty, dark and glazed.

The hum was impossibly loud. It filled Johnny's senses; he tasted ozone. The hard drive hummed louder, and with a sudden inner burst of *knowing*, Johnny *reached out* with his whole being . . .

The electricity took him.

The current jolted through him, but instead of pain he experienced an intense pleasure. The core of this pleasure was the knowledge that he was himself again, and he rode the electric current like it was a river, sweeping him through wires and plugs, along conduits and out into the compound proper.

The experience was the weirdest he'd ever had.

He saw the whole compound, *feeling* it as if it were a physical body, not his own but one assembled at a much higher frequency. The power grid reached through the tunnels of the winter camp, and he felt the whole thing, all at once.

In the kitchen bunker, Bud Arney sits and sips tea and eats dried venison. Johnny can't see him, exactly, but he can feel the older man's presence, just the same.

Hummmmmmmmmmmmmmmmmmmm . . .

In the greenhouse, where an electric current powers light bulbs, a single computer, and an automatic drip unit, Abby Carmichle squats over a hybrid tomato plant, trimming . . .

Hummmmmmmmmmmmmmmmmmmm . . .

Gurgling water splashes over Stark's current-generating river-taps, running between stones and over mossy flotsam. It is here that the electricity originates, and Johnny feels a surge of unlimited power, opening, expanding into the verdant soil, down to the bedrock of the mountain, outward into sky and space . . .

Hummmmmmmmmmmmmmmmmmmm . . .

The current spat him out, just like that. He sat up, disoriented. Around him, the forest chattered to life, alien and weird in its normality.

Hummmmmmmmmmmmmmmmmmmm . . .

He was outside, in the quiet heart of the forest.

It took him a few moments to realize that the hum was no longer coming from between his own ears. It was coming from a nearby power node – an ugly camo-green box he recognized almost immediately. He knew his position now, at least; up-valley half a mile or so from Control, deep in a stand of juniper. The node housed one of the transformers that powered the bunker system.

Fine and good . . . but how did I get here?

The box sat humming quietly.

Twilight began to thicken as the forest closed around him, easing his tension. His mind became quieter by degrees, the questions fading.

As he got to his feet and began to walk, the deeper sounds of the forest came on, all at once, electrifying his senses.

Somewhere in the near distance, water gurgled over stone. In the underbrush, a pair of blue jays twittered and sang, adding a splash of color to the glowing dusk. Ferns formed a natural, lush garden here, interspersed with large bursts of gleaming green clover and twisting viney plants with tiny white buds. And everywhere he looked, the world was limned with a preternatural light; a hallucinatory gleam that made everything somehow more real than real.

The burp and chuckle of water over stones grew progressively louder as he walked, and now he heard another sound. After a moment, he recognized it as a female voice, softly singing. The song seemed to flow within the rhythmic sound of the stream, the melody hauntingly familiar, though he couldn't place it.

Is it Maia?

He'd heard her sing a few times, but only in campfire circles. This voice didn't sound at all like Maia's; in fact, Johnny had never heard *anyone* sing like this.

He parted the overhanging branches of a small, moss-covered tree, trying to peer toward the voice, but he could see nothing. The singing had reached a new pitch, full of strident tones, elegant sweeps, mighty crescendos . . . and all with a bone-chilling softness that made Johnny want to weep. A sense of urgency overtook him, and he pushed aside the tree branches, stepping fully out into the open . . . but the singer seemed to have moved further downstream.

He picked his way carefully along the edge of the water, trying to listen and look and walk all at once. For the first time in what seemed a very *long* time, he was totally absorbed, his strange malaise forgotten. A nearly frantic need had come upon him; a near-compulsion to find the owner of this ethereal voice at all costs.

Small, flat stones lay tumbled along the edge of the water, next to larger, wet-slick rocks with hollowed-out basins on top, like tide-pools. These stood out from the darkly reflective surface of the water at random intervals, creating ripples which moved constantly but never really changed. Downstream, the water deepened, forming a pool, rimmed with swirling eddies. Beneath the mirrored surface of the pool, half a moon floated like a ghost, grinning soundlessly up at its counterpart.

Johnny stopped, transfixed; he sensed somehow that the music was now emanating from the pool itself. He thought that if it didn't stop soon, he would begin to cry. A tangible wave seemed to be spreading from his feet, through his groin and up to his head, an ecstatic vibration that was coming from the song itself. The music seemed to *have* him . . . it was carrying him away, into itself.

With the force of a vision, the singer suddenly became clear.

A woman's figure – or at least her upper half – rose like Venus from the jeweled net of reflected stars in the deep, glassy pool. Her naked skin was opaque and tangible, a swirling bluish-green color that seemed to absorb light, but also to exude it – her figure fairly glowed in the inky twilight. Her body seemed made of liquid – it was as if the river itself had been bound together by some unknown force of nature, until it had somehow fused into this unnaturally flawless form.

But it was her face that held him spellbound. Her eyes were luminescent orbs of deep, smoky jade beneath dark tangles of hair that seemed to gather silver light from the edge of dusk itself. Her hair seemed to move of its own volition, like her skin. Her dark sapphire lips drew out the breathless notes of her song like the tailing echoes of a violin, her nostrils flared slightly.

Johnny felt a strange sensation. It was like she was tugging on a part of himself that he hadn't known about; vaguely, he thought he must be imagining all of this.

But this was too *real* to be hallucination; was, in fact, the *realest* thing he'd experienced since he'd gone to the Falls with Maia, on that afternoon a million years ago. He felt as if every breath in his body was being sucked out, like he was being drained of some vital, liquid essence. More music flowed from her like aural wine; pure, thrumming vibration.

Ecstasy tore from him every desire, and every hope. He felt he was standing on an invisible shore, the music like a vision now. Faster and faster it came, obliterating him, inundating him . . .

There was a loud tearing sound suddenly, like the ripping of fabric.

The vision began to dissipate, like vapor chased before a breeze. Unbelieving, shaking in his boots, he reached out, but felt nothing except a kind of heat where she had been. As he watched, stunned, the vapor seemed to change, coalescing into the figure of a bird. Downy, snow-white wings beat the air as it hovered there before him, cawing and screeching. It was a raven, but with the exception of its red-rimmed eyes, the bird was white as virgin snow. With a loud screech, it flapped away into the night.

Johnny was rooted to the spot. He struggled to think, to make sense of it, but he was strangely numb. Thought seemed impossible; his mind was a perfect blank.

The water shone with a phosphorescent glow beneath the demon moon, tiny ripples standing out in jagged relief like wrinkles on old skin – light and shadow, shadow and light, and deeper shadow still.

33

"Ah, Simon! It's good to speak with you!" Lazaro Sol injected every bit of false good cheer he could muster into his cracked and straining voice, holding back a cough by pretending to clear his throat.

"And you, sir." DaLuge's haggard face peered from the digichrome screen on Lazaro's desk.

"How's our boy? I haven't spoken to him in a few days."

"From everything I've seen, he's exactly what we built him to be." DaLuge looked tired. "I'm sure he'll perform admirably for his mission tomorrow; in fact, there've been a few times when I've thought maybe this assignment hasn't been complex enough to really keep him busy." He hesitated. "Do you have plans for him after he's done with these . . . ahh . . . ." he cleared his throat. " . . . .terrorists? We have to keep him busy for another two weeks, you know."

"Oh, I don't think it will be a problem." Lazaro waved a hand casually. "I have several options open, depending. I'll let you know. In the meantime . . . from what you've seen, how does he shape up for the big picture?"

DaLuge favored him with a rare grin. "Oh, on that score I think we're all right. I'll have to do a thorough physical exam before we plug him in, of course, but I believe he's as good a shot as we've got right now. In fact, I'm actually hopeful for once." Lazaro sensed that his pet scientist told the truth.

He's hiding something.

"But?" he prodded gently, hoping to get it out of the man without having to dig too deep. Gods, but he was tired! His body hung in a delicate, uncomfortable balance; he'd never pushed it this close before. There had always been a young body waiting in the wings, a host waiting to be possessed, but this time there were even more important things at stake than his own continuity – which, naturally, he held in high regard. This time, the Elders' entire future was at stake – and their past as well; centuries of work and toil that justified and paid for all the wars, all the turmoil, all the pain.

Two weeks. By all hell's bells, I can last that long.

DaLuge sighed and ran a hand through his unkempt hair, squinting uncomfortably. "Well . . . " he said hesitantly, "well, now that you mention it, there is one thing. A minor hiccup, I'm sure, but I haven't got it licked yet."

"Ah." Lazaro Sol felt the heat rising in his cheeks. His pulse quickened, and he made a huge effort to bring himself under emotional control.

A HICCUP? The culmination of thousands of years of planning hangs in the balance, as well as my own personal existence, and you want to tell me about a HICCUP?

This thought was followed by another, more diplomatic one.

Delicately, Lazaro . . . delicately. If the artist is to perform, he must be bolstered and indulged.

DaLuge was simply too important; the knowledge between his ears was worth worlds. Lazaro Sol raised his eyebrows, keeping his expression bland and noncommittal.

"I'm listening."

"It's the imaging generators," DaLuge said. "I have been haunted since day one by a notion that there's a problem there. Something causing interference with the clone's abilities to assimilate the master program."

"I was thinking about it last week and decided to run some simulations," he continued, scratching absent-mindedly at the white stubble on his chin. "As far as I can tell, I think there's a decent chance it's been the generators causing the problem from the beginning – or at least a good part of it."

Lazaro Sol allowed himself to take this as good news. "Well?" He returned DaLuge's smile. "So you believe you've pinpointed the problem, then! Good for you! What's the hiccup?"

Simon appeared visibly relieved. "Apparently," he said, warming to his subject, "there's a feedback problem between the internal imaging generators and the sensory response system." He hesitated. "Do you remember when we spoke of it before?"

Lazaro pursed his lips. Truth was, he *did* remember that conversation, but it had happened more than two years prior, and he was hard pressed to recall details.

"Refresh me."

DaLuge frowned, squinted at an imaginary point somewhere above his head. "Well, sir, the problem seems to be one of processing speed. The clones we've built, Daniel included, have a much higher synaptic density than normal, as you know. The extra brain-power makes them smarter – and more neurotic – than an average person, but the extra processing speed doesn't even come into play until they're plugged in."

"The imaging generators rely on signals from the clone's sensor suit, which in turn read the miniscule muscular twitches, generated by the brain, that represent outside commands. *Our* commands."

"Oh yes." Lazaro remember some of this part. "If I remember correctly, that part is hard-wired, yes?"

"Correct. The first thing the installation program does after Contact is to set up the clone's internal 'work-station'. To him, it will appear as a virtual workbench, from which he can make any necessary system adjustments, based on our 'suggestions'." DaLuge eyed his boss warily. "You *do* have this boy under control, don't you? It would be bad if he grasped the scope of what he was and decided to go renegade. I mean, there are fail-safes, as you know – he couldn't do any *real* damage, but he could turn into a huge nuisance if ..."

"Don't worry about him," Lazaro rumbled, throwing up a hand in a derisive gesture. "I believe I'll have the proper leverage when the time comes."

And besides, I only have to get him through the Contact protocols – once the installation is complete, he'll be sedated and I'll take over his body.

DaLuge didn't know that part, of course – from his point of view, Lazaro Sol would be dead in two weeks, having passed quietly during the night, a day or so after Contact had been achieved.

DaLuge paused, raising an eyebrow. "Leverage?"

"I believe so. He's taken a more-than-healthy interest in a certain female among the group in the forest, as you know. I believe he means to take her alive."

"Really." Simon looked thoughtful. "What do you intend to do about it?"

Lazaro Sol grinned, shark-like. "I intend to let him," he said. "In fact, I intend to facilitate the process, and you're going to help me by getting a message to General Kirkland. But not yet – not yet. We'll speak of it later." He twirled two fingers of his right hand in the air. "Continue your blasted explanation before I lose all temper – my head hurts, and all this techno-babble is helping not a goddamn bit. Something about imaging generators, I believe?"

"Right. As I was saying, the program hard-wires the muscular responses coming from the brain to the sensory suit, so that the clone doesn't have to think about - for example - tensing the tip of his right index finger in tandem with a hundred or so other similar neural responses, to do something simple like regulating the satellite grid, or what have you."

"Now, here's where it gets interesting, and I have to say that this is still just a *theory*, but I'm nearly convinced that I'm right about it. The problem isn't the imaging generators themselves – all they do is create the internal 'visual' aspect of whatever the clone is seeing."

"His workstation."

"Right. A giant internal control interface. It's the center of every command, both incoming and outgoing. And here's the problem, as I see it. The processing speed is all wrong."

"The processing speed . . . ." Lazaro's head hurt from trying to wrap his brain around it; he was beginning to wish he hadn't asked.

"Right. The commands coming into the brain can be processed at an extremely high rate of speed – that's where the synaptic density comes in. But the commands *leaving* the brain have to be processed as muscular twitches, ordered and buffered in real time by the suit, which translates them into data and feeds them back into the computer. And his body's neural responses can't keep up with his brain."

Lazaro Sol shook his head. He felt dizzy. "Wait a minute," he growled. "Are you telling me that his brain is *too fast!?* Blast it, man, that was what we were going for, was it not?"

"It's not that his brain is too fast," DaLuge went on. "In order to maintain and process the required amount of information, his brain *has* to be that fast. And there's no doubt we need the sensory suit – it acts as a buffering and data ordering system, which is absolutely imperative. But I believe there's an inconsistency in processing speed, and it's causing what essentially amounts to a feedback loop. If I'm right, well . . . " He shuddered. "Let's just say it's no wonder we lost the first three. No mind could handle that sort of input."

"Tell me about this . . . feedback loop," Lazaro said, hoping he wouldn't regret asking.

"It's simple." DaLuge shrugged. "The initiate brain processes data and issues a command, which goes out through the suit. The program follows through for a micro-second, to see that the command has been carried out, but the electrical impulses in the synapses move much more quickly than those in the rest of the body's neural pathways. The brain thinks the command hasn't been received, and issues it again . . . and throws the program into a loop. The brain can't handle it, and overloads."

Lazaro nodded with clenched jaw, remembering the video feed of the last attempt. "Yes . . . yes, maybe you're right."

"I wish I wasn't."

Lazaro narrowed his eyes. "Simon," he said brusquely, "If the problem has been this . . . this *feedback loop* all along . . . well, did we make a mistake in using the Daniel program, waking him up? Should we have left him a blank slate?"

DaLuge shook his head. "I don't think so," he said slowly. "In fact, the more I think about it, I'm not sure it matters at all. But it shouldn't hurt anything. The boy's mind is resilient. No, I think we did the right thing." He laughed roughly. "It's a gamble no matter what, sir. There's no way to be sure of anything except through continued trial and error."

"Well," Lazaro growled, "I hope we get it right this time. We're all out of clones. We don't have any more room for trial or error."

DaLuge was a good man; brilliant, in fact, but Lazaro Sol wished he'd have let Simon keep all that information to himself. Without opening his eyes, he reached for the bottle of pain medication in his top desk drawer and dry-swallowed two chalky white pills with a grimace.

The screen on his desk *pinged* mellowly, and his eyes snapped open. Randall looked at him from the desk-screen, his gaze flat and even.

"Yes?"

"I assume you're still interested in any information to be had regarding the Ashbro/McElroy situation?"

Lazaro straightened in his chair, leaning forward over the screen. "Of course. What do you have?"

"As I'm sure you're aware," Randall said, "the coming coronation of our young prince is drawing quite a bit of attention from various factions of the Organization. Most of the Twelve will attend the ceremony personally, but Ashbro and McElroy are already here, at Clifftop. They've been reticent, but I've spotted them walking the grounds twice, both times together. They seemed to be conferring."

"Already there?" Lazaro felt the anger rising again. He took a long draught of stale water from the cup on his desk, slammed it down hard and closed his eyes, breathing as deeply as his wrecked lungs would allow. "Now why would they be there so soon?" He growled. "The ceremony isn't for two more weeks." He peered intently at Randall through the screen. "Is McElroy still traveling with an Agent?"

Randall nodded. "Yes, though not as openly as before. I believe he's learning."

Lazaro nodded, eyes narrowing. "Yes, with Sol Ashbro as his teacher, he's no doubt learning many useful tricks. Well, I can do nothing until I arrive, and I'm . . . decrepit, as you can see. You'll have to be my eyes and ears. If they're planning something - a coup, perhaps - then you'll have to do your best to thwart it. Talk to me in a week or so – we'll plan my arrival at Clifftop to be as secretive as possible. Until then, find out what you can."

"Very good, sir. Randall out." The screen went blank, and this time Lazaro set it for no interruption before leaning back in his chair. He closed his eyes. My, but his head did ache!

Two weeks. Only two more goddamn weeks.

34

Daniel sat next to a grounded chopper, his hands shrouded in the fine knit-chain gloves worn by every Controller. His fingers twitched and moved soundlessly over the holographic command board hovering before him in glowing orange, a product of the VR mask strapped to his face.

The chopper sat at the top of a long rise, a low hill bordering the forested training area - a few miles south of Clifftop - where he'd been working out a few last-minute kinks with his team.

DaLuge had engineered this exercise, pointing out that although Daniel's skill as a Controller was gaining a prodigious reputation, the mission in question was to involve fairly rough terrain with many obstacles, including trees, and he'd not yet had his team out in the field.

For once, Daniel agreed.

"Blue group, mark 1," he muttered softly, and the four grunts representing his 'blue' group stopped suddenly, a hundred fifty yards up and over the ridge. With little thought, he maneuvered the other five groups into the positions demanded by the drill, watching absent-mindedly with the swarm feed as they assembled and converged with lightning precision.

His mind was on something else.

Only twenty-four hours until we go in.

His days at Clifftop were filled with order and planning, and the mission had crept up on him silently as he'd fulfilled his various duties and obligations. Now, with the moment of truth at hand, he wondered if he'd be able to go through with it.

I have to go through with it. It's the only way she lives.

He knew this was true, and for what seemed the thousandth time in the last week, he steeled himself and thought of all the reasons why it was so, why it must be so . . . but in the end, reason was hollow, and he was left with a sour taste in his mouth, considering the lives that he knew would be lost tomorrow.

They're not terrorists! They're simple people, and we should leave them alone.

This conviction did nothing to change the facts.

If it wasn't me, it would be someone else. At least this way there's a chance to save her.

As usual, this was the only thought that gave him anything resembling solace, and he clung to it doggedly through the remainder of the exercise.

Later, as the deepening blanket of night closed over Clifftop, he donned his VR gear and found his way back to the forest compound and the red-haired woman, letting the swarm slip in and out of all her favorite haunts until he spotted her.

She sat alone on a boulder at the edge of the river, tossing small pebbles into the water. The image was dark as the forest night, and he had to adjust the internal brightness on his VR mask to make her out at all.

When the picture was clear, he sat back and watched her, wondering for maybe the fortieth time what her name might be. Something about her face tonight stilled him; she seemed sad, and her gaze was far away.

Though she knew nothing of his virtual presence, he was there with her in his mind, and so he sat silently in her company for an hour or more, feeling more calm than he'd felt for a very long time.

After a while, she rose and walked away from the water, and he let her go without following.

35

The roar of the chopper was a heady buzz, drilling into Daniel's brain and making it hard to think. Randall sat stoically next to him, seeming equally unmoved by the passing landscape and the lurch of the chopper as it hit pocket after pocket of dizzying turbulence.

It was a three-seater, one of the smaller ones. DaLuge had recommended using one of the larger command choppers for today's mission, but Daniel had passed on the offer out of hand. Taking favors or recommendations amounted to getting close, and Daniel didn't want to pal around with any of Grandfather's cronies.

The countryside below them was wild and picturesque, and he tried to keep his mind on this aspect, rather than his myriad worries.

A working vacation, that's all this is.

It was a hard sell; his overactive mind would not leave him alone.

Since arriving at Clifftop, a desperate plan had been gestating. Only an idea, truth be told, but he had nothing to lose and meant to try.

She must survive.

He meant to take her, pure and simple. In fact, that was the easy part.

He'd watched her enough to get a good sense of her patterns, and he knew she usually took a walk in the evening, around dusk. The strike was planned for tonight, just after sunset, which meant there was a good chance she'd be away from the main compound when the ground troops arrived. She'd probably try to flee, and this would be an ideal situation. With the swarm, he could track her and put himself in position to take her when the time came.

After that came the hard part.

How to justify such a thing?

First to Randall, whose constant hovering presence would surely demand an explanation; then, if he could get past the Agent, there was DaLuge and Grandfather to contend with.

She must survive. She must survive!

The countryside rolled by, smoothing out his thoughts; groves of poplar and pine, sun-drenched meadows, rolling hills. Coming up quickly, mountains loomed purple in the early afternoon sun. Capping some of the higher peaks, snow glistened against a pale blue sky.

The whine of the rotors shifted in frequency, and Daniel awoke from a light doze as the chopper began to nose in towards the rendezvous point; an old military base on the edge of a thousand acres of flatland, near the foothills of the mountain range which loomed directly to the east.

Looking down and to the right, Daniel saw a long strip of runway, next to a low line of aircraft hangars. The buildings were scrappy and run-down, but looked serviceable. Craning his neck, he looked behind and saw a low air control tower, which emitted no lights.

" . . . and rendezvous with General Kirkland's men," Randall was saying.

Daniel blinked and looked up, realizing that Randall had been speaking to him for a minute or so. "I'm sorry," he said. "I think I must have dozed off. What were you saying?"

Randall smiled without seeming to move a muscle. "I was going over your itinerary."

"Oh." Daniel fought down his irritation. "I have the itinerary right here." He tapped his console screen, set into the back of the pilot's seat. "I know it front and back. I've got it."

He stared pointedly out the window, ignoring the Agent's furtive stares until the chopper touched down a few minutes later.

A team of white-coated technicians greeted them; Kirkland and his men were not yet here, which was fine by Daniel. He dropped to the tarmac easily, shook the obligatory hands all around, and then, ignoring Randall's steely gaze, began walking the perimeter of the old base, hands stuffed into the pockets of his jumpsuit, deliberately taking his time.

The hangars he'd spotted from the air were empty; their doors were like vacuous black eyes, gazing vacantly. Behind the hangars was a row of barracks, looking equally abandoned. Tin roofing hung from the corner of one building, creaking uneasily in the low breeze.

Somehow Daniel found this to be comforting; the pristine-ness of his life, with its rigid schedule, was getting to him. It was nice to see a part of the Elders' world that was in less than perfect condition.

He stopped and looked at the distant mountains. The thought occurred to him, and not for the first time, to simply bolt – to run to the hills and disappear. A laugh burbled from his throat at this insane thought, a harsh sound with no hint of humor.

They'd find me before I made it a mile.

He walked the length of the airstrip, back to the far end where the chopper sat, rotors idling slowly.

Best to continue playing along.

As the sun touched the horizon, shadows stretched long across the airfield, now swarming with soldiers. Daniel's group of clones was already aboard the stealth jet, which sat purring at the end of the runway; lithe and feline, its black engines gleamed dully in the light of the flares that marked the strip.

Closer to where he sat in his chopper's open passenger bay, six or seven large commando helicopters waited for their cargo of special ops teams. Smells of tar and burning fuel came from somewhere nearby, noxious and heady.

One of the choppers started with a roar, and the others followed suit until the air reverberated with the sound. Randall appeared in the cockpit door, a wraith from the gloom.

"Are we ready then, young master?" His coal-pit eyes seemed to mock Daniel.

Daniel nodded and pulled on his VR mask, checking his team's readouts. "Ready when you are, skipper."

Randall eyed him with an odd expression. He seemed about to speak, then abruptly changed his mind and climbed in.

36

Maia pulled her jacket tight with a shiver. Spring was definitely on its way, but the evening air still held an edge of cold. On the riverbank opposite from where she sat in the grass, the trees swayed in the evening breeze. What wildlife there was around the compound must have gone to bed with the sun; she'd been out here half an hour and had seen only a single squirrel, which had soon disappeared up a tree. Somewhere up-valley, a solitary bird gave a solitary call.

She sighed, reached down and tossed a pebble into the water.

Where the hell is Johnny?

He'd promised to meet her at dusk, but that didn't mean much anymore. Over the past few weeks, Perdue had been anything but reliable. His psychosis, whatever it was, had deepened to a point that made her seriously afraid for him. He was so unresponsive, so drawn into his own private hell, that she despaired of ever getting him back. She felt so *sorry* for him – whatever this thing was, it was eating him alive.

She hardly ever saw him any more – he spent his days wandering the forest, usually within a mile or two of the compound, as far as she could tell. When he wasn't walking, he was prone to sitting for hours with his back to a boulder or downed log, completely motionless to the point of near-invisibility.

It was so *weird*. He seemed little more than a zombie, and nothing she or anyone else said made any difference.

Where is he?

It hurt, this thing, nearly as much as what had happened to Karla, and maybe more. No one could blame Maia for what had happened to Karla, but with Johnny . . .

Then again, it wasn't like *she* understood what had happened, either.

In past years, whenever she would 'disappear' for a day or two, she'd always had a sense of peace about it. Even in not understanding fully, she'd accepted these times as sacred; she'd always felt a profound sense of well-being after coming back from the forest.

But this time was different, and she was beginning to wonder why she hadn't questioned it before.

How could I take something like that for granted? Was it the mushrooms?

But that didn't make any sense. Or did it?

Now that she thought about it, most of the times she'd gone into the forest *had* been in conjunction with the mushrooms. Most of those times, but not *all* of them, surely.

Could I be wrong?

For the first time in a very long time she felt real fear, a wrenching in her gut as she questioned herself, trying to see through the veils of memory. She began to breathe faster with the effort, her heart pumping. Cold sweat broke out on her arms, and she hugged herself inside her layers of sweater and jacket.

This was too tiring; she was ready to go someplace warm.

She blinked back tears, looked again for any sign of him. There were none, only a rippling breeze that moved like a snake through the tired, dead stalks of last year's leftover grass. The sun had disappeared completely, replacing the day with cool, dangerous twilight.

Sorry, Johnny. It's too cold out here.

She turned toward the path, suddenly not feeling very well . . . and looking up, she gasped.

"J . . . Johnny?"

Where did he come from?

He didn't answer. He was ghostly and pale in the twilight. His skin was almost luminescent, seeming to exude tiny green sparks. She rubbed her eyes, wondering if she was seeing his aura, but as she approached, he looked a bit more like his normal self.

He sat as in a trance, his back to a tree. He seemed to be staring right at her, but she could tell he wasn't seeing her at all. A tiny moan came from his mouth, a burble in the back of his throat. He seemed like a statue, or a ghost. Fear gnawed at her stomach.

"Johnny?" She didn't know why she was whispering.

He let out a high-pitched sound, a rasping moan that made the hair on the back of her neck stand up. Her heart beat faster, and she took a few deep breaths, trying to calm herself.

"Johnny, wake up! Shit!" She stepped back, searching desperately for an expression, something to tell her what he was seeing. His eyes were sunken, his face like marble. Even his hair didn't move, though a twisting breeze walked between the trees, chilling the cold sweat on her face and arms.

Suddenly she became aware of something else, something she hadn't seen before – a strange shape was coalescing in the air between them. The more she looked at it, the more solid it appeared, until it resolved into a bird – a huge white raven, with snowy feathers and red-black eyes, hovering in the air above Johnny's head. She should have wondered about it, but instead found herself only watching, as if from outside herself.

I've seen something like this before . . .

He drew in a sharp breath and blinked a couple of times, muttering to himself. He noticed the bird suddenly, and lunged for it, moving more quickly than she would have thought possible. It flapped sideways with a high-pitched screech, disappearing between the boughs of a nearby spruce.

He looked after it for a moment, then back to Maia, seeming to really notice her for the first time. He came a couple of paces towards her, stopped, and again looked toward the tree where the white raven had disappeared.

If he could do it, he'd turn into a bird right now and go after that other one.

The thought made no sense, but Maia felt its inherent truth. She got to her feet slowly, disturbed and shaken.

"Are you all right?" His voice was low but forceful. She remained silent, suddenly unsure of the way he was looking at her, his eyes dark and preternatural.

"I've been missing you, Maia."

He came closer – only a step away now. Something about him chilled and repelled her; something very wrong with his eyes, especially. A velvety, hypnotic darkness filled the place where his green-brown pupils should have been, and his skin seemed to glow unnaturally.

"You're not Johnny," she whispered, and went cold with the surety of the truth she spoke. Saying it out loud gave her strength. "You're not Johnny," she repeated, louder this time. "You're something else."

He seemed to shiver. "I *am* Johnny," he said slowly, and laughed. The sound was hollow. "I've just been a little . . . fucked up . . . lately. But I *miss* you, Maia. Goddamn! I've been thinking about you . . . a lot . . . "

He reached out, caressed her cheek with the back of his hand. It was all she could do not to shudder at the cold electric numbness of his touch.

"Look at me," he rasped. "Maia . . . I want to kiss you."

She didn't want to let him . . . but then she did, after all. His lips met hers, delved into her the way a man thirsting to death might plunge into water. His hands groped her body roughly. She gave in to him a little . . . but only a little, and only because she was so *tired*, so vulnerable, and she needed him, dammit! Even if he wasn't himself.

His lips were somehow simultaneously cold and hot on her face and neck as she clung to him, tears welling in her eyes. She couldn't speak past the lump in her throat; she couldn't tell him how sorry she was, and how afraid.

But even as she responded to his fierce caresses, she was put off by him. His whole being seemed cold, somehow, and he was treating her too roughly. And his eyes . . . they were too bright and too dark at the same time, almost feverish, with a heat to match the coldness of his hands as he tore at her blouse, ripping open the ties in front.

"Johnny . . . don't, honey." She pushed at him, but his arms were like stone. "Johnny . . . *please!* Stop it!"

Her blouse was open now, and she nearly cried out when one of his hands, a block of ice, found her left breast, squeezing it like fruit. His tongue was in her mouth, lapping at her face, his body tensed like steel against hers.

"Johnny!"

He wasn't listening. He continued to tear at her clothes, pinning her down, trying to pull her pants down over her hips. His face seemed almost predatory, teeth locked in a feral snarl.

"Johnny! *Stop* it! What's wrong with you!?" She struck out in desperation, aiming for the side of his face, and connected a solid blow that made her hand go numb to the elbow.

And then, suddenly, he *did* stop. His arms and torso simply went limp. He took a deep, shivering breath and fell away from her like something had taken all the air from his body, falling in a heap on the moss-covered earth.

Maia collapsed, holding and wringing out her arm. Her entire body was shaking, tears streaming from her eyes. Angrily, she pulled her blouse back on, tying the strings in front with jerky, violent motions.

He said something, his voice too low to hear. Despite herself, she took a step closer. *"What* did you say?" Her voice carried the full force of her anger.

"I'm sorry." Slightly louder. "I just . . . I miss you, Maia. Something really bad is happening . . . but I . . . I couldn't have . . . you know . . . raped you."

"What do you mean?" She took one more cautious step toward him.

When he looked up, his face was a caricature, so sorrowful that a little of her anger melted. "I . . . I just couldn't," he said. "I just wanted . . . I needed to try to feel something . . . anything . . . that was normal. That's all. I'm so sorry, Maia."

She took a deep, trembling breath and wiped at her face with her sleeve.

"I wanted to know . . . " She began, meaning to ask about the white bird, but his expression had suddenly changed again. His mouth hung open, and he appeared to be listening to something. She held her breath, listening too, but all she heard were normal night sounds.

"What is it?"

"Goddamit!" he whispered. *"Can't you hear them?"*

37

The compound lay swathed in darkness. The smell of rain lingered in the air, left over from the previous night, but somehow it seemed stale and cloying to Marshall Scott as he walked toward Control to start the night shift. The air seemed too still, and somehow stagnant.

The calm before the storm.

He laughed shakily, wondering where this thought had come from.

"Careful, man," he said aloud to himself. "Don't let it get in your head."

He punched in the entry code at the outer door of the Control bunker and let himself in with a final look back over his shoulder at the creeping shadows.

Just the heebie-jeebies. Nothing more.

In the kitchen bunker, behind the large butcher-block that served as a counter, Diana Russell stood elbow-deep in suds, cleaning up from the evening's dinner. The dining hall had been unusually empty tonight, and she had lots of food left over; roasted apples, blackberry preserves and her patented corn tortilla goulash, usually a favorite during the winter months. Tonight, though, the room had only been half full, as if the entire compound had lost its collective appetite.

Only a few people remained in the dining room.

At a table in the corner, Uma Peak, a paragon of calm attentiveness, was engaging Darla Aldridge in a game of gin rummy. How like her, Diana thought with quiet admiration, to quietly fill in where she was needed. Lord knew the poor Aldridge girl had been through a lot lately. Her little sister lay in a perpetual coma, stricken with some horrible, unnamable condition, and as if that wasn't bad enough, Diana had noticed that the older girl seemed to have almost completely disappeared from her parents' radar. It was is if, with Karla sick and probably dying, their older daughter had ceased to exist at all.

The matron was drinking hot anise seed tea, the girl a steaming cup of hot milk with honey. They were bent over their game. Diana wiped her hands on her apron. "You ladies need anything else?" she asked. "I'm almost done here."

Darla didn't look up, but Uma Peak raised her calm gray eyes for a moment. "We're fine, dear. Don't mind us."

"You got any more of that stew back there?"

Bud Arney's voice rumbled from the table in the corner, next to the warmth

of the cast-iron stove, where he and Doctor Tinney sat playing dominoes and drinking hooch, as they did nearly every night during the winter months.

"A little," she said. "But you should eat it now, if you want it. There ain't much left, and it's cooling off pretty fast."

Karla's room was close and dank, the air stale and cloying. Medicinal smells combined with damp earth and sweat to form a musty, unpleasant cologne. It made Allie Aldridge's nose tingle, as if a sneeze was imminent but wouldn't come. An irritating sensation, but one she barely noticed.

Outrage and pain had dulled into a clinging, seemingly infinite grief that was the only real feeling she seemed to experience anymore.

Will it never end?

She wiped stinging tears from her eyes, feeling guilty, as she always did when this thought arose. But Karla was in pain, and it had gone on too long! She would give anything – *anything!* to take that pain away.

Even the unthinkable would be better than this. Recently, a thought had been circling like a wolf, feeling out the vulnerabilities of an unknown prey. At first it was only there in the periphery, a hint of a bad idea. Lately, though, the wolf was closing in. She could feel its hot breath, as its slavering fangs sought the jugular of her sanity.

But could I do it? Smother the life out my daughter? Pull the plug and watch her die slowly? How could I even contemplate such a thing?

Horrible . . . horrible.

She laid her head in her hands and tried to weep again, but no tears came. She sat like that for a minute, listening to the squelch and squeal of the grid shield, another sick background noise she'd come to accept as just part of her life.

She didn't notice that her husband had entered the room until he laid a hand on her shoulder. She looked up, eyes red but dry, and squeezed his hand gratefully. He returned the squeeze and sank heavily into the rickety chair in the corner.

Twice he cleared his throat, as if he wanted to break the quiet, but it seemed no words would come. Finally he reached for her hand, and they sat that way together.

Waiting.

John Stark looked up as Marshall entered the room. "Hey, Marsh. Ready to party?"

Scott offered a wry grin. "Oh, it's a twenty-four hour party around here, for sure," he said. "All paranoia, all the time."

"You seen Perdue?"

Scott shifted uncomfortably, his smile frozen. Johnny had been little more than a ghost in recent weeks; he drifted in and out at odd times, and sometimes seemed to disappear entirely, for a whole day or more. He hadn't covered a shift since he'd been back, and his absence was definitely noticed; Stark had been talking about training a replacement. But they both knew it wasn't his fault. Something strange and terrible had happened to Johnny Perdue - something that had rendered him only a marginal gray shade of his former self.

Marshall sighed, shook his head. "Not today. I spotted him yesterday, out walking by himself. I was going to go say something to him, but he walked behind a tree and just . . . " he shrugged, not wanting to say what he was thinking. The truth was, Perdue had just flat *vanished*. One second he'd been there, walking along plain as day, and the next . . .

He frowned, not wanting to think about it. "I lost sight of him," he finished simply, then: "I don't think he really wants to be found right now, if you know what I mean."

Stark nodded grimly. "Yeah."

He sighed and stood up, stretching his back with a disturbing series of popping noises.

"Christ, John," Marshall said. "You oughta go get that looked at."

Stark grinned morosely as he pulled on his overcoat. "I'll get right on that," he said. "In the meantime, I'm gonna go take a nap. I'm beat." He paused on the way out the door.

"Marsh . . . " he hesitated, then: "I'll have my radio. Call me if you see anything strange. Anything at all."

Scott nodded, distracted. "Okay."

It wasn't until after Stark left the room that Marshall thought just how odd that last bit was; how unlike the pragmatic John Stark. It was obvious, after all, wasn't it? If he saw anything strange, he'd call.

Obvious.

Then why do I feel this way?

He shook his head and went back to work, feeling puzzled and introspective.

Just the heebie-jeebies . . .

· · «‹ ‹ ◈ › › » · ·

Johnny sprang to his feet, an impossibly fast movement. His face was intense, his jaw set.

"They're coming," he said in a low voice. "They're coming from up there." He jerked a thumb skyward. "We have to warn the others."

Without any further explanation, he began moving through the trees, down the path toward the bunkers. Maia hesitated, looking up into the evening sky.

What the hell, Perdue?

"I don't see anything," she said uncertainly.

He looked back impatiently. "Come *on!*" His voice held an imperative. "We don't have much time!"

She sighed and followed, wondering what strange paranoia had him in its grip this time. Her body was still shaky with adrenaline, her heart beating hard from the way he'd attacked her. And now this - a flight of paranoid fancy, serving only to further prove that something was indeed very, very wrong with Johnny Perdue.

He glided like a ghost through the dark forest, seeming almost to disappear at times. He was moving very fast, and she had a hard time keeping up. Twice he took shortcuts she didn't know about, ducking under swaying limbs and shimmying between massive trunks. When she called out to him he turned and looked back for a moment, but didn't stop.

They reached the edge of the meadow in front of the bunkers, and Johnny finally stopped for a moment. Maia was nearly out of breath.

"Get down!" he hissed, pulling her with him to crouch behind a bush. He cocked his head, listening. His face was taut, every sense straining, but Maia couldn't see or hear anything out of the ordinary. She was beginning to feel silly, and cold. Warm yellow light spilled from the kitchen bunker, tempting her with its promise of warmth and something hot and sweet to drink.

"Why don't we go get some tea?" she asked. "We can play some dice with Darby. I know she's been wanting . . . "

"*SHHHH!*" He glared at her fiercely, his face pulled into a scowl. His flared nostrils left widening shadows on his face, and his feverish eyes danced in the last of the twilight. He still seemed to be listening intently, cocking his head to the side.

She lapsed into silence, wondering if she should just leave him here. But he was so unpredictable! He might do almost anything. She'd been really afraid back there . . .

An unnatural noise, a slip of cloth on grass, suddenly galvanized her awareness. Her unfinished thought died in the back of her mind, her own senses tightening, tuning in to the night around them.

There it is again!

The unmistakable *swish, swish, swish* of someone moving steadily through the grass of the meadow. Out in the clearing, movement caught the corner of her eye, but when she looked, there was nothing - only the play of moon-shadows on dead grass and bare branches.

"*What . . . ?*"

Another movement killed the words on her lips. A dark spot had materialized on the grass, less than a hundred feet away. It slithered forward, then stopped.

A moment passed, then a small light winked on, off. Maia watched in gathering horror as the signal light was repeated once, a hundred yards away at the upper side of the meadow, then again, this time from the riverbank.

Johnny leaned toward her, an imperative look in his eyes. "It's too late." His voice was a throaty whisper. *"We have to get out of here. If we go back towards the river we can head up-valley."*

Her heart thudded out of control. The dark shape on the grass in front of them had been joined by another, and now the two moved in concert, creeping silently toward the bunker entrances. A thought flashed through her mind, an image of Karla lying helpless under the care of her equally helpless mother.

I'll never see them again.

A sudden rush, a dark swarming on the level field in front of them.

"Quick now! Come on!" Johnny hissed in her ear, turning back into the woods.

Panic broke over her like a wave, and she followed.

It was a sound that alerted them.

The door to the kitchen bunker was hung with only a heavy blanket, matted on the outside with carefully placed leaves, branches and dirt which served as camouflage. The sound came easily through the blanket to the ears of those inside.

At their table, Darla Aldridge and Uma Peak looked up from their game at the same time. The girl's face was puzzled, questioning. *Did you hear that?*

The older woman's face had lost all color.

Bud Arney looked up from his game in the midst of placing a piece, his hand suspended in midair. His sleepy features were beset by a species of calm terror that Diana didn't think she'd ever seen before. She barely had time to register this before they heard the sound again: the crackle of static from a hand-com unit, followed by a diffuse beep, hard to hear but unmistakably there.

The static crackle of a hand-com was nothing new or unusual; many Compound members carried them, especially those involved with security. No, nothing out of place there – it was the beep at the end that gave it away. The hand-com units used in Compound West made no such sound.

Doctor Tinney broke the silence. "What in God's name was that?" His eyes were bloodshot stains of fear.

Diana stood with her towel held to her throat, eyes wide and scared. Darla cowered on the end of her bench next to the wall, not knowing exactly what was wrong but able to sense something grossly out of place, just the same.

As usual, it was Uma Peak who kept her head. She rose from the table, looking at all of them with daggers in her eyes. She held one finger up to her mouth in the universal 'be quiet' gesture, then motioned with her other arm, beckoning them all to come close.

Outside, distant but moving closer, more sounds could be heard; muffled thumps, a hoarse cough, and again the crackle and beep of the alien hand-com units.

The look on Uma's face was simultaneously frightened to death and grimly determined. "We're trapped," she said. "We have to get out of this room, and fast. Someone get the lights."

"I'm on it." Diana quickly skirted the perimeter of the room, blowing out candles and flicking the lights off. Within moments, the room was plunged into flickering, watery darkness.

The group drew in close to Uma Peak, near the bunker doorway. She'd pulled the heavy blanket aside an inch or two and was peering into the darkness.

"Quick now," she said in a hoarse whisper. "On my mark, all of us together. We go to our left, then up the hill. Try to get under the trees."

There was no time for argument or debate. She looked again, quickly, then glanced over her shoulder at the waiting group.

"All right, *now!*"

⊹ ← ‹‹‹·꜀·◈·꜆·››› → ◂

Marshall Scott hadn't meant to fall asleep. It was just that he'd been so overwhelmed recently – everyone had, really. Last he remembered, he'd sat down in front of the main security monitor. He wasn't even going to close his eyes, was only there to check a few routine settings . . . but the blip . . . blip . . . blip of the screen, showing the topographical relief map and relative positions of his sentinel spinners, was so . . . very . . . hypnotic...

It seemed like only a minute or two had passed when he snapped awake, roused by an insistent sound

BEEEEEEEEEEEEP BEEEEEEEEEEEEP BEEEEEEEEEEEEEP

from the monitor. He shook his head to clear it, thinking for a moment that he must still be dreaming. The screen bore a message he'd seen only once before - on that day, a few months prior, when their valley had been visited by large black helicopters.

. . . SECURITY ALERT! SECURITY ALERT! Unauthorized intruders! . . .

The screen beeped again, as if to insist that yes, you're really awake, this is not a dream. The map of the valley, so peaceful and serene when his eyes had begun to droop, was now crawling with little purple dots.

Panic finally began to bloom, moving from his bowels up his spine and bursting into his head with stunning quickness. He reached for his hand-com, perched on the edge of his desk, and knocked it to the floor, where it skidded under a nearby table.

Cursing, he went after it, face-down on the littered, dirty floor, fingers clutching blindly until they closed on the familiar hard-rubber surface of the walkie-talkie. He yanked it to his face and rolled to his back, not bothering to regain his feet before depressing the send button. *"John!"* he nearly screamed. *"John! Come back! Are you there, John?"*

For a moment there was silence, and Marshall could hear nothing but his own heart hammering into overdrive, pounding a spike through his head that threatened to explode his eyeballs in their sockets. Finally, thankfully, Stark's voice came back, sounding sleep-roughened but ready.

"Marsh, it's John here. What's the problem? Over."

Marshall got to his feet shakily, checking the screen. Most of the purple dots were concentrated in the lower valley, but a few of them had split from the rest and appeared to be heading up-valley, directly towards where he sat in Control.

"John!" he hissed. "John, they're right on top of us. We're screwed, buddy. They're all over the valley. Oh my Lord, John. Oh my God."

For a moment there was nothing, and then Stark came back, sounding tired and alarmed. "In the valley? Are you sure?"

"I'm looking at purple dots, John. A *lot* of them."

For the first time, Scott realized what must have happened. Even considering the fact that he'd dozed off for a couple of minutes, the security system should have alerted long before the bogeys were inside the valley. No one on foot could have come over the ridges, and if they came up the valley, they would have been detected.

"Oh my God," Marshall whispered. How could they have been so stupid? With all the drills and preparations, no one had thought of the obvious.

He keyed the send button again. "They dropped in," he said. "Shit, John, they dropped in from the sky. Parachuted right down on top of us. We've been bushwhacked, old buddy."

"Copy that." Stark's voice cut off in a burst of static, then: "Jeremieah, do you read me? Repeat, Aldridge, come in."

Moments passed with nothing from the hand-com but the occasional static hum. The purple dots on the screen kept moving. Some of them had faded a bit, and were buzzing stoically over the bunker entrances where the living quarters were, just down-valley from the kitchen.

Marshall's stomach sank.

They're inside! The spinners can't get a read on them.

It was only a matter of time before they reached him in Control. Three or four of the dots had already closed the distance.

Stark's voice came over the hand-com, riding a flourish of static. His voice was breathless and jerky – he sounded like he was running.

"Marsh, if you can still hear this . . . oh, *shit!"* The transmission ended, then came back, quieter, a whisper from the void. *"Goddammit, Marsh, they're everywhere. This is gonna have to be my last transmission. The goose is cooked, Marsh. You hear me? THE GOOSE IS COOKED! Oh fuck ... "*

The transmission ended with a long, ominous howl of static, and the unit went totally silent. Marshall Scott stood for a moment, hand-com drooping from suddenly nerveless fingers, head reeling.

Then the finality of Stark's words hit him like a load of wet cement, and he began to move.

The only sounds in the room were the whine of the grid shield and the wheeze of the ancient breathing machine as it made Karla's chest rise and fall, rise and fall, with sterile clockwork precision. Allie and Jeremieah Aldridge didn't realize anything was amiss until guttural shouts arose from the corridor outside the room.

By then, it was far too late.

The curtain over the door was thrown aside, and the barrels of two blast-rifles appeared, followed by the men holding them. Their bodies were bulky with the armor they wore, their large helmets and goggles rendering their eyes glassy and insectile.

Jeremieah leapt to his feet, spilling his chair over sideways and nearly tripping on it. Allie, her eyes huge and frightened, moved her body unthinkingly between the men in the doorway and the bed where her daughter lay. She screamed once, the sound huge and piercing in the close quarters, and then one of them shot her where she stood. Her chest bubbled and sizzled, her last breath coming out her nose in a thin drizzle of reddish foam. Her eyes glassed over, and she folded where she stood.

Jeremieah Aldridge released all his rage and hatred into one long howl and launched himself, headfirst, at the nearer of the men. More blast-rifles had appeared in the doorway, and as his fingers closed around the shielded throat of the trooper, bashing the man's foul metal-encased head against one of the room's angled support beams, he had time for one last thought.

There's too many of them.

He felt the cold muzzle of the blast rifle digging into his side, just below the armpit, and his scream ended in a surprised gurgle as the trooper pulled the trigger and relieved him of most of his torso. Blood and entrails ran down the wall, staining the slick, polymer-coated earth a violent purple shade.

The room was silent again, except for the creak of metal and leather as one or the other of the six clone troopers shifted on his feet. One of them, the group leader, cocked his head, as if receiving a transmission, then nodded to the others.

Three of the clones took up positions beside the door and at the head of the girl's bed. Without a word, the other three turned on their heels and left the room in perfect synchronicity.

A burst of gunfire was followed by another scream. Men were shouting unintelligibly . . . Maia thought she recognized Bud Arney's throaty growl. A low hissing sound arose from behind them, and a yellow flare of light rendered the hillside above the compound a mass of spiny shadows. In the glare, she saw people running.

And another sound; it had been growing in her consciousness, as she ran blindly through the woods, for a full thirty seconds before she recognized the low, reverberating hum.

Choppers!

"Which way are they coming from?" The sloped sides of the valley echoed with rebounding sound, a cacophony of pounding rudders mixed with sporadic bursts of gunfire and general confusion. Ahead of her, Johnny glided soundlessly through the trees. She could see his ghostly form, turning every few seconds to find her.

"*Quick! This way!*" he whispered over his shoulder.

She nodded, motioned for him to lead.

They crawled out from under the trees cautiously, creeping over the muddy riverbank and into the shallow water at the edge. The earth odor was fetid with the sweet smell of natural decay. The stream burbled lightly, unconcerned with any human drama.

Luckily there hadn't been excessive rain in recent weeks, and the water was no more than thigh-high. It was cold – very cold, in fact, but adrenaline prevented her from feeling the worst of it. Using the wet roots of overhanging trees for handholds, they crept along the cut-bank. The murky water caught the fading yellow light of the flares in little swirling pockets, spinning slowly into her mind the horror of what was happening.

The roar of the choppers echoed more loudly. Two of the metal beasts hove into sight over the trees, and further up-valley the running lights of a third and fourth became visible. To their right, another flare, and then another, and they crouched low, holding their breath. They were almost to the clump of trees that would give them cover, but the last twenty yards were a gauntlet of unnatural white-yellow light, casting distorted shadows over the water.

The choppers hung low over the meadow, their spotlights pointed at the bunker entrances. Someone, she couldn't tell who, ran out of a bunker, and a beam of sizzling yellow light flashed from the helicopter. An eerie scream rent the night air and was cut off in the middle, as if someone had flipped a switch.

"*Now!*" Johnny hissed.

Darla Aldridge scrambled up the cold, rain-soaked hill above the kitchen bunker, holding on to Uma Peak's hand for dear life. The night was thankfully devoid of moonlight; grumbling banks of clouds had begun to march down the valley shortly before sunset and had succeeded in rendering the night black as tar.

As her eyes adjusted, she could see just enough to grab onto the occasional root or branch and haul herself a little higher up the hill. The hillside was muddy clay, slippery and difficult to traverse.

"Come on, Darla," Uma whispered, and gave her hand a little squeeze. "There's a path right ahead, it will be easier going. Can you see the others?"

Twenty feet below them, Diana Russell crawled on hands and knees in the muck. Behind her, Bud Arney and Dr. Tinney were moving decidedly slower, helping each other over the rough spots. So far they hadn't been spotted, and Bud supposed that was good, but in the back of his mind he thought they were probably done for.

Ain't never gonna make it up this hill. Me and the Doc, anyhow. The others might have a chance, but the two of us are old and out of shape.

He paused, balancing against the trunk of a young, grotesquely misshapen pine for a look down at the valley floor, through a thin cover of scrub brush and trees. Spotlights jigged this way and that, less than a hundred fifty yards away. Bud thought it very, very lucky to have not been spotted so far.

In the distance, he heard muffled shouts, a woman screaming, and the cries of several children. The valley walls shook and trembled as several more choppers swooped low over the compound, their searchlights stabbing remorselessly at the row of bunker entrances, usually so well-hidden but now looking like open sores in the side of the hill.

They know exactly what they're looking at! They had us pegged the whole time.

He turned to Tinney. *"We gotta keep moving, doc,"* he whispered, and grabbed Tinney's forearm with his slab of a hand. *"We're lucky we ain't been spotted yet, but if we don't move, we're gonna be cooked for sure."*

The old doctor looked terrified – his spectacles hung askew on his nose, one lens cracked – and his eyes were glazed and wild, but he nodded and they began to move again.

A flash of shocking white illuminated everything in a moment of gross relief, accompanied by the thump and scream of flares being deployed. One by one they rose into the night, illuminating the sides of the valley in a sick array of blue-black afterimages.

A moment passed, and Bud thought they might be okay yet, maybe they hadn't been seen . . .

A flash of light came from below, accompanied by a sizzling shriek – the sound of a short-range grenade missile being deployed. He barely had time to duck, and then the hillside erupted around him. He was thrown to the ground, his wind knocked out. He struck a muddy patch and rolled downhill, grasping for purchase and finding nothing but slick rock and wet grass. His shoulder struck something hard enough to cause a blue explosion of sparks in his head, and another string of white flares exploded overhead. They were like muted, ghastly fireworks, a dreary celebration of madness and quick death.

He hauled his aching bulk to its feet by force of sheer will alone. He looked up the hill to orient himself and saw little Darla Aldridge slip over the top of the hill under the darkened trees, scrabbling for balance.

Another round of flares went up, and by their strobing light he saw the Doc, twenty feet away and further down the hill. He started to move, and gunfire stroked the ground around him, bullets thumping into the trees and earth as he slip-slid along the face of the hill, trying to make it down to where the Doc was getting to his feet, his face dazed and bruised in the ghost-light.

Another volley, and Tinney screamed. It was a hoarse, jagged sound. In the fresh light of the new flares Bud saw the doc go down, his body jerking, riddled with bullets, his face caved in. He did a grotesque pirouette, almost graceful, as the bullets continued to slam into him, and then flopped like a rag-doll, his body pitching down the muddy incline in the fading blue after-light of the flares.

"Doc!" Bud's scream was lost as the roar of the choppers redoubled, bouncing from every angle. He said a quick prayer and scrambled back toward the top of the hill, mind reeling and numb but still trying to stay under cover.

Forty feet up and to his left he glimpsed Diana Russell, hanging for dear life to the root of a precariously leaning tree. She'd been knocked from her feet when the missile struck the hillside, and was now in a precarious position. The entire slope beneath her had caved in, leaving her stranded, half-sitting, clinging to a newly exposed root. Beneath her was a sheer drop of almost fifteen feet to a jumble of broken earth, rock and mud. She had no clear path, and he could see that she was going to need help. He—

It was too late. Two of the newest round of helicopters had broken off and were coming toward them, not hurrying. To Bud, they looked like gigantic, glowing wasps, monstrous eating machines that would enjoy the fear of their victims as they picked them off, one by one.

The entire hillside was awash in buzzing white light as the choppers turned their spotlights on full. Bud threw an arm over his face to shield his eyes, and the guns began to hammer. The whole thing seemed to be happening very, very slowly.

Well, I guess that's that. We tried.
This was the last thought of Charles 'Bud' Arney.

Marshall Scott's hands moved like a blur, his mind watching from far away, horrified by what he was doing. Wipeout codes flashed across the screen and were gone in a blink, eating all the data stored in Compound West's banks. John Stark's last words kept racing through his mind.
The goose is cooked . . .
It was a code phrase he'd hoped never to hear – essentially Stark's version of a self-destruct button. Four other compounds depended on secrecy for their survival, and it was imperative that information stored in the compound databanks not find its way into government hands.
Everything seemed to be happening in haunted slow motion. He glanced at the spinner monitor and saw that three purple blips had begun to hover statically over the Control bunker door.
So if they weren't already inside, they will be soon.
He banged in the last sequence and stood up, forehead beaded with sweat.
It's done.
On the screen, streams of information flew by as the compound's entire history disappeared, file by file. From up the passageway, a muffled thump shook the room hard enough to knock a sprinkling of dust from the ceiling.
They've blown the door, then. They're definitely inside.
The main terminal gave a loud, satisfied beeeep and went dead as heavy, thudding footsteps advanced up the corridor. He heard the creak of leather on metal, but the invaders, whoever they were, seemed an eerily silent bunch.
All thoughts of survival had fled, and now there was only the raw moment, the task at hand. Trance-like, he crossed the room and began systematically rummaging through an old storage locker behind the back row of monitors. After a moment he emerged with what he'd been looking for – a handful of impact grenades. He straightened and readied himself.
The footsteps paused, just outside the door. The handle turned slowly.
"All right, you bastards!" he screamed. *"Come on in and get some!!!"*
He hurled the first of the grenades at the opening door and ducked as it exploded in its frame, showering the room with dust and shrapnel. A chunk of something hot and metallic burned its way through his sleeve and into his arm, but he barely felt it.
He flung another grenade through the hole created by the first one, screaming, not caring that they'd begun to fire. The room lit up with arcing surges of sizzling energy, and he was blasted to pieces against the wall.
The last thing he felt was a stunning absence of pain; a relief of a sort he'd

never even begun to imagine. The last thing he saw was a static white curtain that blotted out everything. After a moment, the room was silent again.

Maia slipped once, went down to her neck in cold water, then bounced up again with a gasp as adrenaline racked her body. Within twenty seconds they'd made the stand of pines, crawling bedraggled from the riverbed, shivering and gasping from the cold.

A chopper made a pass overhead, lights playing through the trees, but the heavy evergreen boughs were thick around them, and after a moment it moved on.

"We're not going to make it," Johnny said in a low, toneless voice. He seemed to be lapsing again, into that strange otherness that had taken him lately. "They'll search the whole valley. They'll know if anyone's missing, and they'll come for us."

"Don't say that!" she whispered loudly, angry that he should be talking this way. "Somebody has to survive! We'll follow the Chairman's escape plans, just like we drilled, and meet up with whoever gets away. We have to keep going." Now that she'd rested for a moment, she felt a little stronger. She set her jaw stubbornly. "Come on, Perdue. You got me this far – I'm not leaving you here."

With seeming great difficulty his eyes found hers . . . wavered, and then held her gaze. He took a deep, anguished breath, let it out slowly. "All right," he said, but his mouth sounded like it was filled with mush. He got to his feet.

"It's your turn. You know this valley better than anybody. Lead on."

38

The sounds of the slaughter had faded behind them. With the exception of an occasional faraway yell or burst of gunfire, or the distant clattering echo of the choppers, only the restless voices of the dreaming forest accompanied them now. Maia paused to catch her breath, keeping to the shadows of the ragged, crooked pines that lurked like ghouls beside the river.

Johnny was beside her, quiet as a ghost himself, his skin almost iridescent in the silvery moonlight. His face was expressionless, and he wasn't breathing hard, though they'd come quite a ways now.

In the near distance, the sound of the waterfall was almost a roar. She wasn't quite sure where they would go once they reached the cliff overlooking the Falls – they'd have to turn south there, and she had no idea what lay in that direction, or even whether it was passable.

"You okay, Perdue?" Her voice was a harsh whisper. He didn't answer at first, and she was beginning to think he hadn't heard when he finally replied, his voice oddly flat.

"I don't think I'm actually here," he said. "It all seems like a dream, and I'm not just saying that."

He reached for her, tentatively, as if afraid he would find her turned to vapor. A visible tremor of relief coursed through him as he encountered the warm flesh of her upper arm, and for a moment she thought he would cry. He shivered, closed his eyes and gripped her arm hard, but it didn't hurt – it was more like a fuzzy kind of pressure.

Light clouds wreathed a goblin moon, grinning and venomous. She looked away, shivering.

"We'd better get going," she said. "We need to be completely away from this valley by sunrise."

Her own words shocked her more than anything that had happened so far. *Away from this valley . . .*

This valley had been her home, the only thing she'd ever really known, and now it was all gone . . . and so *suddenly,* with no time to say goodbye. Tears wanted to come, and anger, but instead something drove her to a place of complete indifference, a place of no pity. This quality surprised her, and for a while she wondered at it as they picked their way through bracken and over stone, the gurgle of the river on their left holding them to their course as they climbed.

She must've been more tired than she'd thought; the roar of the waterfall was very close before she realized her mistake. In the sullen, treacherous trance-light of the moon, she'd taken a wrong path, one that led too close to the river. They'd reached a dead end, at the base of a sheer rock face, at least fifteen feet high, slick with moss and condensation. She looked at it, stupefied.

"Which way?" Johnny asked.

Below them, the river dropped off into whitewater – the only place in the valley where there were true rapids. The sound was enough to compete with that of the waterfall, which would have been visible if not for the carapace blocking their progress.

Maia groaned and slapped her forehead. *"Nooo,"* she moaned. "It can't be!"

"What?"

"We went the wrong way! We'll have to go back. Oh, Johnny, I'm so sorry."

He studied her face. "How far back would we have to go?"

She thought for a moment, fighting hard against her rising panic. "At least ten . . . maybe twenty minutes. I'm so sorry, Johnny."

He didn't seem to be listening. His attention seemed riveted on the slick rock face in front of them.

"Johnny?"

His eyes were dark and sunken, his skin shining in a way the moonlight could not account for. Suddenly, he seemed to tense, and for a moment he exuded a glow, a bright burst of phosphorescent light . . . and then he was clinging like an insect to the rock face, seven or eight feet above her head. He began to inch his way up slowly, using his hands and feet in some way she could not discern, shimmying toward the top, some fifteen feet above them.

And then he was standing on top, looking down at her with those strangely vacant eyes.

She gasped, her mind spinning.

What was that?

But it seemed that she knew exactly what Johnny had just done, and even how . . . as if she'd seen something like it before. A disconnected image arose, clear as crystal; a man, with rugged features and shoulder-length dark hair. With the image came a name,

(Milos)

bursting like a momentary light in her mind's eye. The name seemed both familiar and mysterious, but there wasn't time to think about it.

"Give me your hand."

Johnny was leaning over the edge, one hand holding onto the gnarled root of a tree which sprouted tenuously from a crack at the top. The other hand was outstretched to her.

She reached for him, then faltered at the impossibility of what she was attempting.

How high is this wall, anyway?

"Don't think about it."

His voice floated in some mercuric liquid, pooling in her ears. All her attention was on his outstretched arm; impossibly, it reached her trembling fingertips over a distance that must have been at least a dozen feet.

He wrapped his hand around her wrist, and an icy current electrified her. The next thing she knew, she was standing beside him on the slippery, moss-covered rock. He held her arm for a moment as she gained her balance.

"You got it?" He peered at her, and for a moment he was just Johnny again; overly concerned and vaguely unsettled, but all there. "You don't want to lose your balance. That first step's a doozy."

A sudden burst of nostalgia overcame her, along with sudden, unbidden tears. "Goddammit, Perdue, I've *missed* you!"

She wanted to reach for him, to really *feel* him, but he was gone again, lost in himself, his face shining unnaturally. She wiped the wetness from her cheeks, looked down and had to fight a sudden rush of vertigo. From below, she'd thought the rock wall to be fifteen or twenty feet high, but from up here, it seemed much higher. Again, she was struck by the absurdity of what had just happened.

"How—?" She said. "I mean, what the *hell,* Johnny!? How did you do that?"

Johnny mumbled something under his breath. He seemed exhausted.

"What?"

He shook his head. "I don't know. I just . . . did it. Somehow I just knew I could . . . transport myself. And you." He heaved a great sigh, as if the whole thing was simply too tiring to think about. "Something weird happened to me, Maia. I don't know if it's good, or bad, or both, but *something* definitely happened. I keep having this feeling that I'm about to wake up, but I never do." He sighed again. "I don't think I'm even really here."

Those words again. A chill went through Maia's heart, and with it the distinct and unshakable feeling that she knew *exactly* what had happened to Johnny, and what was happening to him now.

In the brush, a bird chirped, reminding her of the coming morning. Above them, the tops of the trees were brushed with the first light of dawn. A chill wind stirred the hair on her cheek, and she shivered, feeling really cold for the first time since they'd begun their escape, hours ago.

"We'd better go," she said. "It's going to be light soon."

Johnny followed her without a word or a sound. They moved slowly at first, until she came upon a familiar path, and after that they made good time.

39

Daniel's team had sequestered the infected young girl in preparation for transport; now, as night moved restlessly towards the first hint of dawn, she lay unconscious in a makeshift medical tent at the edge of their temporary encampment, breathing through a respirator.

The other man – the engineer DaLuge had requested – had been more trouble, but was found within a few hours. Daniel's team had located him, with the aid of the swarm's ultraviolet scanning technologies, then brought him down with a heavy-duty tranquilizer gun. Daniel had, via swarm, personally monitored his transfer to the head of the valley. His immobile form lay beside the girl's, manacled to the hospital gurney in case he should regain consciousness.

Mission accomplished.

Except for one thing . . .

The red-haired woman had responded as predictably as he'd hoped. She'd headed up-valley, away from the conflict, and he was impressed with her speed and resourcefulness. He'd checked on her progress throughout the night, and she appeared to be moving steadily toward the head of the valley, toward himself and his men.

Twice during the night he'd thought he'd seen someone else with her, but he hadn't been able to get a clear view in the moonlight, and infrared wasn't picking anything up. Besides, he was much too busy to worry about a blip on his screen. If someone was with her, that person would be dealt with.

At the moment, he sat resting in the quick-tent that Kirkland's men had so efficiently thrown up when they'd arrived here . . . how long ago? He checked his watch. Nine hours now.

Has it really been that long?

As he pushed the VR mask up to his forehead, he noted with some surprise that the sun was coming up, smearing the surrounding peaks with dull rose and glinting from the quartz crystals embedded in the rocks. The sound of the waterfall boomed across the plain, muted only by the stand of pine which separated them from the cliff's edge, two hundred yards away.

Very soon, it would all be over.

The only reason they were still here was that the General wanted to survey the scene in the daylight, to pronounce the mission officially accomplished before pulling up stakes. A thorough man, Kirkland, and Daniel could respect that. In fact, now that he thought about it, he realized with some surprise that he actually liked the man.

The open-sided tent was mostly a conglomeration of equipment and extra gear, and the only people around were Kirkland and his command team; Daniel noted with some satisfaction that Randall was nowhere to be seen.

Kirkland sat comfortably in a fold-out polyzan flex chair, in front of a sprawling table that held a map of the valley. He was chatting amiably with DaLuge's assistant, Sneed, who had come along as an advisor. Daniel was surprised that he hadn't noticed the thin-faced man's presence before, and had a moment of doubt.

What else have I missed?

Another thought came on the heels of this one, a thought that made him sweat and got his legs moving through the jumble of equipment towards Kirkland and Sneed.

She's close.

His last check had put her less than a mile away; from analyzing her path, he knew she would emerge from the forest, near the cliff, in less than half an hour. Strangely, she *did* appear to have a companion, and Daniel was a puzzled as to why he'd been unable to get any solid readings, either visual or thermal.

No time for that. They'll be dealt with, whoever they are.

He approached the General's work-station, and the conversation slowed, then petered out. The old soldier looked up, his eyes gray and questing beneath his close-cropped burr of white hair.

"Hello, young sir." Kirkland's smile seemed genuine, cracking the blunt features of his face so he looked almost young. "A successful night's work, if I might say so. You performed admirably, and Lazaro . . . ah . . . your grandfather, I mean . . . will hear no less."

"Thank you, sir."

Kirkland seemed to scrutinize him closely. "Is something on your mind, Daniel? You seem a bit preoccupied."

"Well . . . " Daniel was suddenly, painfully aware that the entire group, including Sneed, had ceased all conversation and were watching him closely.

With mounting horror, he realized that he still didn't have a plan for explaining himself. At the last second, he nearly faltered.

"I . . . I've spotted some stragglers, sir," he sputtered finally, determined to simply charge through it. He was, after all, the grandson of the planet's Security Chief, and Kirkland would most likely go along with whatever he said, at least for the time being. They're coming up on our position now," he continued. "I've just picked them up; we must have missed them earlier, somehow. I was thinking . . . "

Kirkland cut him off with the wave of a hand.

"Yes, yes," he said. "I'm aware of them. A young man and woman, I believe?

Our orders are to dispatch the male, but the girl is to be taken into custody. The message came across the wire a couple of hours ago, special orders from your grandfather by way of DaLuge." He looked closely at Daniel. "You all right, son? You look a bit peaked, if you don't mind my saying so."

Daniel's mind was spinning.

They know! They know about her! There's no other explanation!

And then, the bigger question:

Why is Grandfather helping me? What's he hiding?

Time enough to mull these things over later; in the meantime, the pressure was off. He cleared his throat. "Sorry, sir," he mumbled. "I'm . . . a bit fatigued. So . . . the girl isn't to be harmed?"

Kirkland nodded with a smile. "That's right."

Daniel returned the smile, feeling genuinely better than he'd felt in weeks. A huge weight seemed to have lifted from his shoulders. His lungs relaxed, and he breathed deeply of the mountain air, his grin widening.

40

The plain overlooking the waterfall was cracked and arid. Other than tufts of saw-grass, clinging bitterly to life in the cracks between the rocks, only the occasional knobby, wind-stunted pine dotted the scene, a plaintive but stubborn testament to life.

Maia blinked as she stepped out from the trees. The sun was up, full and strong, and now it came out from behind a streaming cloud. Needles of light, reflected from the quartz-encrusted granite boulders strewn across the plain, made her wince and shade her eyes. Johnny came up beside her, seemingly unfazed by the brightness.

"Where to?" His voice was emotionless and fatigued.

She pointed to their right. "That way," she said, with more confidence than she felt. "We have to go south, I know that much, and we should stick to the tree-line . . . don't you think?"

He didn't answer; it was as if she wasn't even there. He gazed at the clouds, floating on the wind, as if he could simply detach from this moment and sail away with them, vapor in the sky. Sadness hit her suddenly, with almost palpable force, and she sat down heavily on the dusty ground. Johnny continued to stand, motionless and staring. The roar of the waterfall was heavy static.

Minutes passed, and nothing changed. As the sun began to mount the bright blue dome of the sky, shadows on the plain crawled back to the safety of the trees and ridges, and the wind sighed mournfully as it swept a surface as dry and cracked as a cast-off snakeskin.

Fighting down a wave of helpless anger, mostly at Johnny for his seeming oblivion, she ground her teeth and regained her feet, swaying unsteadily. Her world rocked, and she was dizzy for a moment. She realized suddenly that she was utterly famished; she hadn't eaten anything since lunch the previous day – nearly eighteen hours ago.

"We should keep going," she said, laying a hand on Johnny's arm. He was ice-cold to the touch, and she recoiled slightly. "We'll need to find some food before too long."

"Hmm? Oh. Yeah, of course. I don't know where my head's at." He peered at her forlornly. "I'm sorry, Maia. I know I'm not much help." He hesitated, and as she started to reply, he spoke again, quietly. "Do you think maybe we could go look at the waterfall . . . just one last time, you know? We can't know when we'll be here again."

This time, she didn't have the strength to fight the sadness that welled in her breast. She tried to reply, but her throat was closing up, choking off anything she might've thought to say. She was leaving her home, probably forever, and she had nowhere to go. No one waiting for her anywhere, and her only companion might as well have been a ghost.

"All right," she said softly. "I wouldn't mind saying goodbye."

They made their way out into the sunlight, picking their way along the boulder-lined edge of the cliff. She shivered in the empty, ragged wind, pulling her jacket tight around her.

Below them, the air shimmered with dancing rainbow-light, refracted through mist that swirled up in hypnotic spirals from the smash of water in the upper pool, some hundred feet below them. Maia could see the small etched shadow of the path that had taken them behind the Falls, and had a moment of cloying nostalgia as she thought of all the happy times she'd spent there.

Johnny's face was pure, radiant reverence. He seemed lost in the scene, enraptured by its wild beauty. Almost angrily, she wondered again how he could possibly feel anything but loss. He shook his head slowly, eyes finding her again. With seeming great effort, he focused on her.

"Maia . . . " he breathed. The look in his eyes stilled her completely; they were glazed and wild and violently penetrating, all at once. "Maia, what happened to me? What happened to us?" A shudder wracked him, a spasm that seemed to coil his body.

She wanted to touch him, to hold and comfort him, but he was so alien somehow, still not quite Johnny, and she pulled back.

"Come on," she said instead. "We'd better go."

They'd only taken three or four steps when she saw the soldiers, coming across the arid plain in a group of six or eight shimmering figures, all dressed in camouflage gear and holding blast rifles. As she watched with mounting horror, two or three of them dropped off to the flank on either side. Her breath stopped cold in her throat, her heart tripping in her ears.

Caught!

She turned to run toward the ledge path that would take her down to the upper pool . . . and immediately tripped and fell.

As Johnny beheld the approaching troops, something inside him snapped.

He let out a low bellow, like a bull about to charge, and then, with no clear idea of what he was doing, ran directly at the soldiers, now lifting their blast rifles in shock and surprise. Shouts rose, and more troops appeared on the far edge of the plain, deploying with unnerving rapidity.

Suddenly he was among them, lashing out, a weapon of blinding energy, whirling like a dervish. A soldier reared up before him, and he smashed the man's face with a single blow. The helmet disappeared in a splash of red mist, and the soldier, now headless, toppled to the ground. In a second he had killed another, and then another, moving with blind efficiency, limbs striking like lightning, smashing everything they encountered into a pulp.

From somewhere nearby there were more shouts. A new unit of commandos streamed onto the field, firing at him, but he continued his blind melee, mindless of all but the anger that had overtaken him.

They'll pay for this – all of them! They will pay.

And yet, some part of himself seemed outside it all, witnessing the scene from above. He kicked a man in the chest, hard enough to leave a smoking hole where his heart should have been, and the trooper went down, twitched once, and lay still.

At least three dozen soldiers had fallen before they cornered him, and in the end, it was only with sheer numbers that the tide was turned. Twenty more soldiers, thirty more; on they came, pumping blast after blast into him, pushing him back. The air was an arcing, yellow-orange glow. He could feel the electric heat filling him, *charging him*, almost, but still he didn't go down. He knew that a single blast should be enough to kill him, but instead he was somehow riding the blasts, welding his own energy to the arcing pulses of the guns.

But, though they could not kill him, he was still immobilized. Helpless, he felt himself being pushed toward the edge of the cliff.

"Maia! Run!" He screamed.

⊶⊷⊶

Maia stood with her heels to the precipice, mouth agape in an 'O' of pure wonder. All thoughts of escape had left her head, and her mind spun, legs suddenly turned to putty. For the third time in twenty-four hours, she was witnessing something unprecedented.

This is impossible!

Johnny was moving faster than any human being could possibly move. He floored a very large, armored trooper with a single blow, then was somehow, miraculously, forty feet away, fighting with three other soldiers. Shocked bellows and screams rent the air, and then he had dispatched them all and moved on.

From just beyond the jut of tree-line on the far side of the plain came a sudden influx of new bodies, and she realized that he wasn't going to make it. There were simply too many of them. They were shooting at him, into him, and his body jumped backwards fifteen or twenty feet at a time with the blasts. She heard his scream as if in her own mind

Maia! Run!

but she was rooted to the spot. She could only watch helplessly as he was blasted, little by little, to the very edge of the cliff. He balanced on the edge precariously, arms pinwheeling, his eyes locked on hers. They were wild and glazed, but they were *his eyes.* He mouthed her name, and an unspeakable feeling passed between them.

A curtain of yellow-orange flame rent the air, and he was blown over the edge, disappearing soundlessly.

Whatever power had been holding her suddenly loosed its hold, and she bolted to the rocky lip, unable to quell the rising gorge in her throat.

"Johnny!" she screamed. She could see nothing below; there was no sign of his body.

"JOHNNY!!!!"

Rough hands held her arms; someone knocked her down, and she felt a bright spot of pain in her right shoulder as someone else jammed a needle into it.

And then, thankfully, thoughts and pain went away, leaving her with only the darkness of her dreams.

41

The cleanup crews were finished, the temporary camp struck by mid-morning.

By eleven o'clock, Daniel's chopper was headed back to Clifftop. He sat in the back, watching the countryside fall away below. He was glad that Randall had elected to sit in the front seat with the pilot, a talkative man who didn't allow the Agent's stolid silence to deter his mouth.

"Easiest mission I've had in a year," the man was saying. "No casualties, no troubles, just a bunch of woods-monkeys who didn't have the good sense to keep their heads down." His shrill laugh faded into the whine of the motor as the craft banked southward.

Daniel could only think of *her*. If decorum had permitted, he would have ridden in the chopper with her, but it was full of medics and technicians, and he didn't want to arouse suspicion. She'd been taken directly aboard the craft, strapped to a gurney and clamped into place next to her two comrades – the old man technician and the sick little girl. He hadn't even caught an actual look at her before the large white-and-blue helicopter lifted off, headed back to the coast.

The questions were driving him insane.

What do they want with her? Do they know what I want with her?

He couldn't guess, but the anxiety persisted.

I know I'll have to talk to Grandfather about this before too long.

What was the old man's game? Was it possible that Grandfather was merely acting from a place of genuine kindness? Had he saved the red-haired girl for his grandson as a kind of gift?

Maybe . . . maybe. But it didn't fit with the old man's methods.

The chopper touched down at Clifftop a little before one o'clock. Daniel stepped out into the bright afternoon, shielding his eyes with one hand. Though he hadn't slept in more than twenty-four hours, he was not tired; his body seemed to be all nerves. The thought that she was here, at Clifftop, was scary but unbelievably exciting. And the fact that Grandfather had somehow known, had stepped in to make sure she was brought in alive, only made his nerves sing to a higher pitch.

And, to top it all off, he was hungry. No, not just hungry; famished. His stomach rumbled as his boots hit the tarmac.

General Kirkland's chopper had touched down a few moments ahead of his own, and now the General approached him, cap under one arm. He was puffing contentedly on a thick cigar, the smoke tailing into the afternoon sea breeze. The top two buttons of his uniform were undone, and his demeanor was that of someone who works hard but knows how to relax. He grinned at Daniel and clapped him on the shoulder.

"Daniel!" Kirkland had to shout to be heard over the roar as three more choppers descended into the semi-enclosed landing area. "Wonderful job today, lad! Me and Sneed, and maybe Maxwell and one or two of the boys, we're all headed over to the officers' lounge for dinner. I was hoping you might join us, eh? What do you say?"

In truth, Daniel's worried mind was on the red-haired girl. He was thinking that maybe he should personally see that she was given reasonable quarters . . . but saying no to the General might be taken as a personal insult, so he only hesitated a moment.

"Sure," he said, forcing a smile. "I'm hungry as hell. Let me just grab a change of clothes."

He saluted and snapped about on his heels, then walked briskly the short distance to his condo. The afternoon was brilliant, and he took a moment to appreciate the view of the ocean and the tangy salt wind on his face as he crossed the flagstone patio and slipped in through the back door.

He changed quickly, wondering if he had time to find out where she'd been taken, and almost missed the alert light in the corner of the wall-screen. It was blink-pulsing with a dull, amber light.

A message.

He didn't have to guess who it was from. He played the message, unable to stop the feeling of revulsion as Grandfather's face appeared, fairly beaming from the screen, his wrinkled face all the more hideous for the smile he attempted.

"Well done, son!" He rumbled. "General Kirkland just informed me of your performance last night, and I've seen some of the footage myself, just this morning. Very, very well done, Daniel. Well done, indeed. Now listen . . . it's . . . " Grandfather's face disappeared off-screen for a moment as he checked something. " . . . it's late morning, where you are, and I realize you're probably not back yet, but do contact me this evening. I have a . . . *surprise* for you." He smiled again, shark-like, and Daniel could tell the old man was enjoying this game, whatever it was. He had an idea where this was going, and he soon found out he wasn't wrong.

"There was a young woman," Grandfather continued, "among that terrorist group. A rare and beautiful specimen, I must admit. I couldn't bear to see her wasted, so I've instructed the General to have her sent back to Clifftop, where she is to be housed and treated well. She will make an excellent addition to your stable, I think, here on Mephisto, once you've been initiated. I thought perhaps you might be feeling . . . ah . . . lonely, shall we say." He smiled again, knowingly. "Anyway, that's all for now. I'll be expecting your call."

The transmission ended abruptly and the screen went blank. In the corner, the message-light returned to a steady green.

Daniel stood where he was, the blood hot in his cheeks. He felt light-headed suddenly, and sat down heavily on the edge of the bed. The sense of relief was overwhelming. He buried his head in his hands and began to shake uncontrollably.

For a moment, his body seemed on the verge of total physical breakdown, but then, slowly, the tide of blood ebbed. He began to smile, and then to laugh. Drawing a great, shuddering breath, he got to his feet, suddenly full of power and purpose, feeling that he was finally, fully alive – perhaps for the first time in his life.

She's here. She's here, and she's mine!

The **Magic** of Science
———————

THE
SCIENCE
of MAGIC

1

The camp lay in smoldering ruins, bunker entrances gaping like empty sockets in a rotting skull. From a few of them, wisps of smoke were still rising, dissipating into the bright afternoon. Between the bunkers and the tree-line that marked the river's edge, the sleepy meadow had been churned into a swath of clumped and broken mud-holes that suggested many soldiers and much machinery.

With a heavy heart, Milos picked his way down the hillside. Four or five trees lay with their roots pointed at the sky, their splintered trunks like broken toothpicks. Shreds of bark and wood littered the hillside and meadow below.

Maia has been taken.

This thought pained him, but he spent no time on remorse – he could only move forward now.

He'd had an ominous, uneasy feeling most of the previous day, and as twilight had come to the doorstep of the hidden house he shared with the others in the high mountains, he'd slipped alone toward the valley below, his uneasiness turning to dreadful certainty the further he went.

He'd heard the helicopters as they came down the valley, had witnessed most of the horror from a hidden spot on the north side of the river, sitting motionless on the limb of a huge oak that dominated the tree-spotted riverbank, opposite the meadow.

The sadness, the sense of loss at this senseless slaughter, was overwhelming; even with his prodigious emotional control, it was all he could do to remain hidden when everything inside him wanted to break cover and try to help. But the damage had already been done; there was nothing one man could do, even if that man was a sorcerer.

There was nothing to do but wait and watch . . . and locate Maia.

If she's still alive.

He ignored this pessimistic thought; he was certain, in some way that defied explanation, that she hadn't been killed in the initial attack. He could feel her in the forest.

Even so, It took a supreme effort to clear his mind enough to use his dreaming body, but somehow he managed it. His consciousness rose out of his inert body, hovering over the water.

He found her only moments later, moving furtively up-valley. He was about to try to contact her – another bit of magic that would have required all his skill and concentration - but before he could, another element of his vision caused him to snap awake with such force that he over-balanced and fell from the low branch, crashing into a nest of moldy bracken below and scraping skin from his elbows. He barely noticed the pain, though; what he'd seen had been strange enough to override all other thoughts. Even the slaughter on the other side of the river was momentarily forgotten.

This can't be! It simply can't!

He leapt to his feet, feeling a sudden surge of energy, and made his way up-valley as quickly as he could. He tried to stay under cover, but in his excitement, it was hard not to run.

He tried to compensate for the differences between his dreamtime vision and the waking world, but he still over-shot the area he was looking for, then wasted half an hour backtracking around an impassable blackberry thicket that covered at least a ten-acre area.

By the time he'd physically located Maia and her strange companion, the main compound was far behind, the night thick and dark. He shadowed them, trying to keep them in sight while navigating the steep, tricky terrain on the north side of the river. There were no paths, and more than once he had to let his dreaming body take over for a few minutes to find them again.

The dawn was painting the forest in shades of silver and gold as finally, exhausted, he climbed the stair-step boulders to the top of the falls, resting for a moment as he shaded his eyes and looked for movement below.

A moment later, he saw them as they broke out of the trees, onto the cracked plain below. Again, his heart quickened as he beheld her companion – the same young man she'd been with that day.

The one who'd been abducted.

The fact of the young man's reappearance was not the source of Milos' sudden excitement, however. Once again, he wondered at the extreme improbability of what he was seeing.

What he's doing is impossible! How is he accomplishing it?

He watched them for a few minutes, using his skills to see Johnny's energy carefully, making certain he was right in his assessment.

Martuk will want to know about this immediately.

He thought of trying to contact his benefactor remotely – Martuk was an adept of the dreaming fields, and wouldn't be hard to find with his dreaming body - and was about to make the attempt when a movement from the cracked plain below caught his attention. Alarmed, he sprang to his feet, muscles tensing, ready to run to their aid if necessary . . .

But it was already too late; once again he could do nothing but watch, angry and frustrated, as the troopers advanced, and in some ways, this was worse than what he'd witnessed earlier.

Maia represented much more than an investment of time; she was more than just a student, or even a friend. Her presence was absolutely vital to their plans; plans for a true sorcerer's journey, one that he'd seen many times over in his dreams. But there was no margin for error – to achieve this journey, not only must the sorcerers' combined intent be flawless, but their configuration must be complete.

If Maia is lost, then so are we all.

A pang of hopelessness passed through him, but he let it go, keeping himself attuned to the moment as his training mandated . . . and so it happened that he witnessed a very strange thing, a thing neither Maia nor the firing soldiers could see from atop the cliff.

Johnny Perdue had not fallen to his death from the arid cliff-top.

Overwhelmed by numbers and firepower, he was finally blasted from the precipice; his body arced out, falling much too slowly through the sparkling, empty space above the pool, and then . . .

Then he'd dissipated; that is, he'd come apart as if he had no more substance than smoke, and then simply disappeared, literally into thin air.

Based on what Milos had already *seen*, he wasn't completely caught off guard . . . but still, it was a strange and frightening omen. Casting a last look at Maia – trussed up, laid out on a white gurney and being wheeled toward a waiting helicopter – he turned and struck into the forest.

In shared dreaming that night, he pondered, with Martuk, the significance of what he'd seen.

When he awoke the next morning, refreshed with the first light, a plan of action had been formulated. Martuk and the others would be traveling even now, heading west, towards the coast and Maia. He planned to catch up with them before night fell, but this morning he was on a unique mission - one that promised to be as challenging as it was strange.

He spent an hour or so sitting on a large rock in the cold sun, examining his memories of Johnny Perdue, and when he felt he had what was needed, he got to his feet and began walking down-valley, following the river.

ABOUT THE AUTHOR

Matthew Asher Wakefield currently resides in the Pacific Northwest with M., his longtime friend, partner, and collaborator, and their two chihuahuas, Maria and Lupe.